ONE FOR SORROW

Helen Fields studied law at the University of East Anglia, then went on to the Inns of Court School of Law in London. She joined chambers in Middle Temple where she practised criminal and family law. After her second child was born, Helen left the Bar, and now runs a media company with her husband David. The DI Callanach series is set in Scotland, where Helen feels most at one with the world. Helen and her husband are digital nomads, moving between the Americas and Europe with their three children and looking for adventures.

Helen loves Twitter but finds it completely addictive. She can be found at @Helen_Fields.

By the same author

Perfect Remains
Perfect Prey
Perfect Death
Perfect Silence
Perfect Crime
Perfect Kill
The Shadow Man

'Grabs you at page one and holds on like a police dog tackling a suspect. Sometimes shocking, often gruesome, always gripping. Ten for thrills!'
Douglas Skelton

'A breathtaking thriller with a devastating conclusion – I defy anyone to read this and come away unaffected. Perfectly plotted and executed with extreme care – I devoured it and can't stop thinking about it.'
Susi Holliday

'From a – literally – explosive start, the pace of *One for Sorrow* never relents. In this cleverly plotted story of disillusionment and revenge, Helen Fields vividly brings to life the failings of the criminal justice system. Thoroughly entertaining!'
Guy Morpuss

'As always, Helen provides relentless pace, devilish cleverness and a laser-sharp focus on plot. Her characterisation is second to none.'
Christopher Brookmyre

'An incredible, heartbreaking, terror-filled, pulse-in-throat thriller. So brilliantly plotted, clever and slick and so, so dark. You will struggle to put it down, and then when you run out of pages, you'll be absolutely bereft.'
Cressida McLaughlin

READERS LOVE ONE FOR SORROW

'If I could award more than 5 stars for this I would, it's an absolute masterclass of a thriller!'
NetGalley Review, 5 stars

'Without a doubt the best book I've read in 2021, probably in a very long time. This is the most gripping, horrific and heart wrenching book I've ever read. I couldn't tear myself away from the pages.'
NetGalley Review, 5 stars

'I think this is the best detective series I have ever read.'
NetGalley Review, 5 stars

'Fast-paced. Relentless. Powerful. Breath-taking. Emotional. Devastating. Heart-stopping.'
NetGalley Review, 5 stars

'This book has it all, brilliant characters, tension, twists and danger from the first page to the last.'
NetGalley Review, 5 stars

'Not only is Helen excellent at suspense. She writes characters that leap off the page.'
NetGalley Review, 5 stars

'Wow! I could not put it down, totally chilling yet expertly written to keep you on the edge of your seat from start to finish.'
NetGalley Review, 5 stars

'Highly recommend this book, series and author!'
NetGalley Review, 5 stars

'This is an absolute page turner of a book with so many twists and turns.'
NetGalley Review, 5 stars

ONE
FOR
SORROW

HELEN FIELDS

avon.

Published by AVON
A division of HarperCollins*Publishers* Ltd
1 London Bridge Street
London SE1 9GF

www.harpercollins.co.uk

HarperCollins*Publishers*
1st Floor, Watermarque Building, Ringsend Road
Dublin 4, Ireland

A Paperback Original 2022
1
First published in Great Britain by HarperCollins*Publishers* 2022

ISBN: 978-0-00-837933-9

Typeset in Bembo Std by Palimpsest Book Production Limited, Falkirk, Stirlingshire
Printed and Bound in the UK using 100% Renewable Electricity at CPI Group (UK) Ltd

MIX
Paper from
responsible sources
FSC® C007454

Acknowledgements

The more books I write, the better understanding I have about the commitment, passion, sweat and tears required from the publishing team for it to succeed. The team at Avon Books and the wider support within HarperCollins is extraordinary. I am grateful every day for the kindness and enthusiasm of everyone who works on my books. A special mention, as always, for publishing director Helen Huthwaite. I've never met anyone who can brighten the room in the way she can, even on her busiest, hardest days. Team Avon, those brilliant book lovers, consists of Becci Mansell, Eleanor Slater, Ellie Pilcher, Elisha Lundin, Molly Walker-Sharp, Lucy Frederick, Cara Chimirri, Radhika Sonagra, Oliver Malcolm, Hannah O'Brien and Catriona Beamish. I owe each and every one of them a debt of gratitude. Hats off to the design team particularly to Claire Ward who made this stand out on the shelves. And, as ever, to Samantha Luton, Tom Dunston and Hannah Avery, who are part of the incredible sales team that talk the talk and get books into shops. A special mention for Laura McCallen who did the copyedit for this book in record time and who ironed out the wrinkles and added the polish.

Big love to the inspiring women at Hardman & Swainson Literary Agency. My agent, Caroline Hardman, is as good as they get, and I'm constantly awestruck by how principled and unafraid, and how efficient she is (not to mention annoyingly slim). Also to the lovely Joanna Swainson, globally talented foreign rights superstar Thérèse Coen, and to the wonderful Nicole Etherington. I have no idea what I would do without each one you.

To the Baumber family who let me talk through this idea over numerous lunches and barbecues without once complaining. Thanks to Margaret, Helen, Mark, Alice and Matthew. Also to my own clan – David, Gabe, Sollie and Evangeline. May the mockery never cease. (Now leave me alone and let me write a few more paragraphs.)

Finally to you, lovely librarians, booksellers, bloggers, reviewers and wonderful readers. A book is not really a book until it's being read. So thank you. Keep turning those pages.

For the Maddison sisters

- Margaret and Lesley -
With all my love

Chapter One

Two women remained in the cemetery after the funeral, one above the ground, one below. Neither could feel anything.

The whole day had passed without sensation. A service, attended in huge numbers, had taken place in a church. The burial had been for close friends and family only. It had been a quiet, dignified affair. Throughout it all – readings, hymns, eulogy, the shaking of hands and slow nods of mutual regret between mourners – Detective Chief Inspector Ava Turner had tried to comprehend what was happening, and largely failed.

She knew her friend was dead. That her body was in the coffin. Never again to share a secret smile. That reassuring presence, forever absent now.

Ava had dim recollections of conversations during the day. People asking if she was okay, expressing sympathy. She felt sure she'd done the right thing, which seemed to be to smile and respond with one of the polite half-truths mourners told one another at such times. Yes, she was fine, thank you for asking. Yes, the deceased was a wonderful woman who had made her mark on the world. No, she would never be forgotten. Yes, the tributes pouring in would have made her proud. No, she didn't need anyone to drive her home. That final one, at least, was entirely true.

Ava lifted her head to find that, at long last, everyone had gone. Some kind person had organised drinks and canapés at their home, but it was the last place Ava wanted to be right now.

Smoked salmon blinis with crème fraîche? No thank you, a woman I loved with all my heart is dead.

The rain was coming down and the fresh grave was liquefying, muddy rivulets running towards Ava's newly polished boots. She watched as the water spattered the leather, making a mess of the hem of her black trousers. She preferred them that way. Life was neither clean nor neat and tidy. It was a shit show, and Ava didn't want to keep on pretending anymore.

Bending down, pushing one hand into the mud, she wondered how cold it was below ground, wishing ridiculously that she could tuck a blanket over her friend's body to keep her warm. Wishing she could hold her one last time.

'You bastard,' Ava told Death. 'How dare you take her from me.' Death, typically arrogant, didn't feel compelled to answer. 'I loved her.'

That was the moment Ava began to feel again, and after that she could feel everything.

Every icy raindrop. Each bite of the whipping wind. The tearing, ripping teeth of grief. The nausea of understanding the timeline of forever. And worse than anything else, the expanding void of pointlessness.

Ava pushed her hands into her stomach and fought the desire to take to her bed and lie there forever. She cried tears that were bitter with hatred and sweet with memories. She screamed into the howling Edinburgh gale, but even the echo of that noise was taken from her as if she was entitled to nothing. Pressing her upper teeth hard enough into her bottom lip to draw blood, she rejoined the world.

There was work to be done, and work would save her. She could bury her grief in custody records and forensics reports, cold cases and door-to-door enquiries. Back at the station, she could encase herself in the Major Investigation Team, hide behind a facade where other officers addressed her as ma'am and didn't ask about her private life. Ava knew that without the life raft of distraction, she would throw a few belongings in a bag, pick up her passport, and simply leave. She still might. But not yet.

For now, there was a case to be solved, evidence to be gathered. A trail to excavate and then follow. Ava swallowed her heartache. It stuck in her throat for a moment, trying to choke her, but she was stronger.

'You didn't win,' she told Death quietly. The anger was gone from her voice. Only a reedy sadness remained. 'You'll never really take her from me. I know she's still here.'

She packed up her sorrow, tucked it away where no one could stare at it, and began the long walk back to those awaiting her leadership.

Chapter Two

Edinburgh City Mortuary was a vacuum of silence. Multiple officers from her team had already viewed the footage Ava was there to see and she'd read their reports, but she still needed to watch it herself.

She was met at reception by an efficient young man she'd never seen working there before, and guided into a spare office where a computer was ready to play the file. She was offered coffee but refused it, then the door whooshed softly shut and Ava was alone.

She pulled out a notepad and pen to record her observations as she went, knowing she would watch the footage a hundred times more before the case was done, but she had to start somewhere. The screen was blank save for a case number in the top left-hand corner. The practice of videoing postmortems had only become common procedure a year earlier in all cases where there was some sign of criminal activity. In this case, the deceased had yet to be identified. Missing persons files had been cross-checked but no one matching the deceased's description or appearance had been reported missing in the previous six months. Putting a name to the corpse was the number one job on Ava's list right now. She pressed play and Edinburgh's Chief Forensic Pathologist appeared on screen, running her fingers over a computer keyboard before glancing into the camera and beginning her work.

'Right,' Dr Ailsa Lambert said, snapping on gloves, 'this young man – identity as yet unknown – is aged between twenty and twenty-five years. Measurements already taken show that he is 5'11" in height, slim build, Caucasian, dark brown hair, hazel eyes. Weight is 178 pounds.'

Dr Lambert pulled back a sheet to reveal a naked body, devoid of the healthy pink colour of life, with a patch of bloody scabs on his upper abdomen. Ava peered more closely at the screen, writing her first question: how old are the scabs?

'The only externally visible trauma is to the abdominal area. It's not clear yet if that was caused accidentally or deliberately but there are remnants of butterfly stitches amongst the scabbing.' Dr Lambert walked towards her computer, unclipped the little camera poised above the screen and walked with it to the body. The viewpoint suddenly switched to first person as a gloved fingertip pointed at tiny white fragments of paper between the scabs. 'Whatever caused the trauma, medical treatment was given, though it doesn't appear to be professional. My assessment is that surgical stitches would have been applied at a hospital, and the extent of the scabbing shows that insufficient care was given to fully stopping the bleeding before the butterfly stitches were applied. Nonetheless, an effort was made to assist this young man.'

Dr Lambert shifted position and made her way down to the man's feet.

'Feet are an adult male shoe size 10, although no shoes were recovered with the body. There are no obvious injuries to the soles, and the skin on the upper surface is intact. However,' Dr Lambert pulled down a light attached to a magnifying glass, positioned it to show the soles, and pointed, 'the general redness indicates a recent irritation. On closer inspection I found patches of what could be either thorns or splinters. Those have been removed and sent for testing to ascertain what plant or wood they came from.'

Ava paused the video file to write herself another note: where are his shoes? Was he running away? As she hit play again, she imagined the pain of having soles full of thorns or splinters and wondered why he hadn't removed them himself. Unless he couldn't.

'Come on, Ailsa,' Ava whispered to the screen. 'Give me something useful.'

'Just above the ankles,' Dr Lambert continued, 'there are bands of faint redness indicating further skin irritation. There's no bruising and no abrasions, but the pattern indicates repeated pressure or rubbing in that area over both ankles. I'll be excising the skin over those patches to take a look below the surface for a better indication. Other than that, the legs have no external injuries.' She ran her hands up and down each leg. 'I can't feel any abnormalities. Muscle tone and condition is within acceptable ranges. No evidence of wasting that would indicate disease or malnutrition.'

She gently parted his legs.

'Penis and testicles are undamaged. Swabs of the skin have been sent away for trace evidence. Around his anus, however, there is substantial reddening and some chafing that forms a drip pattern towards his coccyx. If he had been tied down on his back for long periods and not allowed use of a toilet, that might explain the reddening. It's not dissimilar to nappy rash in babies.'

Ava made herself an additional note to run theories about that past the pathologist.

'No external injuries on the arms. Some older scarring,' Dr Lambert pointed to one or two areas, 'but I'd say those injuries are all more than twelve months old. The wrists have similar vague and broad red lines to the ankles, which I will investigate further. There are no specific pressure points or marks but certainly there's an indication of interference. I'd rule out any hard restraints as the cause of these marks. It's certainly not chain, handcuffs, cable ties or thin ropes. Maybe a wider section of material, strong but soft.'

She picked up his right hand and pointed the camera at the nails, close-up.

'The fingernails on both hands show some damage, some broken tips. Each nail has been cleaned and the contents sent for testing to see if there's DNA from any other person. There's yellowing at the end of each right hand fingertip and between the right middle finger and index finger, indicting both that this young man was a heavy smoker and that he was right hand dominant. Obviously the state of the lungs will inform us better about that.'

Dr Lambert rested the man's hand back down, muttering quietly to herself. Ava paused the footage, rewound it a couple of seconds, increased the volume and leaned in to catch what the pathologist was saying.

'Damned cigarettes. Government licensed murder, that's what it is.'

Ava smiled and sighed. Ailsa Lambert never minced her words. Tiny, fierce, brilliant and a poster girl for old-fashioned values, she epitomised professionalism and kindness.

'There are no visible injuries or sign of disease on his back or his buttocks,' Dr Lambert was saying. 'His throat and neck are unharmed. No swelling, no abnormal movement. I'm going to clip the camera to my pocket and open the mouth now.' She did as she'd said then pulled the light overhead to shine directly into the mouth. Opening the jaw, she ran her fingers around the inner cheeks, looked into the back of the throat, lifted and then compressed the tongue. 'We've already taken dental impressions, which will remain on record for identity checks where necessary . . .' She broke off. Ava sat forward in her chair. Dr Lambert unclipped the camera from her pocket and moved it closer to the mouth, then pulled down the lower lip. 'This might help shortlist candidates to give us this young man's name.'

In spiky script, the legend '60M+' appeared on his internal lower lip. There was no doubt that it was a gang tattoo – few other people wanted to go through the pain of getting a tattoo inside their mouth. That might bring the case to a much swifter resolution. Gang violence often led to premature deaths. It remained a tragedy – there was still a family to be notified – but death in the line of criminal activity was a possibility foreseen on a daily basis by gang members.

Dr Lambert checked his eyes and nose, ran her hands through his hair, clipped a section and bagged it for further testing, then moved the camera again so it was directly over the scabbing. She must have pulled a ruler from her pocket as one suddenly appeared in the frame.

'The scabbing starts two inches below the centre of the ribcage. The injured area is five inches vertically and four inches horizontally. The scabs are in rough patches leading me to believe that the initial injury wasn't a single incision. In that event, the most likely explanation is that these wounds were caused by an accident. I'm going to remove some of those scabs to preserve them, then cut around the wound so as not to damage any evidence that might be concealed immediately below the skin.'

Dr Lambert clipped the camera back onto its original mount on her computer, changed her gloves and picked up a scalpel.

Ava paused the footage once more, stood, stretched her arms and flexed her neck. She didn't want to watch. It was her own fault. She knew she shouldn't have come straight from the funeral to this. It was her job, though. She'd seen plenty of dead bodies before. Pointless being oversensitive now. She sat back down and pressed play.

The scalpel slipped easily into the taut skin just below the shoulder joint. Dr Lambert ran it diagonally downwards to the centre of the chest, returned to the other shoulder joint and made them meet.

'Right,' she said, 'I'm deviating from my normal course.' She pulled out the scalpel, prised up a few sections of scab, bagged them and set them aside for labelling and testing, then picked up her scalpel again. 'The skin beneath those scabs was starting to heal, so I estimate those wounds were made some three or four days prior to death, confirming that this wound alone was not the immediate cause of death. There's no infected tissue around the edge of the scabs or the wound. That was either very lucky, or the wound was properly cleaned at the time the butterfly stitches were applied.'

She dug the point of the scalpel into the base of the Y-section of incision in the chest and began drawing it downwards to open the abdomen and access the lower organs. Ava crossed her arms and took a deep breath.

The scalpel stopped. Dr Lambert frowned then stepped in closer, bringing her head down to the incision to see what the problem was. She tugged once, twice and the scalpel began moving again, then it popped out of the skin. She laid the tool down and slid her fingertips into the incision, one hand either side of the wound, teasing the skin apart, eyes as close to the abdomen as possible to identify the problem.

Ava heard the hissing before she saw anything happen.

Dr Lambert pulled the incision open, and a bloodied circle of metal popped upwards, spinning. There was a visible spraying of tissue to highlight the fact that the gas was exiting under pressure. Red flecks spattered the walls and floor metres from the body. Whipping her head backwards, Dr Lambert instinctively put one hand to her mouth and pressed back down on the canister sticking out of the body with the other.

It took only a second for the horror to register in her eyes. She doubled over, her forehead hitting the corpse's chest before she staggered back, grabbing for the table, a chair, anything to keep herself upright.

Ava looked away, put her own hand over her own mouth as if the gas were in the room with her too, steeled herself for what was to come and forced her eyes back at the screen.

Dr Lambert gave up trying to push the lid of the canister down. She was choking now, gasping for breath. The hissing had grown louder as the metal had emerged from the corpse. Dr Lambert crashed to her knees hitting the edge of a metal trolley as she went down. It shook but did not fall. Fate kept dealing cruel blows.

The small windows into the room were positioned near the ceiling to avoid passersby seeing in. The glass was thick to stop the sounds of saws from echoing through the building to where administrative staff or visiting families might hear. The room was effectively sealed to stop the stench of death from pervading the atmosphere.

Just maybe, Ava thought, if someone had been passing, the sound of a crashing tool cart might have attracted attention. But it wasn't to be. Dr Lambert was on her hands and knees. Even with her limited view, Ava could see she was struggling to breathe. The temptation to rip off her surgical mask to get more oxygen must have been enormous, but Dr Lambert's discipline was greater. She kept the mask on, one hand pressed against it. Did her best to crawl in the direction of the door.

Ava's face contorted in fury. She put her hands up, clutching each side of the screen as if the image might escape, gritting her teeth.

Dr Lambert collapsed onto her side, knees drawn up, head thrown back, beginning to convulse. Spittle began to drip from either side of her mask, her eyes were swelling red. Her head flew from side to side as she fought the toxic gas. Finally, when she must have known she would never reach the door – probably knowing that even if she did, there was no way she would open it and risk the lives of her colleagues – Ailsa Lambert pulled the mask from her face.

Fighting her pain and fear, she turned her head towards the camera.

Dr Lambert looked into the lens, shook her head, took a rasping breath and spoke her last desperate words.

'Ava, I'm sorry.'

Ava's hands made claws against the screen, and she ground her teeth together so hard that her jaw was an agony. Ailsa was apologising to her for something she couldn't possibly have foreseen. Apologising in the knowledge that Ava was going to have to view the footage and witness her dreadful death. Apologising for leaving her.

Still she watched.

Dr Ailsa Lambert, who had celebrated her seventieth birthday a month earlier, who had served the people of Edinburgh and Scotland throughout a distinguished career, took another twenty-six minutes to die. Her body twitched, arms and legs flailing.

No one came.

She vomited, clawed at her face, sucked in insufficient oxygen, until Ava could hear the bubbling rattling in her friend's lungs.

Blood made its way out of Dr Lambert's mouth and nose.

Still, no one came.

The neat, focused, pin-sharp woman who had been friends for decades with Ava's parents, who had been a second mother to her, became a scrunched-up ball of dysfunctional cells on the floor. The tell-it-like-it-was teacher to many a police officer, scenes of crime officer or expert, a woman who didn't suffer fools lightly, perished slowly and in agony. She, who had cared for so many families, carried them through their pain with extraordinary empathy – knowing what information to share and what to spare, understanding what language would soothe and what would patronise. A woman who had dedicated her entire professional career to promoting justice, relief and healing.

The gas finally finished with her at 4.02 p.m., her last expulsion of air a ghastly drumroll of phlegm. Ailsa, who Ava had believed invincible, lay alone on the floor of her own morgue until 5 p.m. when her secretary entered to say goodnight.

Stepping straight back out of the suite when the gas hit her, the secretary called in a specialist crew. The building was emptied, suits with oxygen supplies were donned, and finally, at 5.44 p.m., an attending officer stopped the video camera from recording. Only then could Ava stop watching.

'Fuck!' she bellowed, ripping the monitor from the ties that bound it to the computer stack and throwing it across the room where it hit a wall, denting the plasterboard and landing in a broken heap. The young man who'd shown Ava in raced into the room, took one look at her face, and backed out without a word.

In that instant, DCI Ava Turner made Ailsa Lambert a promise, one she intended to keep no matter the consequences or the cost.

Chapter Three

The incident room was silent – an almost unknown occurrence – as Ava approached it. Police officers stayed sane by using banter at all times. Now, heads were down as eyes scanned screens, documents and photos. Telephone conversations took place in whispered voices. The Major Investigation Team was still in shock. She put her hand on the door, composed herself, and entered.

'Don't stand up,' she said, before anyone could waste their energy. 'I've viewed the full footage from the postmortem murder. Detective Sergeant Lively, I want you chasing up—'

'You are going to be fucking fired.'

Everyone stood. Ava didn't flinch.

'Ma'am,' DS Lively said to the stick-thin, red-lipsticked woman in the doorway who had spoken, 'we're making progress.'

'You speak again before I've finished, Sergeant, and you and the DCI can buddy up revamping your CVs,' Detective Superintendent Overbeck said without bothering to look at Lively. 'Turner, how dare you petition the Procurator Fiscal to sign off the release of a body when we don't have so much as a lead on a murder suspect yet.'

Ava folded her arms and waited it out, so far beyond arguing about her decision that she was already bored.

'You want to give me the silent treatment? Fine with me. I've put up with your subordination bullshit long enough. Pack your fucking things.'

'No,' Ava said.

Overbeck stalked across the floor, her metal tipped stilettos scratching like nails on a chalkboard. Several officers winced and chose to look away. She stopped a matter of inches from Ava, looking down at her, her voice a whisper carefully designed to carry throughout the room.

'Detective Chief Inspector, I am suspending you from active duty. You are facing a disciplinary review. Go home immediately. If you refuse to follow a direct order, the disciplinary tribunal will no longer be required.'

'Ma'am, Dr Lambert's funeral was this morning,' Lively said quietly. In his fifties, an old–timer compared to most of his colleagues and not in the best physical shape thanks to a wicked biscuit addiction, he wasn't afraid of the consequences of speaking up. 'It's been hard on everyone, the Chief most of all. Could we maybe just take a moment . . .'

'I don't need your help, Lively,' Ava said.

'Sergeant,' Overbeck interrupted. 'I need a volunteer to do a three-month rotation giving talks to school children. Congratulations. You're being transferred out of MIT. DCI Turner, last chance. Leave the station now.'

'I asked the Procurator Fiscal to release the body for burial on the basis that Dr Lambert's organs were removed and preserved at the morgue. Ailsa Lambert's death – every moment of it – was captured on high quality video. We have the weapon, we know the methodology, causation has been established beyond question. There is literally nothing any defence team could use to hurt us at trial.'

'They can ask for a second fucking postmortem on the murder victim!'

'They have one. An independent postmortem took place with no police presence before the organs were removed. Every conceivable sample was taken twice, half of them left untested in case a defence team requests them. The only issue at trial will be identifying the person who put a pressure operated toxic gas canister inside that corpse. Nothing else.'

'And what about Dr Lambert's family? You didn't have the right to make the decision to bury her. Just how many lawsuits are we facing?'

Ava dropped her arms and met Overbeck's glare with her own.

'*I* was her family,' she hissed. 'Ailsa left everything to me. Everything she owned, every decision, all the legal authority. Her sister is in a care home suffering from advanced dementia. There was no husband, no children, no other living relatives. Her loyalty was to her career. I had both the legal authority and Ailsa's blessing to make the choice. She wasn't going to lie in a drawer in her own fucking morgue waiting for us to find who did this to her.'

'You stupid girl,' Overbeck muttered. 'Dr Lambert was a consummate professional. She would have been the first and the last person telling you to comply with normal procedure, to do it by the book, and not to make it bloody personal. You're too close to this. You should have walked away from this investigation the second you heard what happened.'

'Er, Chief,' a voice called from across the room.

'Wait,' Overbeck held up a palm in the speaker's direction. 'Turner, I'll give you the time you need to get your notes together and brief whoever your second-in-command is on this.'

'Actually it's important.' Ava looked up at Detective Constable John Swift who was waving a piece of paper enthusiastically in the air. Swift, still in his twenties and prone to bouts of confusion, went red in the face. He ran a hand through his unruly hair as if to make himself more presentable.

'What the hell is it, Constable?' Lively snapped.

'The tattoo on the bottom lip of the corpse: apparently the M stands for "months". Sixty months is the minimum prison sentence needed to be allowed in the gang who use the tattoo.'

Lively looked up at Ava. 'We ran the corpse's DNA through the database. There was no match. If he'd been convicted of a crime or gone through the prison system, his DNA should be on record.'

'DI Graham,' Ava said to a huge man who stood unobtrusively at the back of the room, a gentle smile on his face. 'Liaise with any officers you've worked with who have been undercover in local gangs,' Ava said. 'We need inside information. I'm guessing it'll be difficult to persuade any gang members to talk to us directly?'

'Almost impossible. The consequences for them sharing information are too severe for any of them to break the rules, but I've a few contacts on the periphery from my days on the streets. I don't want to put any of them in danger, but I'll look them up and do my best,' Pax Graham promised.

'I appreciate that,' Ava said. 'Lively, send a photo of the deceased – face only – out to every prison in the UK. He might not have served his time in Scotland. Let's see if there's a prison guard who recognises him. The missing DNA might be an anomaly. The system's been known to fail. Samples could have been mixed up. Also, circulate the details with probation services. Anyone who's served a long stretch will have been allocated a probation officer.'

Overbeck was undaunted. 'I meant what I said, DCI Turner. You're off this case and standing down from duty. I won't have any loose cannons on my team. My office, thirty minutes, with a comprehensive plan for handover.'

There was a quiet knock at the door.

'Dr Carlisle's here,' PC Sandra Biddlecombe announced, fiddling with her watch to avoid making eye-contact with Overbeck. 'I'll show him in.' She stepped back into the corridor, her shortness all the more noticeable as she ushered in a tall, sombre black man with close-shaven hair, carrying an open laptop with one hand as he typed into it with the other.

He looked from Overbeck to Turner, assessed the situation, then made his way quietly to the side of the room and waited until all eyes were on him.

'Good evening,' he began. 'I'm Dr Nate Carlisle, currently acting Chief Forensic Pathologist in Edinburgh, transferred here from Glasgow as an emergency appointment. I know the circumstances are difficult. Many of you will have known Dr Lambert well, as did I. We have some updates, and I know you have twenty-four-hour operations on this case so you'll be getting information as I receive it.'

Ava moved away from Overbeck and perched on a desk in a corner of the room, pulling a band from her pocket and tying back her long curly hair. Overbeck remained where she was, expressionless.

'I appreciate there'll have been some frustration that it's taken longer than usual to get forensic results back. It was difficult to access the postmortem suite safely to begin with, and toxicology testing can be a lengthy process. I can now confirm that the gas released into the morgue was chlorine gas. I've had a reconstruction of the canister used to deliver it made so you can understand precisely what you're dealing with, but let's start from the beginning.'

He linked his laptop into the screen on the wall and it lit up with a photograph of a corpse Ava was all too familiar with. The photo showed the scabbed section of stomach before Ailsa Lambert had cut into it.

'Rough zigzag incisions were made into the corpse's stomach and the flaps of skin would have been pulled back to allow access so the device could be fitted into the stomach cavity.'

'Would it not have been easier to have cut in a straight line?' DS Lively asked.

'It would,' Carlisle replied. 'My theory is that a single neat incision would have been a much more obvious surgical intervention and therefore a red flag to any pathologist. She might then have entered the abdominal cavity via a different route, possibly avoiding the canister completely. We can assume that whoever did this anticipated that the presence of scabbing and stitches would make it look as if the injury had been sympathetically handled, making those wounds appear less threatening than they actually were.'

'What would it have felt like to the victim, having a metal object sewn into his stomach?' DI Graham asked. 'Would it have been painful?'

'The victim was sedated for surgery, and my belief is that he continued to be sedated afterwards, otherwise we'd have seen a lot more damage from his restraints as he fought them. The sedation would have limited both his pain and his emotional distress, but yes, it's likely he was aware of what happened on some level. Now, if you could all stand and gather round, there's something I want to show you.'

They shuffled out from behind their desks, leaving a space for the superintendent. Ava hung back. She had a clear enough memory of what they were about to see.

Nate Carlisle took a plastic box from his case and removed the lid. Beneath it, an object was concealed by multiple layers of taut clingfilm. He handed an officer a scalpel.

'Start at this end of the box. Your job is to get a clean cut all the way through,' he instructed.

The officer got the tip of the scalpel in without a problem, dragged it along until it hit the concealed object, then it snagged and she used her fingers to pull the clingfilm apart. As the film gave way, a metal lid popped up and into view. As the lid came completely free, it began to spin. The natural reaction from the watching officers was to put their faces closer to watch what was about to happen.

A perfumed spray covered them all. They threw their heads back, stepped away, a couple of them reaching out to push the canister lid back down.

'It's all right,' Dr Carlisle said. 'The tech team borrowed the contents from an aerosol deodorant. But this,' he held up the canister itself, 'is both very simple and very clever. The device triggers when the pressure is released from the top of it, same as a landmine. Nothing more complex than a spring, but there's a battery in here too, and a connection is made when the lid's released. The spin mechanism is powered, then the gas is released and circulated using an aerosol. The engineering isn't complicated but the chemical aspect was clever. The wound needed to heal for enough days that there was a good natural pressure seal to avoid the canister going off accidentally.'

'How did they make the chlorine gas?' Lively asked. 'That stuff's got to be a chemical weapon or something.'

'Historically it's been used as exactly that, partly because it's easy and cheap to make. Most of what you need to make it you'll find in a cleaning supplies cupboard. Mix bleach with an acid, even urine. Together, you have a potentially lethal gas. Even at very low concentrations it causes skin irritation and breathing difficulties.'

'And at a high concentration?' Overbeck asked.

'If you lean down into it, if the gas is pressurised, if you take several deep breaths of it and exposure continues?' Carlisle set the canister back in the box. 'It begins with burning inside the throat, nose and eyes. Immediate damage to the bronchial tree.

The gas is very distinctive. Dr Lambert would have recognised the threat immediately which is why her first thought was to try to shut the canister, but the spring only goes one way, then it locks.'

There was a long silence.

'Tell us how she died,' Ava said. 'The mechanics. We need to know what we're dealing with.'

Nate Carlisle sighed.

'In the video, you can see Dr Lambert's face becoming irritated from the gas, the redness and swelling. That would have been replicated internally. Her throat would have begun to swell, she'd have experienced dyspnoea, meaning breathing would have become difficult quickly. Pulmonary symptoms would have started after that: rapid pulse, irregular heartbeat, a lack of oxygen to her vital organs. Chlorine gas is heavy and Dr Lambert was in a sealed room. The initial dose made her fall to the floor which is where the gas would then have accumulated.'

'So she'd have continued to breathe it in,' Lively said.

Carlisle nodded.

'Her breathing would have become laboured, causing secondary effects like cramping. We know that she suffered haemoptysis—'

'Translate,' Overbeck said.

'Coughing up blood,' Carlisle explained. 'There was haemorrhaging of her respiratory tract. Her lungs were so badly damaged that her brain and heart couldn't get enough oxygen. Eventually she suffered a cardiac arrest.'

'So she was burned, bled internally, suffocated slowly then had a heart attack,' Ava summarised.

All eyes were on Dr Carlisle.

'That's about it,' he said.

'The set-up means the pathologist was the target,' Ava continued. 'Whoever did this wanted no one else to interfere

20

with that body until it was in the morgue. They knew the canister would be triggered during a postmortem. And they were willing to kill someone else to use his body as a weapon.'

'It looks that way,' Carlisle agreed.

'So all we have to do is trawl through forty years of cases in which Dr Lambert helped convict murderers, and figure out which one of them might have wanted revenge,' Lively said. 'That's going to take forever.'

'You'd better get started then,' Ava said. 'I want half of you focusing on Dr Lambert's previous cases. Categorise suspects – those released from prison, those still alive, those with the means and capacity to do this, and those still in prison who could organise other people to do this on their behalf. The rest of you follow up the gang lead. We need to identify our corpse. He's the only direct contact to our killer.'

Officers scattered in all directions and got back to work. Nate Carlisle began to pack up too.

'I'm not done with you, Dr Carlisle,' Overbeck said. 'I'd like to know if DCI Turner engaged your support with releasing Dr Lambert's body for burial, because if so, your stint as acting Chief Forensic Pathologist on my patch is likely to amount to a very short stay.'

'I wouldn't have agreed to anything that compromised a case – this one or any other,' Nate Carlisle said softly, looking Overbeck directly in the eyes, keeping any defensiveness from his voice and his stance. 'There were the morgue staff to consider, too. Keeping Dr Lambert's body on the premises was extremely distressing for them. The independent postmortem and storing of the organs was a compromise. It's a break from protocol, but these are exceptional circumstances.'

'It seems I'm the only person left who cares about procedure, discipline and accountability. I'm done having this discussion in public. My office now, Turner,' Overbeck said.

Another man appeared at the door, mid-thirties, dark brown eyes, and even darker hair, enviable looks.

'All units alert,' he said, his words rolled within a thick French accent. 'We've been told to get every available police officer searching the city streets. The message came from whoever killed Dr Lambert.'

'How can you be certain of that?' Overbeck snapped.

DI Luc Callanach held up a piece of paper and read from it. 'Because they said, "No chlorine gas this time. You need boots on the street. One hour."'

Chapter Four

Units rushed out to cover the city in a grid formation, no one knowing what they were looking for, or if there really was anything to be found. Orders were to spread out and cover as much ground as they could, and to be on the alert for anything suspicious.

Ava jumped in an unmarked car and took the wheel, Callanach wrenching the passenger door open and throwing himself in as she pulled away.

'Tell me about the message,' Ava said.

'It came through to a phone number MIT uses for appeals for information. Whoever called used a digital voice changer, so the voice sounds robotic. We can't even be sure if it's a male or a female speaking,' Callanach said.

'We didn't get a warning before the attack on Ailsa, so why are we getting one this time? This could all just be a waste of time and resources.'

'Maybe the attack at the morgue was to put themselves on the map, make sure we were listening. Without that, we might not have responded to this message at all,' Callanach said. 'Listen, I know you don't want to talk about it, but . . .'

'Don't ask if I'm okay. I'm going to do my work. Overbeck can threaten to take me off the job, but she's been in the force long enough that she's got a whole closet of skeletons to worry about. She doesn't want to start picking through mine.'

'I don't care what Overbeck thinks, but you and Ailsa . . . you were almost closer to her than your own mother, Ava. Maybe this isn't the right case for you.'

'That's for me to decide. Ailsa wasn't a blood relative and I'm not implicated in her death, so the protocols don't apply. If we took every police officer off the case who knew her and cared about her, we wouldn't have anyone left to work the investigation. I'm as well placed as anyone else to find out who killed her.'

Callanach watched her take every corner with clinical precision, her mouth set straight, and knew she was in a place so dark there would be no talking to her. She'd been his closest friend, and sometimes more, since he'd left Interpol and joined Police Scotland looking for a fresh start three years earlier. Through it all, he'd never seen Ava like this. Her fury was scorched onto her face.

'All units,' the radio announced. 'Head for the Innocent Railway Tunnel entrance on Holyrood Park Road.'

Callanach grabbed the radio and replied. 'Got that,' he said. 'Please advise, has there been a second message?'

There was some static, followed by the screech of a wheel spin as Ava U-turned the car.

'Yes, sir. The message said, "I changed my mind. You have four minutes." Then it gave the location. We have paramedics en route.'

'Seal off the entrance from the A7 road,' Ava ordered. 'Make sure no one can approach from inside the tunnel. We'll be there in two minutes.'

Luc shut down the call and turned back to Ava.

'Do we need to stop trains? Are we going to find someone literally tied to a train track?'

'There are no trains. These days it's just a path for cyclists and pedestrians, but originally it was the first underground railway passage in the UK. It's tricky to locate if you don't know where to find the entrances.'

The air wailed with sirens as they joined a stream of emergency response vehicles approaching the site. Ava turned up East Parkside, but by then the area was blocked.

'We won't get any closer than this. Time to run.' She stopped the car, left the keys in the ignition in case another officer needed to move it, and they ran, Ava leading the way.

From the residential cul-de-sac they headed onto a footpath, rounded a ninety-degree bend and were met by a crowd of first responders yelling instructions to one another. The sides of the footpath were overgrown bushes and eighty metres ahead was a dark brick arch.

A woman dangled in the archway's mouth, neck in a noose, the origins of the rope hidden in a mass of thorny bushes above the entrance. Her long, dark hair swung to and fro, but there was no breeze. Ava looked down at her body. The woman's fingers and toes were twitching, just barely. And her belly was swollen beneath her shirt.

'Shit,' Ava said, pushing forward between bustling bodies. 'She's pregnant.'

'She's still alive,' Callanach shouted, a head taller than Ava with a better view above the throng. Louder, he shouted, 'She's not dead yet. Get her down.'

A makeshift stool that appeared to be a large toolbox was already being set beneath the hanging woman's feet. Two police officers jumped up, one supporting the woman's legs to take the pressure off her neck and buy her some time, the other holding that officer still so he wouldn't fall and create even more pull on the rope.

Ava stepped aside to allow access to an ambulance crew who were racing in with a stretcher, medical kits and oxygen.

More officers appeared on the bridge above.

'We need wire cutters!' they shouted.

Ava studied the upper section of the bridge, and her eyes located barbed wire, a stream of it, tangled and entwined into the natural foliage, designed to prevent officers from reaching down to the rope from which the woman was hanging. She grabbed binoculars from a uniformed officer to get a better look at the victim's face.

Her skin was the colour of an overused white sheet, lips grey, eyes half-shut reddened slits.

'There's no time left. Cut her down now!' Ava shouted. 'Out of my way!'

Police and firefighters left a path for Ava to get closer to the bridge.

'We need to cut through the barbed wire to get down to the rope,' came the response from the bridge. 'It's been nailed into the brickwork.'

'Get a crowbar under it, you only need to see an inch,' Ava responded. 'Have that stretcher ready. I need officers around her feet in a circle. Everyone's going to fall when the tension's gone. Be ready to perform an emergency caesarean in the ambulance. Move!'

The kick had gone from the woman's legs. Her hands were open-palmed and relaxing.

'Cut it now!' Ava shouted, moving forward again.

Above the bridge, an officer had shoved a crowbar beneath a few strands of wire, enough for another to slide a knife over the visible section of rope.

Callanach took hold of Ava's arm.

'Chief,' he said. 'This is nothing like what happened at the morgue. It doesn't feel right.'

'Not now.' She shook him off, still twenty metres from the victim, and headed forwards.

The knife sawed through the rope. The strands gave way one by one. Ava could see the weight of the body shifting downwards, the officers reaching higher up to make sure they could catch the woman as she toppled forward. A third officer was hoisted up on a colleague's shoulders to add more hands to make sure they caught her.

The officer on the bridge with the knife kept sawing the thick rope. He paused for a moment. Ava wasn't watching the body anymore. The knife-holding police officer cocked his head to one side and opened his mouth to say something.

The explosion was a rainbow that started white and rolled through every shade of yellow, orange and red before engulfing the crowd in grey-black smoke.

Ava saw the officers on the top of the bridge flung into the air before she heard the bang. Men and women fell like dominoes from the blast. Body parts flew over Ava's head and a red mist descended through the smoke. She tasted meaty metal before putting her face to the floor and trying not to breathe in death.

That was when the rumbling began. She looked up and her eyes met Callanach's. He was a few feet behind her in the dirt and already getting to his feet, moving forward. Ava forced herself up to join him, the world tilting left and right as she tried to shake the ringing from her ears.

'Get away from the bridge,' Callanach yelled.

'Go!' Ava shook the men and women dusting themselves off around her. 'Get away from here.'

They stumbled forwards, each able-bodied officer grabbing the arms or legs of a body and hauling them backwards.

It started with a few bricks tumbling from the hole at the top of the bridge, then huge sections of brickwork were falling. A thunderclap heralded the front of the bridge entrance falling forwards, covering those bodies not recovered. Brick dust layered on top of the smoke from the explosives, and the living had no choice but to back away to safety.

New sirens approached until the environment was nothing but sound and hazy light. Civilians were running from nearby houses, collecting the injured and walking them to safety, every home opening its doors and offering shelter until more paramedics could take over.

Ava took the arm of a young, shaking female officer, took her by the chin and looked her in the eyes. 'Focus on me. We have to check the Innocent Railway Path from the other end to see how far back the damage goes and if anyone's injured inside. Call it in for me.' The officer nodded and got on her radio.

Ambulances came and went. A doctor made an attempt to check Ava and was ushered away by DS Lively who'd arrived at the scene late from the other side of the city. Callanach split teams between assisting the scenes of crime crew, guarding the perimeter, and trying to ascertain which first responder units had been in the area at the time.

Ava tried to recall what the hanging woman had been wearing and went looking for her clothes. She found a section of bloodied baggy green hoodie, one hundred metres away in some bushes.

In her head, all she could do was wonder: how many dead? She tried to reproduce the earlier scene in her mind. There had been several officers on top of the bridge, two balanced on the stool, another on his colleague's shoulders. The paramedics directly under the woman, maybe three of them? And how many others gathered around, arms up, doing their duty to the last?

Her shouting, 'Cut the rope now!'

A rope that none of them had considered might be a detonator. Except that wasn't true, either. Luc had taken her by the arm and tried to tell her. She'd ignored him, rushed in, so desperate not to lose another person that she'd sacrificed how many? Luc, who had seen what she too might have seen if she hadn't let Ailsa's murder overwhelm her.

A helicopter buzzed overhead. Not one of theirs. Ava grabbed a radio from the nearest police officer.

'Get that helicopter out of the area right now. Call a judge and get a court order if you have to, failing that just fucking shoot it down.'

'Er, ma'am?' came the response.

Ava switched the radio off and handed it back.

'Chief,' Luc called, appearing in a scenes of crime suit. 'They need your clothes to check DNA for the dead list, and the superintendent's here.'

Ava dragged her eyes away from the pile of destruction and made her way to a hastily erected crime scene centre of operations tent where Overbeck was waiting for her.

Overbeck looked her up and down, didn't comment on the bloody mess Ava was in, and asked, 'How many dead?'

Chapter Five

BEFORE

Quinn McTavish was the sort of girl no one ever noticed. That wasn't true, in fact, but it was the way she perceived herself. The girl in the mirror was mousey and unremarkable, timid and dull. That girl made sure her hair was neat and tidy but never ran straighteners through it, and certainly didn't bother to colour the brunette strands with more eye-catching tones. She wore sensible shoes, trainers whenever possible, high heels almost never. Expletives were a rare eruption from her lips, and only then if she was taken by surprise or enraged by cruelty, particularly towards animals.

At twenty, she still lived with her parents and hoped that they wouldn't mind her staying for a few years yet. Her casual job paid only £10 per hour and her part-time online book-keeping studies were nowhere near completion. Also, she loved being at home. Her parents were, as far as she could make out, an exception. Through school, her friends had moaned about their own mothers and fathers – boundaries, expectations, bedtimes – the complaints had been endless. Quinn had nodded along companionably, but she rarely disagreed with her perfectly reasonable parents, and if she did it was handled with a discussion, good grace and compromise. The reality was that she didn't want to move out because she would miss them. Then there was the baby to consider.

Quinn was well into her nineteenth year when her parents had asked her to sit with them for a chat. That hadn't felt like a big deal until she'd found a pot of tea waiting for her – not just teabags dropped into cups and covered in boiling water, but a proper loose leaf effort – and the really terrifying part of it all, homemade scones with jam scooped from the jar into a tiny dish. Her parents had sat opposite her and neither of them said a word until Quinn had filled her plate and accepted a carefully poured cup.

The thoughts that went through her head were, in this order: a life-threatening illness, financial ruin, they wanted her to get her own place, they'd decided to take early retirement and move to Spain.

'Sweetheart,' her father Simeon had begun, reaching across the table to take her hand.

'Please just tell me you're both okay because you're really freaking me out!' she blurted.

Their faces dropped and they gave one another an incredulous stare.

'Oh no, there's nothing wrong,' and, 'No, no, not at all, nothing like that,' they both babbled at once.

Quinn relaxed.

'Don't do that to me. No scones next time you've got news, understand? So what is it then? Did you two win the lottery or something?' she asked.

'Better than the lottery, but no less shocking,' her father said.

Quinn took in her mother's beaming face and her father's attempt at covering the tears forming in his eyes.

'I'm pregnant,' Cora McTavish said quietly. 'We're having a baby. You're going to be a big sister, Quinn.'

It took her a few seconds to absorb the news. Her parents had tried for a baby for years after Quinn had been born. She'd been endlessly jealous of her friends who'd had wee brothers and sisters to play with, and eventually just accepted that it wasn't going to happen for her parents. They'd done their best to cover their sadness, delighted in Quinn, and had given her the love they'd have given a whole troop of children, and filled their lives with each other.

'How?' Quinn asked.

'No idea, just time and nature and irony I guess,' her dad said. 'It won't be easy with your mother being forty-five and me pushing fifty, but we were hoping you'd stay around long enough to be the sort of big sister who'll go to the park and play games and be less uncool than these ancient parents will be.'

Quinn stood and offered her open arms to her mum and dad who were so obviously delighted and overwhelmed that she could feel only one thing for the baby that was coming – that the little boy or girl about to burst into their lives was going to be the luckiest, most adored child in the whole world.

Six months later, that baby arrived courtesy of a caesarean section, and Quinn had found herself with a sister at an age when she could have become a mother herself. As her mum had slept off the drugs and had father had made phone calls to every family member and friend across the world, bursting with pride and relief, Quinn had held the tiny wriggling thing to her chest, and fallen in love in a heartbeat. The emotion came from nowhere, a confusing blend of honey and tiger-blood, that she would love the girl endlessly and limitlessly at the same time as she would kill anyone who ever dared hurt her.

Still glowing the next day, Quinn went to work at the FastMart supermarket in Gorebridge. Most people only knew the diminutive town as they drove through it on the A7 towards or away from Edinburgh, but it functioned well enough for those who lived there. A few high street shops provided for most day-to-day needs, and there was a school, a couple of pubs, a nice cafe. The McTavish family had lived there for three generations and were making no plans to move. You couldn't put a price on knowing your neighbours, on a community that would rally when you needed them, and that would celebrate with a middle-aged couple who found themselves with a new baby rather than whispering and judging.

There were few customers who went past Quinn on the till that day who didn't send their best, ask for an update, or look dewy-eyed at the numerous baby pictures on Quinn's mobile. She was just slipping her phone back into her pocket when a young man gave a small cough.

'Do I not get to see whatever it is that's making everyone go so soft?' he asked.

Quinn paused mid-scan of his chicken salad sandwich and looked up at him.

'Honestly, I don't think you'll be very interested.' She smiled.

'Ach, come on now, don't judge this book by its cover,' he said. 'Let me guess . . . new puppy, or maybe a kitten, but you look more like a dog person to me.'

His grin was infectious. His hair was down to his collar, dark blond curls that looked effortlessly messy-chic. Quinn could imagine how much her girlfriends would pay to get hair like that.

'Actually, neither,' she said. 'I've a new baby sister.' She carried on scanning the few items from his basket.

'Really, what's her name?' he asked.

'No name yet. Nothing we think of seems to suit her.'

'Come on, solving problems is my area of expertise. Let me see.'

Quinn protested, feeling foolish showing baby photos to a stranger, particularly a twenty-something man passing through who couldn't possibly have been interested. Had there been a queue or anything else pressing to do, she wouldn't have even considered it, but he was charming and persistent. She took out her mobile and showed him five or six photos of the sweetest human being in the world.

He took his time inspecting each image, commenting on different aspects of the baby's face. Quinn knew it was all for show, blushing a little harder every time he looked up from the photos to stare at her.

'Well, she's going to be as beautiful as her older sister,' he said eventually. 'Wider mouth though and squarer jaw, whereas you got those amazing cheekbones. What's your name? Sibling names should complement each other.'

'Quinn,' she said quietly, feeling self-conscious but happy to play along.

'Quinn. Hmm, tough one to beat. That's snappy and attention-grabbing but still feminine and mysterious. The baby will need something different. Maybe more traditional but not common-place. I've got it. She's Dolly.'

'What? No,' Quinn said. 'That's too American and cutesy.' But she looked down at the photo of her little sister, eyes closed peacefully in slumber, a smile playing at the corner of her lips, and turned the name over in her mind. 'Dolly,' she said aloud.

'Give it a day to get used to it,' he said. 'I'll be passing through again tomorrow. You can let me know what your parents think of it then.' He picked up his groceries and gave her a mock salute. 'Always good to be of service.'

'You didn't tell me your name,' Quinn said as he approached the automatic doors.

'Liam,' he said. 'See you tomorrow, Quinn.'

'God, could he have loved himself any more?' Quinn's manager called from the shelf where he was completing a stock inventory. He was only seven years older than Quinn, but his position gave him a certain amount of authority in the town. Mark Devlin enjoyed tinkering with old cars and motorbikes in his free time – he'd always thought he'd have a career in mechanics – but even more than that he'd found he liked retail. He relished the routine and order of it. He also liked Quinn, as oblivious as she was to his attentions.

'I think he was just having a bit of a laugh,' she replied softly.

'He was cracking onto you. Did you not feel his eyes crawling over you? I should've thrown him out, slimy lavvy heid.'

Quinn giggled. Her manager was always quick with the more colourful Scots insults.

'That's maybe a bit harsh,' she said. 'He was just suggesting a name for the babe.'

'Full of crap is what he was.' He checked his watch. 'Your shift's over.' He shoved his hands deep in his pockets. 'There's a band playing at The Queen Mary this Friday night. A few of us said we'd meet there around nine. Will you come?'

'I'll see how my mum and dad are doing, I guess. They might need me at home.'

'Maybe just for an hour,' Mark suggested. 'They wouldn't want you to stop having fun.'

'I know, but I've got to fit my studies in as well. I'll see how I feel.' She closed up her session on the till and took off her tabard, slipping it into her backpack. 'See you tomorrow.'

By the time she arrived home, she'd stopped dismissing the name Dolly as nonsense and was trying it out in different scenarios. Full name Dolly Cora McTavish – they'd already agreed the baby should have her mother's first name as her middle name. But could you discipline a child with a name like Dolly? Quinn discounted that. Her baby sister would be disciplined even less often than she had been growing up.

She approached her mother with it. The newest member of the family was gurgling in her mother's arms, waving tiny fingers and thumbs in the air, discovering the look and feel of the world.

'Dolly,' her mother whispered. The baby gave a wriggle, turned her head into Cora's breast and fell immediately into a contented sleep. 'I like it.'

By the time her father got home from work, it was all over. The baby had transformed herself into Dolly forever. He'd taken her into his arms, kissed her wrinkly little forehead and shrugged.

'Dolly it is then,' Simeon whispered to the baby. 'Dolly McTavish, newest member of our happy clan, welcome to the world my love. May your days be filled with sunshine, your nights be filled with stars and your life be filled with laughter. I can tell you this sweetheart, you've the best two women in the world as role models. If we give you nothing else, we've already given you that.'

Chapter Six

A major incident was declared. Protocols slammed into gear. A multi-agency well-oiled machine took over. Callanach finished coordinating MIT's response and writing his own statement at 3 a.m. Half an hour later he picked up coffee and sandwiches. It was 4 a.m. when he found Ava where he'd known she'd be; sitting on the hillside that overlooked the entrance to the Innocent Railway Tunnel, watching the work continue by floodlight. The bulk of the building rubble had already been shifted so the finer forensic work could begin, and every item of clothing, car keys, mobile phone, watch, ring and stray hair was being mapped, photographed, bagged and tagged.

Callanach sat on the damp ground at Ava's side and handed her a steaming cardboard cup. She took it without a word, her fingertips brushing his in passing the cup. Even at times like this, at the very worst moments, all he wanted was to be by her side. They'd come so close to having a real relationship. Sometimes he'd pulled away, other times she had. But they were always drawn back to one another, and not just because work required it. Ava Turner was gravity to him. He wondered if there would ever be a right time for them to try again.

She blew on her coffee to cool it, then took a careful sip. 'Every time I think I've seen the most fucked up thing I'm ever going to see, someone goes one better,' Ava said. 'At least now I know what I have to do. I've got to stop tempting fate. If I accept that there's still something worse than this, then maybe I won't need to be shown it.'

'When did you last sleep?' he asked.

Ava shrugged and they stared silently into the misty haze. Workers moved, ant-like, from tent to rubble to vehicles and back, criss-crossing paths, methodical and focused. In their white suits, in the dark, it was nothing short of science fiction. Occasionally a larger object needed to be moved, and even from a distance there was no mistaking the discovery of a substantial body part.

'How long is this going to take?' Callanach asked.

'Several days. We're lucky it's dry tonight. There's rain forecast for tomorrow so they're going to start erecting tenting over the area but it'll need scaffolding first. Then we have to keep the water from running down the hillside onto the pathway, which means digging some drainage. How are the press being held back?'

'We've closed all the roads leading to the immediate area and set up pedestrian barriers to keep anyone from walking in. They're being manned full-time until you say the scene is completely processed. As you'd expect, there's a large media presence on Holyrood Park Road getting footage of emergency vehicles going in and out. We've issued a statement saying that no drone footage is to be taken of the scene while it's being worked on, but it's going to be almost impossible to enforce.'

Ava stretched her neck and rubbed her eyes. 'I appreciate you coming to sit with me, Luc. I'd lost track of time. Hey, did you check in on Natasha? I completely forgot to call her.'

'I did. Her exact words were, "tell Ava to get her arse home for a while".'

Normally there'd have been a response dripping with Ava's habitual funny, acerbic wit. Normally she'd have sent her best friend a text to put her right. Normally.

'She seems so much stronger,' Luc said. 'Now that the chemo-therapy's stopped and the prognosis is positive, a weight has slipped from her. Last week she was even talking about going back to work. Natasha's still coping with the emotional issues from the mastectomy, but she's been in touch with a therapist and I think she's ready to start dealing with that, too.'

'You two really did get close since we all started living together.' Ava took a sip of her coffee. 'I know it's been weird. You, me and Natasha living in one house, getting her through the treatment and the surgery, propping each other up. Natasha adores you. Honestly, it's actually started to piss me off.'

'Jealous?'

'Just bored,' Ava said. 'Hand me a sandwich.'

'I'll move out as soon as she's back teaching at the University. If she can cope with hordes of students then she certainly won't need me making her coffee in the morning,' Callanach said.

'She won't want you to go,' Ava told him.

Below them, an officer raised his arm and called for assistance. Luc and Ava fell silent and stood, studying the latest find. Photographs were taken of the item in situ, then it was lifted onto a sterile mat. It resembled a caved-in red football. Only the few strands of long black hair still clinging to it made it recognisable as a head.

Callanach reached into his pocket and pulled out an unopened pack of Gauloises cigarettes, ripping open the top and tugging out a stick. Ava took the pack and put one in her own mouth. They stood, the unlit sticks hanging from their lips, and watched the process unfold.

'Are you ever going to give up not actually smoking?' Ava asked.

'Probably not,' Callanach said. 'Is that the hanging woman's head?'

'I think so. I wonder if she knew what was going to happen to her. Can you imagine, being hanged, and while it was happening, knowing that if anyone rescued you, you'd explode?'

Callanach sucked cold air through his cigarette and blew out a lack of smoke.

'This is going to get political,' he said. 'There'll be enquiries, global press attention, idiots demanding to know why we haven't already caught the perpetrator, speculation about terrorism. There's going to be a lot of pressure on you. Lean on me, Ava. I know things haven't always been easy between us. Maybe we should never have mixed work with our private lives – not that I regret it – but you can rely on me. I want to help.'

The head was being moved carefully to the waiting transport for transferral to the mortuary. Ava turned her attention to Callanach.

'You know, at first, when Natasha was diagnosed and asked us to move in to take care of her, I thought it was all a ruse. That maybe she thought she could get us together as a couple as some last good deed. But it was simpler than that. She had the good sense to reach out when she needed help. Natasha surrounded herself with people who loved her and who could be there for her.' Ava said.

Callanach crushed his unsmoked cigarette in his empty coffee cup and waited for Ava to continue. It was the most she'd spoken about this for months. Not that she was quiet at home, but she'd never really opened up about how Natasha's illness had made her feel. The timing didn't surprise him. There was something about bearing witness to tragedy and loss that made you reassess what was going on in your own life. He took the opportunity to study her in what little light was bouncing up from the floodlights below. In spite of the tiredness etched around her eyes, she looked the same as the day they'd met. Her curly brown hair was tied in a ponytail, as was her tradition for work. Large grey eyes, wide cheekbones and a rosebud mouth gave her face a heart-shape, but anyone who mistook her prettiness for softness was a fool. Her attractiveness came from a deep-seated intelligence and a strong passion for life. Callanach forced himself to look away again.

'When she started losing her hair, the day she decided to shave it, you wore a hat to the hairdresser with us, and pulled it off when she saw herself for the first time . . .' Ava ran a hand through Callanach's hair, just starting to grow back, her fingertips icy cold but gentle, '. . . I saw then what I'd failed to see before. Natasha had known all along that she needed your compassion, your strength around her. She claimed it was backup for me, and she believed it. If anyone ever asked my fierce, beautiful, lesbian friend if she would admit to being reliant on a man, she'd gut them. But she relied on you because you never once treated her as if she was weak.' Ava put her hands back in her pockets and sat down on the frosting ground. 'Watching you with Natasha has been joyful. I know I can rely on you, Luc. Whatever happened between us in the past . . . It's time to let it go.'

Callanach walked behind her, sat down with his chest against her back, and put his arms around her shoulders. She let her head fall against him as they watched the pieces of the dead being gathered.

'What are you not saying to me?' Callanach asked.

'I'm taking some time out, Luc. Once I've found the person who killed Ailsa and when I know Natasha is safe, I'm going away for a while. I don't want to stare down death in its many underhanded fucking forms anymore. I don't want to watch another postmortem or visit the grieving family or take questions from the press about it. It's right there, over my shoulder, at all times and I've got so used it that it doesn't even scare me.'

Callanach wrapped his more tightly around her.

'Where will you go?' he asked.

'I'm not sure yet. Maybe India or Australia, I've heard good things about Panama. Just away. I'd like you to stay with Natasha. It's a lot to ask, and if she starts a new relationship then things might change, but she shouldn't be alone. We nearly lost her. She knows how close she came. It's going to take a while before she feels secure again.'

'I'll do whatever I can,' he said. 'If Natasha wants me there, then of course I'll stay with her. What about this investigation? What did Overbeck say when she was here earlier?'

'Don't worry about that. The evil Overbitch and I have reached an agreement. I said I'd finish up this case given the fact that she can't afford to lose any more police officers at the moment, then I'd get out of her hair.'

'It was that simple?'

'There was one other thing.' Ava extricated herself from him, stood and stepped away. 'I told her that I had no intention of letting Ailsa's killer face trial. No one who causes this much devastation has the right to a comfy cell, gym equipment, a TV and three square meals a day.'

Callanach looked down at the chaos below them, knowing argument was futile.

'And what did Superintendent Overbeck say about that?' he asked.

'Nothing,' Ava said, walking slowly down the scorched grass bank to the pathway. 'She said nothing at all.'

Chapter Seven

The red brick entrance to HM Prison Kilmarnock would have resembled a scout hut if not for the high grey walls extending out either side of it. Ava and DI Pax Graham had travelled west across the mainland to reach it, been greeted unenthusiastically, and were waiting in the legal visits suite for Allan Cronk.

Pax Graham had long hair he wore tied back, a jaw that would have made any man proud and the sort of frame that normally dwarfed everyone around him, but Allan Cronk rendered him average, and Ava positively tiny. He strode in, didn't give them a second look, and waited to be seated and secured. His prison disciplinary record and previous convictions for assaulting police officers meant the governor had insisted on it. Head shaved, almost no skin left untattooed even on his face, he wasn't the sort of cell mate you wanted unless you had plenty to bribe him with.

'Didn't agree to this,' Cronk said, looking at the high slit of window offering a view to the outdoor greyness.

'You don't need to agree, this is a criminal investigation. I'm DCI Turner, this is DI Graham. You're being spoken to today as a witness, not as a suspect. You're not obliged to help us . . .'

'Kind of you, sweetheart.'

'. . . But any assistance you provide will be reported to the governor, and you might find that it's important for you to help us for personal reasons.'

'Lick my balls,' Allan Cronk said.

Ava couldn't even be bothered to sigh. It was all too predictable. She opened an envelope and stared at the contents on her lap, which were shielded by the desk so Cronk couldn't see them.

'Your prison file says you have a numerical tattoo on your inner bottom lip,' Ava said. 'I need to ask you about a fellow gang member.'

'Nah, I wasn't a member of any gang, love. That's just a record of the length of my dick.'

'In millimetres?' Pax Graham asked.

Not normally given to sarcastic asides – within MIT that role was usually reserved for DS Lively – Ava was surprised that DI Graham was getting involved in petty banter, but he was naturally protective and Cronk was off to a bad start.

'You wanna suck it an' see?' Cronk retorted.

'Mr Cronk, do you have any other close male relatives in the same gang as you?' Ava asked gently.

'Fuck me, does this bitch actually expect me to answer that?' he aimed at Graham. Ava ignored the comment, instead pushing a report covered in small print and numbers onto the desk between them. 'What's that then?' Cronk asked.

'It's a DNA match report in relation to an offence that happened six weeks ago.'

'Then someone needs to introduce you to a calendar because I've been in this little slice of paradise for the last three years, so whatever it is you're about to accuse me of—'

'The DNA match that came back doesn't implicate you, Mr Cronk. What we found was a 93% match for you, indicating that the DNA in question is likely to be a close male relative of yours. He also had the same tattoo inside his bottom lip. We're hoping you can tell us his name.'

Cronk picked up the report, made a pretence of reading it for a couple of minutes, screwed up the paper and tossed it backwards over his head.

'Load of bollocks,' he said. 'You think I'm talking to the polis, about anything, ever? You think I'm going to help you stitch up some other poor sucker?'

'You stabbed a man in clear view of a CCTV camera. You were never stitched up,' Pax Graham said.

Ava shrugged. She was going to have to get the information a different way. From the envelope she pulled a photograph of the face of the corpse used to kill Ailsa Lambert.

'Mr Cronk, can you identify this man for us?' she asked.

Cronk's smirk was replaced by a grimace. 'Why are his eyes closed?' he asked.

'I need a name before I can give you any further information,' Ava said. In reality, Cronk's facial expression had given her all the confirmation she needed. He cared about the man in the photo, and he was devastated. There would be files somewhere – with a school or Social Services – that would provide answers.

Cronk balled his hands into fists, his face a snarl of hatred.

'Is he fucking dead? You tell me right now. What cunt did that to him?'

'I can only share the information with a family member. You have to give me a name and a date of birth. If you do that, I'll answer every question you have.'

'Bitch!' Cronk screamed, but by then he was crying too. Heavy tears splashed down onto his chest as he howled.

'The name,' DI Graham said.

'Gavin,' Cronk cried. 'That's my little brother. I'm gonna find who did that to him and I'm gonna make them fuckin' pay.'

'Same surname as you?' Graham clarified.

'What the fuck do you think?' Cronk yelled.

'I need his date of birth to verify his identity,' Ava said quietly. Cronk screeched and hit his head against the desk. Ava waited it out.

'March 3, 1998,' he said.

Ava nodded at DI Graham who slipped out of the room to make a phone call. She didn't need to wait for independent verification of the information Cronk had given her. She'd known they had to be brothers as soon as she'd seen his face. The similarities were stark, and for all the hard man bullshit, Allan Cronk sure as hell wasn't faking his reaction.

'Tell me,' he said.

'The toxicology report showed a lethal amount of heroin in his body. We're not sure yet if the overdose was deliberate or accidental. There was a fresh injection site between his toes.'

'Gavin didn't use,' Cronk said. 'That's bullshit. You're wrong. Trying to make him look like some druggy so you don't have to investigate it.'

'I'm here because we are investigating it.' Ava kept her voice low. 'Are you saying Gavin had never used drugs before, or never injected before?'

'Not fuckin' H,' he said. 'A bit of weed now and then . . . a tab of E sometimes.'

Ava studied his face. Allan Cronk was telling the truth. That much had already been verified in the toxicology report. A hair strand test had shown nothing more than ecstasy and marijuana longer term in Gavin's body.

'When did you last see your brother?'

'He visited me about three months ago. Was supposed to come again in a fortnight. Will I be allowed out for his funeral? Can you fix it with the governor for me?'

'Absolutely,' Ava said. 'But that won't be for a while. Do you have any parents who need to be notified?'

'No idea where our dad is. Haven't seen him for a decade. Our mam's still in Inverness. Her address is on my file. He was always her favourite. This'll fuckin' kill her.'

'I'm sorry,' Ava said. 'I have to ask, was your brother in any trouble? Did he have any enemies that you knew of?' She was delaying the worst of the news until last. Allan Cronk was going to go off the rails when she delivered that blow.

He shrugged, went silent.

'Someone injected a huge amount of heroin into your brother's body, and there's a possibility that it might have been done deliberately. There are also signs on his ankles and wrists that he was restrained for a period of days before he died. Allan, if your little brother was into something he shouldn't have been, I need to know about it.'

Still no response.

'Your brother had a gang tattoo like yours but he isn't on the database as having any convictions. Can you explain that?'

'Dumb shit wanted to be like me,' he muttered. 'He wanted into the gang, but there was no way he was ever going to do anything bad enough. I'd have fucking killed him for starters.' Allan stopped talking, the horrible irony of what he'd said sinking in.

'So he got the tattoo,' Ava said. 'What else?' Silence. 'I can't get justice for your brother without you telling me what you know, and you're not getting out of here any time soon so you can forget reaping any vengeance.' Still nothing. Ava took a deep breath. 'While your brother was being held, someone performed an operation on him. They used him as a human bomb, planting a chemical weapon in his stomach. They kept him long enough for the wound to start to heal, then administered the overdose. His body was left on a pavement in an industrial area of Leith in the middle of the night. He was already dead by then. During the autopsy, the device went off, killing the forensic pathologist.'

Cronk began panting. Tendons stood out in his neck. Ava braced, but he got control of himself.

'Gavin was dealing. He couldn't get a job and his landlord was about to kick him out. Is it . . . is it a rival gang? Do you think . . .' his chest heaved with a sob, '. . . do you think maybe it's because of that fuckin' tattoo in his mouth?'

Ava thought about it, watching Allan Cronk exercise the last vestiges of control he had.

'If it had been a beating, even a shooting, I'd have said yes. But this? The technology was beyond what I'd expect from a gang, and your brother wasn't the end target. If I can locate the place he was abducted from, that might provide some trace evidence or a witness who saw a vehicle.'

'He had a flat on Hyvot Loan, Moredun. I don't know the number,' Allan said.

'I'll find it,' Ava said. 'Did he live alone?'

'He had a girlfriend. Can't remember her name. They were on and off. I need to know if he . . .' He put his forehead down on the edge of the table and stared at the floor.

'If he suffered?' Ava asked.

Cronk gave a slow, sad nod. Ava considered what her reply should be. Under any other circumstances she would automatically reach for the most reassuring reply. This man, though, had taken a knife to another human being. He'd run with a gang who dealt in arms, drugs and prostitution. He'd once hit a police officer over the head with a brick. She put the photograph of his brother's face back into the envelope and left the DNA report on the floor where he'd thrown it.

'He'd have been scared,' Ava said. 'When he was healing from the surgery he might have been in some pain, knowing something was wrong inside him. There were sedatives in his body, high levels, and we assume he was sedated for the whole period after surgery to keep him still as he healed. He wouldn't have suffered after that. His actual death would have been painless.'

Part of her hadn't wanted to offer the comfort. A mean part that refused to see Allan Cronk as a victim even in his grief. The man in front of her had played his part, Ava told herself. What sort of role model had he been to his younger brother? Maybe, if his brother hadn't copied the gang tattoo, then he wouldn't have been kidnapped, used as a bomb and Ailsa would still be alive.

Only that was wrong. If it hadn't been Gavin Cronk, it would have been a different victim. He'd been nothing more than a means to an end. The outstanding evil at play wouldn't have hesitated to have taken another body off the streets.

'I'll make sure your mother is looked after,' Ava said as she headed for the door. 'And I'll let you know when Gavin's body can be released for burial.'

She hated the compassion she felt. Didn't want it.

'Thank you,' Allan Cronk whispered.

Ava left him to his tears.

Chapter Eight

The drive back to Edinburgh took an hour and a half, by which time units had been mobilised to attend Hyvot Loan in Moredun. The property Gavin Cronk had been renting was a studio flat in a divided house. Ava knew the area well enough to realise that the term 'studio flat' was probably going to be more euphemism than reality. South-east of the city centre, the area was a far cry from the historic buildings in the grandiose shadow of Edinburgh Castle and the bustle of Princes Street. Edinburgh was a city of two halves, the one blindingly beautiful, the other no more than a sticking plaster over increasingly deepening social cracks. It was precisely those wounds that Gavin Cronk had been monetising. No more than a few pounds could buy the hopeless, depressed and anxious a salve for a couple of hours. A high, however transitory, however pointless, was still a stairway to heaven in a ravine of unemployment and food bank queues.

Scenes of crime officers waited in trucks while armed units fronted the operation. DS Lively met Ava and DI Graham in the neighbouring road, not that there was any reason to believe Gavin Cronk's murderer was still at the property, but preparing for the worst had become second nature for Ava. Where there were drug dealers, there were weapons, and Ava had been clear that not one more officer was to be harmed in the course of the investigation. Eight police officers had already lost their lives, and that was without taking into account the paramedics and firefighters. 'Caution, caution, caution' was the new mantra.

The house was a two-storey with tiny wooden windows and damp staining the pebble-dash. Gavin's ground floor flat was accessed through the rear door. The windows were shut, curtains drawn, but rap music announced life within.

'What the hell do these kids hear that I can't?' Lively groaned. 'Sounds like utter shite to me. When did music no longer require any sort of tune?'

'Save it for later, Detective Sergeant,' Ava said. 'Right, everyone, minimal bodies inside. We need to preserve what's left of the evidence so no hands on anything unless they're gloved. Secure the access, arrest anyone inside. We'll hold them on suspicion of involvement in drug offences for now. No one leaves from any surrounding properties before they've been spoken to either.'

There was a general murmur of understanding and then Ava gave the go sign.

The external back door swung open as the lead officer knocked it, and armed units filed into the corridor, Ava at the rear. As they raised their weapons and prepared to announce their presence, the internal door opened and a teenager stumbled out, barging through officers and running towards the exit where he promptly emptied his stomach onto the floor.

'Police!' the lead officer shouted as he stepped through the internal door.

Ava waited for the inevitable shouting and attempts to pile out. What she heard instead was a huge cheer then the music got louder.

'Stand back,' Ava said, striding through and forcing her way into the heaving flat. There were bodies everywhere, dancing, sitting, at least seven lying on a bed, several more crammed into the shower room, and others filling the kitchen.

Smoke thick with the unmistakeable aroma of marijuana made the air a dense haze. The lightbulbs had been painted red, and the atmosphere was more night club than bedsit. Everyone was clearly off their faces on various substances. Ava performed a rough count. No fewer than fifty people had turned Gavin Cronk's tiny dwelling into party central. She strode over to a portable speaker and ripped out the plug. The silence stopped the dancing, and every face turned blankly but passively towards her.

'Police.' Ava sighed. 'We don't want any trouble. We're not anticipating any arrests but we do need to search this property. Make your way one by one to the door where you'll be asked some questions by the waiting officers. Is Gavin Cronk's girl-friend here?'

'Who?' the nearest person to Ava questioned, a stupid grin plastered over his face.

'Gavin Cronk. This is his flat.' Ava tried to remain calm in the face of a twenty-something zombie apocalypse without the appetite for brains.

This is the next generation, Ava thought, understanding dawning on her that the world was well and truly fucked.

'Panda!' someone shouted. 'Where's Panda?'

'Kitchen,' the reply came.

Ava pushed a few feet in that direction where a space had been made around a pale young woman with enormous brown eyes framed with the most ridiculous false eyelashes Ava had ever seen.

'Panda,' Ava said, 'my name is Detective Chief Inspector Turner. We need to talk.'

★ ★ ★

One by one they were persuaded to leave the party and go quietly with officers. It was the least violent drug bust on record and Ava had no complaints about that. What was left behind, though, was a disaster. The scenes of crime officers simply stared into the flat.

'Not a chance,' one of them declared.

Ava took stock. Scenes of crime were unswervingly professional. For years she'd watched in wonder as they'd arrived at the worst of events only to plod quietly, painstakingly onwards and process whatever was needed without question.

This, though, was pointless. Even she could see it. Any prospect of gathering meaningful DNA, skin cells, fingerprints or footprints had been eradicated with a party that neighbours were reporting had been raging for weeks, people coming and going twenty-four hours a day.

'Do people really hate us so much that everyone in this road preferred to let this carry on rather than ask for our help? What in god's name is it that we've done wrong?' Ava asked.

DI Graham was the only person present who felt brave enough to answer. 'We arrested drug users instead of drug dealers. We went for the easy targets who were already the victims of a well-organised drug-pushing scheme. And, as a community, we didn't listen well enough when people were in trouble and asking us for help. Policing has changed recently, but not enough to undo the damage from previous generations of law enforcement. Our outreach still needs to improve.'

'You're wasted at crime scenes, Detective Inspector,' Ava replied. 'We should make you Police Scotland's spokesperson.'

'Ach, no. Public speaking's not my thing, ma'am, and someone's got to be here to keep DS Lively in order, don't they?'

Ava smiled. Lively had been out of order since the day Ava had first met him, and Pax Graham was the least likely candidate for maintaining order. At his height and build, she'd

53

never actually seen him have to assert himself. People just naturally wanted to do whatever he suggested.

'Ma'am,' Lively said as he joined them, 'we can't get much sense out of most of them, but the girlfriend – Panda – turns out to be called Amanda, so points both for rhyming and for choosing her makeup spirit animal. She showed me a text and I've confirmed it on several other mobiles. When Gavin disappeared, he sent a round-robin message to everyone in his mobile contacts list telling them he was going away for a while but that his flat could be used until he returned. He even left the door unlocked for them.'

'Shit,' Ava said.

'Aye, whoever took him either accessed his phone or made him send the message under threat. Panda says Gavin liked a party but has never done anything like this before. By the time she arrived, it had already started and she didn't feel able to kick anyone out.'

'So the murderer didn't need to clean up his crime scene, he just let everyone else trash it,' Ava said. 'Is there a drug stash in there?'

'Panda reckons it had been cleared out before she arrived. No idea who took everything.'

'Fine,' Ava ran a weary hand over her eyes. 'I need a thorough search of the property, not that it'll do any good, but we can't afford any screw-ups. Secure the scene and get everyone else on door-to-doors asking when they last saw Gavin and if anything unusual has happened. I'm particularly interested in him getting into strange vehicles.'

'I'll get that organised,' DI Graham said. 'Come on, Sergeant. You've obviously formed a bond with Panda. Let's see if she can provide any more information.' He clapped Lively on the back and they walked away together, banter in full flow. Ava was grateful for her team every day, but never more so than when they were under pressure.

Ava's mobile rang. Callanach was calling.

'Any progress?' he asked. The station's coffee machine hissed in the background, and Ava wished for a few minutes' peace at her desk with a hot drink and some clarity.

'What's the opposite of progress? Never mind, whatever it is, that's what we've got here. Any news your end?'

'Nothing definite,' Callanach replied, 'but a missing persons report just came in. A sixteen-year-old is looking for his thirty-two-year-old mother. She's tall and skinny, with long, dark hair. He stayed a couple of nights with his father, then his mum should have picked him up from school yesterday but didn't appear. He walked the three miles to her house, let himself in, and she still hasn't come home.'

'You think it's the hanging woman?' Ava asked.

'Maybe. I need to go and see the kid, but I thought you'd want to come with me.'

'What's her name?' Ava asked.

She heard Callanach move a piece of paper. 'Maura Douglas. The son gave his name as Jimmy.'

'I'm on my way back into the city. I'll leave Lively in charge here. This is going to take days anyway. We're so thin on the ground with one team still up at the Innocent Railway Tunnel and another here. Stay put. I'll collect you.'

'Ma'am!' Lively shouted from the doorway to Gavin's flat.

'Got to go.' Ava ended the call. 'What is it?'

Lively waved a notebook in the air at her. As she got closer to it, she saw tiny frosted particles around its edges, faintly soggy with damp. Ava drew on gloves and took the notebook from Lively.

'It's his deals book,' Lively said. 'It was in his freezer wrapped in a plastic sandwich bag and shoved into a pack of Brussels sprouts. Theoretically, it was genius. No one who broke in was going to steal Brussels sprouts, but then what sort of drug dealer . . .'

'Eats Brussels sprouts?' Ava finished for him. She flicked through to the last page. The writing and columns of entries were surprisingly neat. 'His last deal was five forget-mes. Is that Rohypnol?'

'Yup,' Lively confirmed.

'That must have been the day he went missing. Sold to someone he refers to as "Sesame" for £100. I want everyone questioned, Lively. Find out who this Sesame is. Start by asking Panda. If anyone wants me, tell them I'm driving to an address where I fully expect to deliver news that will destroy a kid's life. Just another day at the bloody office.'

Chapter Nine

Ava's mobile rang as she was driving. A familiar sense of panic filled her chest when caller ID revealed that Natasha was trying to contact her. She gave the voice command to answer the call on speaker.

'Tasha, you okay?' Ava did her best to keep her voice light. Natasha hated it when she fussed.

'Actually, I was calling to see if you were okay.'

'I'm fine, why?' Ava said.

'I happened to look in your bedroom this morning. You need to talk?' Natasha asked.

'What's wrong with my bedroom?'

'So . . .' Natasha began slowly. 'Your bed's made, all the dirty clothes are in the laundry basket, the pile of paperwork that's been on your desk for months has all been dealt with. Also, you dusted.'

Ava sighed. 'Look, I know I haven't seen you much lately and I'd love to chat, but I'm in the middle of something and—'

'Yeah, I get that. And the room comments were flippant, I know, but not without merit. You thrive at work by letting all your chaos out at home, Ava. What little time you spend here

57

at the moment should be used for eating, sleeping and social-ising. Instead, you've become some sort of robotic neat freak in the space of weeks.'

'You're exaggerating,' Ava said

'You're avoiding,' Natasha responded. 'I've known you longer than anyone except your family. Not at any other point in your life have I walked into a space you occupy to find it looking so immaculate and . . .' she struggled to find the word, '. . . clin-ical. I know you've been through hell with Ailsa, and that you're still processing that grief while you're busy at work, but—'

'Busy at work? Natasha, I'm not going to row with you, but I'd hardly label this investigation anything as bland as being busy at work,' Ava snapped.

'I know that. Even though you've tried to wrap me in cotton wool, I can still read the news. So come home and talk to me. Open up a bit. Don't use the few precious hours you're home for dusting. All those soulless idiots who claim that cleaning is therapeutic forgot that a single hug equates to roughly fifty hours of ironing, forty hours of vacuuming and infinite toilet cleans.'

Ava laughed in spite of herself, in spite of where she was going and all that she'd been through. Natasha, irritating as she was at that moment in time, was right.

'I'll remember that,' Ava said. 'No more cleaning.'

'Well, not none at all,' Natasha said. 'I mean, you're a complete slob at home so a small improvement is welcome.'

'Would you get off the phone already?' Ava asked. 'Luc's waiting for me.'

'Luc's been waiting for you forever. How about putting the poor man out of his misery? And yourself for that matter.'

'That's not what I meant, and you know it. Also, my private life is none of your business. Are we done?'

'Absolutely. I'm off to empty your laundry basket all over your floor so it'll feel like home when you get back later.'

'Would you leave me alone?' Natasha merely laughed in response. 'Hey, Tash, I really am glad you called. Now get some rest and stay out of my bedroom.'

Callanach was waiting for her in Clovenstone Drive, staring up at the shabby tenement building that was shedding plaster like sunburned skin and crying tears from blocked gutters.

'Some of that tourist revenue needs to be spent out here,' Callanach said.

'Out of sight out of mind,' Ava replied. 'Who wants to think about kids waking up hungry when there are bars and museums and galleries to visit?'

'I guess it's the same in every city.'

'Doesn't have to be,' Ava said. 'We all just need to straighten out our priorities. Come on, let's go talk to this boy.'

He watched as she strode away, purposeful, head up, outwardly stronger than he'd ever seen her, and felt concern spread like venom through his veins. Ava Turner had rescued him, physically and mentally, several times in the previous few years. A false rape allegation during his time with Interpol had left him borderline suicidal. His family, friends and colleagues had done their best not to judge but he'd seen the questions in their eyes. Ava had let her gut guide her and led him out of the darkness. That was her natural state, offering a hand, giving a smile, coping. She wore those attributes like a shell. Now it was cracking.

He hadn't wanted to believe what she'd said about going away, even less the implication that she would take justice into her own hands when she found Ailsa Lambert's killer, but the Ava he knew was fading. He wasn't sure about the woman walking in her shoes right now.

The door to the upper floor flat was standing open as they approached.

'Come in,' a voice called. Jimmy Douglas had broken the six feet barrier some time earlier, and looked like a future shoo-in for any basketball team.

'You knew we were here?' Callanach asked.

'The polis doesn't get to stand around in this car park without everybody knowing about it,' he said. 'Have you found my mam?'

'We need to see a photo of her,' Ava said.

He pulled a mobile from his pocket and opened the gallery. Flicking back a hundred or so shots, he reached an image of a painfully thin woman blowing out candles on a cup cake, tears in her eyes.

'It was her birthday,' he said. 'My dad wouldn't give me any money for a proper present so the cake was all I could get her.'

'Looks like she appreciated it,' Callanach said. 'Not many boys your age would have bothered.'

Jimmy gave a grateful smile.

Ava stared out of the window, her face as pale and pinched as the woman's in the photo. All that was left to do was collect a DNA sample for comparison.

'You're not in uniform,' the boy said. 'That means you're detectives, right?'

'That's right,' Callanach said.

'I expected uniforms, the usual couple that come round when there's been a burglary or more graffiti. Why are you two here?' The question was direct but not rudely asked.

'What does your mother do for money, Jimmy?' Ava asked. 'Does she have a job?'

'She's on the social,' he said. 'Still isn't enough for us to live on. She does a bit of babysitting, or delivery work when she can afford the petrol and the car isn't broken.'

'When did you last see her?' Callanach asked.

'Four days ago. When I went off to school, she was still in bed. I stayed two nights at my dad's. She was supposed to pick me up from school and never turned up. You think she's dead, don't you?'

The lie would have been easier, but less fair in the long term.

'We're not sure yet, Jimmy,' Ava said. 'I'm afraid there is a resemblance to a woman who . . . was involved in an incident the same day your mother failed to pick you up. Who's the best person to call? Your dad?'

He looked out of the window. 'I knew it,' he said. 'She's never not come to pick me up when she said she would. Even if she was sick, or working four jobs, or I asked to be picked up at 2 a.m. from some stupid party. She always came.'

'We're not certain yet,' Callanach said. 'But we do need to make sure you're safe and that there's an adult to look after you.'

'Did you find her car?' Jimmy asked. 'She was supposed to do a delivery before she picked me up. If she'd come back, her car would have been down there.' He gestured vaguely to the car park below.

'Did you ever suspect that she might have been involved in anything illegal?' Ava asked. 'As a courier, for example.'

Jimmy shrugged.

'Drugs, Jimmy? Is there any chance your mother could have been delivering drugs? It's a booming new industry. You send a text and get whatever you want delivered right to your door. I'm not saying your mum even knew what she was delivering, just that it would have been easy for her to have been used by people who knew she was desperate.'

'Not drugs. Her brother died of an overdose when he was nineteen and she was like, fourteen or something. She begged me, whatever else I did, never to get into that. I don't want to live with my dad full time. I go there two nights a week and that's more than enough. I'm not sure he'd even want me. Will Social Services let me live on my own, do you think?'

Callanach watched the boy's brain ticking, pushing the

61

oncoming grief aside as he came to terms with the blow he was being dealt. The survival instinct was strong.

'Do you have any other family? Grandparents, aunts or uncles?' Callanach asked.

'No. I mean, you don't know anything's happened yet, so I can just stay here, right?'

'We have no choice but to let both Social Services and your father know,' Ava said. 'We'll do our work as quickly as possible. I'm very sorry about this, Jimmy. If there's anything you need, here's my number.' She handed him a card with her contact details.

'Detective Chief Inspector,' he read. 'Shit. You really do think she's dead.' It was the first time tears had appeared in his eyes. 'She wanted me to go to university. Be the first in the family, all that crap. Dad said it's bullshit, that I should just get an apprenticeship – plumber or electrician. Said I'll always have a job.'

'Maybe you should think about the police force,' Callanach said. 'You'd make a good detective.'

'Perhaps,' Jimmy replied thoughtfully. 'I'd have to move though. You don't grow up here and go off to join the polis. They don't like it.'

Boots echoed from the corridor. Ava had asked uniformed officers to take care of the paperwork and request help from other agencies.

Callanach extended his hand to the boy, who took a deep breath and stepped forward to shake it.

'Don't give up hope,' Callanach said. 'Call if you need anything.'

'I need something of your mother's like a hairbrush or a toothbrush. Is that okay?' Ava asked.

'Her bedroom's through that door,' he said.

'One last thing,' Ava said. 'Was your mother pregnant?'

'No.' He shook his head. 'Why would you think that?'

Ava tried not to feel hope for the boy. Either Maura Douglas was somewhere else and might yet come home, or she was dead and had done a good job of hiding her condition from her son. She disappeared into the bedroom.

'What car did your mother have?' Callanach asked.

'A knackered old blue Beetle,' he said. 'She was a bit of a hippy really. Loved that car. Wouldn't let go of it. Am I allowed to ask what you think happened to her?'

'Let's wait until we know. Right now, she's still just missing,' Callanach said. 'One step at a time, okay?'

The boy nodded and Ava reappeared with a hairbrush in an evidence bag, snapping gloves off her hands.

The two uniformed officers introduced themselves as Ava and Luc slipped out.

'Find anything of interest?' Callanach asked as they took the stairs.

'No drugs, I took the opportunity to have a quick look around her bedroom and the bathroom. No paraphernalia, not even cigarette papers or a lighter. Didn't even see any prescription drugs or paracetamol. There was a novel by her bed, which was neatly made. The clothes in her wardrobe were old but clean and folded. She was living in poverty but hadn't let it drag her down. If she was involved as a drug courier, then I doubt she knew the details.'

'I like the boy,' Callanach said. 'What do you think will happen to him?'

'The system will take over.' Ava sighed. 'If he's not a criminal yet, there's every chance he'll have become one by the time he gets out of social care.'

'That's not inevitable,' Callanach said.

'I love that you're still so keen to see potential instead of believing the statistics, even after this many years in law enforcement.' She put her hand over his as she said it, and they both stopped moving. Callanach stared at her fingers, so delicate lying across his own. She pulled away again before he could cover them with his free hand. 'We need to get back to the station. The superintendent has called a press conference,' Ava said, unlocking her car.

'What for?'

'All the families of the deceased first responders have now been notified. Overbeck's going to release the names of the dead.'

Chapter Ten

BEFORE

Quinn jumped every time a customer entered the shop. She told herself it was just because she wanted to tell Liam that her parents had decided to stick with the name Dolly, but there was no hiding the sense of excitement in the pit of her stomach. It was hard to meet new people in a small town, and she wasn't the kind of girl who bothered going into the city to the late night bars and clubs. Liam arrived just minutes before the shop shut for the night, dashing in breathless then grabbing a bottle of champagne and grinning as he asked Quinn to run it through the till.

'I need to check you're over eighteen,' she said sweetly.

He leaned in low, his voice a rumble for her ears only.

'Sounds to me like an excuse to see my ID and find out all about me,' he said. 'If it helps, I'm twenty-six, I live in Edinburgh, I have my own place – no annoying flatmates – and I drive a Golf GTi. Is that enough to get us started?'

'I didn't realise we were getting started on anything,' she said, closing up her till. 'The shop's closing. My boss is about to ask you to leave.'

'Well, I think our first date is something worth celebrating, hence the champagne. I'll be waiting outside.' He fake whispered, 'Your boss is looking awfully fierce over there!'

Quinn hadn't needed to look at Mark to know Liam was telling the truth. She could feel the waves of disapproval being fired in their direction.

She giggled. 'Fine, I'll see you outside.'

'You can't trust him,' Mark said after Liam had exited. 'I see blokes like that in the pub all the time, the way they look at women's bodies, how they talk about them when they can't hear. You should steer well clear of that one.'

'I think he's okay. Just a bit of a joker, really.' Quinn pulled on her jacket and picked up her bag. It was nice that Mark was protective of her. She didn't have an older brother, and it was good to have people watching her back. Sometimes, though, it would have been nice not to have people – her mum, her dad, her boss, even her uncle – watching her every move. 'See you next week.'

His car was parked outside the supermarket. Quinn looked at the open door, feeling foolish, blaming Mark for making her feel suspicious.

'That's all right,' Liam said, 'I wouldn't dream of asking you to get in. You don't know me. I'm glad you're not the kind of girl who would. I was just fetching these.' He held up a pair of plastic wine glasses. 'Would you mind doing the honours?'

Quinn didn't want to admit that she'd never opened a champagne bottle before. At home her father had always been in charge of the odd bottle of wine or prosecco they'd cracked open. She took it, feeling bizarrely grown up, got a good grip of the neck, and popped the cork. The first fizz overflowed, then Liam was ready with the glasses to catch the rest.

'What's this in aid of then?' she asked, holding her glass up to toast.

'I think – at least, I hope – it's the start of something amazing,' he said. 'Because since I met you yesterday I haven't slept or eaten or been able to think about anything except your face.'

Quinn's cheeks burned red.

'You're messing with me,' she said quietly.

'Are you kidding? You're beautiful. What are you doing hiding away here? God, imagine if I'd never stopped at that bizarre shop. I'd never have found you.'

Quinn found herself suspended in time, her glass in the air, ready to clink against his, expecting a moment of silly fun. Not this. Not for the breath to have been stopped still in her lungs, heart waiting until it felt able to beat again.

'Cheers,' Liam said, his voice low, a soft smile on his lips. 'Here's to getting to know each other. If you want to.'

Quinn gulped in oxygen.

'Cheers,' she replied. 'I do want to. And we have something else to celebrate. You somehow managed to pick exactly the right name for my baby sister. She is now officially Dolly McTavish, thanks to you.'

'You see how useful I am to have around?' He grinned.

They drank their champagne at the side of the road, smiling stupidly at one another and making small talk, until she said she needed to get home. Liam walked with her and left her unkissed at her front door. It was the first real secret she kept from her mother, to whom she told everything, not that she wanted to be deceptive, but Liam – whatever Liam was about to become – was so exciting that she wanted to keep him entirely to herself, for just a little while.

On their second date, they'd met for a walk. Liam had asked Quinn what her favourite place was, and she'd decided on the Royal Botanic Gardens. They'd made plans for a trip there together. As they'd hiked slowly and talked endlessly, the sun had seemed yellower, the trees sparkled emerald, and when she'd arrived home, the mirror showed her a girl who'd gone from plain to pretty in the blink of an eye. Seeing herself the way Liam saw her, had changed everything.

On their third date, she'd climbed into his car and they'd tried to see a movie. Tried, because it was impossible to look at a screen when they could only stare at one another. Holding hands in the dark had been too thrilling. The explosions and special effects unfolding at the far end of the auditorium were nothing compared to the fireworks happening in Quinn's body.

A week later they finally kissed, standing on the Bridge to Nowhere in Belhaven Bay. At high tide the bridge was an enigma – just a structure sticking out of the sea – no path to it, no path from it. As the waters receded it formed a shortcut over Biel Water to the far beach. Quinn thought it was the most beautiful thing she'd ever seen. They'd picnicked there all day, watching the tide invade and recede, and when Liam had finally taken her by the hand, she'd known she was in love. When he kissed her, when he told her he didn't think he'd ever be able to live without her, she'd been sure there would never be another moment in her life as perfect as that.

He dropped her home and she'd taken his hand shyly in the car.

'Would you mind coming in to meet my parents?'

'Sometime, but not yet. Let's keep this magical, okay babe?'

'But they'll love you! And my dad would feel better about me seeing someone if he's met you. I keep having to make excuses and I hate lying to them. Please?'

He kissed her again, leaned across her to open her door, and held her chin in his free hand.

'I'll meet them when I want to. Not before. Now you go and get some rest. You're looking a bit washed out. I'll call you tomorrow.'

Quinn fixed a smile on her face and climbed out of the car. She was such an idiot. No man wanted to meet his girlfriend's parents. She'd pushed him too hard too fast. It wasn't his fault if her parents were old-fashioned. Her mother had figured out there was something going on, but had been careful not to ask directly. At twenty, they recognised that Quinn was entitled to some privacy. But they were protective only because they loved her. She knew they knew, and had been looking forward to sharing it with them. Not right now, though. Their first question would be, when could they meet her new boyfriend? She wasn't sure how to explain that would only happen when Liam decided it was time.

She went in through the back door rather than the front.

'Hey there sweetheart, is that you?' her father called.

'If it weren't, you'd have been calling a burglar sweetheart, which I'm not sure would be the best way to get rid of them.' Quinn laughed.

'I wouldn't be so sure about that! Most grown men around here would run a mile from me calling them sweetheart,' her father replied.

Quinn could hear her mum and dad laughing together at the thought of it. She went into the sitting room to see them. 'I've locked up behind me.'

Her parents were sitting together on the sofa, as they always did, the TV playing but their hands busy. Her mother was knitting Dolly a cardigan, and her father was drafting designs for the doll's house he'd decided to make his baby daughter from scratch. Looking at how elaborate it was, Quinn decided he was right to start work on it before Dolly could even walk.

'You want to come and watch TV with us?' her mother asked.

'Actually I've a bit of a headache,' she lied. 'I'm off for an early night.'

'Shall I bring you a hot drink and some paracetamol, or

maybe a cold flannel for your head?' her father asked, ever the carer. Quinn had always suspected he rather liked it when a family member was a bit under the weather, just so he could tend to them even more than usual.

'No, but thank you. I'll be fine. Just need some sleep. Love you.'

'Love you more!' they replied in unison.

Quinn went to her room and sat on the little stool in front of her dressing table mirror. It was old-fashioned and outdated, but her parents had bought it for her when she was fourteen. They'd only ever treated her kindly. For the first time in her life she felt like she couldn't face them.

Liam was right. She was looking washed out. Dark circles were forming beneath her eyes, and she was paler than usual. Quinn felt the sting of being told to go in and rest, then scolded herself. Why was she hurting over something so trivial? Liam was obviously just worried about her.

A shower would help. It had been a long day in the tidal winds and saltwater breeze. Anyone would be tired. If he hadn't been kind about it, then that was because he was tired too. He'd done all the driving, packed the picnic and kept her entertained every second of the day.

Kicking off her shoes, she recalled the kiss, instead. The warmth of his arms as he'd held her so tight she thought the feel of his embrace would never leave her. The memory was all the perspective she needed. Liam loved her. He might not have said it yet, but she was as sure of it as she was her own name. She would sleep. Tomorrow she'd be looking better. The conversation with her parents could wait a few more days. The most important things should never be rushed. Liam had been right about everything.

★ ★ ★

70

The next morning Quinn woke late. By the time she'd emerged from her bedroom to the sound of Dolly's gurgles, her parents were waiting for her in the sitting room.

'Hello, love, we heard you get up. There's a cup of tea for you,' her dad said.

Quinn hesitated at the doorway. She felt sick with keeping the secret.

'Come on in,' her mother said. 'Dolly missed you yesterday. She wants a cuddle, don't you my wee girl?' She offered the baby, and Quinn was helpless to refuse. She gathered Dolly up and settled on the sofa next to her mother.

'You know we don't like to pry,' her father began. 'But I bumped into Mark from the shop. I know you're an adult and this is your business and no one else's, but he seemed to think there was someone hanging around.'

Quinn sighed.

'Mark should never have spoken to you about it,' she snapped, regretting her tone instantly. Her parents weren't the enemy.

'Maybe he shouldn't have, but your mother and I have noticed things too. We'd never stop you doing anything, my darling, but we'd rather know you're safe,' her dad said gently.

'Mark has been asking me out forever, you know that. He's just jealous and trying to cause trouble. I am safe. I don't know why this is such a big deal.'

'Perhaps for the same reason you didn't talk about it?' her mother offered. 'Your life is your own, Quinn, but you've never been one to keep secrets. So who is he?'

Quinn softened.

'Someone I met at the shop. He was passing through for work but he lives in Edinburgh. He's twenty-six and works for an engineering firm, repairing large machinery. I suppose I wasn't sure if he was serious or if it was going to work out, and I didn't want to jinx it. I wasn't trying to hide anything.'

'Of course you weren't! That's not what we thought. It must be difficult living at home when you've got a job and you're studying. A lot of people your age have already flown the nest. You can have all the space you like, you know that. All we want is for you to be happy and safe,' her father said.

'I am happy, Dad. Really happy. He's amazing. He's respectful, not pushy at all. We talk about all sorts of things. It's not like going to the pub here with my mates and going on about what we've watched on TV or celebrity relationships. Liam can discuss politics and books and other countries. I feel like my world just got bigger.'

Her mother and father exchanged a look Quinn couldn't decipher.

'He sounds impressive,' her mother said gently. 'Will we meet him, do you think?'

There it was.

'Not yet, if you don't mind. It's early days. I don't want him to feel like I'm desperate to get a ring on my finger.'

'Oh no, that's not what we want to do, it's just that I'd rather know who my girl is out with.' Her dad smiled.

Quinn looked at his face. He was grey now, and the years had marked themselves into his skin in lines, but he was still the man she'd clung to every time she was scared, laughed at as he'd thrown her into the air, and cried in his arms when a girl at school had stolen her diary and read it to the class. He was her rock.

'Would you trust me, Dad? I'm not stupid. If I thought he was playing me, I'd have nothing to do with him.'

A few seconds of silence, then her mother patted her hand. 'You're right,' she said. 'You may be twenty but to us you're still just a little girl breaking our hearts every time she gets a scraped knee. Forgive us.'

Quinn smiled back.

'If that's roast beef I can smell cooking, and you promise you'll make Yorkshire puddings, then I can forgive you anything.'

Her mother leaned over to kiss Quinn's forehead.

'Then I've some cooking to do. You stay here with that baby. If I try to move her from your arms now, she'll scream the place down anyway.'

Quinn finally relaxed. Her world had been set right.

Chapter Eleven

Detective Superintendent Overbeck was not herself. She wore uncharacteristically low heels with her immaculate uniform as she took her place in front of the largest press gaggle Ava had ever seen, gathered from every corner of the world. Ava and Luc stood at the back, out of uniform, staying inconspicuous. Overbeck's black hair was constrained in a harsh bun, and she'd rejected her standard full-face makeup for a simple dash of mascara. No lipstick at all.

'She's making sure it's not about her,' Ava said. 'For once.'

There were ten minutes of chaos as cameras were focused and sound checks completed. Photographers jostled for position in the front line, and journalists were poised to ask questions. Through it all, Overbeck sat motionless, staring at her hands, waiting for quiet. She was introduced by the media liaison officer, took a sip of water, and stood.

'Police Scotland is in the process of investigating the attack at the Innocent Railway Tunnel. We issued a statement soon after the incident took place to explain that there had been a bombing that was deliberate in nature, and asking for time to process the scene and any intelligence before commenting further. You were notified then that the blast had taken the lives of multiple victims. The families of the deceased have now all been informed and we hold close in our thoughts the loved ones, relatives and friends of those we've lost. Many other first responders were injured and we wish them a speedy recovery. We will work tirelessly to bring those responsible to justice.'

Overbeck swallowed, tried to speak and gave a dry croak instead. She returned to her water glass, unhurried.

'By way of summary, Police Scotland was notified that there was to be an attack in Edinburgh but given no more details than that. We immediately sent out all available units. Shortly thereafter, officers were called to the Innocent Railway Tunnel. Paramedics and the fire service attended to provide backup. At the scene a woman was found hanging. During the course of assisting that victim, an explosion was detonated causing multiple injuries instantaneously, which was followed by the collapse of the tunnel entrance, making rescue additionally difficult. Several people perished. Postmortems are ongoing. Would you stand with me please as I read out the names of the dead.'

The press grappled with equipment as they got to their feet, not that anyone was going to complain. The room was unnaturally still.

'Four paramedics were killed who were waiting to assist the hanging victim. They were Dylan Rigby, Michaela Donaldson, Wren Brewster and Agathi Ellison. Three firefighters were also killed. They were positioned on top of the bridge and engaged in helping cut through the rope. They were August McKellar, Kevin Phillips and Courtney Burton. Also on top of the bridge were Police Scotland uniformed officers Constable Crofton Bennington and Constable Aengus MacKenzie.' Overbeck paused again and finished her glass of water. No one moved or spoke. 'Below the bridge assisting the rescue process were Police Scotland officers Sergeant McKenna Keyes, Constable

Marsha Thrussell, Constable Areti Smythe, Inspector Vivek Gupta, Constable Desta Zhu, and Sergeant George Williams. In addition, the woman who was the subject of the rescue lost her life. Her identity is still in the process of being confirmed and we will not be issuing any further details about her at this time.

'The fifteen souls lost to the emergency services that day behaved in the most exemplary manner, putting their work before their own safety, and doing nothing less than giving their all to save a life. We recognise their sacrifice and will make sure that these brave men and women are honoured and remembered. We're working with forensics teams and external agencies to draw up a more accurate picture of what happened, and I take full responsibility for ensuring that this investigation draws to a successful close. These were brutal murders, carefully planned and executed. Whoever did this will not escape justice.'

She sat down. There was a vacuum in the room for several seconds, then the air exploded with sound. The media liaison officer stood and raised her arms to bring order.

'We have time for one or two questions. Please wait to be asked, do not shout out. Yes, BBC Scotland, go ahead.'

'Given the scale of the attack and the use of a bomb, are you investigating the possibility that this was a terrorist attack?'

'We haven't reached any conclusions at this point but we're not ruling anything out,' Overbeck said.

'Has any terrorist group claimed it yet?' the BBC correspondent continued.

Overbeck paused momentarily. Ava and Luc caught the moment and glanced at each other.

'There's no firm evidence linking these attacks to any particular terrorist group at this time,' Overbeck said.

'Right, question from *Le Monde* newspaper,' the liaison officer directed.

'Yes, you were alerted only to a vague threat, you say, and yet you put all your officers on the street immediately. What reason did you have to believe the threat was credible in the first place?'

'We take all threats seriously,' Overbeck said. 'Our primary duty is to protect the public.'

'How many threats would you say Police Scotland receives each week?' the reporter pressed.

'I don't have a precise figure but we assess them all as soon as they're received. Next question,' Overbeck said.

'Last one,' the liaison officer decided. '*The Guardian* newspaper.'

'Yes, Edinburgh's Chief Pathologist was murdered in the City Mortuary recently. Are these events linked or is that just a coincidence? Also, why have no details about Dr Ailsa Lambert's death been released yet?'

Overbeck stood. 'Dr Lambert breathed in toxic gas fumes. That's a very different scenario from a large-scale explosive device. You'll appreciate how busy we are, so if you'll excuse me.' Overbeck left quietly, no drama, leaving only unanswered questions in her wake.

Ava and Luc followed her out and caught up with her in the corridor.

'Ma'am, we have a probable identity for the woman found hanging at the bridge. We've organised for the DNA sample to be couriered to the lab. Could I ask . . . You paused when you were asked if anyone had claimed the tunnel attack. Why?' Ava asked.

Overbeck sighed. 'A group called the Brothers of Darkness claimed it an hour ago. They're a fringe group no one knows much about, not religiously affiliated, just anarchists as far as I can tell. New Scotland Yard have put a squad onto it. We can't officially rule it out but they provided no evidence that wasn't readily available online to confirm their claim.'

A senior officer moved in, took Overbeck by the arm and led her away.

'Eighteen people dead including the attack on Ailsa, from multiple agencies, including random members of the public.' From her pocket Ava drew the list of names that had been provided to the press with full details of each of the deceased. To the bottom she added, Maura Douglas, Gavin Cronk and Ailsa Lambert. 'Eighteen. Edinburgh's never been subjected to an attack like this in modern history.'

'Maybe it is terrorism,' Callanach said. 'Perhaps the group claiming it are telling the truth.'

'I don't think so,' Ava said. 'Not the way Ailsa died. Why go to all that trouble to kill just one person?'

'Perhaps it was about showing off their capabilities, to make us take the Innocent Railway Tunnel seriously. It forced us to get as many officers there as possible.'

'That's feasible,' Ava said. 'But I can't shake the feeling that this is only the start. If this anarchist group is responsible, why risk getting stopped at this stage by claiming it?'

'For publicity, funding, to get more followers. The rise of the far right is a global phenomenon, and it's becoming big business.'

Ava's mobile buzzed. She scanned the message. 'We're needed at the mortuary. Dr Carlisle wants to see us. Apparently whoever hanged that woman from the bridge performed surgery on her beforehand. The poor woman's tongue was cut out.'

Chapter Twelve

Ava hesitated at the doors to the Edinburgh City Mortuary. It felt so alien to be walking in there without Dr Ailsa Lambert in charge. There had never been any joy to be found in what amounted to a hospital for the dead, but now there would be no comfort either. Ailsa had been so good at that in spite of her no-nonsense manner. She was the warmth that kept her staff functioning.

Dr Nate Carlisle met Ava and Luc in the reception area and escorted them into the postmortem suite where a sheet hid a variety of lumps and bumps without the coherent form of a human body. They suited up silently and mentally prepared themselves. Every viewing required a steeling. Ava couldn't remember a time when she hadn't had to remind herself that she was there to do a job. It was business best done with a professional eye and dispassionate interest. Her mask was slipping, though. She could feel it, and she knew that Luc could see it. She wondered how long she had left before her resilience wore too thin for her to carry on.

Long enough to catch this bastard, she told herself. Long enough to do to him or her the equivalent of what they did to Ailsa.

'You ready?' Callanach asked.

Ava nodded and drew close to the table.

Nate Carlisle folded his arms and stared at Ava.

'When did you last sleep?' he asked her.

'That's all anyone seems to ask me these days.' She sighed. 'Sorry, we don't know each other very well yet, but you should know I'm not in the mood for advice, however well-meaning. Let's just get on with this, Dr Carlisle.'

Carlisle took a step back and switched on an additional light but didn't touch the sheet.

'You're pale bordering on ashen, your eyes are bloodshot, you look dehydrated – and forgive the rudeness but in my professional opinion I'd say you haven't washed your hair for several days.'

'That's enough,' Ava said.

'No. You're in the mortuary. I'm in charge in here. I expect my team and every other professional that comes into contact with these bodies to be appropriately prepared. That's more than just donning a suit to avoid contamination. My job is to make sure the work I do for each deceased person has value and leads to an accurate resolution. I'm seeing someone who is sleep-deprived, nutrient-deprived and not in a good place to concentrate and be careful in this very sensitive environment.'

Ava folded her arms and gritted her teeth. 'You're out of line,' she said.

Callanach forced himself to stay out of it. Much as he wanted to stand up for Ava, she needed to heed Carlisle's words.

'If I didn't say anything I'd be out of line,' Carlisle replied. 'DCI Turner, the human body has needs. I witness first-hand on these very tables what happens when those needs aren't met. What are your views on sleep-deprived drivers who kill someone?'

There was a pause that lasted an uncomfortable thirty seconds.

Nate Carlisle didn't feel the need to break it, he simply waited for Ava to realise she didn't have a convenient response.

'Point taken,' she said quietly. Her eyes were prickling, but not from the reprimand. 'That's what Ailsa would have said. It was as if she was speaking through you for a second there. Did you know her well?'

'Well enough to know that if I'm ever a fraction as good a pathologist as she was, I'll retire a happy man.' He walked to his desk and called through to reception. 'It's Dr Carlisle,' he said. 'I need a huge favour. Is there any way we can make sure there's a hot pot of coffee for when we finish in here? Apologies for asking you to perform a trivial task like that. I'll make the next pot, I promise.'

Just the thought of coffee helped Ava wake up. Hard as it was to hear, Dr Carlisle was right. She needed food, a shower and some sleep.

'Let's begin. Head first. This isn't good. If either of you is struggling with it, let me know. And don't tell me how many of these you've attended as police officers. I much prefer human beings who don't show off to me about how hardened they are.'

'He really is like Ailsa,' Callanach said quietly as they stepped closer.

The warning had been soundly given. The severed head was barely intact. The mat of hair had provided a frame for the skin to cling to, but the skull was in shards and the soft tissue of the face hung in ragged strips.

'I'm going to give you a minute,' Carlisle said.

Ava picked up her mobile from the counter and flicked through her photos to the one she'd taken of Maura Douglas. She held it up.

'I need to know if this is her. This is a recent photo provided by her son. I've got a DNA specimen for comparison but that'll take twenty-four hours. From what you can see here, do you think she might be a match?'

The blood-stained hair didn't help. Dr Carlisle took a sterile sponge from a pack and washed a few strands, looking at the clean hair under a light.

'I'd say the hair colour is very similar,' he said. 'I haven't been able to age the skull, and there's too much facial damage to do a reconstruction, but I certainly wouldn't rule her out. How did you trace her?'

'Her son reported her as missing, but we don't know when that happened as he also stays with his dad. She had a few casual jobs so we've got a lot of work to do tracing her movements,' Ava explained.

'I can tell you that this woman was held at least briefly prior to the hanging.' He moved in close and turned the head so they had a better view into the mouth. 'Her lower jaw is missing. It would have been blown off in the initial blast when the soft tissue damage occurred. The eyes were forced inwards and effectively liquidised. The nose was lost at the same time. What I can see here though . . .' he pointed at a straight line of flesh at the rear of the mouth, '. . . is that the tongue was cut out, surgically, in advance. It's too neat a line to have been caused any other way.'

'Has the cut started to heal?' Callanach asked.

'There's no sign of that but the mouth was very badly damaged, so any preliminary knitting of the wound could have been reopened anyway.'

'No tongue, no risk of her warning first responders, so I'm guessing she knew what was coming,' Callanach said.

Ava closed her eyes and let that sink in.

'We're still trying to piece bodies together and that's going to take a long time, but we're certain that these hands belong to this victim.' He pulled the sheet back further to reveal a pair of lower arms severed from just below the elbow, cable tie still securing the wrists together, hands badly damaged but intact. 'The hands were secured behind her back so the worst of the blast damage was suffered by her core. If the arms had been tied in front of the body, we'd have substantially less left.'

'So all the explosives were attached to the front of her body, making her look pregnant,' Ava said.

'Quite deliberately.' Dr Carlisle walked to a computer and tapped the keyboard, bringing up a series of photos on the screen. 'This was found at the scene. The rubbery jelly material is a false pregnancy bump, often used in movies and TV. You can get them in a variety of sizes. What you can see here is the back strap with a double Velcro seam. Her spine protected it. I suspect the explosives were packed inside the false bump, so the front must have been completely incinerated. There'll be a more detailed report from the explosives consultant.'

Ava looked back at the body parts arranged over the table. There was a partial section of lower spine, the right leg and foot, and some odd bones. So little to show for a life. Too little to ever explain to a sixteen-year-old. Ava had lost hope that this was anyone other than Maura Douglas.

'Are you likely to get any evidence from the perpetrator – fingerprints, skin cells, DNA?' Ava asked.

'I think you can discount that. There's the bomb blast, some burning to the body, and endless contamination from all the other dead in the vicinity. It's a worst-case scenario in forensic terms.'

'Her kid's only sixteen,' Callanach said quietly. 'What are we supposed to tell him?' He was asking himself rather than Dr Carlisle.

'This won't help, not yet – maybe not ever – but you should know I did find one other thing. At the rear of the brain I identified a large tumour, far enough in that it would have been inoperable. She would already have been experiencing a wide range of symptoms. Certainly dizziness, blurred vision, nausea, migraines, possibly a change in taste and smell, balance issues. I'd be surprised if she hadn't consulted a doctor.'

'How long did she have left?' Callanach asked.

'I'd need to consult a neurologist and maybe an oncologist for that, but compared to other similar tumours I've seen, I'd say just a matter of months. That doesn't help given the violence of her death, but if she was involved in something that got her in trouble near the end of her life, you might want to bear in mind that it's possible she was making irrational or desperate choices at that point.'

They finished up and then drank the waiting coffee. Callanach went off to speak with the victim's doctor regarding her knowledge of the tumour, hoping they would be flexible about the lack of a court order with Maura Douglas not yet even legally confirmed as the deceased. Meanwhile, Nate Carlisle sat with Ava as she made a few notes and took his advice about slowing down.

'It's hard to be in a profession where death becomes an everyday experience. When faced with a personal loss, it can be tricky to process grief, having disciplined yourself to rise above it.'

'I never thought about it like that,' Ava said. 'Rising above grief. I don't think I've ever managed that. The problem with Ailsa's death isn't just how personal it is. My best friend Natasha is in recovery from breast cancer. It was touch and go there for a while. I went to bed every night saying I would give anything, sacrifice anything else, if I could just keep her.' She stirred her coffee for a while, watching it swirl. Carlisle waited. 'I'm not superstitious and I'm not religious, so I don't know who I was begging for a miracle, and I know I didn't cause Ailsa's death, but I guess I feel as if I kind of asked for it.'

Nate Carlisle put his feet up on the coffee table between them and let the thought steep in the air a while.

'Ailsa knew how much you loved her, right?' he asked.

'She did,' Ava admitted. 'We were very close. I never met anyone else like her and I certainly never trusted anyone as much. She never once let me down.'

'That's a gift,' Nate said. 'You can't get over losing someone to such evil. I've come to believe you shouldn't even try. All you and I can do is work to save others from the same fate. That's worth something. What you do every day, is worth a lot more than you'll ever realise.'

Ava took her last sip of coffee and nodded. There was no adequate response, but his words helped. A little.

Chapter Thirteen

'Forty-eight hours until justice is done,' DS Lively read again from the note written by the officer who'd taken the message. They were already six hours into the allotted forty-eight.

'Did we have a chance to trace the call?' Ava asked. She'd slept for twelve hours, eaten the meal Natasha had cooked for her, and spent a full half hour in the shower. In her absence, the message had been received.

'No, it was too short. The recording sounds exactly like the last message though. Same use of the digital voice changer. It was from a mobile, no account. They used a burner phone.'

'Right,' Ava said. 'No more talk about what we don't have and what we don't know. We need to go back to basics with the other two offences. We can forget DNA or any other shortcuts. Assuming the choice of victims isn't random, what do we know about Gavin Cronk and Maura Douglas? They're the only linked parts of this operation.'

'Blunt Sword,' Lively added.

'Was that the next approved name on the code list?' Ava asked. There was generalised nodding. 'Okay then, Operation

Blunt Sword. Lively, what did you get from Gavin Cronk's girlfriend, Amanda?'

'Not much, she just grinned at me a lot. I'm not sure it'd really sunk in that her boyfriend hadn't just gone on holiday and was actually dead. Whatever she'd just taken, I need a stash of it for when this case is over.' There was murmured agreement. 'Anyway, she confirmed that the names in the deals book are the names Gavin remembers his clients by, rather than actual nicknames. Obviously no self-respecting dealer is ever going to write down a real name, but these days they won't even write nicknames down in case the book is found by people like us. Sesame – Gavin Cronk's final drug deal – likely has no idea that's the allocated name. It's just whatever was going through Gavin's head at the time. What we do know is that Gavin had dealt drugs to him on at least five different occasions over the last eighteen months, which is as far back as the book goes. Cocaine, ketamine, Rohypnol and ecstasy.'

'And Amanda never came into contact with this Sesame person?' Callanach asked.

Lively shrugged. 'She says not. Gavin tended to drop drugs off rather than have a lot of late-night visitors to his home address. Didn't want to draw attention from the neighbours apparently. He never took Amanda with him on drug drops.'

'Do we have Gavin's car?' Ava asked.

'We do, as of yesterday. It's in the shop now where the computer team is trying to download the data from the Satnav unit. What we don't have is Gavin's mobile, so we can't double-check messages and calls against drop-off locations. The theory is that the killer has his mobile. It's switched off and can't be triangulated,' Lively said.

'Keep working on that,' Ava said. 'Known enemies?'

'Other drug dealers operating in the same area. There's a turf war going on.'

'There's always a turf war going on, I just don't think any of the local gangs would bother to repurpose a landmine, thereby attracting the attention of every police unit in the UK,' Ava said.

A phone rang at the back of the room. DI Graham answered it then waved to get the team's attention. 'We've got Maura Douglas' car,' he said. 'It's inside an abandoned farm building south of Temple.'

'Get a forensics team out there,' Ava said. 'No one goes in or out until scenes of crime have done their thing. Let's go.'

Half an hour and a few wrong turns later, they arrived. South of Temple Village, out on roads so rural they weren't named on any map, and finally up a gravel track that was more pothole than substance, the barn could be seen, its entrance at a ninety degree angle to the track. Ava and Luc parked far enough away to preserve any other tyre prints, donned shoe covers and made their way to where a forensics tent was already being set up.

Four push bikes had been dropped in a pile against the farm fence. Callanach called over one of the uniformed officers guarding the crime scene perimeter.

'Who do these belong to?'

'The lads in that police car. We're calling their parents now to come and get them,' the officer said.

Callanach motioned for them to be brought to him, and stood, arms crossed, waiting for them to speak.

'We did nothing wrong,' the first said, chest out, head shaved, stance like a bull. Callanach figured he had to be all of twelve years old.

'Aye, and we don't talk to the polis neither,' another joined in.

Callanach said nothing.

'Are we in trouble?' the third asked, hands in pockets, head down. He was the one to talk to.

'What do you think you might be in trouble for?' Callanach asked.

'We weren't stealing the car. We just wanted to start it up and see if the radio worked. That was all, honest.'

'How did you get the keys?'

'They were in the ignition,' he explained.

'Aw, shut up Paulie,' bull stance said.

'Paulie's doing you a favour,' Callanach told him. 'If you answer my questions now, I won't have to take you to the police station. If I take you to the station, social workers will be called, your parents will also have to answer questions, and it'll just get worse from there. Is that what you want?'

Three of them shook their heads. Bull stance remained defiant.

'We didnae want to crash the car into the barn wall. It was in gear when we started it. It just went forward,' the fourth boy said. 'No one owns this barn now anyway. The whole place has been abandoned for months. My mam says the farmer killed himself in the house and it's haunted and that's why no one will buy it!'

'How often do you come here?' Callanach asked.

'Like maybe once a month if we get bored. The barn's a good place to hang out if it rains. Are we going to have to go to court?'

Callanach waited long enough that they were all wide-eyed with anticipation.

'No,' he said. 'But you'll need to help us. I want a statement from each of you explaining what you touched in the car, if you took anything or moved anything, and we'll need finger-prints.' There was some protest at that. 'Calm down. The fingerprints are only to exclude you from other investigations. You're not in trouble, but no more driving until you have a licence. Why were the police called?'

'I made an anonymous call,' the third boy said. 'There's quite a lot of damage to the car.'

'And the barn wall,' the fourth added. 'We felt bad. But then Georgie left his torch here and we figured it had his fingerprints on so we came back to get it. We didn't think the police would bother coming as quickly as you did.'

Callanach held in his laughter.

'All right, go and see that officer there, the really tall one. Give a statement, each of you, and leave nothing out then you'll be allowed to go home. Stay out of trouble, but well done for calling it in. DI Graham,' he shouted, 'could you see to it that these boys are as helpful as they possibly can be?'

Pax Graham responded by putting his hands on his hips, sticking out his chest and making himself look as big as he could, before giving the boys a smile, and waving them over.

'Whoa, he's like a mountain!' one of them whispered.

'Aye, I'm not bloody lying to him,' another replied as they wandered in Graham's direction.

Callanach allowed himself a smile as he put on a white suit to join Ava in the barn.

The pale blue Beetle was half in and half out, the wood slat wall almost completely destroyed and the edge of the roof beginning to bow precariously.

'The farm's abandoned. A group of kids come here to use the barn from time to time. They found the car with the key in the ignition, one thing led to another and now this. Fortunately they're kids with consciences and they called it in, anonymously, only we got here faster than they'd anticipated.'

'So they've already contaminated the inside of the vehicle,' Ava said.

'Look at it this way, if they hadn't we might not have found this car for another six months. Apparently the farmer killed himself. Whoever inherited hasn't managed to organise a sale, which is why the buildings are empty.'

'That's local knowledge,' Ava said. 'Not something a passerby would know, or a far right terrorist group. Even if someone was aware that the farm was up for sale, they couldn't be sure it wasn't being used or inhabited.'

Lively walked up, holding an evidence bag.

'Ma'am, we've got clippings from a rope and also sections of wire. The forensics team think there are blood droplets on the floor at the rear of the barn.' He held the rope up for closer inspection.

'Was any of the rope left intact after the explosion at the railway tunnel?' Ava asked.

'Pieces. Enough to verify if this is a match,' Lively said. 'If it is, then this may be where the bomb was constructed, which means it's also possible that both Maura Douglas and Gavin Cronk were held here.'

They made their way to the far end of the barn where low plastic steps had been strategically placed around small markers on the ground with rulers to give scale as a photographer snapped pictures of various debris and marks.

'Ma'am, this is Sam Vesper, she's a blood spatter expert. Forensics asked her to come down,' Lively said.

Ava shook hands with Sam, a willowy blonde nearing six feet tall who smiled vaguely, already looking over at the pattern on the floor. She hopped onto the first of the square plastic steps designed to keep clumsy feet from messing up the scene.

'This is definitely blood,' she said, shining a powerful light downwards then following whatever patterns she could make out. 'It's old and dried up, but it's dense. You can see how it's soaked up the dust particles around it. We're lucky the floor is concrete, not dirt. The droplets here are an interesting shape.' She pointed at the one closest to her and everyone bent to look.

'This droplet here is perfectly round. It has tiny spatter marks coming out equally from its circumference. It's not part of a pattern either from a stab wound or a knife being pulled from a wound – those droplets become elongated and tend to have one end slightly wider to indicate the direction the blood travelled in. What's interesting here is that each of the blood droplets across the floor has maintained its circular form, meaning it was dropped directly from above.'

She moved from step to step, following the blood droplets to a small side door that opened out onto an untended field covered in thorny brown weeds. Ava bent down and picked a sample of the plant, turning to hand it to Lively for bagging.

'Have this checked against the debris found in the soles of Gavin Cronk's feet. I wonder if he made a run for it at some point,' she said.

'That door handle needs to be checked for prints and DNA,' Sam Vesper called to a forensic technician. 'No one tread here. I need pegs to mark this area out and a tent, please.'

'What is it?' Ava asked, following the route from step to step.

Outside the back door was a folded plastic sheet. A puddle of blood had run off it onto the earth, the outline visible as a dark stain.

'So, an event happens inside the barn over the plastic sheeting, then someone carries the worst of the blood out here with a view to getting rid of it. For a reason as yet unknown, the careful disposal stops there and they simply leave the plastic sheeting in situ.' Technicians appeared, erecting a tent over the area as they began photographing the blood pool.

'If someone performed surgery on top of the plastic sheet then carried it outdoors to dispose of it, that would cause droplets of blood to fall to the ground?' Ava asked.

'Yup, large drops of blood not properly contained by the sheeting would account for the round droplet forms on the journey to the door,' she said. 'Excuse me, I need to get better photos.'

'Douglas was working as a courier,' Callanach said. 'Suppose our murderer called her out to pick up a parcel from the farmhouse. They waited for her, grabbed her when she knocked the door, secured her in the barn, and drove her car in through the double doors so it wasn't visible from the track or from the sky.'

'Cut her tongue out, fitted her with the explosive device, cleaned up but didn't do a thorough job – maybe they were disturbed, maybe they ran out of time – then they drove her to the Innocent Railway Tunnel,' Ava finished.

'He certainly didn't do all the railway tunnel prep in one go,' Lively said. 'No friggin' way, if you don't mind my saying, ma'am. There was a bundle of barbed wire secured over the top of the rope to make it harder for us to access, and a large metal hoop in the brickwork that would have needed a drill. By the time the bomber took Maura Douglas to the tunnel, they'd done the groundwork. Had to. They transported her there with the rope already in place.'

'So he'd been to the area at least twice before,' Ava said. 'Once for a recce and to figure out logistics, again to prep the wire and metal hook for the rope, then finally to deliver Maura.'

'The bomber's as driven as fuck,' Lively said. Ava and Luc stared at him. 'That's scarier than your everyday psychopath who wants their bit of sicko time away with whoever they've kidnapped. This person's in a rage like I can't even imagine.'

'And they've combined that rage with immaculate planning,' Callanach said.

'Aye. There'll be more bodies before we've finished this one. Mark my words,' Lively said.

Chapter Fourteen

BEFORE

They were kissing in the car when Uncle Bob began banging on the window.

'Hey you two lovebirds!' he shouted. 'Come on out and say hello. Quinny, your poor parents are desperate to meet this fella of yours.'

Liam pulled away from her, eyes pressed shut.

'For fuck's sake,' he muttered before recontouring his face into a winning smile.

Quinn's heart sank. She wiped the moisture from her lips and opened the car door to greet her mother's brother. Liam remained in his seat but wound down the window.

'Uncle Bobby,' she said, smiling at the broad-chested red-haired man who was beaming at them. 'I didn't know you were visiting today.'

'Can I not surprise my favourite grown-up niece from time to time? I was missing the wee baby girl, too. It's the Wilson genes, you know. Bonny kids my sister produces.' He extended a hand through the open car window to Liam. 'Robert Wilson, Bob to my friends.' They shook hands.

'Liam,' he replied. 'Nice to meet you.'

'Now what's this I hear about you two not going in to say hello to the folks as of yet? Quinn McTavish, that's no way to treat your parents!' He said it kindly enough and followed the reprimand with a warm hug. 'Your mother's got scones fresh out of the oven and I just popped to the shop for cream. Reckon we can put some weight on these bones, girl. You're skinny as a broom handle.' He held up a bag that revealed the outline of a plastic pot to emphasise his point.

Liam checked his watch.

'I've got to get going. There are people waiting. Maybe next time. Good to meet you, Robert.'

'Ach, your friends can wait. This is important. One day it'll be your daughter gallivanting around with some man, and you'll be wanting to check what sort he is. Two minutes is all,' Bob said.

'Yeah, next time. Call you later, babe.' The window rose to a close and he pulled away fast enough to make them take a step back.

Bob watched him go, hands in the pockets of the khakis he still wore every day in spite of having left the army two years earlier. When the car had finally disappeared, he scratched his head and gave Quinn a curious look.

'Don't start, Uncle Bobby,' she said. 'Mum and Dad have been on at me for weeks now about meeting him. It's just not who Liam is.'

'That's your answer? It's not who he is. You mean, the sort of decent lad who'll give up two minutes to show his face to the parents of the girl he's walking out with?'

Quinn sighed and slipped her arm through her uncle's as they walked towards the house.

'No one says "walking out" anymore, and I know how you used to talk when you were in the army. As much as I love you, let's not pretend you're some knight in shining armour.'

'Okay, busted,' he said. 'I'm no angel. But you're worth a thousand of me, Quinny.' He laid a warm hand over the arm she had tucked through his. 'You deserve someone who'll behave properly and treat you right. I'll not let anyone near you unless he's willing to go the extra mile, and that one . . .' He didn't finish the sentence.

They paused at the front door. Quinn withdrew her arm and slid it around her uncle's neck instead, giving him a swift kiss on the cheek.

'I'm happy,' she said. 'But thank you. It's good to know you're watching over me.'

'Am I being overprotective then?'

'Being protective is never a bad thing. You should have had your own children, Uncle Bobby. You'd have been a great dad.'

'The regiment was my family. And I've got you. You're as good as my own daughter. I've no complaints about my life, but if I don't get this cream to your mother she's going to give me hell.'

The text came while they were sitting around the kitchen table cooing over Dolly and laughing about nothing in particular. Quinn loved seeing her mother and uncle Bob together. It was as if they both became children again, the silliness creeping into their every move and word. She took out her mobile and glanced down to see what Liam had sent her.

Don't ever fucking do that to me again. I live on my terms. Not going to be pressured into meeting your family. Keep your uncle out of my face. You're going to have to do some serious work to make this up, and don't eat any of that cream. Your hips don't need it.

The look on Quinn's face silenced the table. She shoved her mobile deep into her pocket.

'Sweetheart,' her mother reached out a hand, 'is everything all right?'

Quinn did her best to shake it off but the tears had some force behind them.

'Is it Liam?' her father asked. 'I'll not have anyone upsetting you.'

'Dad, please don't. Sorry, Mum, this was lovely.' She pushed the remaining half scone away. 'I've got some work to do. Nice to see you, Uncle Bobby.'

Quinn took the stairs to her bedroom and sat on the floor with her back to the door, as she had during those painful teenage years when the world was such a confusing place. No less confusing now – she hadn't realised it would still be like this. The jibe about her hips was just plain mean, but people only got mean when they were upset. Perhaps he'd had a bad experience in the past with another girlfriend's family. Perhaps he was ashamed of his own family and it was a difficult subject for him. If only Uncle Bob had been able to hang back, but it wasn't his way. Quinn couldn't blame him for wanting to meet her boyfriend. He'd been a second father to her for as long as she could remember.

Pushing her hurt feelings to one side, she determined to do what Liam had asked and make up for the day's problem. She decided to call rather than text, but he didn't pick up. Ten minutes later she tried again, then five minutes after that, telling herself he was just busy and that she wasn't losing him, it wasn't such a big deal. She took a shower. Tidied her room. Caught up on some studying. Her parents gave her the space she needed, knocking her door once to leave a cup of tea and plate of biscuits. Quinn took only the tea.

A message came through at 9 p.m.

I'm down the road waiting for you in my car. Come now. Let's work this out.

Quinn told her parents she was going for a walk, took her

mobile but left her wallet, threw on a jacket and went. Liam drove around Edinburgh to the east, barely speaking a word to her, until they reached Portobello where he parked and pointed at a flat above a bagel shop.

'This is me,' he said. 'If this is going to work, Quinn – and I really want it to – then we need to open ourselves up to each other. I'm going to start. I thought you might want to see where I live.'

'Me too, and I'm so sorry about today. I really had no idea my uncle was coming.'

'I don't want to do that,' he said. 'Apologies bore me. They only ever relate to something in the past. What I'm looking for is a future.'

'With me?' she asked softly.

'I wouldn't have brought you here otherwise,' he said.

They made love on his sofa, then on the floor. It wasn't how she'd wanted it to be the first time, but he'd said it was more spontaneous than the cliché of a bed. Passion, he told her, was supposed to be uncomfortable and raw. She'd admired his ethos, even if the carpet was a little sticky and the sofa made her back ache. It had been, mostly, what she'd expected. Her friends had all crossed that particular bridge years earlier but she was glad she'd waited until she could appreciate the importance of it. As they lay in each other's arms afterwards, she gathered her courage and put her hands around his face.

'I love you,' Quinn whispered.

He kissed the end of her nose and smiled.

'I know you do,' he said. 'You want another drink?' He stood, wrapping the single blanket they had around himself, leaving her naked as he went to pour more wine. Quinn curled up. 'You don't need to be shy anymore. I've seen the goods now.'

He handed her a glass of red. She really only liked white wine but it was okay that he hadn't remembered.

Downing his glass, he picked up his mobile and began thumbing through messages.

'What's the time?' Quinn asked idly.

'Just after one a.m.'

'Wow, really? My parents will be worried. I should be getting back. Do you mind?'

'Are you blind or just stupid? You've sat there and watched me drink four glasses of wine in the last three hours. You knew I wasn't going to be driving, right? It's an hour there and back and I'm knackered even if I wasn't over the limit. Stay the night. I'll drop you home on my way to St Boswell's tomorrow. I'll be leaving here at ten.'

'You're right, I am an idiot. I've just remembered I've got a shift in the shop starting at eight. My dad goes to work early, and he's not going to be impressed if I wake him up and ask him to come and get me now.'

'Uber it. There'll be no traffic at this time of night,' Liam said, walking through to his bathroom.

'I actually don't have an account,' she said.

'Taxi then,' Liam called.

Quinn grabbed her jacket and checked her pockets. 'I forgot my wallet. I guess I didn't know we'd be coming so far from home.'

'You just left it to me to do all the driving, pick you up, drop you off, sort the money.' Quinn bit her bottom lip as Liam dipped his hand into his pocket and pulled out a twenty and a ten. He dropped the cash into her lap and told her the address for the booking. 'I'll call in on the way home from work tomorrow so you can pay me back.'

Home seemed a universe away. Quinn had moved quietly around the flat picking up items of clothing. She'd annoyed Liam again, and he was watching a film in his bedroom. He'd said goodbye in a sleepy voice as she'd exited, clicking the door gently shut so as to not disturb his neighbours. The cab was waiting and the driver was kind but the journey home seemed to take forever. Hopeful of a quiet entrance, she was met by her mother who was nursing Dolly in the sitting room. She kissed her daughter on the cheek and let her retreat to her bedroom.

Quinn didn't need to analyse anything. She was no fool. She'd fallen too easily, and she accepted that nugget of self-criticism. Had given herself to a man who hadn't appreciated her. Been a fool letting herself go out the night before a morning shift. But that wasn't the real problem. Standing in front of the mirror, wiping off what small amounts of makeup she'd been wearing, she accepted what she already knew; Liam wasn't as nice a man as she'd first thought he was. A relationship that started badly never rectified itself. Even with her limited experience of relationships, Quinn was sensible enough to know that. She was worth more, deserved better, and everything her parents had taught her about self-respect had been right. Quinn made a decision, took another shower, told herself she was allowed to cry for fifteen minutes – not a tear more – and went to bed.

Chapter Fifteen

Callanach nursed a beer in The Hanging Bat on Lothian Road and tried to enjoy the plush leather couch and arresting wall murals, but all he could see was Maura Douglas' son's face as he'd visited him the previous evening after leaving the farm. The call to confirm Douglas' DNA had come as he'd been driving home, and Callanach wasn't prepared to let anyone else deliver the news.

Jimmy Douglas had been expecting it, but the words were finite. No more hope. No taking it back. His mother was dead. The world before him consisted of a father who, he'd explained, only had him to sleep over to reduce child support payments, a step-mother who was also exiting his life as soon as that divorce was finalised, and a tired social worker sporting a black eye from some other family who were falling apart.

Callanach's heart ached. In crime there were short-term victims and long-term victims. The short-term ones ended up in body bags, hospitals, and victim interview suites. Jimmy was long-term. He would spend a lifetime thinking – more likely trying not to think – about the agony and terror his mother had suffered. His whole life would change. If he made it out of poverty, if he improved his lot in spite of it all, he would still miss his mother for the rest of his life and see her in the eyes of his future children. You could witness the long-term effects of crime in the face of the partner of a rape victim, in the eyes of the parent whose child had been abused by a scout master, a priest or a football coach. Crime was an airborne virus, touching many more victims than those at the scene.

'Chin up, Frenchie,' Lively said as the rest of the team collected their drinks from the bar. 'You're too pretty to look that sad.'

'I bet you say that to all the girls,' Callanach responded.

'Aye but you're only interested in one, and we all want to know what she's thinking.'

'Sergeant, if you were as good at police work as you are at sticking your nose into other people's private lives, you'd have made Superintendent by now,' Callanach said.

Lively clapped a hand on Callanach's shoulder. 'Still a touchy subject with you then. Say no more. But you've a direct line to the Chief. What're we doing here?' Lively asked.

'Convening,' Ava said planting a glass on the table. 'Away from my desk. I'm not eating any more limp sandwiches from the petrol station.' DI Graham and DS Max Tripp joined them. Tripp, the team's youngest and most health-conscious detective sergeant, set his usual salad and sparkling water down on the table. For once, nobody made a sarcastic comment. 'Right, we've got forty-five minutes. What have you got?' She bit into a huge burger and nodded at Lively to get it started.

They kept their voices low, huddled in a corner.

'Uniforms have canvassed every property in the Temple area and stopped every car driving near the farm to ask who might have seen a vehicle turning in or out of the farm track recently. We got one possible. A dark blue Nissan Qashqai exited from the farm track about two weeks ago. No idea of a number plate, no visual on who was driving. An estate agent saw the

Qashqai and realised it was unusual, knowing the farm was empty, but it was the end of the day, could have been a lost passerby making a three point turn, nothing else suspicious.'

'We've got tyre tracks from the farmyard. There are only two recent sets of prints. One's confirmed as Maura Douglas' Beetle. The other has no known source. We're assuming it's her killer's car,' Tripp said. 'Tyre tracks are all a bit worn on the driver's side. Looks like the tracking is off in the car.'

'All right,' Ava said. 'We've got a potential vehicle make and model, and tyre tracks. How many cars matching the description in the local area?'

'A lot,' Lively said. 'It's been one of the most popular models in the last decade and the blue is their most popular colour, so we're wading through them, cross-checking owners against the database for people with previous convictions.'

'Good start,' Ava said. 'But then I want boots on the ground. There's no reason to assume that whoever did this will have committed similar offences before.'

'I can't think of any serial killer case where they haven't sent a warning shot across the bow first,' Lively said. 'Who the hell converts a landmine into a toxic gas weapon on their first offence?'

'Terrorists,' Tripp said. 'People with access to the knowledge and the technology. Plus these sorts of offences scream group participation. It's too much for one person.'

'It may not be terrorists,' Callanach said. 'But it's definitely a crusade. This isn't some idiot buying grenades and throwing them into a police station. It's meant to be up close and personal. If it's terrorism, it's more like when an army has mistakenly drone-bombed a village full of women and children. The response is classified as terrorism but the motivation is a much more private thing.'

'Do we know any more about Maura Douglas?' Ava asked.

'She hadn't told her son about her brain tumour, but we know she was aware of it. She'd been taking medication and seeing an oncologist. I spoke to the doctor who said that her only concern was how much time she had left in terms of making provision for her son. It looks as if she was taking any work she could get to leave some cash behind for him. No life insurance, no family except his father, and her bank account was almost depleted. She was desperate,' Callanach said.

'Desperate enough to get involved with someone who turned her into a human bomb?' Graham asked. 'Poor woman.'

No one spoke. They sipped their drinks, stared at food that suddenly seemed less appealing, and considered the possibilities.

'Whoever did it also cut out her tongue. If she gave herself up willingly, why would they have needed to do that?' Callanach asked.

'Insurance, maybe?' Tripp suggested. 'In case she changed her mind.'

'I don't believe it,' Callanach said. 'She wouldn't have done that to her son. What mother would do such a thing?'

'A mother who was offered, I don't know, maybe £20,000 when she knew she was already dying,' Lively suggested.

'Then where's the money? Maura Douglas was broke but I don't think she was stupid. She'd have asked for the money up front to make sure it reached Jimmy,' Callanach said.

'We'll have to bear it in mind and double-check. Is there any link between Gavin Cronk and Ailsa Lambert?' Ava asked.

'None that we can find,' Pax Graham said. 'I spoke to Cronk's older brother again. They've never lost a close family member other than grandparents and have never had contact with Edinburgh City Mortuary. We're getting stuck for motive to be honest, ma'am. It's hard to draw any lines between the parties involved in the case. Realistically, we won't be able to spot any patterns until—' He stopped talking abruptly.

Ava wiped her mouth and threw her napkin onto her plate. 'Until there's another death. We need three for a pattern. That's what you were going to say, isn't it?'

Pax Graham acknowledged it with a slight nod.

No one replied.

The camera flashed as they sat there, burgers in some hands, fries in others, a pint of beer being raised to lips. Each of them just sitting there, staring blankly at one another, looking for all the world as if there were nothing more important to be doing than sitting in a pub as the day slipped by.

'Detective Chief Inspector,' a journalist announced smugly, appearing from behind the photographer, 'eighteen people are dead already. Do you even care? Is this lunch being paid for by the taxpayer? Have you made any progress in the case yet?'

Lively and Graham were on their feet in an instant.

'Back up, right now,' Lively said.

'I don't think so, this is a public space,' the journalist replied. 'I'm not committing any offence. You can't tell me what to do.'

Pax Graham shielded their view through to Ava as Callanach pulled on his jacket. 'I'm afraid the Chief's not available to speak right now. You should leave,' Graham said.

'That's all right,' Ava said.

'The fuck it is,' Lively growled. 'Those were our colleagues whose blood got spilled, and this is the shit we have to put up with?'

'Detective Sergeant,' Ava said. 'Let her pass you. Not the photographer.' Lively shot Ava a look that contained a small measure of fury and substantially more questions over her sanity as Graham made sure the photographer stayed well back. 'Please.'

They made a corridor to the table and the journalist stepped through, chin up, taken aback in spite of the pointed questions and the accusatory tone. The last thing she'd expected was access.

Ava stood to greet her. 'Please, sit down,' she said. The journalist sat. Ava didn't. 'Do you see this?' Ava pointed at the water she'd been drinking. 'It's to keep us hydrated. And this, on these plates, this is food. We need that so we can continue to function.'

The journalist began to get back to her feet.

'Stay where you are,' Ava said. There was no mistaking her tone. Only an idiot would have disobeyed. 'This is a table, no different to the tables at the police station. We sit around them and we talk. We discuss what we know and what we need to do. Some of the people around this table are on duty right now, some are off duty but still working, unpaid, because that's what my team does.'

'Is this on the record?' the journalist asked.

'Oh yeah,' Ava said. 'Every word of it.'

The journalist tapped her mobile phone and laid it on the table between them.

'My team is working every second of every day. We've pulled in specialists from other agencies across the UK who are advising. No one is taking leave. Few people are going home to their nearest and dearest. Our police station, our offices, even the corridors, are rammed full of additional officers from other forces brought in to assist. Just to dispel whatever American TV drama misconceptions you may have, there's no cafeteria at our police station. No one's cooking delicious plates of hot food to keep my squad functioning. This place, however, is able to offer that service, which is why you find us here, briefly, continuing to work as we discuss the case and plan our next moves.'

'I wasn't suggesting that you aren't entitled to—'

'Stop talking,' Ava said. 'Because you have only sixty seconds left with me.'

'Fine.'

'So if you're here interrupting our work on the case, thinking that your job to sensationalise the news and drag every last piece of human misery from an already horrific story is more important than leaving us to continue our discussions, then let me disabuse you of that notion.'

'I'm recording this. You should watch how you talk to me,' the journalist said.

'Should I? You see, the fact as you so rightly pointed out, is that eighteen people with families, friends, dependants and communities are counting on us. Those people did the job we do. They wore the uniform we've all worn, they've picked people up from car accidents, heart attacks and our cells, they've dragged people from burning buildings in the middle of the night. The eighteen dead are us. You think I've forgotten about them?' Ava leaned over the table. 'Do you know their names? Go on, tell me their names. List them for me, right now.' The journalist shifted in her seat and looked to check her exit. 'You can't do it, can you? With your fake outrage and your bullshit questions. How dare you.'

'Ma'am,' Pax Graham said.

Other diners were standing from tables further away, watching the scene unfold.

'Leave her to it, lad,' Lively said.

'Let me tell you what it means to actually serve your community. It means attending a scene where you try to save a woman from hanging. It means watching your fellow first responders get blown apart and, rather than running away, rushing forward, even as a bridge is collapsing and threatening to kill you. It means, no matter how physically exhausted or injured you are, staying there to pull bodies from the rubble and pick up evidence. It means bearing witness. Not taking photographs to sell to a hypnotised public, but witnessing the pain and devastation until it's so imprinted into your psyche that you will not rest until justice has been done. It means going to the families of the dead and breaking the news and staying strong to give everyone around you the space to break. So I'm going to ask you one more time. Do you know the names of the dead?'

The journalist stood. 'I've got all I need,' she said, retrieving her mobile.

'Kevin Phillips,' Ava began. 'He was thirty-one and expecting his first child two months from now. Martha Thrussell. She'd just sat her sergeant's exams. She didn't know it yet but she'd aced them. Her commanding officer was going to break the news to her the day after the explosion. A cake was being decorated at a local bakery.'

The journalist had pushed back her chair and was signalling to the photographer to get out.

'August McKellar. He was a year away from retirement. His husband said they were planning to buy a little place in Italy to do up.'

Only the journalist's back was in view now, and she wasn't slow at taking the stairs to the exit.

'Ailsa Lambert,' Ava shouted after her. 'Graduated with top grades from her class at medical school. She gave twenty per cent of her salary every single year to charities to fight the poverty in Scotland that she saw as the cause for so much crime, violence, drug use and early death.'

They'd gone. Callanach handed Ava a set of car keys.

'Ma'am,' Tripp said.

'I think we'll just let the Chief take a moment.' Lively patted him on the arm.

'There's no time for that. A man called Colin Love's trying to get hold of you. He believes his wife's been kidnapped.'

Chapter Sixteen

Eden Lane, between Greenhill and Morningside, boasted one of the most sought-after addresses in the city, with rare spacious garden plots and easy access to tennis courts, a little way from the heavily-beaten tourist trails. The homes were semi-detached rather than terraces. The price you paid for having a private front door was measured in the millions, which was how investment banker Colin Love could afford to be part of the Eden Lane brigade. The reason he was demanding to speak with Ava personally was that his wife, Felicity, was an advocate most often found in Edinburgh's criminal courts. She and Ava had developed a grudging respect for one another over the past decade, as police officers and defence lawyers sometimes did. Felicity had a reputation for fierceness. She pulled no punches, argued her opponents into submission, and excelled at cross-examination. His second wife, the couple shared a four-year-old son and not much more, if rumours were true. Colin, now in his sixties, favoured golfing holidays with his buddies, while Felicity – some twenty years his junior – was more happily married to her job.

Colin Love was in his lounge, sipping brandy when Ava and

Luc arrived. She'd met him at a variety of official city events and fundraisers.

'Detective Chief Inspector,' he said, without bothering to rise. 'I asked you to call me en route.'

'I appreciate that,' Ava said. 'Instead I took the opportunity to make enquiries about Felicity's whereabouts to avoid wasting any time. I gather her mobile's turned off, no one from her place of work has heard from her since Friday lunchtime, and she missed a court hearing this morning. Could I ask where you were this weekend?'

'St. Andrew's, on the green. I left Thursday night. Benefits of early retirement. What do you intend to do about this?' He crossed his legs and looked irritated.

'First, we have to establish a timeline from Thursday onwards. Today's Monday so that's five days we need to cover. I want to know who had access to the house during that period. Where was your son this weekend?' Ava asked.

'His nanny took him to Felicity's parents for the weekend. It's become quite a regular event. Felicity uses the weekend to catch up on reading briefs and preparing for the next week's cases.'

'And when did you last speak with her by telephone?'

He shrugged. 'We don't really do that.'

'Do you know where her car is?' Callanach asked.

'We've a garage at the end of the lane. The Aston Martin's in there. Felicity's mobile is on our bed, as is her handbag. Her wallet's still in there too. None of her cards are missing, I've checked.'

A uniformed officer entered quietly and whispered in Callanach's ear.

'Excuse me,' he said, leaving Ava to continue alone.

In the corridor the uniformed officer pointed to the floor just behind the front door. Callanach knelt down. Two false nails were stuck in the bristles of the door mat. He pulled on the gloves he kept in his pocket, photographed the nails in position on the mat, then carefully deposited them into an evidence bag.

The door was old and wooden, beautifully crafted to fit the uneven doorway, no glass in it. No chain for security, although there was an alarm box on the wall. A long cashmere coat hung from the brass fitting on the rear of the door. Callanach pulled it aside. Behind, the wood was scratched. Three nearly horizontal markings had been left in the varnish, lighter than the mid-brown.

'Pass me a torch,' he said to the nearest officer.

A few seconds later, he was shining a bright light into the scratches and cursing softly in his native French.

'Get a forensic team out here right now,' he told the officer. 'No one uses this door to enter or exit. Everyone goes through the garden instead.' As his commands were being carried out, he rejoined Ava in the lounge. 'Sorry, ma'am, I need to inter-rupt. Mr Love, do you recognise these?'

He held up the bag containing the false nails. Colin blinked hard twice, took another sip of brandy and turned away to stare out of the window.

'They're Felicity's,' he said. 'She had her nails done every four weeks. Always that same shade.'

Ava let him take the time he needed.

'Colin, was Felicity working on any particularly controversial case? Anything she was concerned about?'

'Not that she mentioned, but then we haven't really discussed her cases for a while. We've been living somewhat separate lives – I'm sure you already know that – but I never wanted this. She adores Dylan and when she's present, she's a good mother. Would you mind giving me a moment? I have to call her parents and ask them to keep Dylan a little longer. They should be told what's going on.'

Callanach took Ava to see the scratches on the door. She opened it up to take a look at the front. A tiny black circle above the doorbell was evidence of a camera. Fifteen minutes later they were staring into a monitor in Colin Love's office and scrolling through the security footage.

At 8 p.m. on Friday a motorcycle courier, helmet on, darkened visor down, rang the doorbell carrying a large bouquet of yellow roses. The camera began recording. No one answered the door. As Ava was peering closer to the screen, the delivery person's thumb slid upwards and everything became a darkened blur.

'You're fucking kidding,' Ava said. 'What the hell just happened?'

'At a guess, I'd say that's a smear of engine oil or grease,' Callanach said.

They scrolled forwards. There was only one other clip after that. At 11.17 p.m. the doorbell rang again. The darkness outside and smear of grease on the lens combined to make the footage useless save to show a shadowy, most likely male, figure holding a large object with a flash of white in their arms. He stood waiting for the door to be opened. It duly was.

'Is there no audio?' Ava asked.

Colin Love pressed a key and in crackled the sound.

'Who is it?' Felicity's voice was immediately recognisable.

'Delivery. Urgent case files from Talisman Advocates. I did try earlier but no one answered.' The voice was male, mature, Edinburgh accent.

'Talisman is her legal practice, right?' Ava checked.

Colin nodded.

'Sorry, I didn't get the message that there were papers coming or I wouldn't have gone out. Hold on.' About a minute passed before the door opened. The camera showed vague movement. 'Do I need to sign?'

An arm shot out and then Felicity lurched forward. Arms flew, and for a moment she managed to pull herself back into the house but the man at the door was faster and stronger. They both went down. The lack of screams told its own story.

'He must have got his hand over her mouth.' Callanach spoke Ava's thoughts.

There was a scratching noise, harsh, brutal. It was easy enough to imagine Felicity's false nails pinging off as she gripped the back of the door. Seconds later it was over. The man retreated from the doorway pulling her along the short garden path. After that the video clicked off.

'What happened?' Ava asked.

Colin Love took in a shaking breath, coughed to cover it.

'The video is only set to record for two minutes with each delivery. We never really anticipated . . . something like this.'

'Felicity's been gone nearly three days now,' Ava said. 'We're not going to improve the quality of that footage. Do you know where she went Friday evening?'

'Usually she sees a friend from work, but we can check her phone for confirmation. She uses a shape formation as a security feature. I've seen her do it a million times. She's never off the damned thing.'

Felicity Love's legal chambers, Talisman Advocates, were situated in Parliament Square in the most imposing of areas, between St Giles' Cathedral and the Supreme Court Building with its ground floor arches and upper storey pillars that defied normal architectural rules. It was a place set back in time. Ava had always marvelled at how untouched it seemed, but time had indeed moved on. Largely gone were the old-fashioned advocates' briefs tied with pink ribbon, and the female advocates' wore trousers and strode confidently among their male colleagues.

Talisman's head clerk sat across the table from Ava, consoling another female advocate, Elise Holmes.

'We'd got into a bit of a pattern on a Friday night,' Elise explained. 'Felicity would come over to mine, we'd drink wine or coffee, talk about the cases we'd done that week and what we had coming up. I've got no children so she used to leave Dylan with the nanny if he wasn't with his grandparents. It was never a very late night but she tended to hop in a taxi so she could have more than just one glass. We can't risk breaking the law. She was always fastidious about it.'

'So this wasn't an impromptu plan then?' Callanach checked.

'No, more routine. We'd even joked about it on Twitter, our Friday night sessions.'

'Was she being followed or watched, worried about security maybe?' Ava asked.

'No, nothing like that,' the clerk said. 'And in terms of her cases, Felicity only ever defended. If you're worried that she might have crossed someone dangerous in a case, they were always her client and she was good at her job. I don't think we've ever had a complaint.'

'Could you check your files to see if Felicity ever had Gavin Cronk or Maura Douglas as a client or a witness?' Callanach asked.

'I can check clients but not witnesses; we deal with too many cases to have that sort of information in our records. I'll look this afternoon and let you know.'

'Thanks. And just to confirm, did you send her case papers out late on Friday?' Ava asked.

'No, although it's not unknown. Sometimes a case comes in late as an emergency, maybe an injunction or a family law matter that needs attention over the weekend. But not last Friday. That wasn't us.'

'There were the flowers, too,' Elise added. 'She texted me

when she got home to say she'd received a bouquet of roses without a card.'

'No idea who they were from?' Callanach asked.

'No. All she said was they definitely weren't from Colin. They weren't, you know, very close.'

'We appreciate that,' Ava said. 'Was there anything in Felicity's private life that bothered her? Anything she ever talked about?'

'Not really,' Elise said. 'It was all about the job with Felicity. She felt guilty for not being what she called a "mumsy kind of mum" to Dylan, but he has a good nanny and seems happy enough. The only thing she ever talked about is the same thing a lot of us feel: sometimes she wondered if she'd lost her ability to empathise. Felicity is good at her job. She could take people apart in the witness box in a heartbeat. It was the only thing that ever bothered her. Cross-examining rape victims, child abuse victims, the family of murder victims . . . She was only ever doing her job, but she was better at it than anyone else I ever saw. Recently she'd talked about joining the Procurator Fiscal's office, to give prosecuting a try instead. They'd have jumped at the chance to have her.'

'Thank you,' Ava said. 'Can I just ask what she was wearing when she left your house?'

'Black trousers and a baby blue tailored shirt. Her hair was tied back in a plait. Black shoes with high heels and her long cashmere coat. She never looked less than perfect. Please find her. Felicity's not as tough as she seems. Out of the courtroom, she's not really tough at all.'

Chapter Seventeen

The memorial service in St Giles' Cathedral was humbling. Every seat was filled and those who had never been inside before sat staring, awestruck by the cobalt ceiling over the nave and the historical stained-glass windows that told the story of Scotland's past. The Cathedral, the oldest parts of it, had seen nearly a thousand years of deaths. This was nothing new in the grand scheme of Scots' history, and yet the Innocent Railway Tunnel bombing had been a modern-day massacre, one that wouldn't be forgotten for decades.

The Royal Mile was packed full with those unable to find a space inside. At the last minute screens had been erected to allow the exterior mourners to watch. The families of the dead processed in last. It was cold comfort given that the bodies of the deceased could not be released for burial. Guilt weighed heavily on Ava's shoulders for that. When the only victim was Ailsa, it hadn't occurred to her that a decision to break protocol would be under such scrutiny. Now she had loved ones on the phone daily demanding an explanation for why they couldn't lay their nearest and dearest to rest, and thereby at least begin the long walk towards healing. Every time she explained why the bodies had to be held at the mortuary until there was some sort of resolution, she wanted to crawl under her desk and hide.

Superintendent Overbeck and every senior Police Scotland officer – not to mention every brand of politician and the First Minister – were in the Cathedral. Ava had wanted to tell them it was unwise. There was a monster on the loose who'd like nothing more than to gather everyone in a single place – the very way the victims were so carefully brought together at the railway tunnel – and here they all were again. It was a security nightmare. She had every available police officer out responding to a claim that another victim was to be killed in a matter of hours, and a missing lawyer who might just fit that bill, yet they were simultaneously organising the policing of the city's largest event since Hogmanay. People had flown in from all over the world to mourn with Edinburgh's residents. She'd never seen so many press passes.

'What if the killer had all of this planned?' Ava muttered to Luc. 'What if he or she is in the crowd right now wearing a suicide vest, or is up in one of the overlooking buildings with a stash of automatic weapons?'

'For what little it's worth,' Callanach said quietly as they watched from the edge of the crowd outside the Cathedral, 'I don't think the killer wants to hurt members of the public. We've started excavating the inside of the railway tunnel. Beneath the rubble they found a sign and some tape. Whoever killed Maura Douglas stopped pedestrians and cyclists from going towards the bombed entrance. I didn't notice at the time, but he or she had also sealed off the lane into the tunnel from the road. Did a good job of making it look official – that's why no members of the public got hurt.'

'Or maybe they just sealed off the tunnel so no one could disturb them midway through hanging her,' Ava said.

'Agreed. But then Gavin Cronk's body had a concealed weapon, one that could only have been discovered during the postmortem in a sealed room. The killer could as easily have left a body in the road with a bomb inside it ready to explode while a crowd of onlookers was gathered. Is that a coincidence?'

'I don't know. We have a counter-terrorism unit from London that's taken over half the station and they're pursuing their own avenues. Dr Carlisle says that another forensic examiner briefed by the First Minister has been sent in to double-check his work. I haven't seen Overbeck for days because she's so tied up in red tape, she hasn't had a moment for me to brief her on the operation. It feels like the sheer scale of this thing is what's stopping us from making progress.'

A serpentine hush made its way through the crowd, spreading outwards from the Cathedral. The service began with two minutes' silence. Ava and Luc bowed their heads.

The quiet was then broken by the sound of bagpipes. A solo chorister joined in. The words of 'Dark Island' caught in the throats of the watching throng. Eyes glistened and heads dropped.

Away to the westward, I'm longing to be
Where the beauties of heaven unfold by the sea
Where the sweet purple heather blooms fragrant and free
On a hilltop, high above the Dark Island.

'That's beautiful,' Callanach said.

Their mobiles buzzed at the same time.

'You take it,' Ava told him.

He answered, listened, murmured consent, ended the call. 'We've got the licence plate for the delivery motorcycle. There was enough detail in the footage before the driver put the grease over the camera that we were able to pick it up on CCTV when it turned left onto Morningside Road. We're wanted at the station now.'

★ ★ ★

'The security app on Mr Love's computer gave us the precise time the motorcycle left. A motorbike with a male rider and a darkened helmet turned onto Morningside Road precisely one minute after leaving Eden Lane. There were no other motorcycles in the area at that time so we're confident,' Lively said. 'CCTV from different points along that route has so far traced that bike heading west out of the city. The licence plate is registered to a different make and model of bike that looks to have been scrapped several months ago. We're chasing that lead although theft of a licence plate from a scrap yard that long ago is likely to get us nowhere, if it was ever noticed.'

'So if we're right that the flower delivery was intended only to disrupt the security camera, where do we go from here?' Callanach asked.

'We're already checking every camera along that route for the period when we last saw the motorbike. Every unit, every civilian CCTV centre, plus traffic wardens and other first responders are on notice to check licence plates of all passing motorcycles. We're hoping he'll pop up again,' Lively said.

'Whoever did this knew they wouldn't be able to lure Felicity Love out of her house. She's too savvy for that. They've been watching her for a sustained period. They know she's a lawyer, hence turning up with the files and giving the name of her chambers. They also know she regularly goes out on a Friday night and I'm assuming they purposely waited until her husband was away for the weekend. This suggests long-term surveillance, so it wasn't an opportunistic kidnapping,' Ava said. 'They knew about her doorbell camera. One look into the rear garden would have told them there was a child in the house, so did they also know Dylan was at his grandparents'? Go back to the neighbouring houses in Eden Lane. Ask them about any incident or sightings in the last six months. Vehicles, pedestrians, anyone not recognised coming and going in the road. And cross-reference all our new information with the National Domestic Extremism Database. See if they've had any similar cases or if anyone involved is known to them.'

'Message for you, ma'am,' PC Biddlecombe said, handing over a barely legible note.

Lively continued with the briefing as Ava read it. She thrust it into Callanach's hand and grabbed her bag.

'Check Colin Love's alibi with his golfing buddies,' she said as she made her way towards the door. 'Ask the Procurator Fiscal to flag any cases where Dr Lambert appeared as a witness and Felicity Love was defence advocate. And find that motor-bike. DI Callanach and I will be at the Royal Infirmary.'

'You can't go in yet, I'm afraid. There's a waiting room just down the corridor,' a nurse told them.

Ava strode forwards anyway, her hand outstretched to push the door into the room. She stopped short. The square of glass in the door framed Natasha on a narrow bed hooked up to a drip, machines lighting her with their digital displays, beeping occasionally. A pair of doctors whispered in the corner while a nurse tidied away the debris of emergency treatment.

'Luc,' Ava said, reaching back for him to steady her. He was in no better state. The two of them stood still, watching, hardly daring to ask the question they needed answering.

Professor Natasha Forge was grey against the white sheet, her skin dried out, hands flopped uselessly on the bed.

'She's not moving,' Callanach said. 'We need to find a doctor to explain what's happening.'

Ava knocked on the glass and waved at the medics. A female doctor exited to speak with them.

'Sorry, you are?' the doctor asked.

'Natasha's housemates,' Ava said.

'Both of you?'

'Yes, but only because she needed help while she was getting chemotherapy and surgery. We don't normally all live together. What can you tell me?' Ava asked.

'Nothing, as you're not family, until Professor Forge is awake and gives her consent for me to discuss her situation with you. I hope you understand. I need to go back in.'

'We're police officers. Detectives.' She pulled her ID from her pocket and handed it to the doctor. Callanach followed suit. 'I'd rather not pull any stupid stunt to find out what's happened to my best friend. All I would say is that I'm pretty sure if you check her records with the oncology department, Natasha has me down as next of kin. Her biological family hasn't been involved. So could you, please, just give me the bare bones?'

It might have been the look on Ava's face, possibly the tone of her voice. More likely the shake of her hands as she held up her government identification that showed her to be a detective chief inspector when she more closely resembled a scared teenager. The doctor softened.

'She's terribly anaemic. Her iron levels were virtually non-existent so her body stopped making haemoglobin. That meant her blood wasn't transporting sufficient oxygen to her vital organs. She would have been experiencing exhaustion, dizziness, maybe headaches, weakness, palpitations, feeling generally unwell. Did she say anything about that to either of you?'

They both shook their heads.

'Natasha's stubborn, proud, and a good liar. Also we've been busy with an investigation,' Callanach said.

'Of course,' the doctor said. 'Well, the result was that Professor Forge suffered a type 2 myocardial injury. A very mild heart attack, more of a warning really. She collapsed at the University and was brought here by ambulance.'

'Oh Christ, I've been so distracted. I haven't been shopping or cooking enough fresh meals. I should have seen this coming,' Ava said.

'Ava, don't,' Callanach said. 'That won't help.'

'I agree,' the doctor added. 'Anaemia is a side effect of chemotherapy, and the surgery would have taken its toll. We've given her a blood transfusion and intravenous iron. We're monitoring her heart. When she's conscious, we'll be performing an echocardiogram to double-check that there's no underlying heart failure.'

'What can we do?' Callanach asked.

'Wait until she's more awake then keep her company, reassure her. Having a heart attack – however minor – can be extremely scary and should be a real wake-up call for her to listen to her body. She'll be shocked and probably confused. I'm sure it would help to have the people she loves around her.'

'We can do that,' Ava said. 'What about coming home? Do I need to get a nurse in to look after her?'

'One step at a time,' the doctor said. 'She won't be leaving here today. We're doing extensive tests. We need to get her on more medication and liaise with her oncology team.'

'Please tell me it's not back,' Ava whispered.

'We're waiting for blood tests and, in any event, I couldn't discuss that with you until I've talked to my patient. For now, we have to make sure she's stable, safe, and complete more investigations.'

The doctor slipped away. Ava and Luc stood in the corridor, watching through the glass panel, hand in hand.

'How did we miss it?' Ava asked.

'We were doing our jobs. Natasha obviously decided we had enough on our plates, so she kept it from us. And she's developed a hatred of hospitals. I'm not surprised she opted to stay quiet rather than make yet another appointment,' Callanach said.

'She went back to work too soon. I kept telling her she wasn't strong enough. Why didn't she listen?'

'Ava, Natasha didn't listen because she wanted to go back to work. Maybe she felt she had to choose between her physical health and her mental health.'

She slipped her hand from his and stepped forward to press her face against the window.

'I never feel safe anymore,' she said. 'When there's bad news, I feel like I've just been waiting for it. When there's good news, I don't trust it. I'm waiting for the next awful thing to happen, both at work and at home. It's like walking a tightrope over a pit of broken glass. Sometimes I wish it was me who'd got cancer – that it might have been easier than watching Tasha go through it – but then I realise how awful and ungrateful that is. What the fuck's wrong with me, Luc?'

'Unconditional love is the most destructive force in the universe. Sooner or later it breaks us all.'

Finally allowed into Natasha's room, they set up a chair at either side of her bed and sat talking quietly, filling her head with their voices to bring her back to them. Laying her head on the bed, Ava closed her eyes. Her breathing slowed, relaxed. Finally she slept, her face almost as ashen as Natasha's. Callanach watched her dream and wondered how he could fix the two women who'd become his whole world. It had been a year of emotional torture, yet he'd thrived. Being able to forget his past, the mess he'd left behind in France, by committing himself to caring for other people had been medicine for him. Now they both seemed to be slipping away.

He was in love with Ava. She knew it, too, but they never talked about it. Natasha was the only one who ever dared broach the subject, and then only without Ava present. They'd diced with a relationship almost since they'd met, tested boundaries, pushed and pulled each other. He had no idea what to do about it now. Only that doing nothing was no longer an option.

'I'm pretty sure you two should be at work.' Natasha's voice was laced with the hangover of strong drugs, but medication that could dampen her sarcastic tone hadn't yet been invented.

'Would you keep it down?' Luc said. 'It took a heart attack to get Ava to sleep. Don't wake her now.'

'She looks like crap,' Natasha said. 'I'm guessing that's work rather than too much partying. The last time I saw her looking that bad was when she escaped from boarding school, hid in my closet for two days, and we mixed melon liqueur with cherry brandy. By rights, neither of us should have survived— Wait. Did I really have a heart attack? Holy shit!'

'I have a theory that you faked it to get a bit more time off,' Luc said. Natasha pulled her hand from under his and made a gesture he usually only saw drunk men make in the cells late at night. 'So you're feeling better then.'

Natasha gave a tired grin.

'Is she properly asleep?' She nodded in Ava's direction.

'She's stopped giving me orders, so yes.'

'Good. Luc, I'm so worried about her. She's like . . .' Natasha closed her eyes and fought for the words. 'You know when you were a kid at school and you drew something really badly, then rubbed it out so you could start again, but there was this line drawing left there, almost invisible but kind of pressed into the paper. That's what she's like. A line drawing someone did of her then rubbed out. She's just a messy outline of her former self.'

The vivid description of Ava made Luc's stomach drop.

'Yes.' It was all he could say.

'Something has to give, Luc. She can't go on like this. Ailsa's death hit her so hard, then there was the incident at the tunnel. I know she's trained for it and believe me, I get that Ava is capable of anything, but I think she's forgotten that the essence of being human means being breakable.'

Ava breathed in sharply, twitched and sat upright too fast, steadying herself by grabbing the bed.

'Seriously, you came to make sure I was okay but got so bored you fell asleep?' Natasha asked her. 'Did you at least bring me grapes?'

'You hate grapes,' Ava muttered.

'Not to eat, to throw at you. Now that you're awake, let's fast forward. Apparently I had a heart attack, they obviously gave me some sort of sedative, so how long have I been here and how long have you two been here?'

'You about four hours, us about three. You had a blood transfusion. You're due some more tests this evening. And you're staying in for a while.'

'Yeah, right. You think I'm sleeping in a single bed hooked up to Mr Beepy? Ava, tell them you're taking me home. I can come back tomorrow for whatever they need to do,' Natasha said.

'You're staying here,' Ava told her, stretching her arms above her head. 'I'm not arguing about it. If I have to, I'll handcuff you to Mr fucking Beepy.'

'Wow, so you're always grumpy when you wake up? It's not just first thing in the morning?' Natasha asked.

'Tash, you're so anaemic that you've been experiencing exhaustion and dizzy spells. Why, for the love of god, did you not tell us?' Ava snapped.

'Because eighteen people died, and although it's not your fault, you'll say they died on your watch. Because those eighteen people each had a family, friends and neighbours. If I know anything about you and Luc it's that you'll be torturing your-selves and feeling like you're failing those people by not being able to turn back time so none of those people ever died. That's how hard you are on yourselves. And because, if I'm honest, when it all started happening, I felt a sense of relief. You were finally both so busy with something that you stopped watching me every second. It felt so good to have you both behaving normally again that I didn't want to break the spell.'

'Natasha, you had a fucking heart attack. Do you not get it? This isn't a game. If you didn't want to talk to us, you could at least have told your doctors,' Ava shouted.

'If you don't calm down, there'll be two of us on the cardiac unit,' Natasha said. 'For the record, I do get it. I cheated death once this year. I shouldn't have pushed my luck. If it makes you feel any better it really bloody hurt and it was really bloody scary.'

'Shit,' Ava said. 'I'm sorry. Can we pretend I came here with flowers and a reassuring smile, and told you everything was going to be all right?'

'Aside from the fact that I'd think you'd been bodysnatched? I prefer the authentic you. It's when you're not a pain in the arse that I get really worried.'

Callanach's mobile rang.

'How long ago?' he asked after answering. 'We're on our way. Set up a perimeter, no one goes in until we know it's safe. Do not approach the victim. Call in the bomb disposal squad. We're not taking any chances this time.'

Chapter Eighteen

BEFORE

He drove past first, slowly. Liam could see Quinn sitting at the till. From the movement of her head, he decided she was talking animatedly to a customer. That was part of her charm, the innocence of not understanding how her energy affected people. Men, in particular. She needed to be controlled. Women who weren't took advantage faster than a mouse trap snapped shut, and he wasn't going to be one of those poor fools who ended up a slave to a woman's every whim. Train them early, his father had taught him. No one ever needed to get slapped if a hefty dose of respect had been injected into a relationship early on.

He could have any woman he wanted. Liam knew that. The right smile, slightly distant charm, some teasing. Women liked men to be playful, and to let them respond with coyness. Quinn was the queen of coy, but she'd dropped her knickers quickly enough the previous night. Not that he'd ever had any doubt that she might refuse him. What he'd learned over the years was that if you held off on the kissing, made a woman really wait for it, let her think you were a prince, then the rest of the clothing came off as soon as you whistled.

Liam liked Quinn. Really liked her, in fact. He was pretty sure she'd been a virgin until he'd given her what she'd so desperately wanted. Not that he'd asked her about it. It would have become a big deal, he'd have had to act obsequious and grateful. She might even have shed a few tears. All that bullshit. Instead, he'd shown her that she needed to remain independent. Let her get herself home. She hadn't realised it the night before, but he was doing her a favour. It was quite clear that she'd been babied. To be the ideal girlfriend – pretty but not vain, intelligent but with a carefully planted seed of self-doubt, adoring but not needy – she had to look after herself without bothering him.

It had been a long day. As much as he was looking forward to seeing Quinn, he was too tired to hang around and wait for her to finish her shift. He'd have to go into the shitty little FastMart to get the money from her. It wasn't that he needed the cash. His job paid well and his father had avoided paying tax for years, so money was never an issue. The point was that Quinn had left looking rather dented. Today, he needed to remind her who was boss but also that, when she played by his rules, she got to see him again.

Liam parked the car and walked round the corner to the store, checking his reflection in the glass as he went. He and Quinn made a good couple. He'd shown off photos of her to colleagues at work and they'd been suitably impressed. Now, Quinn needed to quit her stupid part-time job and get her book-keeping qualifications. Much more impressive to say his girlfriend worked for an accountant.

The jerk who laughingly called himself the boss was there, as was another woman stacking shelves. It was like an episode of a third-rate sitcom. He half-expected to hear canned laughter when he entered. Quinn looked up, noticed him, and frowned. It wasn't the greeting he'd wanted but then she was probably tired. It had been a late night, after all. The manager walked closer, loitering as Liam went to see her.

'Hey, babe,' he said. 'I wished you'd decided to spend the night. You look exhausted.' He made it loud. Loud enough that the skinny wannabe wearing the 'I'm Mark. How can we help you today?' label would get a technicolour picture in his head of what he and Quinn had been up to.

'Hi,' Quinn said, pushing one hand deep into her pocket. 'I've got your money. Here you go.'

'I appreciate that.' He took it and gave her the smile that made her weak. 'That wasn't the only reason I came in. We didn't organise our next date and I cannot wait to pick up where we left off.'

He leaned over the counter and went to kiss her. She dodged sideways, looking to her manager who nodded briefly.

'We should talk outside,' she told Liam.

'You going to be okay?' the manager asked.

'Sure,' she said.

Was that a simpering half-smile she gave the loser? What the fuck was that bollocks? She was right. They did need to talk outside.

'Did you have that all set up?' he began once they were alone. 'I don't like it when people have been talking behind my back. I won't tolerate it, Quinn, you need to learn that about me. Now, I like you, but there have to be some rules.'

'I can't do this,' she said, looking at the ground as she spoke. He almost thought he'd misheard.

'I'm sorry, you can't do what?'

'Us,' she said. 'I wanted it to work, but it won't. We're very different people. I can't see you anymore.'

'I beg your fucking pardon?' he said. 'Did you just decide we're over?'

129

Long pause.

'I did,' she confirmed.

'What, so you're dumping me?'

He wasn't sure what was happening. Women didn't dump him. Certainly not mousey little Quinn.

'Not dumping. Just being honest about the fact that we're not compatible. You'll be better off with someone more like you. I've got to go back in. My shift ends in a couple of minutes and I need to close my till.'

He put a hand on her arm.

'What you need is to give me an explanation. What's going on, Quinn? Are your parents pissed off because you got home late, or is it Uncle friggin' Bobby, that nosy bastard? Is your manager giving you a pay rise to let him feel your tits behind the canned goods, or are you just feeling guilty for enjoying a fuck last night?'

'That's enough,' Quinn said. 'You've helped me see that I'm making the right decision. I want you to leave me alone.' She headed for the shop.

'You don't get to tell me what to do,' Liam said.

Little bitch wasn't stopping.

'Get back here. We're not done.'

She was at the shop door before she paused to answer him.

'We are,' she said. 'And it was my decision alone. I didn't need anyone else to tell me what a huge mistake I'd made.'

She went in. By the time Liam reached the door, Mark the manager was standing there, arms crossed, looking like the weediest bouncer in the world.

'I want to speak to her,' Liam said.

'Not here, not now,' Mark said. 'And you're permanently banned from this shop. I don't want to see you here again.'

Liam laughed.

'Did that feel good, mate, exerting your little bit of power?

Better than selling bog roll to old ladies for once.' He got up into Mark's face. 'I bet you think about her when you're whacking one out. You ever ask her to do a late night stock take in the hope that she'll give you a quick blow job in the loading bay?'

Mark stepped back and let the automatic door close in Liam's face, flicking a switch so it would remain shut. Quinn was inside being consoled by the shelf-stacker.

Liam folded his arms and watched as they played out their domestic drama. He gave her three hours – four, tops – before she was on the phone begging for him to take her back. He'd ignore the first few calls. Let her leave some voicemails. It would sink in when she was no longer the centre of attention.

Before him, she'd had nothing. A crappy job where she saw the same faces each day. No social life except Friday night at the local pub. She'd moaned about it to him. Movie nights on a Saturday. Sunday lunch with the parents. Tales of what the baby did today. He'd tried to tell Quinn that it was time for her to leave, but she was either too brainwashed or too lazy to get her own place.

The lights in the shop went off, and they filed away to exit through the storeroom. Liam went to his car. He wasn't prepared to have Quinn think he was waiting for her. She had to come crawling back.

A car went past, Quinn in the passenger seat. Her father, Liam guessed, driving. Neither of them looked at him. Someone must have called daddy to pick her up. He wondered if that had been Quinn herself, or if she'd had Mark do it as she'd milked her victim status for all it was worth.

Give the girl her due, he hadn't thought she had it in her to finish with him. He was usually a better judge of character than that. He liked his women pliable. Who the hell wanted one who talked back and had opinions? Maybe it had all been an act – the reticence and persuade-me eyes. Quinn McTavish needed to be taught a lesson. He liked that idea. Just as soon as she'd apologised and begged him to forgive her. Like all bad girls, she was going to have to learn the hard way.

Chapter Nineteen

'Did you find the motorbike?' Callanach shouted to DI Graham as he and Ava ran into the industrial area, putting on bomb vests and helmets as they ran.

'It was left on the ground here, on its side. The driver was obviously in a hurry. We've got units surrounding the area and we spotted the victim by flying a small drone overhead. The quadrangle she's in has only one access point via a footpath at the side of a building,' Graham explained, running with them. 'We're checking it out now before we authorise anyone to enter. That should only be another couple of minutes.'

Ava and Luc stopped where directed. The bomb disposal unit was getting set up. Around them was a sprawling, abandoned industrial site. Lochend Road in Newbridge sat to the west of Edinburgh near the airport. Housing in the area was sporadic, thrown up in small plots, fitted in ramshackle sections along the road. There were green fields, too, but they appeared unloved, merely filling in the space. No tourist was ever going to do more than drive past on the way to or from a flight.

The three-storey industrial red brick building had lost enough small windowpanes to make it the perfect home to birds and rodents. There was a scorched earth smell to the grounds, and the grass hadn't bothered to grow back through the cracks in the asphalt. Low level buildings were dotted around the outside: a gatehouse, garages, storerooms and a security office from the days when there had been sufficient cash coming and going for such corporate accomplishments. The main structure sat far enough back from the road that no passerby would have been alerted to an ill-minded presence.

'Bolt cutters were used on the front gate,' Pax Graham explained. 'The motorcycle is being examined by forensics, emphasis on fingerprints and DNA.'

'Do we have confirmation that it's Felicity Love in there?' Ava asked.

'I'm afraid so. We have several photos of her provided by her husband. It certainly looks like her, and the build and height match,' Graham confirmed.

'What sort of state is she in?'

'Scared, of course, but unharmed, no obvious injuries at least. She's wearing a long white gown, no blood on it,' DI Graham said.

'She hasn't been made to look pregnant then?' Ava checked.

'No sign of it. Excuse me, ma'am, looks like there's progress.'

Ava and Luc watched Graham go as an ambulance arrived, set itself near the gate and threw its doors open, ready to jump into action. A fire engine entered a minute later and did the same. No one was taking any risks. DI Graham had done a good job of keeping the centre of the scene clear. Ava made a mental note to thank him later.

DS Lively strode across to them, face like thunder.

'Press have got hold of it already,' he said. 'I've just had the first call. There'll be helicopters overhead within minutes. What's the hold-up with getting to the victim?'

'We're being slow to enter the scene in case any explosives have been set away from the victim,' Callanach explained. 'Do we know who told the press what was happening?'

'Too many agencies involved. We'll never trace the leak,' Lively said. 'I need to talk to you about the way the motorbike was left, ma'am. I don't like it.'

'DI Graham said it had been dumped at the side of the building,' Ava said. 'What's the problem?'

'The first units that arrived following the phone call to the station checked the site before sealing it off, and that was thirty-five minutes ago. There was no one here then.'

'So the driver came here, did whatever he had to, then got out as quickly as possible,' Callanach said. 'He either had another vehicle stashed somewhere, got picked up or left on foot.'

'Aye, I'd figured that much out, sir.' He folded his arms. 'But why bother? He'd already brought the victim here. She sure as hell wasn't riding pillion. Coming back here on the same bike that was seen at Felicity Love's door was a huge risk. We're working on the assumption that this is someone with real skills. They're familiar with the area so you can bet they'd already checked out the CCTV points.'

'They're letting us into the quad now,' Callanach said. 'We need to get moving. Detective Sergeant, if you're coming in with us you'll need to get some protective gear on.'

Ava set off, leaving Lively trailing behind.

'He brought us here, ma'am,' Lively said. 'This fucker knew we'd trace the motorbike. He's controlling everything, our knowledge, where we go, even what time we arrive.'

'I'm listening, Lively, but find a bomb vest first then catch up.' She jogged to the small footpath leading to the quadrangle. It had previously been secured by a wrought-iron gate, chained and padlocked. Bolt cutters had cleared the way.

'Passageway clear,' the first officer called back.

One by one they filed in, first a bomb disposal unit to disarm the device, then a squad of armed police in case the suspect or suspects appeared, followed by a handful of uniformed officers to assist and the MIT contingent to oversee.

The quadrangle was a vast space, formed in the midst of the four walls of the main building. In its working days, the quad would have provided a valuable light source onto the factory floor and the offices above. Employees would have eaten lunch or taken their cigarette breaks there, gathered to enjoy the sunshine or shelter from the winds. It was a thoughtful place for the employer to have provided, sacrificing floor space and square footage for better working conditions.

A couple of wooden benches and some plant pots devoid of life were all that remained of that time. Graffiti from youths whose forefathers might have worked within the same walls. At the far end, positioned on a roughly constructed dais, was Felicity Love as Ava had never been seen her before.

'No one approach until we've completed an assessment,' the bomb squad team leader instructed. 'Stay at the far end with your backs against the wall.'

Ava didn't think she could have moved if she'd wanted to.

Felicity Love's eyes had been bound in a gold coloured silk scarf. Silver tape covered her mouth. Her nostrils flared with the effort of breathing, the tendons in her neck were taut wires straining against the softness of her throat. Her arms, outstretched at either side, had been taped at the wrists to a beam running horizontally behind her. In her right hand a sword was held aloft. In her left, a simplified set of scales. The robe she wore was a white sheet, draped over her shoulders. Her feet were bare. On her head was a faux crown, its five spikes pointing heavenwards, the weight of it pressing into the skin of her forehead. Every part of her was bound or taped in place.

Perhaps she was really unharmed, but what lay beneath the

robe, only Felicity knew. It was possible that her tongue had been cut from her head, that she had suffered the same fate as poor Maura Douglas, but there was no sign of it in her face.

'What's she supposed to be?' Callanach asked.

'Lady Justice,' Ava said. 'Sometimes blindfolded, sometimes not. Could you find me a loudspeaker?'

Callanach hustled away.

Ava stared up at Felicity. More careful inspection of the silk scarf showed damp blotches, from perspiration possibly, but more likely the tears of a mother terrified that she might never see her son again. Her muscles were quivering. Ava wondered how long she'd been there. Even with the tape holding the sword and the scales in her hands, she'd be in pain. The crown was painfully tight on her head. You could see a roll of skin where it had been forced down. Callanach reappeared, speaker in hand.

'Felicity,' Ava said. The speaker spat out feedback and she turned the volume down as the words echoed around the quad. 'This is Ava Turner. I'm here with several police officers and other agencies. The site has been cleared. You are among friends. There will be a delay while we assess your bindings but we're doing everything we can to free you as quickly as possible. Paramedics are on standby. Any injuries you have will be looked at in a matter of minutes.'

A bomb squad officer ran towards Ava, reached a hand up to flick off the loudspeaker, then whispered in her ear.

'It's going to be a few minutes, ma'am. There are some wires leading into the crown and we think we've identified what seems to be a sealed battery unit. The tape over her mouth goes all the way around the back of her head and holds the wires in place, so we can't touch the tape yet either.'

'Take the scarf off her eyes – she needs to see some friendly faces – and cut a hole in the tape over her mouth to help her breathe.' He nodded.

'What precautions do you need me to take?' Ava asked.

'The quad is very long. We're not seeing any mass of explosives so this may be a device designed to kill the victim only. As a precaution, I'm having a line of anti-explosive shields set up between you here and the victim, which would minimise the force of any blast. At this distance, with what we're seeing, I have no concern if your officers remain against this back wall.'

'Okay,' Ava said. 'Let's get this done and save her life.'

Officers began jogging into place with high blast shields, positioning them a few metres in front of the wall. Only the few essential bomb squad officers stayed at Felicity's side, one of whom pulled the scarf from her eyes and carefully cut a slit into the tape over her mouth. She blinked hard then looked around until her eyes met Ava's.

'Felicity, I want you to know that Dylan is fine. He's at home being cared for by your husband and the nanny. He's looking forward to getting you home. I know it'll feel as if this is taking a long time, but the officers are working to make sure they can get you down unharmed. It's a delicate operation.'

'There's no way the killer would set all this up, then have no means of witnessing the event,' Callanach whispered.

Ava let the speaker drop to her side. 'Lively said the site was cleared before we came in,' Ava said. 'They can't have missed anyone.'

'But this is the payoff. That's an elaborate tableau to have created if you're not going to see it play out.'

'What are you thinking?' Ava asked.

'You said it's personal. This killer is targeting people within first responder ranks, so maybe it's someone working from within. It's possible this is a revenge campaign by someone with an axe to grind.'

'It's not a first responder,' Ava said. 'There's not a paramedic, firefighter or police officer who would let this happen to their colleagues. They're not capable of it.'

'With mental illness and the right trigger,' Callanach said, 'anyone is capable of anything. You know that.'

That was when Felicity Love began to scream.

Chapter Twenty

The bomb squad officers around Felicity jumped back and braced. Everyone behind the barrier shields ducked. It was the sort of scream that made you want to look away rather than at the source of the noise.

'It's the crown,' a bomb squad officer shouted.

Felicity fell silent then sagged against the beams that held her up. The bomb squad approached again. Someone put fingers to her wrist and flashed a quick thumbs-up sign. She was still alive, but just below the makeshift crown was now a thin band of blackened skin. The smell of charred meat wafted on the breeze and officers tried not to be obvious about covering their noses.

'Get that crown off her,' Ava commanded via the loudspeaker. One of the bomb disposal experts ran the length of the quad to brief Ava.

'Ma'am, there's a whole tangle of wires. We don't know yet if the battery pack contains an explosive device. It's likely that we're expected to remove the crown to stop the electrocution but there may be a pressure trigger under it which could blow the whole thing as it's lifted. This is going to take some time.'

'How much time?' Ava asked.

'Our best estimate is thirty minutes,' he said.

'I want your boss's permission to stand with the victim,' Ava said.

'That's a no go, ma'am. Makes our job harder if we're worried about additional bodies. We're talking to her and explaining what's happening.'

Ava sighed. 'Fine, get back on it. Someone get a paramedic fully suited up against a potential blast. I want Felicity Love's vital signs monitored. If she starts fading, we'll have no choice but to pull our people back, risk the explosion, and find a way to remotely remove that crown,' she said to the uniformed officers waiting with her.

An officer ran out of the quadrangle in the direction of the ambulance as Lively, his protective gear straining around him, pushed through to stand next to Ava and Luc.

'Do they not make these vests in normal bloody sizes?' he grumbled. 'What did I miss?'

'The crown's working like a taser,' Callanach said. 'The victim was just given a shock. We don't know if that was accidental or the operator has eyes on what we're doing. Bomb disposal is worried about a sealed battery pack that might be a bomb and possible pressure pads under the crown.'

'Wee fucker,' Lively said. 'If it's eyes-on, then the person controlling the crown is either here with a remote in their pocket, or they've a camera rigged in place.'

'Check it out, but don't make anyone nervous. If you're wrong, I don't want to piss off the people working with us. If you're right, I don't want to make whoever's doing this any twitchier,' Ava said. 'And be careful, Lively. I'm not losing any of my team today.'

A drone appeared high over the building, the mounted camera visible by the light reflecting off its lens.

'Get that thing out of the sky,' Ava said to Callanach.

'That may be how the killer's watching what's going on. If so, the control unit will have to be within a certain distance.'

'What if it's the press?' she asked.

'They can't publish any footage where the victim is seriously injured or dies,' he replied quietly. 'Let me take a team and see if I can find the drone operator. I'm no use here.'

'Okay, I've got DI Graham as second in command. Just watch your back. If the drone operator is our bomber, there's every chance they'll have a weapon. Take an armed officer with you.'

'Ma'am,' Pax Graham tapped her arm as Luc walked away. 'There's a call for you. It's been routed through the station.' He handed her his phone.

'Who is it?' Ava asked. DI Graham shrugged. 'DCI Turner,' she said into the mouthpiece. No reply. 'Hello?' The line wasn't dead. She could hear rustling and distant noise. 'Pax, how did this call get through to you?'

'PC Biddlecombe said a call came in for you. It was supposed to be information about this situation.'

Ava's belly churned. She walked into the corner, facing the building to shield her ears from outside noise. 'Who is this?' she asked. A single outward breath was the response, low, deep. 'You said you had information about what's happening. Is there something you can tell me that will help?' Nothing. He – Ava was convinced that it was a male – simply listened. 'You knew I was here, so you know I'm trying to save Felicity Love's life. Do you know about her son, Dylan? He's only four years old.' She waved madly in Pax Graham's direction, pointed at the handset and mouthed the words, 'It's him.'

A burst of static came from the mobile as DI Graham grabbed a radio from a uniformed officer and requested a trace on the line at the police station through which the call had been routed.

'Are you there?' Ava asked.

'Yes,' he said.

That was something. The opening of communications. Perhaps he really didn't want to go ahead with hurting Felicity. Why take the risk of making a call otherwise?

'Is there any way of stopping this?' Ava asked. 'Tell me what it is you want.' A cough, or was it a laugh? She couldn't tell. Ava jammed a finger into her free ear to help her focus. 'Perhaps we can agree a pause?' she continued. 'Give us half an hour. I'll stay on the line with you. I'd like to understand why you're doing this. How about we—'

A crackle of static hit the air before Felicity's dry croak turned into another scream. The bomb disposal experts hit the deck and every officer at the far end of the quad behind the shields instinctively curled their bodies, faces to the wall. Three seconds later it was over. Felicity was shaking and dragging air noisily into her lungs. Every alarm on the hastily erected vital signs monitor was beeping wildly.

Ava gritted her teeth to keep the fury from her voice.

'Please,' she panted, 'please don't do that. If you can't tell me what you want, then I'll just stay here and listen until you're ready to talk. All in your own time. No bargains. No negotiation. You're in control.'

New sounds. Digital buttons, like a text being sent. Then a computer rendering of a voice.

'Ten.'

From the far end of the quad the cry came. 'Timer!'

Ava heard it in tandem.

'Get her down!' she yelled.

They tried. Nine seconds to go and they all knew it would take five of them to sprint across the quad to the safety of the protective shields.

'Everyone on the ground!' Ava shouted to the officers around her.

'Eight.'

'Clear the area!' the lead bomb disposal officer shouted.

Felicity Love was going to die. There was no doubt in Ava's mind. She was either going to fry as the electric current destroyed her brain then stopped her heart, or more likely an explosion was going to blow her apart.

Bomb disposal officers sprinted towards the safe end of the quadrangle as Ava pushed through the barriers to run forwards. Pax Graham grabbed her arm but she wrenched it free.

'Ma'am, no!' Graham shouted.

'Stay down!' she ordered, starting to run.

'Six.'

If she could just get the crown off Felicity's head. The possibility that it might be rigged with springs that would detonate a bomb no longer mattered. Every other officer was going to survive any blast by virtue of the shields. The remaining distance along the quad was maybe thirty metres in length. There was still a chance that she could make it.

Ava's hand was already in the air to grab the crown. It occurred to her that she was almost certainly going to die, at the same time she reached the conclusion that it didn't seem such a terrible way to go.

'Five.'

She'd covered half the length now and Felicity was screaming again, not from any electric shock but with the realisation of what the numbers meant.

'Four.'

Ava was just a few strides away. Voices were yelling for her to get back, to get down, that she couldn't make it.

'Three.'

Ava stumbled but managed to power back up before she hit the deck.

'Two.'

Then she was in front of Felicity, dropping the mobile phone,

144

and clutching the crown instead, only it was pinned and wired around her skull and into her hair. She could feel the hair tearing from the roots.

'One.'

The electrical charge hit her hands and Ava was thrust up and through the air. For a moment she was suspended in time, blown first away from Felicity, then back towards her and spinning out of control. She couldn't feel anything.

There was no pain at all. Ava thought she'd heard the start of a sound, only it turned immediately into an empty silence. She flew past Felicity, onwards and into the wall behind her. She had time to wonder why she was flying in the wrong direction, and how the blast could be magnetic. When she hit the brickwork, the impact was shoulder and hip, her head whipping to one side. She left long scrapes of skin on the surface as she slid down, knowledge crashing over her.

The pressure from the blast had not come from in front of her at all. The bomb that had gone off had been behind them all. Ava closed her eyes and embraced unconsciousness.

Chapter Twenty-One

The quadrangle was silent, only that couldn't be right because Ava could see people running in, lifting debris and kneeling next to bodies. Something moved in the dust at her side. She reached out and found fingers, a hand, an arm. Jolting forward, she rushed to uncover the remainder of the body. Felicity Love, the beams she'd been tied to broken apart by the force of the explosion, was still alive, just barely. Her face was a charred mess, the crown that had been modified into a taser finally gone from her head, tattered remnants of silver tape hanging from her lips.

'Felicity,' Ava tried to say, only she couldn't hear her own voice. She shook her head and tried again. The explosion had deafened her and she had no idea whether or not Felicity could hear either. Setting a hand either side of Felicity's face, she looked directly into her fluttering eyes. 'Felicity, we're going to get you to a hospital, but I need to know who did this. Did you see the man who kidnapped you?'

Felicity managed to return Ava's gaze. Her upper body was a bloody mess. A section of wood had pierced her ribcage, and she was wheezing noisily. She was dying and they both knew it. Ava tried again.

'Who did this to you? Can you give me a name?' Ava wasn't sure if her words were coming out clearly. She kept her speech slow, her voice straining.

Felicity said something Ava couldn't hear.

'I have to lip read.' Ava pointed at her own mouth. 'Say the name again.'

Felicity tried. She moved her lips once, twice, but Ava couldn't hear and Felicity was slipping away to a less painful place.

'Medic,' Ava yelled. People looked up from the far end. 'Help!'

Felicity's head fell sideways. Ava stroked her face, wiping away the blood that had come from her mouth, nose, even her eyes. She leaned forward and gave Felicity a single kiss on the forehead.

Standing was impossible so Ava crawled to the side wall for balance then made it to her feet.

The floor was a light show. Every surface sparkled. Where there had originally been the odd smashed pane in the vast array of windows, now there were only gaping holes within the window frames. Along the length of the quad was a colour gradient, from dusty grey and wood chip brown where Ava had fallen, blooming pink in the middle and darkening to crimson at the far end. She took a few steps, frowned, tried to figure out what she was seeing, then Callanach and Lively were running into the quad, charging forward to catch her as she began to fall, taking an arm each and propping her up. Ava had time to be grateful that she'd sent them both out of the area to follow up other leads before the bomb went off.

Callanach said something. Ava shrugged and pointed vaguely in the direction of her ears. Pain was finding her. She knew that when it got a hold, it would become an agony but for now, she needed to understand what had happened. One foot in front of the other, she forced herself forwards into the organic chaos.

Lively did his best to shield her from the carnage, but there was no stopping her. Stretchers were appearing now. Men and women were being lifted carefully and carried out to ambulances.

Ava stilled her feet near the thickly-coated line of protective shields and finally understood what had happened. They'd been played.

The blast had come from behind the row of officers waiting to assist once Felicity had been cut down. The protective shields had only contained the force and made it stronger. As everyone else had stayed within shelter, Ava had run away from death.

She grabbed Lively's hand and pulled him round to look at her.

'Pax?' she asked, pointing to where she'd last seen her detective inspector.

'Shit,' she lipread Lively's response. He left her being supported by Callanach and ran forward, stepping through bodies, or parts of them, moving the debris he could. Down on his hands and knees he wiped blood from the faces of the fallen, and Ava could see him talking as he went. He stopped suddenly, getting a closer looking at one particular body, turning a face to get a better view, immediately shifting his gaze away.

Callanach pulled Ava closer to him but she pushed him away again, found her balance, and walked forwards on shaking legs. Lively put a hand up towards her, palm out, his message clear.

She wasn't going to be told not to look. Bearing witness was the very least she could do in the circumstances. It was her who'd told DI Graham to stay put. Her who'd left those men and women sheltering in what should have been a safe place. Her who'd failed to accurately assess the threat, and her who'd failed to keep good people alive.

Ava stepped through the bloody mess on the ground. Lively reached out a hand to guide her, before sliding an arm around her waist to help her bend down to see the body.

Pax Graham's lifeless eyes were open and staring skywards. His lips were frayed, and his nose was a crater into his skull. Ava hadn't been prepared for the awfulness of it. It would have been easier had he been unrecognisable, she thought, but enough of his features were intact that he remained the good-looking, rugby type she'd transferred to MIT after his stint undercover. Now, every inch of skin was peppered with nails and embedded with tiny shards of glass. Lively wiped away tears, and Ava squeezed his hand.

Pax Graham had been a giant of a man. To start with, Ava had found it impossible to believe that he'd ever been credible in an undercover role, but he'd slotted into the MIT team seamlessly, often so quiet that he was easily overlooked in a meeting. He was a listener. In spite of his height and bulk, he had an ability to fade into the background that made people underestimate him.

Ava ran her hand down his left-hand side, finding his neck drenched in clotting blood, the nails having found a soft spot to enter a vein and finish him.

'I'm so sorry,' she whispered to him. She found she could hear the words now, although muffled, as if she were listening to someone else talk through a closed door. 'I let you down.'

'Ma'am, we need to let other people in here,' Lively said. 'We can visit the DI at the mortuary later.'

Ava nodded and stood. She faced the wall from where the blast had come, literally blindsiding them. The brickwork was cracked but had stayed in place, a testament to building work erected with such skill that it could withstand the worst of shocks.

'The bombs must have been placed internally behind the windows,' Lively said. 'Pipe bombs, judging by the nails. More than one of them.'

They stepped away from the bodies. She could hear more now. Screaming from a stretcher. Groans from the ground.

149

Crying. People yelling instructions, talking on radios. Sirens incoming, their wail a precursor to much more wailing to come from loved ones.

Ava gasped.

'The phone,' she said. 'I had Pax's mobile. I was talking to the bomber.'

She retraced her steps to the far end of the quad and stopped where she thought she'd been standing when she'd dropped the handset. It took several minutes scrabbling around in the dust until Callanach found it on top of a bomb disposal toolbox.

Ava grabbed it from him, jammed it against her ear, and listened.

'Hello?' she said. 'Are you still there?'

Quiet, but not silence. White noise, but not nothing. Then it went dead.

'He was on the phone with me when the bomb went off,' Ava said. 'I think . . . I think he wanted to hear it.'

'Let me take it,' Callanach said. She handed it over and he slipped it in his pocket. 'We have to get you checked out by the paramedics. No argument this time.'

'Felicity knew him,' she said. 'I asked her for his name, but I couldn't hear anything. She tried to answer me. We need to check every case she's done in the last couple of years.'

'Ma'am, the DI's right. We can sort this out later. We have to get you to an ambulance,' Lively said.

Ava ignored them. 'How many dead, do you think?'

Callanach thought about it. 'There were perhaps fifteen people behind the barriers when I left. Some of them survived but they're injured. I suspect we've lost another ten.'

'The bomb squad were in there, too,' Ava said. 'They ran behind the shields when the countdown started.'

'They had the best personal protective equipment on,' Callanach said. 'They might all have survived.'

'Ten more dead, plus Felicity. The beams to which she was tied were shattered in the blast and it looked as if the wood punctured her upper body. Someone needs to visit Colin Love and let him know.' Ava fought the squealing sound that wouldn't stop inside her head. 'Do either of you know who Pax Graham's next of kin is?'

'He talked about his parents a bit,' Lively said. 'They're both still alive. I'll make enquiries.'

'Press blackout until we've notified the families. Would you get started, Lively?'

The detective sergeant nodded and walked away.

'At least get checked out by paramedics here,' Callanach said. 'I'm not expecting you to go to the hospital.'

'I'm not hurt,' Ava said. 'Couple of paracetamol for my ears will do the trick. I was further away from it than anyone else; at Felicity's side. He fried her when he set the bomb off. He'd never intended that she should survive. It was only the line of protective shields that kept us from fully experiencing the blast. All the nails stayed in that tiny area down there.'

'What were you doing up here when the countdown was about to end? I mean, I'm glad you were, but everyone else stayed behind the shields. Ava, what did you do?'

She shrugged. 'I couldn't let her die like that.'

'You were running into death,' Callanach said. 'Every one of us thought that the danger was at this end of the area. If the bomb had gone off here, you'd have had no chance of surviving at all. What were you thinking?'

Ava shook her head vaguely. 'I wasn't thinking at all. I just knew I couldn't watch from behind a shield while a woman died in front of me. I tried to get the crown off her head but he'd wound the wires into her hair.'

'Ava, look at me.' Callanach positioned himself in front of her. 'I'm worried about you. Natasha's worried about you. I have to ask . . . did you run to Felicity thinking you'd survive, thinking that maybe you'd die, or not caring either way?'

She gave a tiny shake of her head. 'Luc, I'm not suicidal if that's what you're thinking.'

'Are you sure about that?' Callanach asked.

'Tell me this: why did I survive? When the countdown began, I told everyone to stay put, and yet I ran. I keep wondering if I subconsciously knew something they didn't. I had the killer on the phone, after all.'

'That's ridiculous. There's no way you could have known anything. That's not why you ran towards Felicity and you know it.'

'I don't know anything except that I failed to do my job properly and now we'll have nearly a dozen more bodies stacked in the mortuary. For every dead man and woman here today there'll be another set of grieving parents, a partner, children. Pax Graham is dead and I should have been on the ground next to him.'

'Don't say that,' Callanach said. 'What good would your death have done? It wouldn't stop the pain any of those families are going to feel tonight.'

'That bomb was meant for me, Luc. I can feel it. Me surviving by breaking the rules wasn't fair. It's not right.'

'That's not something you get to decide,' Callanach said. 'You survived. Whether it was fate, or an accident or something in your subconscious doesn't really matter. I'm never going to stop being grateful that you did.'

Chapter Twenty-Two

BEFORE

It began with tulips. The first delivery came in shades of violet, orange and white. Quinn had told Liam they were her favourite flowers when they'd visited the Royal Botanic Gardens together. Three days later there was a delivery of sweets. Every type of childhood sweet they'd discussed, crammed into an old-fashioned glass jar. Five days after that, a bottle of champagne with a cuddly toy was left on her doorstep. No cards or letters. No text messages. Quinn gave it all away. There were plenty of elderly people living on the poverty line in Gorebridge who appreciated a treat.

Twice, she saw Liam's car drive past the shop. It wasn't a surprise – he'd been working south of her home on a long contract – but it was unsettling. He never stopped though or beeped his horn as he went past. Quinn wasn't going to change her mind, but it did feel as if it had just been a moment of madness, and that perhaps she'd been culpable of allowing herself to get carried away too quickly. She told herself it was the right thing for her to shoulder some of the blame.

Her parents were appropriately supportive without lecturing or prying for unnecessary details. She was enjoying being at home more often and spending time with Dolly who, at three months old, was changing every day. Liam had been such a distraction that she'd barely seen the baby for a few weeks. Her studies also grounded her, providing a routine and allowing her to focus her mind. Uncle Bobby visited every other day, often staying over. Suffering none of her parents' natural understanding that they should respect a twenty-year-old's boundaries, he probed and questioned. It was done with love and a smile even though he'd made his dislike of Liam clear from the first and had been proved a better judge of character than Quinn. Her father, ever the peacemaker, gently told Uncle Bobby to give Quinn some space. As concerned as Simeon McTavish had been about his daughter, he'd neither said a bad word about Liam nor lectured Quinn about making better choices, and she loved her father for it. Her mother was so lucky. She'd known a good man when she'd found one, and tied herself to him without hesitation. Quinn wished she'd had the same luck.

Even so, there was a part of her that missed Liam. They'd shared good times and being with him had given her a sense that she was growing up. It had felt good to shake free of the constraints of childhood and consider what lay ahead. But she wasn't stupid. Toxic relationships didn't change. Her parents had raised her to be aware of such issues. The fact that she didn't appear worldly didn't mean she walked around with her eyes closed. If Liam was treating her disrespectfully so early on, the future held nothing but misery.

She was pleased when the gifts stopped. It meant that she could close the chapter and feel as if he had too. It was possible the deliveries had been nothing more than an apology and a goodbye.

Running into him in person was an event for which she was unprepared, but when it happened it was almost a relief.

Something about laying her demons to rest and moving on. He looked more startled than her when she rounded a shelf in a bookshop on Princes Street and found him browsing in the cookery section. He was sheepish.

'My aunt's birthday.' He held up the selection of books he was choosing from. 'You?'

'Just finished watching a TV series and fancied reading the book it was based on,' Quinn said.

The awkwardness was broken. After chatting for ten minutes, he'd invited her for coffee. Had the cafeteria not been in the same store, Quinn knew she'd have said no, but it was just one floor up and she was dying for a drink. It seemed churlish to refuse.

They sipped black coffee – Liam said the staff had reported an issue with several of their cartons of milk and he didn't want to risk drinking it – and looked out across the road to the gardens, appreciating the view of the castle against a yellowing sky that promised a storm to come.

'Listen, I behaved like a jerk,' he said. 'My ego got bruised and I think I was scared about how much I liked you. I don't know what the hell I was trying to prove, but you didn't deserve the things I said. Will you forgive me?'

Quinn smiled. 'It's history. And thank you for the gifts. They really weren't necessary.'

'I felt bad,' he said. 'Did you tell your parents everything? They must hate me.'

'I didn't,' she said. 'They realised we'd split up. That seemed to be enough. Uncle Bobby didn't let it go as easily but then you've met him so you can probably imagine.'

'I bet,' Liam said. 'Hey, I'll get us a refill. Why don't you go and pay for your book?'

'Thanks,' she said. He'd left the cookbook downstairs. She didn't think about it until later. By the time she'd fought through the queue, he was halfway through drinking his second coffee and hers was starting to cool. She drank it straight down.

They made small talk a while. Discussed films, music, their dream holidays. The things normal friends discussed during a chance meeting. It was nice. Quinn hated conflict, even the memory of it. Being able to resolve the worst she'd experienced felt like a gift.

The first sensation was a tingling in her calf muscles. She flexed them, cursing her choice to wear heels rather than trainers. A shopping trip around Edinburgh meant covering a lot of miles. When the room didn't stop moving after she turned her head, she was more concerned.

'You okay? You're looking pale,' Liam said.

Quinn shook it off. 'I should have eaten a proper lunch, that's all.'

'Let me get you something now. They've got paninis or pastries.'

'It's nothing. I don't want to make a fuss. I think I'll just head for the loo, though.' The headrush when she tried to stand was worthy of a whole night of cocktails. Quinn sat straight back down. 'Maybe not.'

'You're really not well. I'm going to get you home. Come on, lean on me.' He pulled her coat over her shoulders and picked up her bag. 'It's probably just a twenty-four-hour bug. Do you want to stop at a chemist and pick up some medicine?'

Quinn's head was swimming and she was struggling to concentrate. There were definitely stairs and Liam was helping her down them, but she couldn't feel her feet connecting with the ground and her body felt too big for its skin.

'Nearly there,' he said. 'I'm going to get us a taxi. I didn't drive into the city, but if we get back to my place I can take you home from there. You can close your eyes.'

Quinn did her best to reply, but her lips were numb and

she wasn't sure if anything she was saying made sense. By the time the cold outside air hit her face, she was standing still but the world was moving past at speed. She was floating, watching her body from above, aware that the change in perspective couldn't be real but unable to figure out how to get back into her body.

Liam helped her into the taxi, one gentle hand on the top of her head, an arm around her shoulders so she could rest against him as the driver headed for Portobello. There was a conversation, some laughter. At one point she caught the driver's eyes in his rearview mirror and thought he gave her a wink. A slow wink, suggestive. She didn't like it, but her head was too heavy to lift and Liam was chatting again.

They took a roundabout that Quinn was sure they went round four or five times, approached traffic lights at lightning speed, flying across the brows of hills. Conversation paused. Liam kissed her forehead.

That wasn't right. She hadn't wanted to start things up again. Tilting her head upwards she took a deep breath, ready to ask him to respect her decision. His face came down, lips closed on hers. The kiss seemed to go on forever, the wet invasion of it, but she did nothing.

'Young love!' the driver said. 'I wish my wife still kissed me like that.'

Liam laughed along with him. Quinn closed her eyes and wished the car would stop. She wasn't sure how long the journey took – it might have been two minutes or two hours – but at last it ended. Liam reached down into her bag, took out her cash card, and waved it over the machine to pay. Then they were walking upstairs into Liam's apartment. Her vision was limited to a single vertical strip in the middle field.

'I'll get my car keys,' he said, lowering her onto the sofa. 'You should sleep for a few minutes. I've a couple of calls to make before we go. I had plans this afternoon but it's not a problem. I can cancel. Shut your eyes.'

Quinn fought it. Her body was a lead weight but there was a woodpecker inside her brain doing its best to tap her a message. She tried to decipher it. There was a chance it was the most important message she'd ever received in her life, but she wasn't sure what the woodpecker was doing inside her head.

Quinn was warm, then cold. Sitting up then lying down. Comfortable then fighting to breathe, too much weight on her chest. Face up, then face down. Asleep but not. Everything she saw was a dream. She touched things that her fingers couldn't feel. There was no sensation except that she was shrivelling inside. Then nothing. Not the semi-awareness of natural sleep. This was the vacuum of death.

The clocks ceased to tick the time away. The sun neither rose nor set. There was no sound, not a bird nor a passing child. She didn't roll over, stretch and reposition as sleep normally allowed. There was nothing. Quinn felt as if she was nothing at all.

She awoke in Liam's car, southbound out of the city towards home. Her head ached and her mouth was dry. He opened a bottle of water and passed it to her. Quinn drank half of it before trying to process what had happened.

'What time is it?' she croaked.

'Nine o'clock,' Liam said. 'You passed out on my sofa. I figured it was best to let you sleep. There was no way I was going to be able to carry you down the stairs. How you feeling? I was worried about you.'

Quinn checked herself mentally. Nothing was hurting except for the dull thump in her skull. She felt uncomfortable, no doubt from falling asleep on a sofa, but she was warm enough. Everything was as she remembered. Her coat and shoes were on, her handbag was in her lap. Even the book bag was at her feet.

'I'm fine,' she said. 'Sorry for ruining your evening.'

'That's all right. My girlfriend understood. I'm lucky she's not the jealous type.'

Quinn registered the word girlfriend, felt a flash of relief and an equal dash of guilt. For a while back in the bookshop, she'd been concerned that Liam was trying to win her over again. When he decided to be charming, he was hard to resist, and her ending up senseless on his sofa wasn't going to create the right impression. Him having a girlfriend made everything a lot less complicated.

'Would you apologise to her for me? That's never happened before.'

'Aspen thought it might have been a severe migraine. She gets them sometimes too, puts her in bed for a whole day and she can't do anything but sleep. Hers are brought on by food allergies.'

'Right,' Quinn said. 'A migraine.'

The nausea began when they were just one road from her home.

'Could you pull over?' she asked.

'It's dark,' Liam said. 'You should let me get you to your door.'

'Please,' she groaned. 'I don't feel good. You have to stop.'

She managed to get the passenger door open before she was sick, saving the inside of Liam's car. That was something to be grateful for. He leaned across and rubbed her back gently.

'Poor you,' he said. 'Definitely a migraine. Vomiting is a pretty common symptom, Aspen said.'

Quinn didn't want to hear any more about Aspen's diagnosis. What she wanted was to be at home in bed.

'I can walk from here,' she said. 'You've been so kind already.'

'No way,' Liam said. 'It may not be far but you're unwell. I should make sure you get back safely.'

Quinn insisted. She didn't want her parents looking out of the window and seeing Liam's car pull up. She wasn't sure how she could explain that one. Liam gave a fleeting smile, tinged with a concerned frown.

'Do one thing for me? Text when you get home and into bed. Let me know you're okay? If you do that, I'll leave you be.'

That was fine. Anything to get away and find a quiet bush to be sick in unwatched.

'Sure,' she said. 'I promise.'

Liam drove away quietly, no engine revving to disturb the neighbours and make curtains twitch. Quinn was grateful. As his car turned the corner, she ran for a garden hedge and lost what few stomach contents remained.

She walked home slowly, holding onto fence posts as she went, staggering up the side path to enter through the back door. Leaving the light off as she went in seemed like the best plan, but then her uncle's voice boomed at her from the far end of the kitchen table.

Quinn let out a scream.

'Christ, I'm sorry girl, I didn't mean to scare you. Would you sit with me a while?'

There was no holding it. She ran for the downstairs toilet and threw herself to her knees. Her uncle got a towel and a glass of water, waited until she'd finished then guided her back into the kitchen to take a seat.

'What was that then? It's not like you to go off into the city and come back drunk.'

'I'm not. I think it's a bug, someone said maybe a migraine. I'll be fine now.'

'You don't look fine,' Bobby said. 'Don't tell my sister I said

160

this, but you look like shit, and I don't say that to my gorgeous niece lightly.'

'I think I just need more sleep,' she said. 'Do you mind? Sorry to be antisocial.'

'More sleep?' he asked.

Quinn sighed, too weak to lie. 'Please don't overreact. I bumped into Liam. We were chatting then I got ill. He let me crash at his place then drove me home. I don't know what would have happened if he hadn't been there.'

Bobby crossed his arms.

'Indeed,' he said. 'And you're okay? He didn't upset you this time?'

Quinn made her way quietly to the bottom of the staircase hoping she wouldn't wake either her parents or the baby.

'I never told you he upset me the first time,' she said softly.

'Aye, that's right, you never did tell me that. Do you think I don't know when something's wrong, sweetheart? You're so like your mother when she was your age. Quiet and strong, too concerned about everyone else's feelings to be mindful of your own.'

'I'm fine,' she said. 'But I'm glad you were here. Thanks for looking after me.'

'I always will,' Bobby said. 'Family first.'

'Family first,' Quinn repeated, holding fast to the bannister as she climbed the stairs.

She sneaked past her parents' room, paused outside her sister's door to make sure Dolly wasn't stirring, then made it to the sanctuary of her own bedroom. In the kitchen below she could hear her uncle filling the kettle and getting a mug from the cupboard. He was a night owl. Claimed it was from taking watch in the army. Listening to his stories when he returned from being posted abroad was one of Quinn's favourite child-hood memories. He had his own place but then, like now, her parents opened their home to him whenever he felt like staying. Everything felt safer with Bobby around.

Slowly, carefully, as if she'd been in a car crash, she pulled off her clothes. Each item was intact, unmarked, but they felt worn and dirty. She'd day-slept in them, that was the problem. Clothes lost their freshness as soon as they'd seen a few hours on a couch, and she'd sweated while she was sick.

As much as she wanted her bed, it was the shower that was calling to her. Everything felt . . . she struggled to find the words. Her body didn't feel like her own. She wished she'd never gone into Edinburgh. What did she have to show for it? A book and a virus.

Taking hold of the bag, she let it slide out onto her bed. The front cover fell open to reveal a handwritten inscription on the title page.

My Darling Quinn, What a lovely day together. One to remember. Liam x

She flipped it shut and pushed the book across her duvet where it fell to the floor. She didn't want his writing in her book. It didn't feel as if it had been a lovely day. She couldn't remember most of it. What she wanted was to sleep then wake up to find that none of it had ever happened, but she'd made a promise and she would keep it. The last thing she did was text to thank him for the ride home, and to let him know she was safely back in her own bed.

Chapter Twenty-Three

Callanach had found the drone operator and seized the footage. Journalists had eyes everywhere, even if they couldn't be there in person. The use of a drone to remotely view the brutal deaths of innocent people was a step too far, but it had alerted MIT to one thing – there was such a heavy press presence in the city that they were effectively patrolling now, keeping their teams mobile to be at the next incident in a heartbeat. This time it had turned out, unwittingly, to be a resource. Every investigating officer was in the incident room, standing room only, to watch.

The drone footage began from the side of the quadrangle above a wooded area some distance from the industrial buildings. It hovered at a height that gave it a wide view, including the waiting ambulances. Callanach fast-forwarded to the first time Felicity was shocked. There was no sound with the recording, to everyone's relief.

Ava studied the screen as officers moved up and down the quad, twice throwing themselves to the ground before getting up and continuing to work. Felicity was hooked up to the vital signs monitor. She saw herself take the mobile from DI Graham.

Even from above and at that height, Pax Graham was larger than anyone else. People moved out of the way for him to get through, but there he was with a gentle hand on each shoulder, a clap on the back as he went past. Somehow, even with the incident room as crowded as she'd ever seen it, it still felt as if there was an empty space reserved for him to walk in and join his team.

A hushed gasp went through the viewers. The countdown had begun. The bomb disposal squad ran one way while Ava ran the other. She watched herself give Pax Graham the last order she would ever issue to him. He obeyed, loyal and unquestioning, as he always had, doing his job to the best of his ability. Then she was at the far end, pulling at the crown on Felicity's head until the shock hit them both. Callanach set the remaining footage to play in slow motion. As Ava was sent flying through the air, all eyes were on the far end of the quadrangle.

Three windows erupted at the same time, spraying out tiny shards of glass followed immediately by a cloud of grey that became a scarlet aerosol. The lucky ones were those already on the floor, heads close to the wall and protected by the brick-work. Anyone still standing or who had their heads up to watch Felicity got hit by a blanket of metalwork.

Ava watched Pax Graham reach for the person closest to him, trying to shield them as his own face was shredded. She saw him drenched by a red river that sprang from his neck. He toppled onto his face, hands grasping to pull himself forwards, still fighting, still working. At the far end, alone and alive, Ava tried to sit up, holding her head while every other person in the courtyard fought for their life and many lost.

An explosives expert took to the incident room floor as the drone buzzed away into the distance and the screen went black, no doubt at the moment Callanach caught up with its operator. The lights went back on. No one in the room spoke.

'What we have is three improvised explosive devices – pipe bombs – each small enough to fit into the old air-conditioning units that had been positioned on the inside of the windows in the main hall of the factory.' On the screen the expert brought up an image of mangled metal. 'Each bomb was made from a section of steel water pipe. The pipes were filled with one inch nails and low level explosive powder. Brass caps were welded onto each end. There was an electrical fuse with wires leading to a cheap mobile phone used as a timer and a trigger. The same phone handset was found attached to the battery pack and timer rigged up to Felicity Love. Same wire type as well, so forgive me for stating the obvious, but that means we're concluding that the same person put all the devices together.'

'Have you seen these specifications of bomb before?' one of the anti-terrorism officers asked.

'No, but it's not the sort of bomb where we'd be expecting a specific maker's design. IEDs like these have blueprints that can be downloaded from the internet. The battery pack and crown actually have more sophisticated electrics. The main problem with building pipe bombs is that they're notorious for going off during the build. The explosives can be unstable and the pressure within the pipe is hard to accurately gauge.'

'Would you say they were built by someone with experience?' Lively asked. 'There must be lists of people known for explosives expertise.'

'I wouldn't say this took expertise. All they need is someone clear-headed who can follow detailed instructions. There were no additional features that made them particularly complex, for example. If the bombs had been found in time they could have been made safe. It was their placement that made them so lethal, so you can assume the factory was thoroughly recced. You're looking for someone with a reasonably technical brain and the time, not to mention a private place, to build the IEDs.'

'What about the crown?' DS Tripp asked.

'Modified from a taser. Clever red herring sealing the battery pack and attaching a timer. It could easily have contained explosives and it was what threw the disposal team off. The important thing with the crown was the remote control, also via phone handset. As I say, not expert level electronics, but it would have taken a while. That certainly wasn't thrown together in a day.'

'What sort of equipment are we looking for in a workshop?' Ava asked.

'Bare minimum: drills, saws, clamps, welding equipment, wire cutters and access to electrical wire. If it's in an area not used to that level of noise, you could expect soundproofing to have been fitted. There would also probably be debris from test attempts and modified equipment. Given the care taken with the bombs, you might find a sort of clean area, which might just be a small constructed box rather than a full lab.'

'How did the bomber know when to start the countdown? Was that just chance?' an officer asked.

'He phoned us,' Ava said. 'The police switchboard got hold of DI Graham who gave me his mobile. I believe, although he didn't identify himself, that the person who made that call was responsible for the bombs. I was trying to negotiate with him when the timer started counting down. He was able to hear both my commands and the chaos that ensued. It meant he could hear the bombs going off. I guess it was as close as he could get to the action. The call couldn't be traced.'

Detective Superintendent Overbeck stood, a clear sign that she'd had enough of the briefing and wanted everyone to get moving.

'Three things,' she said. 'First, I've commissioned a psychological profile of the bomber based on the three events we believe them to be responsible for at this stage. To that end,

I've asked a forensic psychologist who assisted in a previous case in the city to prepare a report as soon as possible. She'll need access to our materials and I've given the necessary security clearance, so expect to assist Dr Connie Woolwine with any requests. She's American and I don't like her, but she's good at what she does.'

'When can we expect her?' Ava asked.

'Today,' Overbeck snapped. 'Second, the forensics team found a hair. It was sealed inside the battery pack connected to the crown on Felicity Love's head. There was a substantial amount of glue used therein, and there's some speculation that the hair got picked up without the bomber noticing it. The battery pack did not blow up, it being at the far end of the quadrangle, so the hair is intact. It may be nothing, but then again it might also have come from the bomber. Testing is underway to see if DNA is retrievable.'

She paused.

'Finally, we lost nine more lives to the pipe bombs and two others are still critically ill in hospital. The families have been notified and we'll be making a public statement releasing the names of the dead later today. Many of you in this room will have worked closely with Detective Inspector Pax Graham who was a member of MIT, and I would like to say this to my team. Now is not your time to mourn. You have a job to do. Your work, not unlike revenge, is a dish best served cold. If the loss of a fellow officer devours you, you will not see straight. When anger controls you, you will miss the obvious in favour of what might be a distant illusion. Allowing your heart to control your head will – and I do not exaggerate – fuck-up every procedure that has been painstakingly put in place over a period of years. Do not let DI Graham's death be a catalyst for mistakes, because I want the monster responsible behind bars, and if you let the defence use poor procedure against us, I will not be forgiving when your mitigation is grief. Buckle up, people. Police work is shitty and hard and fucked-up, and if you didn't realise before that that's what you signed up for, then you know it now. No excuses. Get it done.'

Overbeck took Ava's breath away. The woman had a way with words. Usually that way was visceral and deeply unpleasant, but she'd never once failed to get her point across. Today Overbeck was a lighthouse in the pitch dark of Ava's mind. The mourning had to wait. Insomnia had to be conquered in favour of a necessary amount of sleep. The fury had to be vomited out to stop the poison working its way through her system. Pax Graham deserved the best of her. Overbeck was right, no excuse was good enough. When Ava had released Ailsa's body for burial, she'd been thinking only with the grieving parts of herself. No more. There was an evidential trail and she'd had first-hand contact with a suspect. If Ava couldn't make progress with that, she thought, then she wasn't fit to call herself a detective at all.

Chapter Twenty-Four

Ava stood opposite forensic psychologist Dr Connie Woolwine who had asked to be in attendance to get what she'd called, 'a proper hands-on feel for the case'. Between them on the mortuary table was the body of Gavin Cronk. Nate Carlisle was supervising. The two women, both in their thirties, one tanned, one pale, each haunted by their work, let their thoughts fill the silence as they stared at the body. Ava did her best not to imagine Dr Ailsa Lambert cutting open the cadaver only to be sprayed with toxic gas in that very room. Connie Woolwine was imagining nothing else. They'd spent the previous two days together at the police station poring over documents and videos, then going to each of the bombing locations for Connie to do as she was doing once more. Drinking it all in, giving nothing back. Ava had listened to the American mutter to herself, watched her dash endless notes into a pad, seen her look at a photo, turn it over, then whip it quickly back face up as if to surprise herself. It had taken forty-eight hours to get used to the profiler's quirks. Ava had thought there was nothing left by which to be surprised.

'I need you to open him up,' Woolwine directed at Nate

Carlisle. 'Just the abdominal cavity will do. Don't worry about the chest, and the brain doesn't interest me.'

'I can do that,' Dr Carlisle said. 'Was there anything in particular you wanted to ask me?'

'I'm still thinking about that,' she replied.

It took a while. The incision had been loosely stitched rather than stapling because of the original wound Ailsa had attempted to avoid. The cadaver had been inspected a second time to remove the toxic gas device and to complete the parts of the investigation that Ailsa hadn't concluded. Nate carefully opened up the abdomen. Ava took a step back whereas Woolwine moved forward, watching Nate's work.

'You're very gentle,' she said. 'Respectful. Tell me how you feel when you do this.'

Nate gave her a long look which Woolwine met with her cool, direct gaze.

'I'm doing my job, which requires me to be professional and to see the body as evidence, as a road map if you like, but I never forget that this was a living, breathing human being. They have relatives somewhere who will have to imagine this process. Even though they can't see what I'm doing right now, I still feel a responsibility to behave as if they could see me.'

'One of your parents was a physician,' Woolwine said. It wasn't a question.

'My mother was a nurse. How did you know?'

'When students learn to be doctors, they often develop a brusqueness in their manner, their touch or their speech. That's behaviour they've been taught to put on, the same as their scrubs, to protect themselves. It's why seeing a doctor can feel uncomfortable, like they're trying to pull away while we're trying to open up. It's different for children who've watched a medical parent – a good one, anyway – because they see the dedication, the passion and the kindness of the profession from a loved one. They emulate rather than learning. Your mother was a good nurse. Her patients liked her.'

Nate Carlisle looked both taken aback and fascinated by Woolwine in equal measure. 'She's retired now but many of her patients keep in touch. What is it you want to see?'

'Touch, not see,' Woolwine said. 'I'm going to be getting my hands dirty. I'm a firm believer in walking in a killer's shoes every step of the way. I'm trying to recreate their experience in my mind to get inside theirs. I guess everything in the abdominal cavity has been removed so there's no risk of me causing damage?'

Nate frowned slightly and looked at Ava who simply shrugged.

'You'll need to put different gloves on. You can bin the ones you're wearing and replace them with a pair from the pink box. They have a longer sleeve.'

'Could you get them for me?' Woolwine asked, stripping off the gloves she was wearing. 'I'm not being demanding,' she smiled, 'I'm achromatic. I only see in shades of grey, no colours,' she explained for Ava's benefit.

'Genetic?' Nate asked as he handed her the new gloves.

'The unfortunate result of neurosurgery performed to return my speech after a head injury,' Woolwine said. She was bending down over Gavin Cronk's corpse. 'You were alive,' she said, lifting his left eyelid and staring into the cloudy eye socket that already bore little resemblance to a living man. 'But sedated. Why did the bomber do that?'

Ava and Nate Carlisle exchanged another look, both wondering if either was expected to answer the question. Neither did. Dr Woolwine simply continued, transported into her own world where out loud conversations with the dead seemed to be entirely normal.

'I need you. I chose you for a reason but now, everything's changed. I have to do something, I'm not a professional so I've never done it before. I don't want you to move or scream because that will make my job even harder.' She put one hand either side of Gavin Cronk's face and spoke to him directly again. 'Am I worried that I might not have the stomach for it?'

Connie Woolwine went to the abdominal opening, stared in, mimed making the cuts that had been allowed to heal before Gavin had finally died, pretended to wipe away any surface blood, then plunged her hands deep into the cavity, letting her fingers feel everything, listening to the noises, bending low to breathe in the smell and closing her eyes. Minutes later, her hands outside once more, stripping her gloves off and depositing them in a bin, she returned to Gavin's head to look at him quizzically.

'You weren't even human to him by then, were you? That must have been the scariest thing of all. Knowing you were nothing but a vessel. That was when you realised there was no way you were going to survive.' She glanced up at Dr Carlisle. 'I'm done here.'

'Fine, I'll have someone stitch him back up,' he said, pulling the cover over the cadaver. 'Was there anything else you needed?'

'Yeah, Felicity Love. There was no sexual assault, right?' He confirmed that there hadn't been. 'And no injury other than those directly attributable to restraining her and fixing the crown, the sword and scales, correct?'

'Correct,' he said.

'What were her hydration levels like? Was there food in her stomach?'

'Bread in her stomach, not much else. It would have been consumed after she was kidnapped. She showed no sign of serious dehydration so you can assume her kidnapper also gave her water.'

Woolwine folded her arms and stared into Dr Carlisle's eyes. He returned her look for several seconds before turning away and beginning to clear up. She remained where she was, gazing into nothing. Ava checked her messages and wished for coffee.

'So these are just vessels,' Woolwine said abruptly. 'Gavin Cronk, Maura Douglas and Felicity Love became this bomber's postal service. There was no mistreatment of any one of them prior to and excluding the specific purpose he needed them for. If you're about to remind me that Ms Douglas had her tongue cut out, I believe that was simply to prevent a warning from being given.'

'So they were chosen at random?' Ava asked.

'Oh god, no, far from it. The bomber – the serial bomber, we should say, and the distinction is vitally important – is telling you a story. He might know he is, or he might be consciously unaware of it. But there's nothing random here. It's clinical; perhaps the most clinical series of crimes I've ever assessed.'

'So they were just vessels but not randomly chosen? That doesn't make a lot of sense to me,' Ava said. 'Surely it's one thing or the other.'

'That's because our normal thought process is to decipher every decision as a positive. So you're looking to figure out the attributes of each victim in terms of why them? Sometimes it's more helpful to ask why not someone else?' Ava's head was aching and she was afraid her face wasn't hiding her frustration very well. 'Don't get pissed at me. Follow this through. Have any random members of the public been hurt by any of the bombs? The answer is no. And not through blind luck. The papers indicate that the bomber was careful to actively exclude anyone other than first responders from the scenes.'

'All right, I get that,' Ava said.

'So he had specific targets. Your bomber is careful. He or she is not leaving bombs in a cinema or a shopping mall. I think you can assume they don't want to hurt anyone outside of their chosen target categories. If you apply that logic to the

173

three vessels, then he's using them because they're people who he does not deem to be innocent. They're expendable, and so he hasn't felt the need to protect them. He has some knowledge about them or has had some contact with them that allowed him to use each of them in a way that left his conscience free.'

'That actually makes sense.' Nate Carlisle sounded halfway between impressed and incredulous.

'But what he did to them was barbaric,' Ava said. 'Appalling. The first responders at least had the throw of the dice to survive in terms of where they were standing, which way they were facing. Cronk, Douglas and Love were never going to survive.'

'True, but if he'd had a really deep-rooted hatred of them I believe we'd have seen it in the treatment they received before their deaths. The bomber didn't lose his temper, they were given food and drink. They were treated like a means to an end, which we now know is exactly what they were. These people were delivery systems and they needed to remain intact. If I had to categorise them I'd say they were his secondary victims.'

'You think it's possible the bomber had contact with each of them before he chose them to be the so-called vessels?' Ava asked.

'Maybe not direct contact, but some knowledge of them that meant he was able to think of them as less than human. They may well be your stepping-stone to discovering the bomber's identity, but it would be wrong for you to consider them his primary motivation. You know, we all have these people. We carry a list of them in the messy part of our memory that reaches up at night when you can't sleep and makes you replay the bad moments of your life. The person who conned you out of money, the girl who spread a false rumour about you at school, the boss who belittled you knowing you couldn't afford to lose your job, the partner who mocked you to friends behind your back. People we care nothing for, who made themselves less than human to us. For most of us, operating within normal social and legal boundaries, those people are safe from retribution. But when there are no boundaries, where the trigger's been pulled, who are you going to go looking for? It'll be those people you know can be mean and hurtful and just plain nasty. Those less than innocent ones you can allow yourself not to care about. It's the same reason I don't think we're dealing with a psychopath. This is someone with his own twisted but still existent moral code.'

'I won't accept that,' Ava said. 'This person slaughtered Dr Ailsa Lambert as she stood where you're standing now. They took her in cold blood while she served the people of this city.'

Connie Woolwine unfolded her arms and went to stand in front of Ava, less than a foot away. Close enough that Ava could feel the warmth of her in the cold room.

'I met Ailsa,' she said. 'I worked with her on another case. The pain you're carrying is a crippling burden. All I can say from my brief dealings with your friend, is that in my opinion she was worth every bit of the agony you're in. The extent of grief is the marriage of the greatness of the person we've lost and the enormity of the love we felt for them. Your grief feels unbearable because the two things combined are a tremendous force. When you're able, you need to make time to understand how privileged you are to have felt such pain. Too few of us ever find a love that devastates us like that.'

Chapter Twenty-Five

The incident room was only half full when Dr Connie Woolwine arrived the next day to talk through her deductions.

'You know who I am and why I'm here, so we'll dispense with the boring stuff,' Woolwine began.

'Stop,' Superintendent Overbeck said. 'DCI Turner, where is everyone?'

'Every team was sent the memo,' Ava said. 'We're missing the specialist squads.'

'Send an officer to get them. We'll wait.' Overbeck perched on the edge of a desk and let her long, stick thin legs show off six-inch heels. One by one a steady stream of officers entered, looking either annoyed or embarrassed. Overbeck didn't move until every seat was filled. Only then did she stand. 'Senior officers for each squad, you knew about this meeting. Is there a reason why I had to wait for you to grace us with your presence?'

Someone who felt that their life was insufficiently exciting at that particular moment, chipped in.

'We're not actually governed by you. Our units are in attendance at the request of New Scotland Yard, and we have our own brief to fill here. For the record, there's still a lot of doubt about the validity of profiling.'

Overbeck replied with a smile that made every Police Scotland officer sit well back in their chair and hold their breath.

'And it's lovely to have you here. But you're in Scotland, working with my officers, to figure out who killed people who served the Scottish people. While you're here, you will be courteous to anyone I ask to assist in this investigation. I've always found that police officers who are so prideful that they close their minds to learning new skills end up falling flat on their faces, often in a steaming pile of shite. Dr Woolwine, don't make me regret anything I just said.'

Connie Woolwine stood and leaned between Ava and Overbeck to whisper into Overbeck's ear. 'You know, if Police Scotland doesn't appreciate you, there are some openings at Guantanamo. They'd love you there.'

Overbeck rolled her eyes. Woolwine had spoken just loud enough for Ava to hear. For the first time since she'd been given the news of Ailsa's death, she allowed herself a genuine smile.

'Okay, let's do the sceptics first. Listen carefully, it's a potted history and I'm going to skip over the dull parts. Criminal profiling doesn't always work. If it did, there would be no unsolved cases out there. It's relevant only to certain categories of crime, realistically only where there has been a series of crimes. To some extent we work with statistics, and inevitably sometimes we don't hit the percentages right. So when does it work? Honestly, it's only useful when you keep an open mind, apply your knowledge of the facts to the guidelines I give you, and you work with me.'

'Has it ever worked in a bombing case?' DS Tripp asked.

Woolwine grinned. 'In fact, yes. Serial bombers are rare but there was one operating in New York in the 1940s and 50s. They called him "The Mad Bomber". After sixteen years of trying to identify the bomber who'd planted homemade devices in cinemas, libraries and subway stations, police turned to a psychiatrist called James Brussel.' Woolwine looked at Overbeck. 'You want these guys to hear this or shall I skip it?'

Everyone was leaning forward in their seat. Police briefings were rarely silent like this. Woolwine had everyone's attention. Ava's view was that it was worth educating the squads about the value of the science if they were to have any faith in Woolwine's conclusions.

'Finish the story,' Overbeck directed.

'Great, I promise it'll be worth it. So, Brussel refused at first. Profiling wasn't even a thing then. He was busy with patients and worried that he might make the case worse by giving wrong information which, now that we're talking about that, I too am very much aware of. Anyway, the police were persistent. Eventually Brussel caved and agreed to have a look at the letters the bomber had written, the photos of the crime scenes, police notes, you name it. They dumped it all in Brussel's metaphorical lap and left him to read through it.'

'How long did he take?' Lively asked.

'Rumour has it they all just sat there while he read it, that day. Just sat in his office silently while he started thinking it through. But remember that these bombings had plagued New York for a while. Brussel would have been familiar with the crimes through the newspapers and he was also experienced in dealing with what they called the criminally insane. I'll summarise: no one ever doubted that the bomber was male, but a peculiarity of the handwriting and the prior use of bombs in Middle Europe indicated that the bomber was a Slav. The content of the letters allowed the psychiatrist to deduce that he was a paranoid schizophrenic. As most schizophrenics don't reach the peak of their mental instability until they're thirty-five years old, Brussel figured the bomber had to be at least in his mid- to late-forties, if not a little older.'

'What did Brussel get right that was more about psychiatry?' Tripp asked.

'Brussel, from both the letters and the use of the bombs, decided The Mad Bomber was very particular. He had a father he'd competed with for his mother's attention, was obsessive, difficult at work, felt powerless and at the same time superior to others. He concluded he'd never had any successful relationships and was probably a virgin. Brussel told police they'd find the bomber living with other unmarried but older family relations. He directed police to a town in Connecticut that had a large Slavic community but that had easy geographical access to New York.

'The first bomb was placed at the Con Edison power company, but those that came after seemed not to be linked. Brussel said that was just the spreading of the bomber's paranoia and that they should be looking for a former employee of Con Edison. The bomber would be neat, tidy, without close friends. But the really interesting thing is this: as the police officers were leaving, Brussel predicted that they would find the bomber wearing a double-breasted suit jacket. Asked why, he explained that the lack of regular work meant The Mad Bomber would be unfashionable but wanted to be perceived as neat and smart, but also that he would favour clothes that wrapped around him and felt protective, giving him the sense of comfort he'd craved from his mother.'

Dr Woolwine sat back in her seat.

'Come on then, how much did this Brussel guy get right?' someone asked.

'George Metesky – a Slav – was 54 when he was arrested in January 1957. He was living in the town Brussel suggested to police. He was single, always had been, and lived with two older spinster sisters. He'd worked for Con Edison. Obsessive, tidy to an extreme, with a superior attitude. Smug and condescending. Poor employment history because of a tendency to create petty disputes. Disliked by his neighbours. Brussel got it all right. The bombs were an attempt at making himself feel powerful while expressing his pent-up rage.'

'All right, I'll be the one to ask. What was he wearing when they caught him?' Lively said.

'Pyjamas,' Woolwine said. 'Done right up to the neck. Not a hair out of place.'

There was a round of laughter.

'But you should know that when police allowed Mr Metesky to get dressed before they escorted him to the police station, he exited his bedroom, precisely as predicted by James Brussel, in a double-breasted suit jacket. All wrapped around him, buttoned up and neat as a pin.'

The laughter stopped.

'Are you taking the piss?' Lively asked, his tone amazed rather than aggressive.

'I am not, I promise. Look it up,' Woolwine said. 'And all that is a long-winded way of saying that to ignore the insights of profiling is short-sighted, but don't treat it like a Bible. Brussel got that case so right it's kind of spooky, but there were other cases where he admitted he went off in the wrong direction. So if you're willing to listen, I'll tell you what I think about your Edinburgh bomber, and you can take it or leave it when I'm done. Okay?'

There was a general round of nodding across the room.

'Right, general information and parameters first. Let's talk about what we know about serial bombers across the range.' Woolwine pressed some keys on her laptop and the screen on the wall came to life.

Ava looked across at Callanach. He met her gaze with raised eyebrows. They were both surprised at how well the various teams were taking Connie Woolwine's intervention, and Ava

180

had to admit, it was a breath of fresh air to have someone assess the case from outside. Woolwine's methods were eccentric bordering on genuinely weird, but it didn't feel like nonsense. Right then it felt more like they were being thrown a lifeline.

'Can I ask, how long have you been doing this?' Lively interrupted again.

'I'm in my thirties. If you ask my exact age, I will psycho-analyse you in front of the entire room and you will not enjoy that.' Lively responded with a brief grin. He liked her, Ava thought. 'I've worked with the FBI, CIA, Interpol, MI5, Police Scotland once before in fact, and other forces around the world. I'm a consultant, so I go where the work takes me. No more small talk. Serial bombers are not like any other type of murderer. They have very specific, categorisable motivations. Let's take a look.'

A bullet point list flashed up. Across the room there was a rustle as everyone grabbed a notebook and pen.

'For the purposes of this assessment, I'm treating the initial incident at the mortuary as if it were a bombing. Notably the device of choice was an altered mine. And this is how we start. Bombings – and this is going to sound offensive given how many of you have lost colleagues and friends in these events – are regarded as passive-aggressive acts.' A few angry murmurs erupted as Woolwine had predicted. She shut the lid of her laptop and took a single step closer into her audience. 'All right, I'm going to say some things you won't want to hear, but we – you – do not have time for this. I'm going to be talking about body counts, details of deaths, intentions, and I'm going to do it all as if none of it is personal because that is the mode you need your brains to be in. So you get an apology from me now, one time only but, as of this second, pull up your big boy pants, slap on your thickest skin, and get with the program.'

Lively turned in his seat to stare at Ava and gave a subtle thumbs up that no one else could see. Woolwine was right. A bit like The Mad Bomber, Ava thought privately that the psychologist might not have that many friends, but she could cut through crap like a cheese wire, and right now it was her approach they needed. Woolwine was pointing at the wall and waiting to make sure she had everyone's attention.

'Bombing is passive-aggressive because the bomber does not need to be personally involved in actively causing deaths, that is to say there's no knife-wielding, gun-toting or strangulation. No getting his hands dirty or looking his victims in the eye. Quick note, this excludes suicide bombers. Totally different. Whatever you've read about that, disregard for these purposes. Remotely controlled or timer-based bombs allow a killer to think clearly, plan and execute without their motivations getting the better of them in the moment. They also do not have to see death first-hand, which allows them to escape taking full responsibility for the misery and suffering they cause. This is why a serial bomber is so dangerous. They escape the consequences of their actions.'

'So you don't think there's any possibility that . . .' Ava paused, wondered if she was about to start a riot, then decided the question was so important that a riot was irrelevant, '. . . that the person responsible is someone on the inside who was at both the railway tunnel and the industrial site?'

No objection. No muttering. Only a moment of held breath. Apparently Ava's team weren't the only investigators who had been considering the possibility of an inside job.

'That would be extremely unusual,' Woolwine said. 'Impossible? No. But my gut instinct says that's not what's going on here. That doesn't seem to be the Edinburgh bomber's motivation. They couldn't have been present at the mortuary event, so the first incident wouldn't have fit. It's unlikely therefore that he or she would have chosen to be a first-hand witness at the second or third event. Also, because the targets don't fit with a compulsive bomber.'

She pointed to the top of her screen.

'Our first category is compulsive bombers. They use bombs for the excitement and the power. They like the flames, the chaos, the mess and the noise. It's psychosexual thrill-seeking with a sadistic element. That's not what's happening in Edinburgh. Your bombs are so specifically targeted that there's no real chaos. Your victims are disciplined responders who simply continue doing their jobs. A compulsive bomber is looking for somewhere like a night club where people are given thirty seconds to get out of two exits, one of which he's blocked. Very different scenarios.

'Likewise, we can rule out some of the other motivations or psychologies straight away. These bombings aren't military or suicidal. It's not for the purpose of a criminal enterprise. I'm also ruling out a political or ideological motivation.'

That got a few objections.

'Hear me out,' Woolwine said. 'I know a far right group claimed the first attack but it hasn't been validated by your intelligence services, unless you know something I don't. The reason I say this doesn't fit is because of Gavin Cronk and Felicity Love. Attacks in non-public spaces with no wider audience. That's not what terrorists, domestic or otherwise, are looking for. They prefer an equal amount of witnesses to those injured. They want to cause widespread panic. These bombings are too much effort for a terrorist, with too little reward. Argue with me later if you want, but let's carry on down the list.

'So is this psychotic behaviour? No, not at all. Whatever this is, it's deeply rooted in the real world. This is thoughtful, subject-specific killing. Let's cross psychotic off. Sociopathic? This is where it gets interesting.'

At that, Woolwine brought up an image of Maura Douglas hanging from the Innocent Railway Tunnel shortly before the bomb exploded.

'The baby bump troubles me. It suggests either the work of a deeply disturbed mind or a genius. I tend to think it's neither. But sociopathy suggests this bomber can't empathise. If that were true, why go to such lengths to protect innocent members of the public?'

'Was the baby bump not just a convenient method of delivering the explosives then?' Superintendent Overbeck asked.

Woolwine sighed. 'Looked at individually, each of the bomb-delivery victims seems to be unimportant. DCI Turner and I have discussed this. I consider them to be vessels for the bomber to carry out his mission. The Edinburgh bomber does not care about them. They are disposable. But when you consider them in sequence, see them as they were in life, perhaps the bomber is telling us a story.'

She brought up an image of the three human so-called vessels, each next to the other.

'Gavin Cronk was dead when he was found. He was inevitably going to end up at the mortuary. There was no mistaking the state he was in – especially given his relative youth – for death by natural causes. But what do we know about Cronk in real life? He was a drug dealer. His drugs created addicts and ultimately many drug addicts die from the substances they take. So Cronk is presented as a dead body.'

Ava wasn't sure if that was an overreach but Woolwine clearly had more to say.

'I see your frowns, people, and I may be getting your bomber's story wrong, but if you think there's no story here at all, then you don't get how much your subconscious mind controls every decision you make. Bear in mind that the bomber may not even be aware of the choices he's making right now. So, on to Maura Douglas. She's a courier. She delivers things. What else do we deliver?'

At least a dozen people in the room muttered the word

'babies' under their breath before they could stop themselves. Suddenly, there was a renewed hush to the room.

'This is very literal. Actually, I think it's too literal, but all of this is also too much of a coincidence for you to have the luxury of ignoring it. By the time we reach Felicity Love, the subtlety of the messaging is gone. This time, the bomber wants you to know what she's done to offend him. She's his most personal vessel so far. Cronk and Douglas might have been replaceable choices but I don't think Love was. If you're going to find the bomber based on the information you currently have, you're going to find it in a link to Felicity. The Lady Justice outfit did two things simultaneously. It gave him the perfect mechanism for delivering the electric shock while sending you a message too. He hated her not for her personal life or her personal choice, but for what she did as a legal professional. Forget worrying about her husband or child, there's no mysterious lover to hunt down, no secret debts or hidden identity. The bomber both distracted you with that costume and satisfied his own needs with it. What were the needs?'

Woolwine pointed at the remaining words not previously addressed on the original slide as she brought it back up.

'Mission-oriented bombings, possibly dispute based, possibly revenge motivated. This is the personal category, and it is the only one these three attacks all fit into. The attacks have a sense of entitlement and of purpose. I'd guess they will be time limited. The bomber will reach their goal at some point. Bombers, and this crosses multiple categories, often feel they have a righteous power to punish, a sort of divine standing. That's certainly evident here. There's a sense that his victims deserve what they got. Questions?'

'What's the normal gender for serial bombers?'

'Predominantly male. Almost always male in fact, except in terrorism cases where there have been a few notable exceptions.'

'So is he going to be much like that Mad Bomber you were talking about then?' Lively asked.

'This bomber's motivation, if he is male, is different,' Woolwine said. 'But there will be aspects where there are similarities. The Edinburgh bomber has a good ability to follow instructions, think things through, to be careful and logical, to plan and execute cleanly. As of yet there have been no false moves or mistakes.'

'Apart from the hair that got stuck in the battery pack glue on Felicity Love. If we get DNA off that, it'll have been a major cockup,' someone offered.

'Yeah, you see, that's bullshit,' Woolwine said. All eyes flew straight back to her. 'That wasn't a mistake. He packed three pipe-bombs, made an electrocution crown, used a pressurised device to deliver toxic gas. No fingerprints, none of his DNA, no errors, but there's a hair inside a unit he knows won't be destroyed in the explosion. You're not giving this person anything like the credit you should. That's going to be very dangerous indeed. You think he's that sloppy? Think again, or there are going to be a lot more bodies in that mortuary.'

Ava stood. 'Are you saying he planted that hair there for us to find?'

Woolwine took a deep breath as she considered it. 'Too prosaic,' she concluded. 'I think it's part of his story. Just another chapter in everything you've already been told.'

'Parameters then,' Ava said. 'Be our Dr Brussel. Who are we looking for?'

'Adult male under sixty-five, lives within driving distance of Edinburgh, no previous convictions and he's probably never even been in trouble before. You're looking for a trigger. Something happened to start this and when you find it, you'll know immediately what the motivation is. It will all make sense. He's bright but not genius level, well-organised, decent amount of time on his hands. I wouldn't discount someone with good community ties and a normal upbringing. Will recently have been on sick leave or administrative leave, something that gave him the opportunity to do this. He understands how to keep his head down and avoid detection. Remember this: he is not crazy but he is crazed. It's the most important distinction in this case, and that's not medically or politically correct language but it's the best way to keep it in your minds.'

'And what will he be wearing when we catch him?' another officer shouted from the back.

Woolwine didn't crack even the slightest edge of a smile.

'It won't matter what the bomber's wearing,' she said. 'By the time you're within spitting distance, the Edinburgh bomber will be dead or dying. Given this extraordinary campaign, I'd say death is the very last thing they fear right now.'

Chapter Twenty-Six

BEFORE

It wasn't hard to find a courier to do exactly what Liam wanted. Forget the big companies. Go to one of the poorest areas of the city, ask around in the local shops, look at noticeboards. He'd needed someone desperate and he'd struck gold. It had cost him an arm and a leg, the courier wasn't afraid to negotiate. Liam had given her a script that she had to read word for word, and a cheap phone containing a video file that he'd arranged to have returned by the end of the day. Most importantly, the content of the video wasn't shareable. He had only one regret: that he couldn't be present to see the faces of the recipients. That was a shame. They'd had enough time to gloat about destroying his relationship. It was time to get even. The only box not ticked for the day, was composing a message for Quinn. It needed to be persuasive without sounding threatening. Not easy with a girl who required a firm hand, especially given her family's influence, but he'd find the words. Pretty soon, she'd see her life would be better with him in it.

Liam headed for work, avoiding the route that took him

through Gorebridge. Today wasn't the right moment for seeing Quinn in person. Soon though. She'd be ready once she properly understood his motivations.

Friday morning, Maura parked her Beetle in the Gorebridge public car park as directed and waited until she saw Mark Devlin's vehicle pull up. He was easy to spot. She'd been told the recipient worked in a local shop that kept antisocial hours. Even so, she'd have been glad of that work rather than the piecemeal living she was making. Her head was throbbing again. The pills her doctor had prescribed to keep the pain away had long since ceased to be effective, but the next step was to go onto oral morphine and in her head that spelled the beginning of the end. Once she was taking that stuff she could kiss goodbye to her driving licence, and she didn't want her son Jimmy seeing her high on legal opiates either. The thought of him made her flush with guilt. They were past due a conversation about what was wrong, and there were plans to be made. Every week, she found a reason to delay telling him about the brain tumour. Let him stay a kid, unafraid, for just a few more days. He deserved so much better. He'd always deserved more than the life she'd provided for him, not that he'd complained. She'd only taken this job for Jimmy. It was all just cash to stash away for when he needed it. When the time came, she'd direct him to the bag at the bottom of her wardrobe containing the savings she'd scraped together.

'Excuse me, Mark Devlin?' she called to the young man locking up his car.

'Yes?'

'I was asked to show you this. I'm just the courier,' she added. Those words hadn't been in the script and she had no idea what was in the video, but the client creeped her out

189

and she had a sick feeling in the pit of her stomach about the job.

'Sorry, I'm late and I need to open up a shop. You can follow me and do this there if you want but—'

The video began to play. Mark Devlin's expression went from hurried to horrified in a half-second.

'I'm not watching this. You'd better get out of here right now or I'm calling the police.'

'Hold on,' she said, pulling the required sheet of paper from her pocket. 'Sorry. There was a longer message. It says . . .' Maura swallowed hard and kept her eyes down. 'Watch the footage to the end. If you don't, I'll post it on social media for everyone to see. Quinn and I were meant for each other. This was taken on Saturday. You're never going to have her. I'm the only one who can give her what she really wants.'

The four minutes that followed were excruciating. Maura looked away, but she couldn't do anything about the audio.

'Do you love me?' a man asked. She recognised her client's voice.

'Mmm,' a young woman said.

'You don't mind me making this video, do you sweetheart? I'll stop if you ask me to.'

A sort of mumbled groan, but no protest. The camera kept on filming.

Each time she glanced up, the heads were out of shot, but there was plenty of body action. Maura felt like she needed to shower for a week. Finally, it ended.

'You're disgusting,' Devlin said to her.

Maura would have been shocked if she hadn't agreed.

'He didn't show it to me,' she said meekly. 'I was just supposed to deliver it.'

'Yeah?' he said, making fists with his hands. Maura wasn't scared. Taking a punch seemed like a fair response to what he'd just been shown. The girl was obviously someone he cared about. It was shitty making him watch her having sex with another man. 'Are we done?'

Maura nodded. She thought she could see tears in his eyes, although that might have been the fact that she was looking through the tears in her own. He left and she retreated to her car, collapsing her head against the steering wheel as she screamed inside. Desperation had brought her too low. Even so, she knew she would honour the agreement and deliver the second viewing. Her boy was going to need the money, and the memory of what she'd done to get it would die with her.

She drove twenty minutes to the second address and checked the name she'd been given. Robert Wilson lived in a tiny house that looked orderly but soulless. It was still a palace compared to the flat in which she'd raised Jimmy. Before she ruined another person's day, Maura took a moment in her car thinking that the front door would have been more striking painted a deep shade of blue, and that the pebbledash front needed a fresh coat of cream paint. None of the windows had curtains. He had to be single. She only hoped he wasn't prone to violence. Think of the money, she told herself. Think of Jimmy alone. His father wasn't going to do the right thing, never had. It was all down to her.

Wilson opened the door with a broad smile.

'You're an early bird,' he quipped. 'What I can do for you?'

'You have to read this,' Maura said. She wasn't prepared to read another message out loud. 'And watch this.' She held up the phone the client had given her and pressed play on the same few minutes of footage.

Wilson's eyes narrowed but he didn't look away, not for a second. His face took on the qualities of granite. He folded his arms, chin up, and gritted his teeth.

Maura turned her head away and tried not to listen a second time around. It took forever to end, and by the time it did she felt more ill than she ever had before. The journey ahead of her to get home seemed impossibly long. Eventually she was able to put the phone back in her pocket.

'Why did you do this?' Wilson asked her. 'Why would anyone get involved in something so terrible? Is Liam your son?'

'He's not mine! My son is good. I didn't raise a man like this.'

'No? You were willing to take his money and do his dirty work, though. You go back to that son of a bitch and tell him to start running because I'm going to find him, and when I do he's going to regret this.'

Maura saw the truth of the words in the set of his mouth. This wasn't a man you wanted to mess with, and he certainly didn't want to hear her reasons for being involved. She decided that the best thing to do was get out of there as fast as possible. He followed her to the Beetle, pulled out his own mobile phone and took a photo of the number plate, then walked away. Maura Douglas had no intention of delivering his message to her client. It was their mess, not hers. All she wanted now was to climb into bed and forget all about it, and once she'd returned the mobile phone, that was exactly what she intended to do.

Mark Devlin arrived at Quinn's house during his lunch hour to find her parents and another man in heated conversation while Quinn sat pale and silent in their midst.

'Now's not a good time I'm afraid, Mark,' Simeon McTavish told him at the front door. 'Something's happened.'

'Is it . . . anything to do with a video? Because that's why I've come round too.' The chatter in the sitting room stopped immediately.

'You'd better come in, lad,' her father said, stepping aside.

Mark walked through to join the family. 'I don't think you've met my wife's brother, Robert.'

'Hi,' Mark said quietly.

Quinn was crying softly, leaning against her mother's shoulder.

'I'm sorry,' he began. 'A woman came to me this morning as I parked my car. She showed me a video, said I had to watch it all or it would be put online. I didn't want to risk it. I thought you should know.'

'I saw it, too. That little motherfucker raped her. She can't even remember it.'

'Bobby,' Quinn's mother cautioned. 'This isn't helping Quinn. Let's keep our language and our voices under control. We need to figure out what to do.'

'I've got the woman's licence plate, and a photo of her getting into the car. The police will be able to trace her,' Bobby said.

'That's a start,' her father replied. 'We can take that to the police, tell them what happened. They can do some tests, get the video.'

'But then I'll have to give a statement,' Quinn said. 'I'm not sure I can. I'd end up having to go to court, be cross-examined, have all those people listening to it.'

'Quinny, darling, you can't let yourself be treated like this. You said yourself, you can't remember a thing about what happened. It seems clear to me that he slipped something into your drink. What if he does it again to another girl? What if you're – heaven forbid – pregnant?' her father asked.

'Stop!' Quinn's mother said. 'You can't put all of this on her right now. It's too much. What she needs is some space to come to terms with it.'

'Aye, but the man who did this to her has to face a reckoning. Quinn's owed that at least,' her father said. 'I won't sit here and do nothing. I can't.'

'It'll be a damn sight more than a reckoning,' Bobby said.

'Come on, Simeon. We know people who'll help us out. That boy shouldn't go another hour without paying for what he did.'

Quinn sobbed even harder and her father collapsed onto the sofa at her side, wrapping his arms around both his daughter and his wife.

'There now, you shouldn't be hearing this talk. I'm sorry. I'm so sorry, my darling.' Simeon McTavish had tears in his eyes as he rocked them both back and forward, the three of them wrapped together into one giant hug.

'I'll get your shifts covered,' Mark said. 'Don't even think about work. And I'll see if there's any CCTV footage of the woman showing me the video. The florist at the back might have a camera.'

'By the time the police do anything about it, Liam will be long gone. Trust me, I've dealt with bastards like this before. He only understands one language. We have to teach him a lesson. Quinn, I want his address. You don't need to know anything about it,' Bobby said.

'No. I don't want you in trouble Uncle Bobby. I don't want any of you involved in this. It's my mess. I need to deal with it myself.'

'No, baby, you shouldn't have to. What happened wasn't your fault. He's evil, that's all there is to it,' her mother said, clutching Quinn hard.

Quinn's mobile beeped. She blanched.

'It's a message,' she said, 'from him.' The room was silent as she read it. '*Quinn, I hope everyone understands what we mean to each other now. Maybe they'll finally stop trying to keep us apart. Saturday was magical. Let's do it again this weekend. Love you, Lx.* He's not going to stop. He must have been following me, that's why he was in the bookshop. I thought he'd got the message but he's totally deluded, to do this today and then ask to see me at the weekend.'

'Sick in the head, is what he is,' Bobby said. 'And dangerous. Let me sort it out, Quinn. You know I'll do anything for you.'

'Bob, you can't break the law. As much I appreciate and agree with the sentiment, we have to stay on the right side of this,' her father said. 'Violence won't help Quinn, in fact it'll just make things worse. She's my daughter and I'm going to make sure that man pays for what he's done.'

'Come on, Simeon, how often do you think people like him really get what they deserve? You and I know the score. By the time there's been an investigation, even if they do charge him, there'll have to be a trial, months will go by, and then what? If you want justice, the only way to be certain about it is to hand it out ourselves.'

'I won't let my family be reduced to that,' Simeon said. 'We've always been better than men like him. I know you're angry, Bob, I feel the same, and I can't trust myself to go anywhere near him. But I won't risk my family by doing something stupid, and that includes you.'

'I'll sort it out,' Quinn said, sitting forward, gently pushing her parents' protective arms away. 'I've got no choice. Uncle Bobby, Dad's right. I need you to stay away from Liam. I can't face it today but I'll go to the police station first thing in the morning. Mum, would you come with me if Dad looks after Dolly?'

'I will, if you're sure that's what you want to do.'

'I'm sure,' Quinn said. 'I've got nothing left to lose.'

Chapter Twenty-Seven

Six of them sat around the table at Talisman Advocates. On one side Detective Superintendent Overbeck had positioned herself to be flanked by Ava and Luc; on the other was the head clerk, the head of chambers, and Felicity Love's close friend, Elise Holmes.

'On behalf of Police Scotland, I'd like to say how sorry we are for your loss. Felicity was a well-respected advocate. We're here today to ask for your help to find her killer,' Overbeck opened.

'May I ask the current state of the investigation?' the head of chambers asked. 'Not to put too fine a point on it, but I have other advocates asking if they're safe or if they need better security arrangements in place at work and at home.'

'There's no reason to believe that there's a general threat to members of the legal profession. Felicity's death appears to be linked to that of a known drug dealer called Gavin Cronk and a courier called Maura Douglas. In the circumstances, we believe that the choice of Felicity as a victim is linked to her specifically. The threat should not extend to anyone else inside Talisman Advocates,' Ava said.

'Unless any of your other lawyers were involved in the same case that caught Mrs Love's killer's attention. That's why we're here today. We need your assistance,' Overbeck said. 'You've kindly provided a list of the cases Mrs Love undertook in the last two years, mainly criminal and a few civil law matters. We've obtained the case files for the criminal cases from the Procurator Fiscal's office and we'll shortly be obtaining court transcripts from the actual hearings, but that only takes us so far.'

'What else are you looking for?' the head of chambers asked.

'We want to cross-reference the names of the other victims, their addresses, personal information et cetera against Mrs Love's cases. It's vital that we find the connection between Felicity and the other two,' Ava said. 'We'd also like to look through Felicity's case notebooks to see if there's anything useful that we're not getting from the prosecution papers.'

'You can't,' the head of chambers said. 'Anything said in conference between an advocate and their client is privileged. There's only one way of getting you access to the case note-books and that would be for each client involved in each case to waive privilege and allow you to access the notes for these purposes. Some will be serving prison sentences and will not feel disposed to assist, the remainder who were found not guilty won't want you to know their secrets, and almost all will have a deep mistrust of the police.'

'Could we pay for another advocate within these chambers to look through the notebooks and simply notify us if any relevant references are found?' Callanach suggested.

'I'm afraid not,' the head of chambers replied. 'Client advocate privilege is limited to the one single advocate instructed. The case solicitor could look through the notes, but they would still be stopped from telling you if the names you've mentioned also happened to be mentioned by a client in the course of giving instructions.'

'They couldn't even give us a case name so we'd know where to start?' Ava asked.

'Not even that,' Elise Holmes explained. 'Legal professional privilege is absolute and deep rooted. The privilege – the right to confidentiality – belongs to the lay client not to us. It's not ours to waive. I should advise you in a friendly capacity, that you do not want to be obtaining evidence through breached confidentiality rules. It won't help you in court.'

Overbeck leaned forward and put a smile on her face that always reminded Ava of *Chitty Chitty Bang Bang*'s Child Catcher calling the children out of the houses with sweets.

'I'm actually quite familiar with the law,' Overbeck said. 'But, you see, as of this morning's count, thirty people are dead, Felicity among them. More people will likely die as there is no sign that this campaign of terror is over. Indeed, the killings are growing more complex and sophisticated with each incident. The notebooks are no doubt somewhere in this building, just sitting there doing nothing. They may contain the crucial detail that will allow us to save other lives. You cannot seriously be suggesting that there is absolutely no mechanism for allowing access to those notes. That would not simply be unjust, but utterly perverse.'

'Superintendent,' the head of chambers said. 'I knew Felicity Love from the first day she set foot in court. She was a close personal friend and an outstanding colleague. You and I have often found ourselves on opposing sides in the courtroom, but I can assure you now that I would like nothing more than to help identify the man who killed Felicity and put him behind bars. However, I cannot – I will not – allow you access to those notebooks. There is no exception to the rule that would apply in these circumstances. Speak to each of Felicity's clients. See if they'll waive their rights. For any that do, we will gladly hand over the information you seek.'

'You must be plagued with people asking how you defend the deviants you do,' Overbeck said. 'I understand, of course, that every defendant is entitled to a fair trial and proper representation. But this is not that. This is an opportunity for you to save innocent lives.'

'And I wish I could, but the rules are clear. Our hands are tied,' he said.

'So be it,' Overbeck replied. 'And may I wish you the very best of luck living with that decision the next time a bomb goes off in this city.'

Chapter Twenty-Eight

BEFORE

Sexual Offences Liaison Officer, PS Tricia Baird was assigned to the case. Within two hours of reporting Liam Cook for raping her, Quinn found herself in a hospital unit being examined by a sympathetic doctor, as her mother waited anxiously outside.

'We're going to check your body for bruises, injuries and signs of force. We can take a break any time you need. I'll also need to do an internal examination and take swabs. Have you had a bath or shower since this happened?' the doctor asked.

'Several, I mean, it happened nearly a week ago but I didn't realise it until yesterday,' Quinn explained.

There were endless forms. Scrapings from beneath her nails were taken, as she explained they wouldn't find anything. Her skin was in perfect shape, not a scratch or a contusion on it. The internal checks revealed nothing that would suggest the use of force and there were no injuries. Through it all, Quinn did her best to explain that they weren't looking at the sort of rape where there would be physical evidence. The process continued anyway, as the doctor explained that they had to make every possible effort on

Quinn's behalf. Finally, blood and urine samples were taken.

'Will you check to see if I was drugged?' Quinn asked.

'Of course. Can I just confirm the date of intercourse again?' the doctor asked.

'Six days ago. Last Saturday, in the afternoon,' Quinn said.

'Then it's possible that any drugs will have left your system. Chemicals might not show in either your urine or your blood. How many hours of conscious memory did you lose?'

'Two or three maybe, I'm not sure. I slept for some of it.'

'It sounds as if you were given a relatively small dose, in which case it will have left your system faster. We'll try hair strand testing in nine days – it takes that long to get through into the root – but for a small dose of drugs it might not show up clearly or the actual drug might not be identifiable. Do you have any idea what you were given?' the doctor asked.

'I didn't know I was given anything at all. If I'd had any idea what was happening, I'd have left.' Quinn pulled her clothes on. 'I'd like my mum to come back in now, please.'

'Of course,' the doctor opened the door. 'The results will be sent to your liaison officer and she'll talk you through them. If you think of any questions later, do get in touch. We're here to help.'

'You okay, love?' her mother asked as they walked to the car. 'Stupid question, right?'

'No, it's not. I just feel like no one gets it. I couldn't have reported it any sooner. I didn't know I shouldn't have showered. Of course I don't have any defensive injuries or his blood under my nails. Why do they keep asking questions when they know my answer's going to be negative?'

Her mum slipped an arm around Quinn's shoulders.

'I guess they just have to. For what it's worth, I'm proud of you. You're being so brave. It'll be worth it in the end.'

★ ★ ★

By Friday evening a video interview suite was available. Quinn left her mother in yet another waiting room, ignoring the ancient magazines and biting her nails to the quick.

She swore to tell the truth, gave her personal details and explained what she knew about what had happened. PS Baird was patient and understanding, but by the time Quinn was halfway through retelling the events, it became clear that she was facing an uphill battle at such a steep angle it would prove impossible to climb.

'So, it was your boss at the shop and your uncle who were shown the footage. Do you know why Liam chose those two people in particular?'

'Liam thinks Mark – my boss – is interested in me as more than just a colleague.'

'Have you ever had a relationship with Mark?' PS Baird asked.

'No, but I guess he might be a bit keen. My uncle was pushy about Liam meeting my parents. It was kind of embarrassing and Liam reacted badly.'

'So can I go back to you and Liam having coffee in the bookshop cafe. You did that willingly? No reservations?'

'I think I was pleased we could talk again without any awkwardness. I don't like conflict so the chance to get resolution seemed like a good thing.'

'And you consented to getting in the taxi knowing you were going to his house and that he would be driving you home?'

'I was getting ill by then so yes, I knew where we were going but I just felt so sick I didn't know what else to do,' Quinn said.

'I understand. So you believe you were given some sort of drug at the coffee shop?'

'It must have been then. I was fine while I was shopping. Things only went wrong after I met up with Liam.'

'Can I check, and this is no reflection on what happened, but during your relationship with Liam had you previously had sexual intercourse?'

Quinn felt her stomach plummet. She wanted to leave.

'Yeah,' she said. 'Only once though.'

'That's fine,' PS Baird said. 'We just need to know in case we check Liam's apartment for bodily fluids and DNA, those things might have been there from a previous event. Is that right?'

Quinn sighed. 'Yes.'

'You mentioned that at some point during the video, Liam explains that he's filming, and asks for your consent to carry on, and that you appear to agree, or at least don't ask him to stop.'

'I didn't know what was going on,' Quinn said. 'I still can't remember it now. If he hadn't shown Mark and Uncle Bobby the footage I'd never have known.'

'I appreciate that, I'm just trying to build up a full picture,' PS Baird said. 'Is there anything you think it would be helpful to add at this point?'

'He left a message in the book I bought. I didn't see him write it, so he must have done it when he said I was asleep,' Quinn said.

'What was the content of the message?' PS Baird asked.

'He called me darling, then said something about having had a lovely day together and wanting to remember it. He signed it with a kiss.'

'So nothing threatening or abusive? No reference to having had sex?'

'No, but it's weird, right? I mean, we've split up. The message was like nothing had ever gone wrong between us.'

'I see,' PS Baird said.

Quinn wasn't sure she really did. PS Baird announced the

time and that she was going to stop filming, then Quinn's mother was brought in.

'Be honest,' Quinn said. 'What do you think will happen?'

'Drug-facilitated sexual assaults are notoriously difficult to prove,' PS Baird said. 'If we find something in your system that would explain your lack of memory then that will take us a long way. Without it, we can't prove you were drugged, and Liam has a video where you're not unconscious but moving and responding to his speech.'

'But I didn't know what I was doing!'

'Which is why we're going to check the CCTV from Princes Street, see if we can track the taxi you got into and get a statement from the driver. You were feeling ill and not behaving normally by then, so maybe he'll have noticed something. Has Liam contacted you personally since last weekend?'

'Just a text message,' Quinn said. She took out her phone and read the message out. 'It's like he doesn't even realise what he did to me.'

The look on PS Baird's face told the whole story. The text message made proving the case harder rather than easier.

'Quinn, I don't want you to think this is a waste of time,' PS Baird said.

'Are you going to arrest him?' Quinn's mother asked.

'Not yet. I need to get the results of the tests back before I interview him.'

'So you'll definitely arrest him after that?' Quinn's mother continued.

'Not necessarily. Once we've gathered all the evidence, I'll run the case by the Procurator Fiscal's office. They'll make a decision as to whether there are grounds for charging him, and one of the things they'll take into account is whether or not a conviction is likely.'

'What's your gut feeling?' Quinn's mother asked. PS Baird

hesitated. 'Come on, you're the expert. My daughter's put herself on the line here.'

'If there's no medical or forensic evidence then it's going to be Quinn's word against Liam's and in those cases it can be hard to persuade a jury that they can be certain enough to convict. That doesn't mean we won't try, and it certainly doesn't mean that we don't believe you. The process is harsh.'

'I didn't agree to have sex with him,' Quinn said. 'I don't care if you believe me or not. He threatened to put the video on social media. Why would I willingly have sex with a man like that?' Quinn stood and began frantically pulling on her coat.

'It's very frustrating. We feel the same. It's our job to prove everything. He can sit back and watch us chase our tails. But please don't give up. Let's go through the process and see how far we get. Okay? I'll keep in touch. Just hang on in there.'

They left. Neither of them said a word during the journey home because there was nothing to say. Quinn wasn't sure what she'd expected, but not the brick wall she'd hit already.

They waited the right number of days then Quinn provided the hair sample as requested. PS Baird kept in touch to see how the family were doing, offered to help arrange counselling. A support group called to see if Quinn wanted to join. Liam waited two more weeks before he contacted her again. The message came at midnight as she lay sleepless, wondering what she could find in the medicine cabinet that would knock her out.

Hey, I miss you. You never replied to my last message. I hope you're not angry with me. Can we talk? I'm sure we can patch things up.

Quinn lobbed her mobile across the room and screamed into her pillow. She wanted to call her uncle and tell him Liam's address. She wanted to call Liam herself and tell him exactly what she thought of him. She wanted to take a knife and cut that smug grin off his face. She wanted to get the bottle of brandy her parents only ever used to set the Christmas pudding alight and drink it all.

PS Baird had told her to keep a record of any contact made. Screen shots, notes, voicemails. Save it, let the police know. Under no circumstances should she respond to any of it. That was the key thing, or it might jeopardise the case. Only there was no news about the case. No progress. Quinn knew nothing about the law, but she wasn't a fool. It wasn't fair. Liam should be the one feeling stressed and scared. He should be spending sleepless nights worrying about an arrest. He should know that she was prepared to face him in a courtroom.

Quinn got out of bed and stormed across the room.

Reported you to police. You're under investigation for rape. Don't contact me again.

Forty-eight hours later Quinn was back at the police station accompanied by her father. PS Baird met her at the front door, offering smiles and warmth but Quinn was cold. The chill had crept in some days earlier although she was unable to identify the precise moment. She couldn't shake it. Nothing helped. No amount of hot baths or bed covers could stop her shivering.

They were taken through to the family suite where comfortable sofas and hot tea were waiting. A man joined them after a minute, in his forties but prematurely grey, with smeared glasses that spoke of too many hours reading late at night.

'I'm John Raskin from the Procurator Fiscal's office,' he said. 'PS Baird referred this case to me to make a decision about prosecuting Liam Cook for rape.'

Simeon McTavish reached out and held his daughter's hand. 'I hope it's good news,' he said.

'There were some problems with the evidence,' Raskin replied. And that was that. Whatever he said afterwards, Quinn knew it wasn't going to make any difference.

'Isn't it your job to make sure there aren't any problems with the evidence?' her father asked. 'My daughter was raped. She came to you people for help. I don't want to hear about problems. I want you to tell me what you're going to do to make this work.'

'Mr McTavish, the lab couldn't find any drugs in either Quinn's blood or urine. Too much time had passed and the dosage can't have been high enough to have remained in Quinn's system. I would guess that Liam had read up on it and made sure he didn't deliver the video until he was sure there'd be no forensic evidence in the event that you reported him. The hair sample was inconclusive. It often is in cases that involve the use of Rohypnol, which is what we suspect he gave you. If we can't prove that Quinn was drugged, then the consent she appeared to give on the video would be extremely problematic for a jury.'

'What about witnesses?' Quinn asked softly.

'We traced the taxi driver who took you from Princes Street to Liam's address. He says you looked tired but fine and he got the impression that you and Liam were a couple. He reports seeing you were kissing at one point and that there was no suggestion you were being coerced. That doesn't mean he was right, only that he saw what he expected to see. Unfortunately it means that there are no witnesses to corroborate your version of events. Then there was the text message you sent him. Please don't take this as a criticism, Quinn. We completely understand the frustration that victims feel when they're going through this process.'

'How . . . how did you know about that?' she asked.

'Liam turned up at the police station the next morning,' PS Baird explained. 'He asked to speak with me, showed me the message and said he wanted to clarify matters.'

'He was manipulating you,' Quinn's father growled.

'I'm sure that's right, but he offered to make a statement and be questioned under caution without a lawyer present. In the circumstances, it would have been counter-productive to have refused. I have the interview on this laptop for you to view, but don't feel you have to.'

'Show me,' Quinn said.

'Sweetheart, I'm not sure this is—' Her father took her hand but she slipped hers back out of his grasp.

'I brought it on myself, Dad. I may as well know what he said.'

PS Baird dispensed with the legalities at the beginning of the video, and suddenly there he was. The good-looking face Quinn had once believed she loved, leaning forward, eager to listen and to help, nodding sagely as the officer explained that he wasn't obliged to speak with them or answer questions, checking that he understood the caution, advising him that he really should have a lawyer present. Liam was the picture of polite concern and grave concentration.

'Why don't you explain what happened the day you bumped into Quinn at the bookshop?' PS Baird suggested.

'Sure, I was in the cookery section browsing for a present. I'm useless at gifts so books always seem like a safe bet.' He gave a rueful smile that made Quinn feel nauseous. 'Quinn came round a corner and pretty much bumped into me. Things had been awkward, I'd behaved like a bit of a jerk when we'd temporarily split up but I'd made the decision to give her some space. Actually it was a bit painful meeting her like that. I was pretty emotionally invested in our relationship. Quinn's amazing. Not the kind of girl I ever expected to end up with.'

'In what way?' PS Baird asked.

'She's smart, funny, kind and has absolutely no idea how cool she is. Nothing fake about her. Most girls these days are plastered in makeup and false eyelashes, but Quinn never needed any of that. She's real.'

'Okay, so back to the bookshop. What happened next?'

'We chatted for a while. One of us – I'm not sure who – suggested coffee and it seemed like a good idea. I remember Quinn saying she'd be glad to take a seat as her feet were aching. She got a table while I bought coffee and we sat down by a window and talked. I was under the impression that she was enjoying my company. She seemed relaxed and was smiling a lot. Have you checked the CCTV footage from the store? They must have cameras.'

'We have, in fact,' PS Baird said.

'Thank god, then they'll bear out everything I've just told you. Did the footage show me doing anything wrong or illegal?'

PS Baird paused. 'No, the CCTV didn't capture anything we would regard as part of a criminal act, but the view in the cafe area was limited and we wouldn't necessarily have been able to see any . . .' She considered her choice of words. '. . . Small actions.'

'You see? No criminal act.' He put his hands out in a gesture somewhere between protesting his innocence and asking for sympathy. PS Baird didn't respond. 'Anyway, we were chatting for so long that we both wanted another drink. I had plans but I still had just about enough time to make it to my girlfriend's later that afternoon. I can give you her name so you can double-check that. It's Aspen Gibbs. I'll look up her mobile number for you when we're done.'

'I'd appreciate that.'

'Not a problem. Anyway I bought a second round of coffees, and that's when Quinn started feeling ill, which was awkward because I needed to leave by then but I didn't feel able to go. She was looking a bit wobbly and I felt bad. It's quite a journey back to Gorebridge.'

'The taxi driver says he saw the two of you kissing in the car. Why do you think Quinn went from feeling so ill she couldn't get herself home, to wanting to be that close to you?'

'Honestly, I don't know. I was looking after her, feeling very protective. And I . . . Listen, I don't want to say anything that'll make Quinn out to be a liar. I care about her too much.'

'You've come here to talk, Mr Cook. This is your opportunity to give your version of events. Go ahead,' PS Baird said.

'Well, I wasn't sure she was quite as unwell as she was saying she was. I don't mean that in a bad way. We'd had a really good time together, I'd mentioned my new girlfriend, and then all of a sudden Quinn needed help, needed my arm around her, head on my shoulder in the car and then I turned to speak with her and she just kissed me. I wish I could tell you I was a stronger man, but I couldn't resist her. She drives me kind of crazy.' Liam gave a lopsided grin and ran his hand through his hair. 'I was as surprised as you when she started kissing me.'

'He didn't mention his girlfriend until later,' Quinn said. 'I was already feeling ill by then.'

'But you do remember him mentioning her in the context of being a new girlfriend?' Raskin asked.

Quinn flushed and nodded.

'What happened when you got back to your flat?' PS Baird asked Liam.

'I helped her up the stairs – it's on the first floor over a retail unit – then I put her on my sofa. At that stage I realised there was no way I was going to make it to my girlfriend's and I'll be honest with you, after that kiss I didn't feel like I could face Aspen anyway. I went to get Quinn a glass of water and I messaged Aspen while I was in the kitchen.'

He took his mobile from his pocket and passed it over the interview room desk.

'For the record, I'm reading a text message sent from Mr Cook's mobile to a contact named "Aspen" dated a week ago on Saturday at 4.46 p.m. It says, *Hi Babe, Sorry I can't get there today. Bumped into old friend in town. Call you tonight. Make it up to you x.'* PS Baird handed the mobile back. 'Continuing, what happened next?'

'Quinn seemed half asleep when I took her the water so I put the glass on a table next to the sofa. She didn't look that comfortable so I went into my bedroom to get a blanket to put over her. I'd thought about putting her in my bed, but I didn't want her to wake up there and think I was trying to take advantage.'

'What the hell is this rubbish?' Quinn's father asked. 'He's painting himself as some sort of saint, and it looks like you're falling for it.'

'I had to let him go through it, Mr McTavish,' PS Baird explained. 'Can you imagine a jury being told the defendant turned up voluntarily at the police station and the officer in the case refused to speak to him?'

Back on the screen, PS Baird was making notes before asking her next question. Liam was looking more relaxed than ever but stopped short of smug.

'Did you put the blanket over her?' PS Baird asked.

'I tried but she pushed it off and put her arms around me. One thing led to another. We started kissing again, took each other's clothing off, I guess by then we were on the floor. And I – shit, this isn't great – I asked her if I could video us. You've got to understand, I was missing her and I honestly thought from the way she was acting that our relationship was fully back on. She agreed, and I was careful about it, you know? I even did a consent check while the video was going. She was a bit distracted because by then we were properly going for it, but she definitely agreed. We were moving around, changing position – this is all a bit embarrassing – but she certainly didn't mention feeling ill while we were having sex. It was amazing. I guess all in all it was about half an hour.'

'Did you use a condom?' PS Baird asked.

'I did. I'm too young to be a dad, and there are a lot of STDs out there. Better safe than sorry.'

'What happened afterwards?'

'We both got dressed and we were tired. We cuddled on the sofa for a while and Quinn fell asleep. I wanted to tidy up and I had some housework to do so I didn't wake her. When she woke up, she seemed a bit out of sorts again. I wasn't sure if she was ill or just regretting what we'd done and maybe worried about telling her family and friends that we'd got back together. Anyway, I drove her home. By then she said she was sick and wanted to get out of the car before we got into her road. I tried to persuade her to let me get her to her door but she was insistent,' Liam said.

'And you didn't think that was a strange way for her to end the evening after you'd had sex?'

'Look, Quinn's family and friends are her Achilles' heel. She gets stressed just talking about them. She didn't even tell them she was seeing someone to start with. I felt like a dirty little secret. The impression I got was that no one was ever going to be good enough. The uncle and the boss had made positive efforts to split us up and that was when everything was going fine. I know you want to ask me about the video I sent them. I came here today to explain that. It was a poor choice, I know, but I wanted them to see that we were back together and that we were in love. I suppose I knew Quinn would find it hard to make them see the truth.'

'You threatened to put the footage on social media if they didn't watch it all the way through,' PS Baird noted.

'Yes, I may have worded that badly. I meant as in, if they didn't watch it then I'd send them the file via a social media app instead. I didn't really mean that I'd post it publicly. I'd never do that to Quinn, and honestly I don't want my private life splashed all over the internet. I realised later that they may have got the wrong impression,' he said.

'Why send the footage with a courier?'

'I was worried about there being physical conflict if I turned up in person. It seemed a less confrontational way to do it.'

'Where's the video footage now?' PS Baird asked.

'I deleted it when the courier delivered my mobile back to me. I felt bad by then, realised I'd gone about proving our relationship in a clumsy way, and Quinn didn't return my text. I figured the best thing to do was to make sure no one else would ever see it. Please tell her it's gone. I don't want her to be worried about it.'

Quinn let out a laugh she could no longer contain.

'Would you be willing to allow us to inspect your mobile to check for the footage and take a copy if we find it?'

'Absolutely,' Liam said, handing his phone over again. 'Anything you need. The PIN code is 1010.'

PS Baird took a moment to pull an evidence bag from her pocket, slipped on gloves, and put the phone inside.

'Mr Cook, did you administer any drugs to Quinn McTavish at any stage?'

'No way. I'm in love with her. The last thing I'd do is hurt her.'

'Did you have sex with her without her consent, video her without her consent, and give her drugs that prevented her from giving her consent?'

'This is awful. I hadn't realised how bad the pressure on her was. I feel terrible that she's having to say things like this,' he said.

'Could you answer the question, Mr Cook?'

'I didn't and I wouldn't do that. Not to Quinn and not to any woman ever. Best will in the world, I've never had to drug a woman to get sex out of them.'

PS Baird stared at him from her position across the interview room. Liam stared back.

'Did you buy the recipe book if that was why you were in the shop?' PS Baird asked.

Liam frowned and took a moment to think about it, giving a brief glance into the camera. Quinn could have sworn he knew she'd be watching.

'No,' he said.

'So you weren't particularly intent on buying the book then?' PS Baird continued.

'Not at all. It's true that I'd forgotten to purchase it while I was with Quinn but I remembered once I got back from dropping her home. I ordered it online that night and sent it off to my aunt the next day. I can show you the receipt and give you my aunt's name and address. Would that help?' He gave PS Baird a quick wink.

'Smug bastard,' Simeon McTavish muttered.

Quinn stood. 'He raped me,' she said. 'And you're not to going to do a thing about it. I'd like to go home now please, Dad.'

'Aye, sweetheart,' he said, standing up and slipping his jacket over his daughter's shoulders. 'Let's go.'

Chapter Twenty-Nine

The Balmoral Hotel overlooked the commuters who raced in and out of Waverley Station, its clock lying about the time with the intention of getting travellers to their trains with three minutes to spare. Callanach wandered into Bar Prince looking for Dr Connie Woolwine who was already there, head stuck in a book. Even from a distance the air she gave off was pure Americana. An elaborate belt buckle attached to a worn brown leather strap topped legs clad in faded denim, stretched out as if she were relaxing in her own lounge, white linen shirt untucked and just slightly crumpled, hair long and loose with a tan that had no hint of bottle about it.

She didn't bother to stand when she saw him, just waved him over to join her with a lazy smile.

'It's Callanach, right? Funny, you don't sound Scottish. Can I order you something?'

'Luc, and coffee would be great. My father was Scottish but my mother's French. I lived in France until I transferred here a couple of years ago. Thanks for agreeing to meet me. I understand you're checking out today.'

Woolwine motioned towards a barman and pointed at the

coffee pot he was holding. 'Yes, a friend of mine is leaving the Met police. Today's his last day and I said I'd take him out to dinner, which is really just a cover for the fact that I have a proposal for him.'

'No such thing as a free lunch,' Callanach said. A steaming cup of coffee appeared miraculously in front of him. 'What's the proposal?'

'I'd like us to work together. He's a better investigator than people give him credit for and he brings out the best in me. We don't find those people very often. It takes a combination of intellectual compatibility, egos that don't clash, plus that chemistry it's impossible to properly define. Anyway, if you need me I'll be in the UK for a few more days.' She sipped from a bottle of water. 'How can I help you?'

'The trigger,' Callanach said. 'You said there'd be one. I want to know more about it. Any examples if you have one, how it would work, why the target might be first responders. We're so used to patterns in police work that it's hard to investigate a case without them. If there's a rape we're usually looking for someone who started with lower level sexual offences like indecent exposure. Psychopaths usually have a history of disturbed behaviour with animals or generalised cruelty. It occurred to me that I'd never considered a trigger in a serial offences case. A one-off, like killing in self-defence, I understand. Not this.'

'Killing in self-defence isn't a trigger, it's a reaction. It's momentary and switches itself off again naturally when the danger's passed. The trigger you're looking for is one that has caused a factory reset inside the killer's brain. It's not an impulse or a reaction. It's bigger than that, and it has fundamentally altered the killer's perception of the world around them, what's right and what's wrong, and destroyed the normal social constraints that make us law-abiding citizens.'

'Where does free will come into it?'

'Very few killers truly have free will. Most are simply responding to what their brain is telling them they want or need. They can no more switch it off than you and I can stop feeling hungry when we haven't eaten for a day. The best example of when that's not true is when siblings conspire to kill their parents to access their inheritance early. That's not a response to a trigger, it's not psychopathy – not usually anyway – it's avoidable and intellectually constructed. See also when automotive companies decide not to recall a line of cars they know is faulty because the recall will cost more than any damages they'll have to pay when five people in a hundred thousand die as a statistical consequence.'

'But free will when there's been a trigger?' Callanach asked.

'You're asking so you understand his criminal culpability?' He nodded. 'That's tough to answer. If the trauma runs deep enough then sometimes the only other option is suicide. The most fundamental trigger is when a young child witnesses a parent systematically abusing and then killing the other parent. It can actually alter the functionality of that child's brain so their pathway to psychopathy is something of an inevitability unless serious intervention takes place to teach avoidance and self-control. Radically changing an adult though, which the Edinburgh bomber obviously is, takes an even greater force. You're looking for someone so deeply damaged that other people may not have survived what they went through. You hungry?'

'No,' he said, 'but please go ahead. You said this person would be crazed but not crazy. I get the principle but I don't see what the neurological difference is.'

'Could I get some olives, humous and pitta bread please?' she asked a passing waiter. 'Luc, what's the single most traumatic thing you've ever experienced?' He sat back. Sharp intake of breath. 'I have very few boundaries. Hazard of the job.

217

Psychologists are either super-sensitive or totally blunt. If you really want to understand what your bomber is going through, all you can do is bring the experience as close to a real-life event you've experienced as possible. You can trust me.'

He finished his coffee and waited until he was ready to tell it. 'When I was working at Interpol, I was falsely accused of rape by a female colleague. I was arrested, put on leave, jailed for a while before the trial. My friends deserted me, even my mother, although she had her reasons. The evidence was problematic. My accuser had . . .' he swallowed hard, '. . . injured herself internally. I'd been out on a date with her, she hadn't wanted me to leave her apartment and she'd attacked me so I'd defended myself. We both had injuries. I didn't tell anyone about it, in fact I lied to my best friend who also worked with us, saying I got hurt in an accident. Technically, it ended when she failed to turn up for the trial but by then it was too late to clear my name. I ran away from France, came back to the country where I was born, and had to start all over again. It was—'

'You don't need to find an adjective to describe that experience,' Woolwine said. 'There probably isn't one. Was it your face that made her obsessed with you? You're physically perfect. Hard to live a normal life when you stand out like that.'

'I suppose so,' he said.

'Sometimes disfigurements come in the most surprising forms,' Woolwine said. 'What do you see when you look at yourself in the mirror now?'

Callanach thought about it. 'I see my past. I see a liability. When I was young I used my looks to get whatever I wanted. It feels like I've been paying for it ever since.'

'And in your darkest hours, what did it feel like inside your head? Really get yourself back there for a moment. The things you never told anyone, the revenge you fantasised about taking. The fury inside you. Emotional pain is largely comprised of guilt, fury, humiliation and loss. You didn't have the guilt, but the rest of those emotions would have been overwhelming, particularly during incarceration.'

'Just fantasises,' he said. 'Nothing I'd have acted on, but they were very real to me at the time.'

'What?' she asked.

'I wanted to kill the woman who accused me. I remember thinking about how I'd do it, how I'd get away with it, what I'd say to her before I did it. The fantasy changed almost every time I thought about it. Revenge on my friends, too, not hurting them but proving them wrong and humiliating them the way I'd been humiliated. I wanted them to know how it felt to lose everything. Damage their reputations, let them know how it felt to walk into a room where no one's willing to meet your eyes. To feel judged before having a chance to explain yourself. When the allegation's rape, people look at you as if you might infect them. I wanted them all to suffer. I – this is terrible – I imagined them being told they had terminal diseases. I'm not sure this is helpful.'

'Luc?' Woolwine waited for him to escape the memories. 'Was it helpful for a short time though? Did those fantasies allow you to process your own emotions and continue to function? Did they serve a purpose?'

'I suppose they kept me sane,' he said. The waiter set down the plate of food. 'Could I get more coffee?' Luc asked.

'It kept you sane for a very specific reason,' Woolwine said. Her voice was uncharacteristically gentle. 'You had over-whelming emotions and nowhere to put them. Do you know what happens when we don't role play and fantasise away our emotions? Mental illness happens. We think role play is some-thing children do with dolls or when they talk through the stories in picture-books. Really, those are just stepping stones to teach us how to use our imagination as adults. We never stop using storytelling to process our experiences and our feelings. We just learn to do it silently, on the train to work, in our car, in the bath, as we're folding the laundry. Most of the time we're running through past or future scenarios that feel either stressful or unfinished. That's how we prepare and process. Extreme scenarios, like the one you experienced, prompt the most vivid fantasies for processing purposes. What went on in your head may not have been pretty but it was absolutely necessary. People who find it hard to use their imagination get frustrated fast, faster than the rest of us, and the information they're trying to process can come out as a non-imagined reaction. It spills over into the real world, and then people actually do get hurt. Are you okay?'

'Actually, yes,' he said. 'I've never talked about that before. It helps to hear that it was . . . can I say, normal?'

'Most definitely. Your fantasies were normal. Your processing of it was normal. You're through to the other side.'

'I think I finally am,' he said. 'So where does that get us with our bomber? How does my experience relate to his?'

'You're not done yet. Now I'm going to ask you to do something even more stressful. I want you to imagine that your life raft never came. Your accuser turned up to the trial and she gave evidence. She was amazing. There were tears, she couldn't look you in the face, could barely get the words out at the crucial point. It was an Oscar-worthy performance. You had to watch as the prosecutor detailed all of the injuries, the way you allegedly treated her. Your best friend would have been called to explain the lies you told. You were convicted, sentenced and would be starting to serve what?'

'Probably around twelve years,' Callanach said.

'Twelve years. Not easy having been in law enforcement. You'd have been on a special wing with sexual offenders only, with those people you dedicated yourself to putting behind those very bars. Few visitors. Who would want to be associated with you? Maybe your mother would have come around eventually, but who knows? All for a crime you didn't commit. You told the truth. Your life is over, not just while you're serving the sentence but you know how it'll be when you get out. If you get out alive. An Interpol agent and a convicted rapist? How long before someone slips a knife into you in the shower?'

Callanach was breathing hard.

'But it's the injustice of it that's the trigger, because it's always the thing you can't come to terms with that breaks you. The fantasies aren't enough. They no longer help you process the endless stream of emotions. You can't get out. You can't get help. The nightmare is everywhere, every moment, and you are powerless. Then, all of a sudden, you escape. You're free physically but everything you're feeling follows you. There's this moment when you don't know anymore what's fantasy and what's reality, but you do know that you're in pain all the time. Even while you sleep. Without realising it, you're broken psychologically. Nothing feels wrong because nothing feels real. The consequences of your actions don't matter because all you can think about is stopping the pain, and are you dead or alive? Half the time you're not really sure.'

'Sorry, could we stop?' he asked.

'Sure,' she said. 'Just look at me for a moment. Luc, look me right in the eyes.' He did as she told him, glad to have only to follow instructions. 'This isn't your reality. It's a pathway to understand someone else's. Remember it. Use it. Then let it go.'

He stared at the full coffee cup in front of him as if it had appeared from nowhere. He had no memory of the waiter coming back and pouring him a refill. He'd been in a French prison, dying a twenty-four-hour death each day, and losing his mind.

'I'm not sure what I'd have been capable of,' he said.

221

'Bullshit,' Woolwine told him.

Callanach shrugged. 'I'd have been dangerous when I got out. The anger would have taken me. More likely, I'd have found a way to take my own life.'

'But what if you were too angry to take your own life? If your mind wouldn't let you do that until you'd dealt with whatever had happened to you. What might you have been capable of then?'

'Still not the things the Edinburgh bomber has done. I couldn't do anything that evil.'

'Here's the truth, and you've earned it. No one knows what they're capable of until they actually go through the process of breaking down mentally. No one can predict what the people around them are capable of, either. The Edinburgh bomber may not have been a good person before this process started. Not a criminal necessarily. Not a killer, probably. Just not the sort of person you'd want in your dorm room at college, or moving into the apartment across the hall. Or he might have been your average Joe, nice as pie. There are no rules governing this.' She checked her watch. 'I should go. My train to London leaves in thirty minutes. Time for one last question though, if you're desperate?'

'Yes,' Callanach said. 'How can you tell if someone is about to break?'

'Got anyone in mind?' Woolwine asked.

'Not particularly.'

'They may start cutting ties, becoming distant. Self-care will suffer. Their usual routines will become irrelevant. Often they'll practise avoidance of the people they love, and the places they're rooted in because those things are too painful.'

'How do you stop it?'

Connie Woolwine scribbled her initials onto her bar tab and stood. 'You stop it with love, persistence, honesty, and by making yourself as vulnerable to them as they feel to the rest of the world. Nothing says "I love you" like being prepared to go down with the sinking ship. You've got my number. Call if you need me. And sorry in advance for the insomnia. It should fix itself in a couple of nights. Take care, Luc.'

Chapter Thirty

Ava and DS Lively were wearing the white protective suits that had become second sets of clothes to them. The garage was cold and smelled of engine oil and chemicals. Forensic vehicle examination was a specialist field. First of all the vehicle had to be checked for fingerprints, DNA and trace evidence, then the plates and chassis number needed cross-referencing, and finally the engineering itself occasionally yielded results.

'Give me something I can use,' Ava told the lead forensic investigator.

'This is a Suzuki RM125. The paintwork has been covered in matte black, badly, but the original paint is still underneath. New, it would have been bright yellow. You've got the usual problem we have with bikes. They're open to the elements, the driver wears gloves, legs tend to rub off a lot of prints, and apart from that, when they're parked other people have a fascination with them, so you'll find endless random fingerprints and skin cells.'

'What about the plates and chassis number?' Lively asked.

'The licence plate is a homemade effort and it's not linked to a motorbike at all. Chassis number is more interesting and shows that the main body of the vehicle was scrapped two years ago. There's damage consistent with that, too. This bike wasn't ever intended to get very far. Someone bought it, put on a couple of new tyres, made sure the tracking was okay and did an amateur job of getting it roadworthy. Whoever you're looking for in relation to this offence is not a professionally qualified mechanic, but they've got some basic skills.'

'That'll reduce the lists of suspects then,' Lively sniped.

'Did you find anything personal on the bike?' Ava asked, cutting Lively off before he could go full throttle into sarcasm.

'No panniers, no bag attached. Just a keyring but the provenance is unknown. It could have been with the keys since the bike was first purchased or added by a later owner. You want to see it?'

'Please,' Ava said. The investigator wandered off to a locked evidence area. 'You know, Lively, it's no one's fault that we're struggling to get any leads. It doesn't help when you put people's backs up.'

'Ma'am, with all due respect, this is fucked up. How many officers are working on this now? A couple of hundred. And what have we got to show for it? Edinburgh's under siege. This may be the first time I've ever agreed with the bottom-feeders who make up the headlines each day.'

'All we can do is work the scenes and gather the evidence, same as any other crime. The scale is different, and it may be personal for a lot of us, but the way we work the case doesn't change,' Ava said.

'Someone out there knows something,' Lively said. 'Why has there been no public appeal? If ever people had a reason to help the police it's now. No one's safe.'

'You think a public appeal will work? I agree that someone knows or suspects something, but what am I going to say that would make a person currently sitting on useful information come forward if they haven't already?'

'So scare them into action. Threaten that if they don't disclose information and we find out later, they can be charged with acting as an accomplice or something.'

'I can't lie and I don't think we should threaten people. If we make the bomber nervous, he may just decide to get rid of everyone who might suspect him in one massive blast. You heard what Dr Woolwine said. He's not crazy but he is crazed. We have no idea what he's going to do next. You want to light that fuse and see how it ends?'

Lively rubbed his eyes. 'No,' he said. 'But Pax Graham is dead along with plenty of others. I worry about what their families are thinking.'

'I get it,' Ava said. 'Pax is one of many reasons why we can't screw up here. I will not lose a trial because we contaminated the chain of evidence or ignored proper procedure. So put out the fire that's no doubt raging back at the station.'

'What influence have I got?' Lively asked.

Ava put a hand on his shoulder and looked him square in the eyes. 'What influence? More than anyone I know. More than the brass, that's for sure. The old crew have known you for years. You have their ears and their respect. The younger ones see you and know you've put in the years, put criminals in jail. The bullshit – your bullshit – the comments that make them laugh in briefings, the piss-taking, the insolence – that has real power. You control MIT, Detective Sergeant. I give the team orders then leave the room and they look to see your reaction before they get moving.'

'You're exaggerating—'

'The fuck I am,' Ava said. 'This is the way it's always been. Senior command has the authority, but it's the officer right next to you, kneeling on the floor, hands in the blood, turning over the body, who you trust. Nothing happens without your say-so in MIT. If you and I didn't get on the way we do, I might be concerned about that. For now, I need you to help me out. Make sure no one cuts corners. No one makes free with their fists to get that bit extra out of a suspect. Lead the pack. Can I trust you to do that for me?'

Lively shrugged. 'You can trust me for anything, ma'am. You know that. I've worked under a few DCIs now. Most of them I've been lucky enough to call friends. You're as good as any of them, better than many. I know I joke around. It's just how it has to be.'

'I wouldn't have it any other way,' Ava said. She smiled. 'Thank you.'

'Here you go,' the investigator turned up carrying an evidence bag. 'It's been through forensics already so you don't need to worry about blurring any prints. The key was still in the ignition when the bike was dropped.'

Lively took the key ring.

'The bike itself,' Ava asked. 'Was it still in working order? It hadn't run out of petrol or burst a tyre?'

'No, as I said, it was in rudimentary condition but still drivable when we seized it.'

'So the driver – we're assuming the killer – could have left the area on it rather than on foot?'

'Absolutely,' the investigator said.

Lively passed Ava the keyring. There was only a single key attached by a small chain to a plastic section with the capital S of the Suzuki logo inside it, the paper slightly discoloured on the edges.

'How old's the bike?' Lively asked.

'First sold in 2007, so the value was low even before it was scrapped.'

'And is this the type of keyring that would have been handed out with the bike when it was first sold?' Ava asked.

'Depends on the garage,' the investigator said. 'Quite often

227

the original seller hands out a keyring with their own branding on it. I can tell you that this bike was first sold by a dealer in Wallyford. They're still operating. Might be worth contacting them.'

Lively drove as if there was another bomb on a countdown, and Ava didn't ask him to go slower. Instead, she flicked on the blues and twos to give other traffic fair warning that they were in a hurry. Emergency or not, every second counted. At some point they might be glad to have rushed when they could.

DS Lively hesitated at the door.

'You all right?' Ava asked.

'Not much of a fan of bikes, if I'm honest,' he said. 'Every young man's dream in my day – not to be sexist, but there weren't many women motorcyclists at the time. I put that down to women being the more sensible of the sexes.'

'Did you ever have one?' Ava asked.

'No, but my older brother did. I was at home with my ma when the call came to say he'd hit a patch of oil on the road.'

'Oh god, I'm sorry, did he—'

'Survived. Lost his left leg from the knee down. Nowadays I reckon they'd be able to save it. Back then, though . . . poor kid was only twenty-two. I worshipped him. Seeing him like that was the worst thing I thought I'd ever have to deal with. If police work gives you nothing else, it gives you perspective.'

'You want to stay out here? I can do this. Wait in the car.'

'Will I fuck wait in the car,' Lively said.

Ava couldn't help but smile. 'Will I fuck wait in the car, ma'am,' she corrected him.

Lively grinned and opened the door for her.

The manager was wearing a leather jacket that might have fit him a few years and a few burgers earlier, but somehow he still just about carried off biker coolness. They introduced themselves and showed their ID. Ava fished the evidence bag with the keyring from her pocket.

'You sold the bike this came with to its original owner back in 2007. I appreciate you probably weren't here then, but do you know if it would have been sold with this exact keyring at the time?'

'Just to clarify, there's no suggestion that we were in any way negligent or committed any offence?' the manager checked.

Ava tried not to roll her eyes. There was defensive then there was paranoid. 'Just the keyring, that's all we're interested in, for information only,' she said.

'Good. Don't want any trouble with the law. Can I take it out of the bag?'

'I'd have to ask you to put gloves on,' Ava replied. She handed him a pair and he slipped them on before taking the keyring out of the bag.

'It's possible this keyring was handed over as-is. A lot of people took these apart and put their own things in. Originally, I'd have expected the Suzuki logo one side and the dealer's logo on the other. The second side of this is blank. Waste of advertising space. All you had to do was slip your nail between the two sections of plastic, separate the two sides and pull them apart.'

There was a faint snapping sound then the keyring was in pieces in his hands.

'Bloody bollocks,' Lively said. 'It was worth coming here after all.'

'Did I help?' the manager asked, cheeks glowing.

'I think you did,' Ava said. 'Just like finding the hair in the battery pack.' She held up the section of photo booth print with a young woman's face visible, the other half ripped away. 'No mistakes, no coincidences. He wanted us to find it. Now we just have to figure out who she is and why she was important enough to end up in here.'

They raced back to the station, Ava issuing orders by phone the whole way. Back in the incident room, the team were sitting at their desks working while surrounded by half-consumed packets of prawn crackers and cartons of steaming Chinese food that made Ava's stomach rumble noisily. Every spare hand had a fork or chopsticks in it. Lively grabbed the nearest food container and dived in without bothering to ascertain the contents.

'Ma'am, tell your friend thank you. I'd forgotten what decent food tastes like,' DC Swift said through a mouthful of noodles. He passed Ava a handwritten note.

Just because I'm confined to my bed doesn't mean I can't order takeout, and I was feeling sorry for your team. When did you last let them eat? Whatever you're doing, however busy you are, pick up some food and consume it. That's an order. Somewhere there's a chilli beef with your name on it, and a death threat for anyone who tries to steal it from you. Natasha x

Ava took a deep breath and controlled rising tears, issued Natasha a silent thank you, and began the search for her food before she prepared a media briefing.

Chapter Thirty-One

BEFORE

That stupid bitch, Police Sergeant Baird, who'd interviewed him needed to be taught a lesson. It had been no contest since the second he'd smiled at her. Women, generally speaking, were pathetic. Quinn was the only one who'd ever broken the mould. Police Scotland had returned his mobile and found nothing incriminating on it. He'd cleaned the memory thoroughly before taking it with him. It was no good just deleting a file. So many people had no idea just how much the police could get from a phone's memory. Liam did a complete wipe and reset regularly, even if that meant getting a new SIM and changing his number. It didn't take a particularly technical brain to be able to follow instructions to the letter.

Quinn was the one who'd suffered. The police either hadn't believed her, or they knew the prospects of getting a conviction against him were so low that they weren't going to put her through a trial. It had been an exciting prospect, standing opposite Quinn in a courtroom, the jurors looking from him to her. A battle of wits and believability.

It wasn't going to happen now. He'd been too clever. The police had phoned his aunt and checked his story about her birthday and the cookery book. After that, they contacted Aspen who'd confirmed every arrangement, every text message, and the details of their wonderful new relationship to which he appeared utterly committed. As far as Aspen was concerned, Quinn had made up the rape allegation to punish Liam for ending their relationship. His new girlfriend didn't need to know about the sex tape. She was convenient, and she didn't mind him doing things to her that Quinn would have thought degrading, but that was where his fascination with Aspen ended.

As bad as he felt for Quinn, it wasn't as if a rape charge would have been justified. All the time they were chatting in the bookshop, she'd been smiling at him, teasing, flirting. When he and Quinn had kissed in the taxi, she hadn't pushed him away. Sure, she'd been compliant during sex, but that was pretty much how she'd been the first time too. And she'd enjoyed it. He'd been with enough women to know whether they really wanted it or not. The Rohypnol had just sealed the deal. She might as well have taken her knickers off the second he'd apologised for being a jerk. That was all she'd been holding out for. It wouldn't be long until she forgave him again. What he needed to do now was show her that he wasn't going anywhere.

She'd blocked his number, which was sweet. He'd changed his SIM and got a new number. They danced around that one for a while before she changed her number instead. Liam was careful. The messages he'd sent were non-threatening and apologetic without once admitting any specific wrongdoing. He'd talked about the good times, brought up only the best memories. If he had to kill her with kindness, then he would.

Liam proofread the letter he'd written Quinn before sealing

it into an envelope. Text messages were fast gratification, but there was something so intimate about composing a letter that made it a far more delicious experience.

Quinn, baby, you're cross with me. I wish you weren't. You must be under a lot of pressure from your family. I understand that while you're studying you can't afford your own place and have to respect their wishes. So let's keep this letter between us. I guess your uncle persuaded you to change your mobile number. Fair enough. I like the old-fashioned way of telling you how I feel.

I want you to know that Aspen and I aren't serious. Honestly, I think she's just using me to have someone fun to hang out with at weekends. We always had the best weekends, didn't we? The smallest things were special when we did them together. Remember skimming stones on Glencorse Reservoir? We wore our lips sore kissing as we picnicked. And playing hide and seek in the supermarket when they asked us to leave. I don't think I've ever laughed that hard.

I miss your laughter. Your smile. I miss it when you blush after I've paid you a compliment. I miss the way you run your fingers over the back of my neck as we drive. I hope you can see a day when we'll do those things together again. How's work? I drove past the other day and saw you.

More than anything else I want you to know I'm sorry about the misunderstanding with the police. I think we were just approaching that from different angles. All I ever wanted was to make you happy and to let you know that you're loved and respected. I think in the end we'll find that we're both searching for the same thing.

Soon, Liam x.

He pushed the paper into the envelope, thought about it, pulled it back out. Pushing a hand into his underwear, he pulled out a single hair. She would see it and think of their bodies intertwined. Dropping it into the envelope, he licked the gum and sealed it. There was no need to go to the post box. He was visiting Quinn's house this evening, but not until the sun had gone down. There was something special about sitting a few houses down from hers, in the quiet and dark.

Quinn's room had blinds rather than curtains. He caught the occasional glimpse of her through the slats as she walked around, could see the back of her head as she sat at her desk. He kept a notebook to record the household's comings and goings. Quinn's father left for work at 7.45 a.m. Monday to Friday. Home at 6 p.m. give or take a few minutes. Saturday mornings Mr and Mrs McTavish did their main shop of the week, taking Dolly with them. Quinn's mother took the baby out Tuesdays and Thursdays, presumably to some mother and baby group, leaving at 8.30 a.m. Liam wasn't sure what time she got home. He too had to leave by then for work.

Liam wasn't sure when the simple act of driving by to see if Quinn was in her bedroom had become all-consuming. A mate had agreed to swap cars with him from time to time which allowed him to watch unnoticed, but he was increasingly taking the risk of using his own vehicle. The power of watching when she had no idea he was there was addictive. At first all he'd done was invest in binoculars and spend an hour at the house after work. Then he'd begun leaving home an hour early to see if she was up yet. At weekends, when Aspen wasn't demanding attention, he was able to spend the whole evening there, climbing into the back of the car with its darkened windows. A pillow and blanket had made that experience more comfortable.

Sometimes they were all out. Those days, he would pretend to be delivering something and stand at their door. From there, he was able to see directly into the lounge. He knew which newspapers they read, and which baby toys were most played with as they were the ones left out of the box. Quinn's books were piled onto a side-table with more personal items – a hairband, her watch, a necklace – and he longed to touch them.

In the small hours, when every curtain had been long since drawn, he would let himself into the McTavish's back garden, sit on their doorstep, peer into the kitchen and imagine the evening's chatter around the dinner table. Quinn was sleeping one floor up, oblivious to the fact that it had become his habit to try the kitchen door, just to check if perhaps they'd forgotten to lock up.

Not that he had anything planned. Not that he would enter, even if he found it unlocked. Just to see. To smell her in the air.

Maybe just to know that he could – if he wanted – climb those stairs, slip gentle fingers onto her wrist, and feel her pulse as she slept.

Chapter Thirty-Two

Police Scotland's media team leapt into gear. The photo found in the keyring was going public that evening. Now Ava was waiting to enter the same hall where Overbeck had faced the press days earlier, a script in her hand and new hope in her heart. If the bomber had wanted them to find the photo, then he was laying a pathway to being identified, and it wasn't unreasonable to assume he ultimately wanted to be stopped.

The room fell silent as she entered. The lights were painfully bright in her eyes, but they needed the cameras and the booms, the online editions and TV anchors. For once, they were all on the same side.

'I'll keep this brief,' Ava began. 'At the conclusion, each media outlet will receive an email containing a photo and the official press release with a free phone number, which anyone can contact Police Scotland on to provide information.'

Ava kept her left hand in her pocket as she spoke. In it was the evidence bag containing the Suzuki keyring from which the photo had come. There was still a possibility that it was an incidental finding. The motorbike had come from a scrap yard. The bomber's attention would have been on making it drivable, and perhaps he'd never really noticed the keyring, but it didn't feel that way to Ava. The man was a stickler for detail and symbolism. The care he'd put into constructing Felicity Love's Lady Justice costume had been astounding. Then there was the hair he'd left in the battery pack. DNA tests had confirmed only that the hair was from a Caucasian female. It wasn't listed on any police database. It was possible that the hair belonged to the woman in the photo. Only time would tell.

'We're trying to ascertain the identity of this young woman.' The screen behind Ava flicked on and the photograph appeared. 'In this picture she appears to be in her twenties and Caucasian. We can't give an estimate of her height as the photo is a head-shot only, but we believe she's of slim to medium build. In this image her hair is a pale shade of blonde but that may not be natural and it may not be the same shade it is today. Her eyes appear a blue-green colour, although the photo is slightly damaged and it's hard to be certain.'

'Is she wanted in connection with the bombings?' a journalist asked.

Ava looked down at her notes. It was important to get the wording right. Too scary and the woman might not come forward, too vague and she might not be bothered.

'This young woman is wanted as a witness only. There's no suggestion that she has been involved in the planning or execution of any crimes. Her photo was obtained in the course of pursuing leads regarding the Edinburgh bomber. This woman might not even be aware that she has information that could help, but we do need to identify her, find her and talk to her. We're appealing to anyone who might recognise her, to please get in touch. Calls can be made anonymously. If you don't know her name then you can leave an address, a place of work, or a location this person frequents. The smallest piece of information might help us find her. She's not in any trouble, so please don't worry about calling.'

'Detective Chief Inspector,' a journalist from BBC Scotland called out.

'We'll be taking questions in just a minute,' the media liaison officer said.

'This can't wait,' the journalist continued.

'Her image can also be found on the Police Scotland information page and we'll be circulating it on social media, but we are asking the media to assist us with—'

'DCI Turner,' the BBC journalist shouted. 'There's a man on my mobile asking for you. He's been put through from our offices.' Ava stood. 'He says it's about the bombings and that he wants to be put on speaker.'

'Please don't do that!' Ava said.

The journalist pressed the speaker button anyway and a man's voice burst through.

'Can she hear me now?' he demanded.

'This is DCI Turner,' Ava said. 'Who am I talking to?'

'I'm the man you're looking for,' a voice came through loud and clear, with the unmistakeable metallic edge of a digital voice changer. 'I called to warn you.'

He paused.

'Warn me about what?' Ava asked.

Officers were pushing between the rows of journalists to take control of the phone handset.

'What's coming. What you brought on yourselves.'

Ava didn't want to ask the question, but there was no way to divert or deflect. 'And what is that exactly?'

'It's not over yet. Two more. Get ready.'

'Wait! Don't put the phone down. If you want us to listen to you then give us a chance—'

He was already gone, as Ava had known he would be. At

once, the room was a mass of bodies pushing to get to the door, to give the first live news update and redraft the next day's front page. Journalists climbed over chairs as photographers hurried to pack their tripods. The media liaison officer made her best attempt to get them to retake their seats and listen to the end of the briefing, but the moment was gone.

Interrupting the press conference had been the ultimate publicity stunt. The bomber's intention was not to provide a warning but to spread fear and confusion, and to flood the police switchboards with paranoid reports by a terrified populace. Brilliantly, he had also pushed the unknown woman's face to page two, nothing more than a secondary story that might or might not matter. The whole press conference had been turned on its head, playing out to only one man's advantage.

The Edinburgh bomber wanted the world's eyes on him, and he had them.

Chapter Thirty-Three

BEFORE

The courtroom wasn't particularly intimidating but the woman cross-examining Quinn most certainly was. Even the advocate working on Quinn's behalf had taken a sharp intake of breath when she'd appeared.

'Who's that?' Quinn asked.

'Felicity Love,' her advocate advised. 'I thought someone else was representing Mr Cook.'

'It's a non-harassment application, right? Give me five minutes to get up to speed,' Mrs Love said tersely. 'My colleague's car has broken down and he won't make it in time. I've been asked to cover. Won't take me long to read the brief then I'll speak with Mr Cook and we'll be good to go.'

Felicity Love was a world away from the woman Quinn thought she might grow to be. Poised and sophisticated, with ankles that would never dare wobble in her high heels and a spine that could not have been straighter, she moved fast without looking hurried.

'What's she like?' Quinn asked.

'Efficient. Let's run through what will happen so there aren't any surprises.' Her advocate was kind and softly spoken, familiar with the case and professional. Still, Quinn couldn't help but wish that Felicity Love had been on her side.

Quinn gave evidence.

'Miss McTavish, on what date did you instruct Mr Cook by letter or text to cease all communications with you?' Mrs Love's cross-examination began. It wasn't that her voice was aggressive or even unfriendly, more that the brusqueness of it made Quinn feel as if someone had set her blood on fire.

'I'm sorry?' Quinn muttered, trying to find anywhere to look that wasn't directly into Mrs Love's eyes.

'Put simply, Miss McTavish, you complain – among other things – that Mr Cook has written you letters and sent gifts. I'm asking at what point in time and through what means, you communicated to him that he should not do those things.'

Quinn looked to her own advocate for some reassurance, but she was concentrating on taking notes.

'Um, I'm not sure I really had to, I mean, it would have been obvious in the circumstances.'

'Which circumstances? I'm trying to establish a date, you see.'

'I suppose from when we first split up.'

'Thereafter, he sent you a few gifts but you did not indicate to him that those gifts were unwelcome. At that stage he was apologetic and hoping to repair the relationship?'

'I guess,' Quinn said.

'As many young men and women do, wouldn't you agree? Make a mistake, regret breaking up and do something to win their partner over.'

'Yes,' Quinn accepted.

'So not harassment at that stage, then. Just normal relationship behaviour, none of it abusive.'

'I didn't say it was harassment then,' Quinn took a sip of water.

'And then . . .' Mrs Love flicked through several pages in her brief, '. . . we come to a day when you bumped into Mr Cook in a bookshop in Edinburgh.'

Quinn nodded.

'Several days later, you alleged to the police that you'd been raped and the police declined to prosecute, correct?'

The atmosphere was stifling. The jacket she'd worn was way too hot and her tights were making Quinn's legs prickle painfully.

'Miss McTavish, could you answer Mrs Love's question, please?' the judge prompted.

'The police believed me,' Quinn said. 'But they said it would be my word against Liam's.'

'But the police had interviewed Mr Cook when he attended the station voluntarily without a lawyer and allowed them access to his mobile phone, correct?'

'He set it all up,' Quinn said. 'He followed me to that shop, invited me for coffee and put something in my drink—'

'But nothing was ever shown to have been in your blood, or your urine. Are you saying Mr Cook made up the story about buying his aunt a cookbook for a birthday present, because he might have made up the former but not the latter.'

'I don't follow,' Quinn said.

'His aunt's birthday.' Mrs Love gave a condescending smile. 'You're not saying he made that up, are you?'

'He sent the video for my boss and my uncle to see. No one wants the people they love to see those things. That's when I knew I'd been raped.' Quinn was getting angry, and it felt good.

'Surely if Mr Cook had raped you, the very last thing he would do would be to show footage of the event to those closest to you? Why expose himself to that level of legal risk?'

'He's your client. Why don't you turn around and ask him?' Quinn said.

'Miss McTavish, please simply answer the questions rather than taking that tone in my court. I can assure you it never helps,' the judge cautioned her.

Quinn's heart sank. She looked behind Mrs Love to where Liam was sitting. It would have been easier if he'd been grinning or gloating, but his face was the picture of sympathy and concern.

'Bastard,' she muttered.

'Miss McTavish, I'm not sure if that was aimed at me, Mrs Love or Mr Cook but you will not behave like that in my courtroom. If this continues, I will dispose of the case very quickly indeed,' the judge said.

'I didn't mean you, or Mrs Love,' Quinn shouted. 'Why am I being treated like I've done something wrong? I've been through hell and she's accusing me of lying about it.'

'I am simply trying to ascertain the facts, Miss McTavish. You and Mr Cook differ about the events leading up to inter-course, but he has accepted that he sent the footage to Mr Devlin and your uncle, Mr Wilson. The footage was not posted online and was destroyed shortly thereafter, and you received an apology from Mr Cook for his poor decision. He explained that he was trying to prove that you were still in a relationship, isn't that right?'

'That's what he said, but it's rubbish,' Quinn said. 'Why would he need to show both my uncle and my boss that disgusting video to prove it? He was torturing them.'

'Indeed, a poor decision that he will say reflected the strength of the feelings he had for you. So let me ask you again, you received an apology for it, did you not?'

'The apology was to stop him getting in trouble with the police and to make him look like a half-decent human being, which he definitely is not!'

243

Felicity Love ignored Quinn's raised voice and simply continued.

'Do you accept that the video was made on the day you met Mr Cook in the bookshop, rather than at some other time?'

'Yes,' Quinn muttered. 'So what?'

'So when Mr Cook said he only made the video to prove that your relationship was back on, that would fit into your timeline as being after the date the two of had paused your relationship.'

'I didn't pause anything. It was over.'

'And yet you still had coffee with him the first opportunity you got. What impression do you think that gave Mr Cook about your feelings towards him?'

Quinn glared but didn't answer.

'Very well, I'll move on to my next question,' Felicity Love said. 'Since then you say you've received ten messages from Mr Cook that you did not want, correct?'

'Exactly.'

'And were the tone of any of those messages unpleasant, threatening or abusive in any way?' Mrs Love asked.

'That's not the point. I don't want him to message me at all.'

'And he's stopped, correct? You've received no messages for at least a month.'

'I changed my mobile number so he sent a letter instead. It had a pubic hair in it. Is that abusive enough for you?'

Mrs Love took off her glasses and set them on the desk, a tiny wrinkle at the top of her nose as if she were smelling something offensive.

'You had it tested?' she asked.

'What? No. It was in the envelope. It had to be his.'

'Let's break that down. Did you see it when you first took the letter out?' Mrs Love asked.

'No, it wasn't folded into the letter itself. I read the letter, put it back in the envelope and put it away to show my parents when they got home.'

'So that letter touched your hands. Any other surface in your home?'

'I put it down on my bed while I was reading it, maybe on my table. Why?' Quinn asked.

'Because hairs – pubic hairs in this case – can adhere from other surfaces. The hair in question might have been on your bed, your table, even your hands when you touched the letter. That's possible, isn't it?'

'It was his. I know it was his. He put it in there to make me feel . . . violated.'

'Miss McTavish, isn't this just a case of you blowing hot and cold in a relationship then using every excuse to make Mr Cook look like the bad guy?' Mrs Love asked.

'He had no business writing me a letter in the first place. He put it through my door himself. There wasn't a stamp on it.'

'But he didn't knock on the door? Attempt to see you? Harass anyone who lives at your house?'

Quinn folded her arms and didn't bother to answer.

'Let me ask about the contents of the letter, then. Were there threats or anything you had cause to complain about?'

'I already said, I just don't want him writing to me at all. And that's not the only thing. He's sent messages other ways.'

'Such as?' Mrs Love asked.

'He's had other people pass me on the streets and say things like, "Your boyfriend misses you" and "He just wants you to call him". It's freaky. I don't feel safe anywhere. It's like I'm always being watched.'

'People just pass you in the street and say these things,' Mrs Love said slowly. 'Have you got any photos of those people or recordings of the things you claim they said?'

'No, I don't know they're going to say it then it's too late,' Quinn said.

'And where has this happened?'

'Once outside the shop where I work and another time in my local pub. Again when I took my baby sister to the local park.'

'But Mr Cook wasn't there, and you didn't see him in the vicinity?' Mrs Love asked.

'No, but he's obviously arranging it,' Quinn said.

'Miss McTavish, I'm going to suggest that you're either making this up or you're experiencing pressure from your family. Isn't that right?'

'No! Liam uses people, he manipulates them. If he wants something he doesn't stop until he gets it.'

'This is just a relationship gone wrong. A classic example of poor communication, of two young people unable to separate from one another, then throwing everything at each other they can. That's the reality.'

'You think I didn't make myself clear enough? Then I'll communicate it here,' Quinn said, looking behind Mrs Love to Liam. 'Stay away from me. Don't come to my house, don't write to me, don't send other people with messages. And don't you ever come near my family again or I won't be responsible for my actions. Just leave us all the fuck alone!'

'Miss McTavish, I warned you before about your language. I won't tolerate it, and I will not sit by and listen to threats being issued. You do not want to find yourself in contempt of court. If your advocate doesn't have any re-examination, I think we could all do with a break,' the judge ordered.

The case continued after the break but Quinn didn't even listen. Liam had his chance to speak and was remorseful about the footage, humble, swearing he would never make such a bad choice again. One mistake, he accepted, but only one. For the non-harassment order, the judge needed to find two. He didn't. The judgement was far from kind about Liam's part in it, but it was ambivalent about Quinn. Hardly typical of a victim, was how the judge found her demeanour. Capable of being threatening in her own right, he said. More than able to communicate clearly when she felt like it, he decided, which was what she should have done long ago if she didn't want Liam bothering her. Overall, it was a case of six of one and half a dozen of the other. He warned Liam to stay away from Quinn, and Quinn to mind her temper and steer clear of Liam.

Mrs Love didn't gloat when the application for a non-harassment order was dismissed. She didn't offer Liam any congratulations or even bother to say goodbye to Quinn's advocate. She merely threw the brief into her bag, checked her watch while looking bored and frustrated, and walked out. Chin up, head high, already on her phone as if it had all been nothing. As if Quinn were nothing. Only Liam stayed at the end, offering apologies for the way Quinn had been treated in court, explaining that he hadn't asked his advocate to behave like that. Only Liam said the words Quinn was thinking – that Mrs Love was a supercilious bitch who had no idea what it was like to be in a courtroom for the first time ever.

'Stay the fuck away from me,' Quinn told him. 'If you ever cared for me at all, I'm begging you now, please, just leave me alone.'

Chapter Thirty-Four

The building that housed the Camera Obscura attraction sat at the feet of Edinburgh Castle and at the top of Castle Hill. Tourists loved it, although the locals rarely gave it a second glance.

'You ever visited?' DS Tripp asked.

'Optical illusions aren't really my thing,' Callanach replied. 'You?'

'School trip while we were studying Edinburgh's history. As far as I can remember, the whole thing started with just one telescope. Does she know we're coming?'

'No. It was a co-worker who called the name in and they were asked to keep quiet until we'd spoken to her. Let's go.'

They cut ahead of the queue causing audible grumbling from those waiting to get in out of the rain. The young woman they were looking for was visible immediately. Her hair had changed but the piercings hadn't.

'Is that her?' Tripp asked quietly.

'Looks like it,' Callanach said. He took his ID from his pocket and held it up. 'Are you Aspen?'

She looked behind her, realised her manager was standing right there, checked the exit and took a step back.

'If you're thinking about running, don't,' Callanach said. 'We're here about a photo, that's all. Whatever else you've got going on isn't our problem.'

Her expression changed in a heartbeat.

'What photo?' Aspen asked.

Tripp held up an enlarged copy for her to see. She shrugged. 'Have you not read a newspaper or turned on the news in the last two days?' he asked.

'Excuse me, could you do this elsewhere? We've got bookings,' the manager said.

'I'm afraid we'll need to borrow Aspen for a couple of hours. Let's go,' Tripp replied.

She accompanied them to the police station and agreed to sit in an interview room so anything she said could be recorded, her status as witness only confirmed to her several times. Arms folded, poker-faced, she chewed her bottom lip. Tripp provided a drink and a packet of crisps, and broke the rules by letting her smoke, all of which was a small price to pay for the help they needed.

Callanach put on his best disarming smile and began.

'Aspen, the photo we showed you is a copy of one found in a keyring.' He handed her the evidence bag with the original photo inside. She leaned forwards to glance at it, sipping from the can. 'We had no idea who was in that photo, so we asked the press to help. We made it clear that we were only trying to ascertain your identity as a witness to help with our enquiries so your reputation will be intact.'

She gave a snort of laughter forgetting she had a mouthful of drink, and wiped liquid from her nose with her sleeve.

'I have a few questions, and I hope you don't mind that we're recording this so I don't miss anything. Stop me for a break or if you need anything, okay?'

Aspen nodded but didn't speak, swapping the can out for a cigarette and taking a leisurely first drag.

'Could you confirm your full name for me please?'

'Aspen. I go by a couple of surnames.'

'Is Lyle one of them? The person who contacted us wasn't quite sure,' Callanach said.

Aspen blew a cloud of smoke into his face. Occasionally the smell of tobacco still made Callanach want to light up himself. Today, it was simply irritating.

'Lyle might be one of them, yes.'

'So what other surname do you go by?'

She paused and made a show of thinking about it.

'Peston,' she said. 'I'd like a lawyer before I say anything else.'

'You're not under arrest and you're not in any trouble, so you really don't need a lawyer. I don't want you to feel worried about this conversation.'

'But still, I'd like a lawyer here. It would make me feel better,' she said. 'And another can of Coke would be nice.'

'Listen, Aspen, we're under some time pressure. We want to speak to you in relation to some very serious matters we believe you might be able to—'

'But lawyer first, yeah? I'm thirsty and I don't feel like talking right now,' she said.

'Do you have a lawyer in mind you'd like us to call?'

'Naw, I can't afford a bloody solicitor. I'll need you to pay the bill.' She grinned. 'Until you do, I'm not sayin' a word. Right now, I'm not even sure it's me in that photo. You give me what I want and I reckon my memory'll get a whole lot better.'

Two hours later, DS Tripp had obtained the services of a perplexed solicitor and rounded up sufficient cans of Coke to get through what was shaping up to be a very long afternoon.

The solicitor spoke with Aspen alone first, then reappeared looking much less confused.

'Without making any admissions or concessions, Aspen has asked me to inform you that there may be an allegation outstanding against her. She hasn't been contacted by the police or arrested, but if you were to check outstanding matters an offence relating to theft and destruction of property, you might find a complaint lodged by a woman called Sally approximately six months ago relating to a block of flats on Calder Grove.'

'Is your client saying she was involved in some way?' DS Tripp asked.

'For now, she is merely saying that you should obtain the file. When you've done that, my client would like to have what she called a "scratch-each-other's-back talk". Until then, she's withdrawn her consent to assist in your investigation.'

Half an hour later again, file in hand, Callanach was back in the room with both Aspen and her solicitor, wishing it was him with the cigarettes.

'Aspen, as per your request I have the file. There was a falling out between two tenants in a house share. The complainant's key went missing during a late-night drinking session. The next day her room had been ransacked, various items had been stolen including jewellery and gift cards, and several pairs of her jeans had the rear areas cut out of them. She says a woman she knew as Aspen was responsible.'

He flipped the file closed and waited for Aspen to reveal where the conversation was going.

'For the record, the following conversation is not under caution and nothing my client says should be taken to amount to any sort of admission,' the solicitor said, sounding just as irritated as Callanach felt.

'Aspen, is there anything you'd like to tell me about this allegation?' Callanach asked.

'It's all a lie. I mean, if it were about me it would all be a lie, 'cos I didn't do nothing.'

'You're not currently under arrest for this, so how do we move forward?'

'I want my rent deposit back,' she said. 'I had to move out of there real fast. I knew she was gonna accuse me, so I just got the hell out. I want my money and I want to make sure I'm never going to be charged with that.'

'So you accept you were living there at the time and that the allegation Sally is making refers to you?' Callanach clarified.

'No,' Aspen said. 'But if it did, I'd want it shut down forever. Like I said, I want my deposit back. And an apology, in writing, from big bum.'

'Again, to reiterate, that's in no way an admission,' the solicitor said, a general sense of disappointment dripping from his tone.

'How much was your rent deposit?' Callanach asked.

'Two hundred quid,' she said. 'I want it in cash today.'

'Aspen, this is not a game,' Callanach said. 'These things take time. I'll have to get the Procurator Fiscal to look over the papers and authorise a decision, the victim may have to be consulted, as well as your landlord. What we're doing here is attempting to save lives. I'm going to need something from you before I start negotiating, or my boss will tell me to forget it.'

'Well, fuck you very much, I'll be on my way then,' she said, standing up.

'I just need you to confirm that it's you in the photograph. Without that, there's no reason for us to negotiate. Plus, we now know who to speak to about the Calder Grove burglary, so I'd take a seat. You won't be leaving the police station any time soon.'

The smirk dropped from her face.

'I didn't admit anything,' she said.

'You didn't, but I'm sure Sally would be able to pull you out of an ID parade and that would be enough for us to charge you, so whatever false surname you gave to your previous landlord won't protect you anymore.'

She tutted and slouched back down in her chair. Callanach held up the photo taken from the keyring again.

'Aspen, is this you in the photograph?' he asked.

'Yes,' she said. 'I'd just had my lower lip pierced.'

'Can you tell us exactly when it was taken?' Callanach continued.

'Between six months and nine months ago,' Aspen said.

'The photo has been ripped in two. Do you know who was in the other half?'

'That's where my memory gets all fuzzy,' she said. 'I think now would be a good time for you to make some calls.'

Three hours later they were nearing the end of the normal working day. The Procurator Fiscal wasn't prepared to drop the case and sign off on the deal until he'd studied the file properly and spoken with the officer on the case. Aspen's landlord wasn't prepared to refund her deposit as she'd skipped out without paying her final month of rent or giving notice. The solicitor had gone away and needed to be recalled. By the time they got started again, Callanach was wishing he hadn't bothered.

'Aspen, I can't give you a final answer until tomorrow. I need you here at nine a.m., by which time we should be ready to proceed. I'll need an address where you'll be tonight, but also a little more information.'

'I already told you—' she started.

'That's enough,' Callanach said. 'The information you have might be worth nothing, so don't overestimate your own importance. I'm going to ask you some questions, and you're going to answer them. If you don't, then forget the deal. I'll arrest you for the burglary. You're not half as smart as you think you are. You left fingerprints all over the cans of drink from earlier and there were also prints left at the scene of Sally's burglary. Can you do the maths?'

Aspen said nothing but glared at her solicitor.

'Do you remember that photo being taken?' Callanach asked.

'Aye, it was one of them photo booths. Must have been at Waverley Station,' she said.

'Who were you with?'

'How the hell am I supposed to know? I told you, it was ages ago and I can't say for sure. I get photos taken with my mates all the time.'

'Think about it,' Callanach said. 'Man or woman?'

She stuck out her bottom lip. 'Probably a man.'

'Boyfriend, close friend, family? Who can you remember going into a photo booth with during that time period?'

'Tomorrow,' Aspen said. 'That I keep 'til tomorrow, if you do the deal.'

Callanach sighed. 'All right, but I need to know if you've ever heard of any of these people, met them, bought anything from them, used their services, or even just heard other people talking about them. Gavin Cronk. Maura Douglas. Felicity Love.'

'Aren't they all dead now? Just who is it you think I've been shagging who'd kill people? This is sick. I'm nothing to do with that.' Aspen pulled up her hood and withdrew into it.

'We don't think you're anything to do with it, Aspen. This is a whole different league. But you might, inadvertently, have come into contact with someone very dangerous. I'd like to protect you from them. Do you need the names again?'

'No, I bloody don't. I don't know anyone who's anything to do with this shit. That's messed up. I want to go home now. I've missed a whole day of work and I'm tired.'

'Fine,' Callanach said. 'But nine a.m. and don't be late.'

Aspen walked out, already texting her ex-boyfriend from her pocket. Tired or not, there was no way she was going straight home. A day's lost wages was a fair sum of money, but luckily she'd just figured out a way to recoup it several times over without lifting a finger.

Chapter Thirty-Five

BEFORE

Quinn was trying to listen but finding it hard to concentrate. Uncle Bobby was talking about the complaints he'd made to Police Scotland, and to the Crown Office and Procurator Fiscal Service. He was using a lot of acronyms and increasingly raising his voice. The pile of papers in front of him that he occasionally waved in the air then slammed back down were tatty from handling. They comprised all the case papers Police Scotland would release, correspondence, medical reports, the scant evidence they had and, finally, responses to his complaints.

Whilst Police Scotland is extremely sympathetic to the situation Ms McTavish finds herself in, we cannot proceed to trial without the agreement of the Procurator Fiscal who in the circumstances felt there was insufficient evidence to make a conviction for a charge of rape likely. We do consider victims when these decisions are made. Court proceedings can be very traumatic and we do not pursue trials where a conviction is unlikely in part to avoid the stress of giving evidence and being cross-examined. In the circumstances, we will not be taking any action with regard to this complaint . . .

The Procurator Fiscal conducted a careful study of the available evidence and voluntary statement made by Mr Cook and has regretfully reached the conclusion that a conviction would be unlikely. We appreciate that this was not an easy decision for Ms McTavish to come to terms with, and if further evidence comes to light then we would be happy to reconsider the matter. Until then we have reviewed the case and reached the conclusion that the Procurator Fiscal acted properly at all times, and that his decision was correct. In the circumstances, we will not be taking any action with regard to this complaint . . .

Blah blah blah. That was all Quinn had read in the letters, and – much as she loved him – all she could hear now as Bobby fumed and railed.

'No one's accountable, absolutely bloody no one!' Bobby shouted. 'It took three months for the police investigators and review commissioner to reply to me. Guess what she said? No prizes for this.'

Quinn met her mother's eyes. Neither of them tried to stop him. Bobby was doing everything he could to get justice, and had been left banging his head against a brick wall. The very least he deserved was to be allowed a decent rant about it to get his frustration out.

Having carefully and fully reviewed all the papers and interviewed the officers involved, as well as considering Police Scotland's reply to your original complaint, I find no procedural or substantial irregularity in their handling of the case, and no fault in their actions. As such, with respect . . .

He screwed the letter into a ball and lobbed it towards the fireplace.

'With respect, my arse. They've no respect for anyone. Maybe if your father had drafted the complaint, Quinn. He's the writer in the family, after all. I'm just an army grunt. Perhaps I didn't put the right words down. My grammar probably wasn't good enough for them,' Bobby raged.

'Bob,' Quinn's mother soothed. 'It wouldn't have made any difference who wrote the complaint. Cases like these can be difficult. I, for one, am glad Quinn isn't going to appear in court. Can you imagine going through all that, only to have a jury fail to find him guilty?'

'That's the problem,' Bobby said. 'How do we know the trial would have resulted in him being set free? We've only got their word for it. There's every chance the jury would see what a good person Quinn is and what a scumbag Liam is. I reckon they'd convict him in seconds. As soon as he opens his mouth you know the wee bastard is lying.'

'I didn't,' Quinn said.

'What, sweetheart?' her mother asked.

'I didn't know he was a liar. Or a . . . a rapist. Am I stupid? How come you saw it, Uncle Bobby, and I didn't?'

Bobby stood. 'Quinn, I shouldn't have said that. He's a clever boy who only showed you what he wanted you to see. I didn't mean to suggest—'

'Everyone thinks I was stupid. I fell for it the first time, then I gave him the opportunity to drug me. I let myself be taken back to his flat and I still didn't realise what he'd done to me. You know, I actually felt bad that I'd ruined his afternoon? I apologised to him.' She began laughing and crying at the same time.

'Quinn,' her mother went to her. Quinn pushed her arms away. 'No, Mum, I'm fine. It's funny!'

'Quinny, it's all been too much for you,' Bobby said.

She clutched her sides and doubled over. It was hard to breathe and she gasped air between fits of laughter. It was all so ridiculous. Everyone sitting around moaning about what a terrible thing had been done to her. She couldn't even remember it, for fuck's sake. As far as she was concerned she'd had a long afternoon nap on her ex-boyfriend's sofa. When is a rape not a rape? Her brain offered up the joke unbidden. She laughed harder and harder. Red spots appeared on the carpet.

'I'll get a cloth,' she heard Bobby say. He disappeared off to the kitchen.

She was on her knees and the laughter was controlling her. It wouldn't stop until it was done. Maybe until she was unconscious. That would be okay. Whatever Liam had slipped into her drink, she wished she had a great big pile of it to get her through the next twenty years, because she was never going to get a good night's sleep again.

'Stay still Quinn, we've got to stop this nosebleed,' her mother said. She tried putting a cloth beneath Quinn's nose and an ice pack over the top of it, but the laughter had her on her side now.

Her stomach muscles were aching, and the pain was a relief.

'Can you imagine me in front of a jury?' Quinn giggled. 'Some posh lawyer would ask me to tell the jury what happened.' That prompted a whole new pitch of hysteria. 'And I'd say, I have no idea!' Blood sprayed onto the carpet and trickled down her throat.

Now she felt sick, and that wasn't good. Even so, she couldn't get control of herself. 'I'm sorry, I'll stop. Give me a second.' She pressed her lips together but they wouldn't hold. A mouthful of blood hit the wall with the next laughing fit, her tears running streaks through the redness. The world was spinning.

'Shall I call a doctor?' Bobby asked.

'Sure,' Quinn giggled, trying to wipe the blood off the wall and succeeding only in making a smeary mess. 'Ask him if you can have me put down.'

'Stop that right now!' her mother ordered. Quinn's laughter died in her throat. Her mother had almost never spoken harshly to her, not in all of her twenty years. She held a hand up to catch the blood that was flowing from her nose, but her mother took hold of her hands instead and pulled her close. 'Don't you ever say that. You're more precious to me than life, and while I cannot even start to imagine what you've gone through and what you're still going through, I will not accept you talking about dying. I will spill my own blood before I let you hurt yourself, do you hear me? This pain you have, this terrible emptiness and hurt, it will start to subside. It's going to take a long time, but there will come a day when you feel happiness again, and it will take you by surprise when it does, because you think it's never going to happen. But you don't give up, do you hear me? You don't give up. Don't let him win. Please. Please, because I don't know how to live without you.'

Her mother's face was awash. Quinn leaned forward and put her head onto her mother's shoulder. Uncle Bobby moved in, sheltering them both in his enormous arms, his own head turned away to hide his tears.

'I don't know how to get through it,' Quinn said. 'I keep trying but then I see myself in a mirror and . . . and it's like I'm a ghost and I'm haunting myself.'

'One day at a time,' her mother said. 'One hour at a time, if that's how it has to be. With us by your side, knowing you're loved and that this doesn't define you. It only defines him. This is what he is. You are the goodness in the world that he can't feel, and he wanted to ruin it. But he hasn't, baby girl. He hasn't. You mustn't let him.'

Chapter Thirty-Six

Aspen sat with her solicitor and gesticulated wildly. Callanach watched through the small glass pane in the door, unable to hear the conversation, not that audio was necessary to understand that the young woman was unhappy in the extreme. Her solicitor nodded sagely from time to time, with a practised expression of understanding on his face. The patience of defence lawyers, Callanach thought, under circumstances that would test a saint. He gave them another minute then knocked.

'We need to get started,' Callanach said.

'No tape this time,' Aspen said. 'I don't want to be recorded.'

'It's in your interests,' her solicitor advised. 'If we reach a deal we may need the tape for reference.'

'I don't want them having my voice. Switch it off!' she snapped.

Callanach did as she asked.

'All right, Aspen. This conversation is not being recorded, but I will be taking notes, as will your solicitor. The Procurator Fiscal has agreed that the case with regard to Sally's clothes can be closed as long as you comply this morning. That means doing your best to answer every question. There will be no apology from Sally.' Aspen smirked. 'As for the rent deposit from your landlord, he will not be paying that back. However, we recognise that yesterday we cost you a day's wages and that you're unable to work again today. You've also had travel costs and time going to and from the police station. My superintendent has agreed to pay a total of one hundred and fifty pounds to make up for those losses. You can collect that in cash on your way out if you've been helpful.'

'I said two hundred.'

'You can be charged with theft and destruction of property, or help us, take the money we've offered and go home knowing there are no criminal charges pending,' Callanach said. 'Choose.'

'Fine, don't get your fancy French knickers in a twist. What are you doing in Scotland anyway? You don't belong here.'

Callanach ignored her comment. 'Yesterday I asked you who appeared in the other half of that photograph. Have you been able to remember who it was?'

'I actually haven't. Like I said, I messed around in that photo booth all the time.'

'Okay, deal's off. I'll step out, call in an officer to charge you—'

'I didn't say I couldn't help,' Aspen said. 'You can be a right prick. I got it down to a list of five. Sort-of boyfriends, fuck buddies, close mates. I was hanging around with a bunch of different people back then.'

'I need details,' Callanach said. 'Let's get started.'

'Johnny Ray. Guitarist. Smoked too much weed. He might not remember me at all. He was off his head most of the time. In his thirties, lived in Oxgangs. Then there was Jacob someone or other, his birthday was on 1 January, I know that because he had this amazing New Year's party. He was Jewish, if that helps.' She lit a cigarette, and her solicitor backed away. Callanach wanted a double espresso and wished he'd asked DS Lively to interview

Aspen instead. 'Then there was Denny Duncan, only I don't think that was his real name. He was a right laugh but he got into a ton of debt and disappeared off the face of the earth. Bit of a gambler. Had this awesome tattoo of a rat on his neck.'

'Next?' Callanach asked.

'Liam . . . I've been wracking my brains for his surname but it won't come. I wasn't with him long. Mid-twenties, good-looking, had a flat in Portobello.'

'Can you remember the address?'

'You'll be lucky. It was this one-bedroom place, nothing too fancy but not a shithole either. Over a shop but I can't remember which one. He usually came to mine. I think I only went there once. The last one I can think of is a guy called Bobby. Older than the others. Bit of a wanker. Had a temper and a free-flying hand when he was pissed. He was from Hopefield. Didn't like me asking questions.'

'Have you got an address or phone number for any of them?' Callanach asked.

'Nope. Once someone's out of my life, I get rid of their details. No looking back. But I'm sure it was one of them in that photo.'

She was lying about something but Callanach wasn't sure what. The sly grin at the edge of her mouth, her too-casual delivery, the practised reeling-off of the list of men.

'I want as much as you can give me,' he said. 'Physical descriptions. Age, build, accent, skin colour, nationality, associates of theirs you knew, where you used to go regularly. You can prepare a document with your solicitor.' He waited for her to nod in agreement. 'Did any of them ride a motorbike to your knowledge?'

A flicker across her face. A genuine memory, unplanned.

'One of them, for sure. Can't remember which one though. Definitely not Denny. He'd have sold it for the cash.'

'Think about it,' Callanach said. 'I'd like to know about their jobs, too. Do you still have the same mobile number you had back then? We'd like to check your call log for the period.'

'Nah.' She laughed. 'I could never afford a contract. Just get a pay as you go, use it up. Mostly burners my friends get for me cheap.'

Callanach took a deep breath.

'Were any of those men ever in trouble with the police that you knew of?'

Aspen studied the end of her cigarette before tapping ash on the floor.

'Probably all of them,' she decided. 'I don't go for good boys. They're not as much fun.'

'But anything specific that you heard about?' he pushed.

'I knew someone once who was investigated for a rape. Who was that?' she made a play of looking around the room. 'It just won't come. My memory's terrible. Might not even have been one of those guys, to be honest. If it comes to me, I'll be sure to let you know.'

'You do that,' Callanach said.

'Are we done here?' the solicitor asked. 'I'm due in court later today.'

'One thing I did remember, that name you said yesterday, Gavin whatsit. Small time drug dealer, right?' Callanach waited. 'I knew some folks got their gear from him. Never met him myself, but definitely some of the names I just gave you would have known him.'

Callanach left them to write out more detailed descriptions. Aspen knew something. He'd already assigned an undercover team to track her after she left the station. In the meantime, there was a lot MIT could do with the information they had. Aspen hadn't been lying when she said she'd recognised the name Gavin Cronk. The public had never been told he was a drug dealer. She was going to slip up. He just hoped it would happen soon enough to be useful to them.

The solicitor handed her a copy of the papers stating that the case against her had been dropped, she had one hundred and fifty pounds in her pocket and was waiting on a call. Last night she'd wasted her evening and a bus fare going to Portobello and back but he hadn't been home. She'd also tried Liam's number but he wasn't picking up. At least voicemail had been working.

Her message to him had been simple. The police were asking questions. As of that moment, his identity hadn't been revealed, but she needed a reason to make sure nothing came back to her. She'd suggested a sum that he wouldn't pay, but Liam was a tough bastard. He'd negotiate harder than that dick of a policeman had. The money was going to ensure she forgot his surname and address permanently, otherwise . . . She'd left it there. He knew perfectly well what the otherwise was.

It was his own fault, leaving a photo of her around. She was owed the cash for having been hauled into the police station and questioned. It was a shame, really. Liam was a catch. His own place that he didn't share. A nice car and a job. He always paid for her to eat after he'd fucked her, and rewarded her when she did him a favour. He'd even referred to her as his girlfriend for a while. Under any other circumstances she might have given it a second try. But now he was a cashpoint, and it was time for him to pay out. She'd given him until midnight, and left an address where he could find her. Aspen was already counting the notes in her head.

Chapter Thirty-Seven

BEFORE

Small things continued to happen. An item Quinn had long since considered lost would be found on a shelf in the shop – things she had no reason to believe she'd ever taken to work with her – such as a bracelet or a half-read book. Strangers would suddenly, randomly, take her photo in the street then disappear. Postcards would come for her in handwriting she didn't recognise with nothing but her address on. Anonymous parcels would be delivered containing harmless, useless contents that she would stare at then throw in the dustbin outside, only to find that they'd disappeared the following day.

The morning Quinn woke to the scent of Liam in her room, she knew that one of two things was inevitable. Either she needed serious psychiatric help, or Liam had finally taken matters so far that she had to remove herself from her parents' home. The latter involved shutting down Liam's interest in her forever.

She sat upright in bed, breathing in through her nose and out through her mouth. She could hear her mother rattling dishes in the kitchen to Dolly's background gurgle-chatter. Her father would have left for work already. Her room was as it always was. She was tidy, as a rule. Dirty clothes went into the washing basket, clean laundry was put away. Makeup was returned to the drawer after use, and books were stacked neatly on her desk. Nothing was out of place, but everything was wrong.

Cedarwood and clove clouded the air. The notes of Liam's favoured aftershave. Quinn drew the bedclothes up over herself, grateful she'd worn pyjamas to bed. It was impossible. She'd stayed up late watching a film, her parents having chosen to retire early while Dolly was sleeping. Her father had told her he'd locked up. Was that right? Or had he told her to lock up when she was done?

The panic started as a cramp in her abdomen, rose to produce excess bile, and rushed into her mouth as a flood of bitter saliva. She swallowed it back and inched out of bed. The scent of him followed her. Quinn checked every drawer, her wardrobe, under her bed, looked for signs of him everywhere. He had taken nothing, left nothing. Perhaps he was inside her head now. Every moment her mind wasn't occupied, it staggered back to him. She needed to fight harder. It was that or antidepressants, sleeping tablets and long sessions in therapy. Either that or running away. Take her passport, pack a bag and go. She had some savings that would be enough for a youth hostel while she found a job.

Grabbing a backpack, Quinn began throwing clothes onto her bed. There was only space for the bare minimum. She'd need to go to the bank and get some euros. Her father kept her passport in his bedside table, but she knew which drawer it was in.

'Quinn?' her mother asked quietly from the doorway. 'What's going on?'

'Can you smell him?' The words burst from her. 'I can. He's been here. He was in my room. I have to leave, Mum. I can't stand this anymore.'

She'd shed so many tears that she was sure they'd run out, but here they were again. Apparently they were never going to stop.

Her mother sniffed the air. 'I'm not saying you're wrong, but I can't smell anything, darling. Last night, your father asked you to lock up when you came to bed. Did you maybe forget to do it, realise in your sleep and wake up panicked?'

'No, that's not it!' But her voice was fading away into self-doubt already. She had forgotten to lock the kitchen door, but if Liam had been in the house, surely one of them would have heard him. And what were the chances that he'd been waiting for the opportunity?

'You look shattered,' her mother said. 'Are you still not sleeping?'

She shrugged. 'A bit. I wake up a lot.'

Her mother nodded. 'Were you going somewhere?'

Quinn frowned. 'I thought some time away would be good. Maybe France or Spain. I'll get a job washing dishes or picking fruit.'

'I think that's a good idea. Let's plan it properly. Maybe your dad would travel with you, find you somewhere safe to stay. He loves Europe. He could do with a holiday, too. Dolly is gorgeous but, my goodness, having a baby at our age makes you appreciate how much easier it was when we were young.' Quinn's head hung towards the floor. She couldn't lift it to respond to her mother. 'What's the worst thing about it? The thing you can't get out of your head. Share the darkest moment so I can take some of the weight,' her mother said, sitting on the edge of Quinn's bed.

Quinn loved her so much. It was impossible not to. She knew her father felt the same. His eyes were on her, whatever she was doing. She'd be peeling potatoes and Quinn's father would be there, newspaper open in front of him, but he'd just be staring at her mother with this smile on his face. She was everything. That sweetness, the kindness, the extraordinary capacity to love.

Quinn sat down next to her.

'It's when I get dressed each morning,' Quinn said. 'It feels like, whatever I put on, everything I'm wearing is dirty. I feel like I'll be wearing dirty clothes every day for the rest of my life.'

Her mother let out a choking sound, bent forward clutching her stomach, trying to stop herself from being sick. Quinn reached out a shaking hand to rest on her mother's back.

'It's okay, Mum,' Quinn said softly. 'I'm going to find a way to be okay again.'

'I want to kill him,' her mother said. 'I'm so angry. I never knew I could hate like this.'

They cried together as they had before, as Quinn knew they would again. It helped. Her mother's arms were all the therapy and medication she needed. Her passport could stay where it was. Maybe there was a trip abroad in her future. Right now, she had a letter to write.

Liam, I'm writing to tell you that you've won. I was never sure what game we were playing or what the rules were, but still, you've won. I went to the police but you were a step ahead of me. I tried again when you harassed me, but they weren't interested. The court wasn't sympathetic. We even made complaints to Police Scotland, the Procurator Fiscal and the Police Investigations and Review commissioner. The latter was particularly scathing in her reply. I'm telling you all this so you understand there's nowhere else to go. There are no more points to be scored. I hope you got what you wanted.

It has to stop here. This road is a dead end and you have bigger fish to fry. I know how ambitious you are. There's no point sending anything to this address anymore. I'll be moving out. I'm in a new relationship. As scared as I was to trust anyone again, I've found that there are still good men who understand what it means to love and be loved.

So this is our goodbye. I'm being completely honest with you in the hope that it will set you free from whatever made you so obsessed with me. I'll be giving up my job, too, so I won't be at the shop either. There are other people out there. I hope you find someone who's right for you.

Quinn

She pulled on loose jeans and a grey hoodie, didn't bother with makeup, and spent just a few seconds dragging a brush through her hair. Her destination was the shop, not that she had a shift, but there was something she needed to do. She slipped the letter to Liam into the post as she went.

A few customers smiled as she entered, expecting her to go to a till or put on her tabard. Instead she walked along the aisles until she spotted Mark.

He smiled broadly, as he always did when he saw her. He'd been a constant visitor when she'd taken time off, and that had continued after her return to work. If she was on a morning shift, he popped in on his way home with a cake or some meat, letting Quinn's mother talk him into staying to eat or watch a movie. Quinn liked him being there. It meant more conversation, more noise, less time in her own head. It felt safer. He and Uncle Bobby got on like a house on fire. Sometimes her mother had to tell them to be quiet before they woke Dolly up.

Quinn knew Mark's feelings for her hadn't diminished in spite of what she'd been through. He'd only ever tried to protect her, and he'd been right about Liam. That had stung for a while, but now it felt good to have him looking out for her.

He said he would do anything for her. She knew he dreamed of them being together. It wasn't a fairytale, and they would both know she was using him, but Quinn hoped she could give him enough in return to make it fair.

'Are you picking something up for lunch?' he asked. 'There's some lovely lamb that's just come in. Put it on my account.'

'That's not why I'm here, but thank you,' she said. 'Mark, this is sudden, I know, and it's a lot. I need somewhere to stay and it could be for a while.'

'Yes,' he blurted. 'Stay with me. I don't care if it's for a night or a month or a year. My place isn't huge, but we can make it work. I'll get an alarm fitted. I know you haven't been sleeping well so that'll make you feel safer when I'm not there.'

'Are you sure? I was going to give you some time to think about it, to talk about what I can contribute to the rent, see when works for you—'

'Tonight. Or tomorrow. As soon as you can pack. I'll just need to tidy up first and give you some drawer space. And I don't want rent money.'

'I need some time to get my parents used to the idea, so you've got a couple of days to get ready. We'll have to talk about the money, though. I've no intention of taking advantage.' She smiled. It felt good, discussing something in the future. It felt like waking up from a bad dream. 'There's something else I need. You're going to think I'm not right in the head.'

'Anything,' Mark said. 'You know that already. I'd do anything for you, Quinn.'

She took him by the hand, led him out of the shop to the main road where she'd seen people taking photos of her before.

Winding her arms around Mark's neck, she kissed him. It was a slow, sweet kiss, lips closed. A return to a former stolen innocence. Mark put his hands on her waist and kissed her gently back, keeping his body distant from hers. No pulling. No dominating. No demands.

When she stepped away, he took a deep breath.

'I'm not expecting anything from you just because you're moving in. You'll never owe me. You mean more to me than that. I mean, it was nice, obviously . . .' He gave a shy laugh. 'But I respect you, Quinn. All I want is to help put you together again, if you'll let me.'

'I hope you can,' she said. 'I'd really like it if you could.'

Chapter Thirty-Eight

DS Lively was driving so Ava took the opportunity to close her eyes for a few minutes as they made their way east out of Edinburgh to Gullane, on the southern shore of the Firth of Forth.

'Signal!' Lively shouted at some random car. Ava lurched fully awake. 'Sorry, ma'am, didn't realise you'd drifted off. Whereabouts in Gullane is the house we're looking for?'

'Junction of Sandy Loan with Marine Terrace. I'd have sent a courier except it's after-hours, these are sensitive documents, and the commissioner wanted to read them over the weekend. I'm on strict orders not to piss her off. It's bad timing, but out of respect for the dead, the least we can do is be transparent and help the review go smoothly.'

'Who made the complaint?' Lively asked.

'The wife of one of the dead paramedics from the Innocent Railway Tunnel. Can't say I blame her. Technically the complaint is still under review internally by Police Scotland but the current commissioner, Zara West, said she wants to be kept up to speed. It's a tricky one. Arguably we should have secured the scene before letting paramedics anywhere near it.'

'I feel for all the relatives, but you can't put this on yourself, ma'am. You'd no way of knowing there was a bomb inside that baby bump. We could live a dozen lifetimes and never be confronted by evil like that again. So why are you here?'

'The commissioner has some questions for me, so I thought I could kill two birds with one stone, only I know I'm too tired to be behind the wheel and there are too many boxes for me to carry alone. I'll buy you fish and chips once we're back in the city if you promise not to tell anyone I used you as a courier and driver for the evening.'

'Ach, I'm off shift so sadly my union's not going to be interested in this one. It's a yes to the fish and chips though, but I get to put as much salt on as I like without you giving me a lecture. We're here. Bloody hell, this is where the Police Investigations and Review commissioner lives? Nice work if you can get it.' The high wooden gates stood slightly open but Ava got out and pulled them all the way back so Lively could get the car in. The period house was surrounded by high walls on three sides, with an unimpeded view of beach and sea on the other.

Lively took the parking space closest to the front door, ensuring the three other cars on the driveway had access to the exit, pulled up and opened the boot.

'I'll unload. You go on in and answer her questions.'

Ava rang the bell and as it chimed with solemn depths and echoed through the house, she felt a burst of jealousy. Zara West's home was so peaceful – an oasis away from the city, and the clamour of Ava's existence. Oh to be able to fall asleep each night and wake every morning to a view of the rolling waves. Gullane was a small village with limited amenities, but at that moment it was everything Ava wanted. She would sell her house, she decided as she waited for Zara West to open up, and move to the coast. It was within commuting distance of the city centre, but it would be a proper escape at the end of the day. She rang the doorbell a second time.

Lively was already piling boxes by the front door ready to shift into the hallway.

'Maybe she popped out,' Lively said.

'She said she'd be in all evening,' Ava replied, peering through a side window. 'I'll give her a call.' She took out her mobile and dialled. As they waited for the commissioner to pick up, the sound of a phone could be heard in an upstairs room.

'I'll go round, see if there's a back door I can knock,' Lively said.

'Let me.' Ava grinned. 'We don't want her calling the police to report a suspicious man in her garden.' Lively climbed back into the car and put the radio on. 'Hello there?' Ava called as she went. 'Mrs West, it's DCI Turner. Hello?'

The back garden was small and no light spilled into it from the kitchen. Ava reached out to knock the rear door only to find that it was a fraction open. Running her hand down the door edge, she found the rough wood where the lock had been tampered with.

Ava took a step back to call it in as a woman screamed from inside. She entered, reaching out for anything to use as a weapon. A woman was crying in a room to the right. Her hand found a heavy wooden chopping board which would have to do. The crying had turned to hysteria.

Ava put one hand on the doorknob and pushed it open. The fist that hit her wasn't meant to take any prisoners. Her head flew backwards, catching the edge of the door as it swung.

A woman screamed as Ava fell to her knees, nose exploding in a bloody mess, vision reduced to a kaleidoscopic blur. Whoever had punched her, pushed her face down into the carpet and jumped over her. She reached out a hand to try to grab his foot but caught only air.

Footsteps tore through the kitchen then faded outside the house. Seconds later, an engine revved on the driveway and tyres spun. Ava got to her knees, dizzy and bleeding, the headache already burning a hole in her temple.

'Lively,' she muttered to herself. 'Front door.' She did her best to push up from the floor, but the room had taken on funfair qualities.

Then there was a hand on her shoulder. 'Don't move,' Zara West said. 'I'm calling an ambulance.'

'Got to,' Ava said, making it into an upright position. 'Help me.' Mrs West put an arm around her waist and guided her to the front door.

Lively stood at the edge of the driveway looking into the road, hands on hips, yelling obscenities into a space filled only with the smell of burned tyres. Skid marks showed the direction of exit. Lively turned around, glimpsed Ava's face, and his jaw dropped.

'Oh crap,' he said, running forwards to help hold her up.

'Call it in,' she said. 'We have to stop that car.'

The Wests' lounge was packed with paramedics, police and scenes of crime officers.

Jonathan West shouldn't have been at home that evening. A bad stomach flu had prevented him from getting on a plane to a medical conference in Paris. Now he had both a gastrointestinal virus and a fractured skull from a direct hit with a vase. His wife was being treated for shock.

The ambulance crew weren't taking no for an answer from Ava either, in spite of her best efforts to wave them away. Her right eye socket was badly swollen and they were insisting that she get an X-ray. They'd grudgingly administered strong painkillers when she'd promised to attend hospital under her own steam rather than in the ambulance, even though she was still holding onto the wall as she walked.

'It's important that you stay awake for the next few hours. You shouldn't be alone. Is there someone who can stay with you?' the paramedic asked.

'I live with friends,' Ava said. 'Thanks for the advice.'

'That's a possible fracture. You need to get it checked in case it's displaced. I'd say probable concussion too, Detective Chief Inspector. How's the headache now?'

'Yeah, fine, getting better,' she lied. 'Excuse me, I need to talk with my sergeant. Lively!'

He waited until the paramedics had taken the hint and cleared out of the way.

'DI Callanach is riding in on his white steed.' He smiled. 'I'm going to have to tell him to take you to the hospital.'

'If you do, you're fired,' she said, changing the position of the ice pack on her temple. 'How the hell did he get past you and out of the driveway, and what were you doing watching him go like that?'

'Why didn't you come and get me before entering the property if it was obvious that something was wrong?' he countered.

'Because I thought someone was about to get murdered and there wasn't time. Stop deflecting. What happened?'

'The radio was on so I didn't hear anything, and I might have closed my eyes for a while. I didn't see him go past, didn't hear him get in the car. The first thing I was aware of, was some idiot kicking up gravel and revving the engine too hard as he turned out onto the road.' Lively looked sheepish. 'I had no reason to think I should follow him.'

'Did you get a look at him?' Callanach asked, appearing behind Lively and sounding utterly pissed off.

'Neither of us did,' Ava said. 'What type of car was it?'

'Nissan Qashqai, dark blue,' Lively said. 'I didn't catch the plate but then I didn't know what I was looking at.'

'So, the same make, model and colour of the car that was seen near the exit to the farm used to hold Maura Douglas?' Callanach reminded him.

'Fucksticks,' Lively muttered. 'I didn't even notice it when we drove in.'

'Nor me,' Ava said. 'We've got to get everyone out of here so the scenes of crime team can get working without inter- ruption.' She called across the lounge to the sofa at the far end. 'Mrs West, could we speak with you, please?' Ava waited until Mr West had been evacuated by stretcher then went to the commissioner's side.

'I'm just about to follow my husband to the hospital,' she explained.

'Have you been reviewed by the paramedics? You really shouldn't drive.'

'No need, I'm unharmed. Shaken, yes, but nothing physical.'

'I'll have officers drive you to the hospital and remain there to guard you. They'll stay here when you come home too,' Ava said.

'I don't understand. No burglar's going to come back again after that,' Mrs West said.

'It seems more likely that the intruder was here for you. Did you see his face?'

'No,' she said. 'I was upstairs and I heard my husband raising his voice. By the time I got downstairs, my husband was already on the floor bleeding and there was a man standing over him. He was dressed in black. Jeans, I think, and what looked like a winter jacket. Balaclava and gloves. I couldn't give you an age. Medium build. He only said a couple of words, but he had a Scots accent. Then we heard your voice and he went to the door. All he said was, "Warn her and I'll kill your husband." I'm sorry. I was so scared I didn't know what to do.'

278

'That's fine,' Ava said. 'You did the right thing following his instructions. Did he say anything else that you can remember?'

She thought about it for a second, then shook her head.

'Why is it you think he wanted me?'

'The car he was in has similarities to the one we're looking for in relation to the Maura Douglas murder,' Ava explained. Mrs West did her best to hide her shock. 'Detective Sergeant Lively will organise a police escort for you. I'm sorry about your husband.'

'Don't apologise,' the commissioner said. 'I believe you saved my husband's life. And mine.'

They cleared the room to preserve the scene.

'In my car,' Callanach said. Ava didn't fight it. 'Hospital then home. You can issue all the orders you need on the phone while I drive. If you say a single word about not going, I'll call the superintendent, tell her you're speaking nonsense and that I believe you're concussed and should be relieved of authority in the case.'

'Luc—'

'Not one word,' he said. 'Just get in.' He held the door open for her.

She used the time to make calls and organise the squads. A helicopter had been scrambled and units had come from the city, but the car was long gone. All they were left with was the prospect of checking endless cameras to figure out its route, but that far out of Edinburgh the chances of tracking it weren't good.

After a heated debate with a doctor, Ava was allowed to leave. Natasha was in bed by the time they got home, and Ava and Luc both agreed that the last thing her heart needed was to see the mess Ava's face was in.

'Right, I'm off for a shower and bed,' Ava said. 'You headed back to the station?'

'No. Overbeck has gone in to formulate a plan of action, and all the heads of squads have been notified. I'm staying here with you. The doctor said you shouldn't sleep for another three hours to make sure you're not concussed, and you're not allowed to be left alone tonight. I'll cook while you shower, then we'll watch a movie in my room. As soon as it's turned one a.m. you can sleep on my bed, I'll take the chair.'

'You're sure this isn't just a ploy to get me into your bed?' She grinned.

Callanach walked over to her, put his arms gently around her shoulders and turned her to face the mirror on the wall behind her.

Ava took a step back and grimaced. 'Okay. Point taken. Not at my most attractive. I'll get that shower now.'

She was letting hot water wash the day away when her ensuite door opened.

'Holy boiling bollocks,' Natasha said. 'You look like that time we tried out all my aunt's makeup in one go. What the fuck happened?'

'Well, it looks as if I surprised a mass murderer – having failed to notice that the suspect was right under my nose – and let him teach my face a lesson then get away without a scratch on him. Do you ever knock?' Ava asked, turning off the shower and wrapping a towel around herself.

'Nope. Have you seen a doctor? Are you concussed? Where's Luc? Why didn't you call me?' Natasha folded her arms and frowned.

'Yes, probably not, downstairs, and because you had a heart attack. Does that cover it?'

'Ava, if you're glib about this I will have you kidnapped and held hostage until I can be sure you're fully recovered. I shit you not.'

'That's not nice language,' Ava said, pushing past Natasha to get out of the bathroom and into the bedroom.

'Oh, I apologise. I shittest thou not, if you want it in fucking Shakespearean. Have you seen your injuries?'

'Yes, actually, which, coupled with the fact that I feel as if someone tied me by the ankles to a windmill sail in a storm and let my face repeatedly smack the ground as it went round, means I have a fairly good idea of the state I'm in. I knew there was a reason Luc and I decided not to wake you up.'

'Luc agreed to that? Traitor,' Natasha said.

'We'll break Natasha's rules and eat on the bed,' Luc called from the staircase. 'Oh! Hi, Tasha. We thought you were asleep.'

'I gathered that. What's the plan?' She motioned towards Ava.

'I'm going to watch over her, make sure there are no signs of concussion, and ensure she's fit for work tomorrow,' he said, looking from Ava to Natasha and back again.

'And you'll wake me up if you're concerned about her?' Natasha asked him.

'I'm right here!' Ava protested.

'Yes, I will, I promise. Cross my heart,' he said.

Natasha looked unconvinced but left them to it, shaking her head in true mother hen style as she went.

'Thanks, Luc. I'm not sure what I'd do without you right now,' Ava said.

'I'm not going anywhere,' he said. 'And just in case that was an underhanded attempt to manipulate me, I'm choosing the movie. It's not going to be black and white, and it's not going to be from the 1950s.'

'Damn. I felt sure that was going to work,' Ava muttered as she got comfortable. 'What's a girl got to endure these days to get control of the remote?'

Chapter Thirty-Nine

BEFORE

Mark had come for dinner, and they'd set out their plans to Quinn's parents who could see that it was exactly what their daughter needed. Mark had smiled all evening and reassured Simeon McTavish that he was a decent guy who intended nothing other than to look after his girl. Simeon had shaken his hand, given him a sombre look and told him that it was no small thing, saying you would look after someone, and that he would hold Mark to his word. Mark had given a thoughtful nod in response. Before Mark had left, he'd hugged Quinn long and hard, but hadn't tried to kiss her, which was when she'd known that she was in truly safe hands.

Uncle Bobby had been out with his army mates for the evening but Quinn had called him to ask if he wouldn't mind helping out the following day, transporting her to Mark's. That night she managed a couple of hours' sleep, and hoped it was a promise of more to come. After breakfast she had a huge clear-out planned. It was the best possible time to put away childish things, and the charity shop needed clothes, books and bric-a-brac. Bobby was arriving at lunchtime to fill his car and take away anything she'd decided could go. After that, she would strip her bed and wash the bedding to save her mother the job, then pack her suitcase.

Quinn felt some slight melancholy as she started going through her childhood treasures, but the greater sensation was that it was time for a change, even if it had been forced upon her. There were a few precious toys she'd always resisted throwing away, and those she set aside for when Dolly was older. Her father would put them in the loft until it was time.

Into a sack went the few short skirts she owned, the tight tops and her pair of high heels. Those were followed by two dresses that hugged her figure and attracted men's attention. Quinn knew what she was doing, and she resented it, but she couldn't wear those things anymore. She didn't want men to notice her. Not that the way she'd dressed – the way any woman had ever dressed – had been what had got them into difficulty. It wasn't that. She just no longer wanted to exist as an object of desire for anyone. Her world had grown immeasurably more private. Quinn McTavish was in charge of her own destiny, and that meant controlling what other people got to see of her.

The only toy she left in her wardrobe was Bippo, a hippo-potamus her father had bought her at the end of a zoo visit when she was four years old. She'd fallen in love with the cuddly toy from across the shop, hadn't been able to keep her eyes off him, and her father had noticed immediately. Bippo had slept in her bed every night for the following twelve years, accompanied her on sleepovers, school trips, and had been a regular visitor at Uncle Bobby's house. Eventually, of course, Bippo would go to Dolly, but for now Quinn needed him to remain in her childhood room where she could picture him. All he needed was a freshen-up before she put him away. The years had made him dusty.

She drew up her blinds and opened her window wide to hold Bippo out and give his fur a hard ruffle. A cloud lifted from him into the air and sparkled in the morning sunlight. Quinn gave a small sneeze and laughed, for a few seconds able to delight in the toy and the memories of a blissful childhood. Below, her mother pulled into the driveway, got out of her car to open the garage, and gently parked the car inside. Quinn looked up the street that had been her home forever. She would miss it, but it wasn't as if she wouldn't be back a couple of times a week. Her parents would be heartbroken if she didn't.

A car caught her eye at the far end of the street, largely obscured by the shade of an overhanging tree. Quinn pulled her head back inside, rubbed the dust from her eyes, and told herself sternly that she had to stop seeing Liam everywhere. But the image wouldn't leave her. She looked again. There he was, staring, not even trying to hide himself. Her throat tightened. Even if he'd been in disguise she'd have recognised him from the forward-thrust of his chest and arrogant tilt of his chin, in the smirk at each raised edge of his mouth.

Quinn dropped Bippo at her feet. The pressure – part memory, part fill-in from her imagination – was back on her chest. Her clothes were being tugged. Once again she was dragged down into sleep as her body was dragged off the sofa.

'Fuck you,' she whispered, seeing the words like ghosts, float along the air to the car he was in. She thought she saw Liam smile just a little more broadly.

Downstairs, her mother was calling out. 'Hello, you two. Little help getting everything out of the car?'

Quinn stuck her head further out of the window, took a lungful of air and yelled. 'Fuck you! Fuck you, fuck you, fuck you!'

Liam sat forward. Their eyes locked. Quinn wanted to run to the kitchen, grab one of her mother's precious chef's knives, storm down the road, rip open the car door and plunge that blade into Liam's chest. Keep on stabbing again and again until she could wash the memory of him away in a river of his blood.

She could taste it already in her mouth.

Turning to her mirror she watched as a stream of watery red trickled from the corner of her lips. Her tongue waited a moment to send her brain the signal that she'd bitten into it, and then the pain was an explosion. She let her hand relax from the fantasy of wielding the knife, and knew that if she didn't move, didn't get out and get away, she would actually do it. As much as she wanted Liam dead, she didn't want to spend a lifetime paying for her fury. Taking the stairs two at a time, she fought to keep from screaming. There was a tsunami of emotion building inside her that would destroy anything in its wake, and no one was safe.

'Quinn,' her mother said, 'are you okay? We heard you shouting and—'

Quinn grabbed the car keys from her mother's hand as she ran past into the garage. The driver's door was standing open. She jumped in, ramming the keys into the ignition, turning the engine. Wheels squealed and she lurched backwards out of the driveway, her mother running after her and waving madly in her rearview mirror, but she had to get away. There was nothing good left inside her, no positive emotion, however hard she was trying.

Then she was passing Liam's car. He stared as if she was possessed, mouth slack. No smart comments now. She put her foot down and went, heading north towards the city. All Quinn needed was a long, fast road to open up the engine and burn herself out.

Liam caught her up as she neared the Edinburgh bypass, the sprawling jagged oval that encircled the city. Quinn had known he would come for her. She'd always known. It was never going to be over. Slamming the base of her palm into the radio button, she switched on music to drown out the thumping in her head. Onto the bypass now, heading west, speeding up, weaving in and out of the traffic, foot pressed to the floor.

Quinn had no idea where she was headed, only that away from him was the only possible option. Her rearview mirror flashed with the image of Liam changing lanes to fit in behind her. As fast as she was driving, his was the more powerful car. There was no way she could lose him on a long, straight road. She needed options, turning places. The Clovenstone junction was coming up. Waiting until the last possible second, she swerved into the exit lane then headed in towards the city.

Kingsknowe was nearby. A friend from school had moved there and Quinn, aged nine, had been to visit her. The memory came in strong. Her friend's bedroom, the princess bed complete with curtains, them both lying in it giggling, safe from the world, whispering about what they wanted to be when they grew up, nothing unobtainable, happiness guaranteed. Perhaps her friend still lived there. Perhaps that room with its warmth and its memories was all she needed to feel safe and hopeful again.

Quinn spun the wheels to turn into Kingsknowe Road. She thought that perhaps she'd be able to find it, the route a dim recollection, the outside of the house still a perfect imprint in her mind. Her friend's name was proving elusive but Quinn was sure she'd remember it. She sped up and took a slight turn, keeping the golf club on her left, the clubhouse followed by long sections of green – she was going the right way, it was familiar.

Liam was behind her, so close she could see him mouthing at her to stop. Well, fuck him. Foot down as far as it would go. The twenty mile per hour markings on the road were swallowed beneath her car. He kept pace, right on her bumper. She took a bend with houses either side, but all she could see was him in her mirror.

Quinn saw the barrier too late.

Remembered the level crossing too late.

Saw her friend's road just a little way down past the canal.

Slammed her foot on the brakes too hard, the wheel slipping through her sweating hands as she fought the car for control.

She just wanted to be back in that princess bed again, draw the curtains, go back a decade in time, feel whole and clean and safe again.

Liam's face was the cover of a cheap horror novel, a frozen scream, eyes so wide Quinn could see the arc of them bulging.

The front of her car hit the barrier, the back of the vehicle swinging out to one side, too much velocity to bring it to a halt. The barrier bent, gave way, and Quinn's car kept going, bumping down once, twice. Something exploded beneath her and she was thrown forwards, smacking to a violent halt on the tracks. In the distance, something terrifying was hurtling towards her. So much noise.

Then came a high-pitched cry. Familiar, but awful in this time and place.

The memory of her mother, car keys still in hand, asking for help to bring everything in from the garage. The realisation that Quinn had grabbed the keys before her mother had a chance to get Dolly out.

Quinn looked up the tracks to face the oncoming train. She turned the ignition key to be greeted by the sound of silence.

Everything was vibrating, thrumming, through her head, her stomach, her feet.

Quinn thrust open her door. It stuck at first. She kicked it, leapt out.

More crying, louder now.

Both front tyres had exploded. Shredded rubber lay in stinking ribbons at her feet.

Quinn prayed she was in a dream. That she'd fallen asleep

on her childhood bed, holding Bippo, and was hearing Dolly crying from just down the hallway.

She ripped open the rear passenger door. Dolly's seatbelt was locked, the mechanism jammed. Quinn's hands shook as she tried it again and again. The noise was so close, the onrush of air, the furious beep of a monstrous horn.

Instead, she tried to lift out the whole seat, even as she saw it had been too badly damaged in the crash. It was stubborn, immovable. There was nothing more to be done.

Quinn covered her baby sister with her own body, held her close, told her she loved her and laid gentle fingers over her eyes.

That was all.

Chapter Forty

Elise was waiting for Ava in the bar of The Angel's Share Hotel on Hope Street, one empty glass in front of her as she sipped a second cocktail and stared at the black and white prints of Scotland's most famous and beloved sons and daughters. Ava ordered a tonic water from a passing waitress and went to sit down.

'Is your job always that hazardous?' Elise asked, staring at Ava's swollen cheekbone and nose.

'There was an attempted attack on the commissioner,' Ava explained, slipping off her coat. Elise had left a cryptic message about wanting to talk. Ava hoped she wasn't having her time wasted. After the last frustrating meeting with the defence advocates, she hadn't been thrilled at the prospect of a second session.

'You were there? Sounds like you all had a lucky escape. Is it linked to the bombings?'

The lawyer's voice was wavering and reedy, not at all like a woman used to dealing with judges, juries and the toughest players in Scotland's crime scene. Her hand shook as she picked up her glass. Ava reassessed the importance of their meeting.

'Elise, is everything okay?' she asked.

She nodded. 'Fine.'

Ava left it there. She didn't want Elise to clam up.

'The commissioner's attack is definitely linked to the bombings.' Ava decided to reveal information not yet in the public domain, but it was obviously important to Elise. 'There was a vehicle at the scene linked to the Innocent Railway Tunnel investigation.'

'That's pretty conclusive then,' Elise said. 'So you think it's just going to carry on? That there'll be more deaths?' She sounded desperate.

'I do,' Ava said. 'The commissioner is fortunate that the attempt to kidnap her was interrupted. She was the target. Her husband was simply in the wrong place at the wrong time.'

Elise drained her glass, waving the empty at the waiter as Ava took her tonic water.

'I'm sorry we couldn't help you with Felicity's notebooks,' Elise said, her voice so quiet that Ava had to lean forward to catch the words. 'We wanted to. The code we work by can seem frustrating to the outside world. Your superintendent wasn't happy with us. It's not a choice, you see. If we make exceptions then no defendant will ever trust us again. They have to know they can talk in confidence or the whole system breaks down.'

'I get it,' Ava assured her. 'Confidentiality to you is what procedure for evidence gathering is for us. You break one rule and the whole house of cards comes tumbling down.'

'Exactly,' she said animatedly. 'There was no way any of us could have revealed what was in those notebooks, whatever was at stake.'

'Elise, I'm glad we have a chance to talk. I liked Felicity and I'm sorry you've lost such a good friend. I hope you don't mind my asking, though, what this is about. I don't want to rush you, but we're all pulling back-to-back shifts.'

'Right, of course. You know, Felicity was careful about

confidentiality too. She only ever talked about her cases in vague terms, never used names, only discussed what was on the public record, and she wasn't easily fazed.' Ava smiled politely and left space for Elise to continue. 'She did talk about personalities sometimes though. No breach of confidence, just her own feelings. I remember her once telling me how she'd spent endless hours in cells with people accused of the most dreadful crimes. Some of those would have been your cases. There was only one man she ever represented who she seemed to really hate. Normally she was completely dispassionate when she talked about her clients, but this one guy . . . I remember her saying very clearly that she loathed him.'

Elise's new drink arrived and she didn't let it touch the table before putting it to her lips.

'What was it about him that made her react so strongly?' Ava asked.

'Nothing specific. She was just freaked out by him. I think she got the impression that there was something . . . monstrous below the surface.'

Ava considered the information. 'This man, I don't suppose you know what happened to him?' Elise shrugged. 'You can't give me a name or any other identifying detail?'

'No,' Elise said.

Ava rubbed her eyes. Her head was throbbing, she had a mountain of paperwork to complete and Elise's information, while interesting, wasn't helping.

'I don't mean to be rude, but I'm going to have to go,' Ava said. 'If you think of any details that might move things forward—'

'Do you read the papers much, DCI Turner?' Elise interrupted.

'The papers?'

'Yes, the popular press. Sometimes we disregard them as valuable sources of information.' Ava folded her arms and looked at Elise intently. 'You should. I often do when I'm briefed in a new case. I find it useful to know how a crime has been reported, what picture the media paint of my client. Media reports sometimes throw new light on what the case papers reveal.'

Ava let it sink in. Elise wanted to help. Ava just needed to try harder to understand how.

'Do you think I should look at the newspaper reports relating to Felicity's cases?'

Elise gave a small sigh. 'Maybe not the coverage of the cases themselves. Perhaps cast the net a bit wider. I think of it as reading around the edges.' She checked her watch. 'I should get back to work. I volunteered to go through Felicity's room and pack up her notebooks. I started a couple of days ago, but there's still more to do.'

'Her notebooks?' Ava suddenly needed to get back to work too.

'They have to be kept for a certain number of years in case there's a query about a case. I've been flicking through them to make sure no personal effects were accidentally stuck between the pages. Not reading them, you understand.' Elise gave Ava a long, serious look. 'That would be unethical. Legal privilege extends even to other advocates reading the notes. Just packing everything up.'

'Of course,' Ava said. 'I understand.'

'The victim Maura Douglas . . . she worked as a courier, right?' Elise left cash on the table to settle the tab. Ava's breath caught in her throat. 'Good luck, DCI Turner.'

Ava reached out a hand to put over Elise's. 'Thank you.'

'Don't thank me,' Elise said. 'We met by chance. I haven't helped you. I haven't given you any information. I believe in the ethical constraints of the legal profession, and I don't want to sacrifice my career. We just had a drink.'

'Okay,' Ava said.

Elise gave her a quick, unhappy smile. 'Catch him.'

Ava waited until Elise was out of the bar before sitting down to call DS Lively. 'Get a team to compile a list of key players in Felicity Love's cases. We're not interested in direct case reporting, but cross-reference the people in each case against wider media reports. Check what they were up to and what else had happened to them. There's a link between someone in one of those cases – a male, I think – and the bombings. Read widely and think cryptically. Don't tell anyone this came from me. You figured out that it would be a good idea to use the psychological profile to look for anyone in Felicity's cases who fit the outlined type.'

'You mean I can actually take credit for something?' Lively asked.

'Find me this bastard, and you can take all the credit you like,' Ava said. 'Just do it fast.'

Chapter Forty-One

BEFORE

Liam couldn't hear himself screaming but he knew he was. The train hit so fast he didn't have time to close his eyes. It had tried to slow down, been running its horn for a good fifteen seconds prior to impact. The barrier between road and railway lay in pieces at his feet. Sirens warbled in the distance, and he could see the faces of passengers – horrified, terrified – at the train windows. The driver was climbing out and running to the mangled metal lump that had been thrown further down the tracks. Liam wanted to go and help, but his legs wouldn't move. Strangers ran past him, shouting instructions, on their phones, running to help passengers down and away to safety.

No one was helping Quinn. The train driver was a solitary figure standing in the middle of the tracks, staring at what remained of Quinn's car and shaking his head. Liam wondered if he could see her, how beautiful she was, how extraordinary. The driver would never know what he'd taken from the world.

Liam saw emergency vehicles rushing towards him and stepped aside for them to get as close as possible to the tracks.

The paramedic team pulled up next to him. The driver and his partner jumped from the ambulance and ran onto the tracks.

The driver held out shaking arms, collapsing to his knees before they could reach him. One paramedic stayed at his side while the other made his way to Quinn's car, looking briefly into the rear of the vehicle – what was left of it. Liam watched as the paramedic pulled out his mobile and made a call.

'Sir, is this your car? Sir?' A police officer was speaking to Liam. He frowned, dragged his eyes away from the scene on the tracks.

He nodded confirmation to the officer. 'So the car on the railway line was directly in front of yours, is that right?'

'Yes,' he said. 'The driver . . . is she dead?'

'No one could have survived that,' the officer said. 'I'll need to take your name. Officers will want to contact you at a later date to take a full statement. I'll just note the details of your vehicle.'

He hadn't wanted to give his name but if they were taking his registration number, they'd find him anyway.

'Liam Cook,' he said.

'Write your address and phone number here for me, please, sir.' The officer handed him a notebook and pen. He provided the details and passed them back. 'We'll be clearing the road shortly so you can turn your car around. Bit of a detour to get the other side of the tracks, I'm afraid.'

'Doesn't matter,' Liam said.

Quinn was dead. What point was there driving anywhere now? She'd consumed his thoughts, day and night, for months. He wanted to return to her bedroom. His last perfect contact with her had been there.

The opportunity he'd dreamed of had finally materialised. Following his nightly routine, he'd waited until the McTavish house was quiet, then tried the kitchen door, fully expecting the usual resistance. Instead, it gave a satisfying click, and Quinn's world was accessible to him.

Stepping over the threshold, Liam could smell her instantly; jasmine soap, fresh linen, vanilla and innocence. Those things he'd done with her hadn't tarnished her at all. He sat for a moment at the kitchen table and imagined himself watching Quinn in a kitchen of their own, making dinner. She turned and gave him a shy smile, knowing he was studying the slimness of her waist and curve of her breasts.

His imaginary Quinn washed her hands and moved into the hallway. Liam followed, checking out the lounge and the armchair where she'd sat to watch a film that evening, a blanket she'd wrapped around herself left unfolded. She must have been tired. It wasn't like her to be so sloppy, not that Liam was complaining. It explained the carelessly unlocked door.

The stairs were the most dangerous part of the house. He had no idea how much they might creak. Taking them two at a time but gently, up he went. Past the spare bedroom that seemed to belong to that bastard uncle, then her parents' door, the box room they'd given to the baby he'd named, and lastly to Quinn's room.

How badly he wanted to wake her with a kiss. Instead he sat on her floor, studying the rise and fall of her chest. He might have run his hands through her lingerie drawer, possibly taken something precious to keep. He might have put his hands between his legs as he stood over her. But those were all acts of love. Normal red-blooded reactions to the beauty he had once possessed and was determined to have again. She just needed to be reminded of what they had.

When he knew he could stay no longer, his last act was to spray a tiny amount of his aftershave into her hair. When she awoke, all of her thoughts would be of him. She had said so often how much she loved the scent of his skin.

'You'll be mine again soon,' he'd whispered.

'Sir, are you all right? Do you need a paramedic?' the police officer asked, bursting Liam's memory bubble. He'd been lost in the past, reliving every beautiful moment.

The paramedics were walking back to the ambulance, accompanying the train driver. A large white van pulled up as they opened the back doors and helped the driver climb in. The paramedics greeted the male who exited the van. His lanyard proclaimed him to be an assistant pathologist at the Edinburgh City Mortuary.

'I hate train line suicides,' the pathologist said as he passed the paramedics. 'So many lives wrecked. It really is the most selfish way to do it.'

'Amen to that,' one of the paramedics agreed.

Liam made fists of his hands, teeth bared, veins standing out in his neck. How dare they judge her. It had been an accident. Quinn would never, never take her own life. To talk about her in those terms, calling her selfish. They didn't even know her. Only he really knew Quinn. Only he had really appreciated her.

Just that morning he'd received her letter. Finally she'd reached the realisation that her parents' house was too restrictive for the life she was destined to live. By telling Liam her plans, he knew she'd been inviting him to intervene.

Now Quinn was gone forever. Quinn who he'd adored and treasured, and tried to save. Everyone had failed her. Liam climbed into his car, made a clumsy five-point turn and left.

The police were idiots. They'd fallen for his tale of cookbooks and coincidences. So-called detectives, duped by his voluntary statement and his humble smile. How could they have failed Quinn so miserably? She'd gone to them for help and they'd sent her away, tail between her legs, refusing to prosecute him. Then, when she'd stuck to her guns and taken him to court on her own account, his bitch of a lawyer had brutalised her. He'd taken no satisfaction from his victory. Watching Quinn being cross-examined had been a painful experience. She'd appeared so tiny, so vulnerable, entirely unable to protect herself. He'd wanted to wrap her in his arms and ask if she understood now that she needed him, that she was no match for the world. He'd hoped when he gave his evidence that Quinn would be able to see how much he loved her, to understand his true intentions. He wasn't perfect, far from it, but he believed he was perfect for her.

Quinn wasn't made for conflict. She was no more a warrior that a lamb frolicking through a field unaware of the butcher's shop that would sell its parts for Sunday lunches.

Liam raged.

After all that, his girl had been refused the dignity of having her complaints taken seriously by the police and the Procurator Fiscal. If any of them had listened, if just one of the miserable, condescending, incompetent bastards had done their job properly, Quinn might still be alive.

It had been left to Liam to achieve what Quinn had been unable to. He would expose their incompetence once and for all. She was gone now. He had nothing to fear now from a rape charge or a non-harassment order, but he could honour the woman he'd loved. He would make every single one of them weep for what had happened. He was going to show them all how very wrong they'd been.

Chapter Forty-Two

Ava was at her desk. Around her office sat DS Lively, DS Tripp, DC Swift, and DI Callanach.

'I don't even know what we're looking for here,' Lively said, knocking back his tenth coffee in four hours and ripping open yet another packet of biscuits.

'I've got a guy who was a celebrated community champion for his charity work before he bludgeoned his elderly mother to death,' Tripp said. 'But he's inside.'

'There's a children's entertainer, formerly the UK's best juggler, who poisoned his five-a-side football team,' Callanach said. 'He went missing before they could sentence him. Probable psychiatric issues.'

'Any link to our victims?' Ava asked.

'None that I can find, and he'll be getting out of the area as quickly as possible rather than waiting around to start a twenty-year stretch,' Callanach said.

'I've got a young woman who committed suicide on a level crossing,' Swift said.

'How does that relate to a criminal case?' Ava asked.

'It wasn't criminal. The case file says it was an application for a non-harassment order. Felicity Love stepped in at the last minute for another advocate. She represented the man who was supposed to have been harassing the deceased. He won. No order was made.'

'Another dead end,' Ava said. 'No reason for him to have had a grudge against Felicity if he won, and the applicant's dead so it wasn't her. Anyone else?'

'Nasty bastard though,' Swift said. 'It started life as a rape case. Poor girl should've got her order.'

'How does a rape case turn into an application for a non-harassment order?' Lively asked.

'She claimed the bastard drugged her, according to the case papers. Couldn't remember a thing, but he filmed them having sex then showed the tape to a member of her family. Problem was, he asked for her consent during filming and she was heard to reply. They couldn't prove the rape. She applied for an order to keep him away from her afterwards.'

'Is that why she killed herself?' Lively asked.

'The news report said after a police investigation and post-mortem, it had been deemed a suicide. She must have been pretty disturbed though. Had her baby sister in the back of the car when she went through the barrier into the path of the train,' Swift said.

There was a long silence.

'What was his name?' Callanach asked.

Swift looked back down at the case papers on his lap. 'Liam Cook.'

'Wait,' Callanach said. 'I've got someone called Liam, surname unknown, as the possible other half of the photo found in the Suzuki keyring.' He pulled up his notes on his laptop. 'Lived in Portobello. No precise address.'

Swift rifled through more papers. 'Yup, the case papers have him at a flat in Portobello,' he confirmed.

'There's still no motive,' Ava said. 'Why would Liam Cook have been pissed off with Felicity Love if she won the case for him? That makes no sense, and we've got nothing to link him to the other victims.'

'Maybe we do,' Lively said. 'Gavin Cronk was a drug dealer. If the girl— What was the victim's name, Swift?'

'Quinn McTavish,' Swift replied.

'Right, if Quinn was telling the truth about being drugged, maybe Liam got his Rohypnol from Gavin Cronk,' Lively said.

'Cronk used nicknames for his buyers. We're never going to be able to prove that from the paperwork we seized from his house,' Ava said.

'The last buyer Cronk dealt to before his disappearance . . . the nickname was Sesame, right?' Lively said.

'And?' Callanach asked.

'Due respect, sir, have you never watched any friggin' TV in your life? Liam Cook probably got called Cookie Monster every day at school. As in the Cookie Monster from *Sesame Street*?' Lively said.

Everyone dropped the papers they had in their hands and moved to form a tighter circle.

'Lively, you could actually be right,' Ava said. 'What were the details of the final drug deal?'

Lively didn't need to check his notes. 'Cronk supplied him with five forget-mes. Rohypnol.'

'Constable Swift, when did Quinn McTavish die?' Ava asked.

'Six months ago.'

'The timing fits,' Ava said. 'It's a possible link. I want everyone on this. You've got three hours. Work backwards from what we know about Liam Cook to each victim, sift through all the evidence again. See if you can find any other ties to Cook. Callanach, get a team to his address and bring him in. Swift, get me the original file on the alleged rape and talk to the officers involved. I'm going to need a hell of a lot more than just *Sesame Street*. What I want now is a motive. Let's go.'

Two and a half hours later, they were back in Ava's office, the atmosphere as charged as it had previously been hopeless. Backs were upright, pens were poised to take notes. Ava had briefed Overbeck on the new line of investigation. She swept into the room just as they were about to start information sharing.

'Off we go, then,' she said, taking Ava's seat behind the desk. 'What have we got?'

'It was your find, DC Swift,' Ava said. 'Why don't you start?'

He looked nervously at Overbeck and did his best to stop his hands shaking. 'I spoke to the officer who handled the original rape complaint against Cook. She described him as a creepy bastard . . . Sorry for the language, ma'am.' Overbeck simply sighed. 'Anyway, he was a clever one. Came in voluntarily, gave up his mobile for checking, explained everything away. Said sex was consensual, filming was consensual, never posted it online, agreed he shouldn't have arranged for other people to see it. Apologised. The officer said he used a delivery person to take the video and show them. Because Cook admitted it all, they didn't need to pursue that, so they never got the delivery person's name, but . . .'

'Maura Douglas,' Overbeck said.

'They couldn't prove the drugging,' Swift continued. 'There were no injuries, no forensics, no witnesses. A cabbie said Quinn and Liam looked pretty loved up in the back of his car. The file was sent to the Procurator Fiscal who decided that the chances of getting a conviction was too low to justify charging him. The case was dropped. The Sexual Offences Liaison Officer did say she received a nasty letter from Cook after Quinn's death. No specific threats so they didn't action it. She remembers thinking it was very strange in the circumstances but put it down to part of his obsession with Quinn.'

'Next,' Overbeck said, tapping her fake nails on the desk.

'Callanach?' Ava prompted.

'I couldn't get hold of Aspen, the girl from the keyring photo. We've been trying for two hours and I've still got an officer calling every few minutes, but her phone seems to be dead. She did say she only uses burners. However, I double checked the original rape file DC Swift obtained. Liam Cook named a girlfriend as a sort of alibi to show that he'd made plans for the night of the alleged rape. That girl was Aspen. Police spoke to her and she confirmed his version of events. When I spoke to her she couldn't recall Liam's surname or any useful information. I had her followed after her release. The undercover officer said she appeared to be waiting for someone that evening but they never showed. It's possible that she was going to ask him what was going on.'

'Or for cash to keep her mouth shut,' Ava suggested.

'More than likely,' Callanach agreed. 'Officers attended Cook's address an hour ago and remain posted outside awaiting further orders. There was no reply and neighbours say they haven't seen him for a long time. We need authorisation to enter and check his flat.'

'At the moment he's a potential witness, nothing more. No motive and no direct evidence means no smashing down doors,' Overbeck said. 'Someone give me something I can use.'

'I spoke to Panda,' Lively said.

'Is she another character from the children's programme you're basing this case on?' Overbeck snapped.

Lively muttered words no one could make out, then continued louder. 'Panda – real name Amanda – was Gavin Cronk's girlfriend. As most people in the criminal world do, he also used burner phones, but she gave me the mobile number

Cronk was using when he died. If our theory that Liam Cook is Sesame is correct and we can obtain Cook's phone records, we might be able to establish . . .' he looked straight at Overbeck, '. . . a direct link between one of the victims and Liam Cook. That, combined with the link to Aspen, would put Cook right in the middle of this case.'

'In the middle of the case, I'll concede,' Overbeck said. 'But not as a suspect. Sadly there isn't the faintest whiff of a motive in this tangled web, so while all of this is very interesting, I can't see that we're any closer to an arrest.'

'I might have something,' Ava said. She picked up a sheet of A4 paper that she'd been balancing on her lap. 'Fifteen minutes ago, I spoke with the Police Investigations and Review commissioner. She remembered Liam Cook's name from a letter she'd received shortly after Quinn McTavish's death and emailed me a copy. I'll spare you the introductory paragraph and cut straight to the interesting part: *Quinn McTavish did not commit suicide. We were still in love. Many young people face tough times at the start of their relationship, but there's no way she would have chosen to die. We were destined to be together and you took that away from us. The police didn't listen, the lawyer and the judge made her look stupid, you and the Procurator Fiscal rejected her complaints. The paramedics and pathologist didn't even see her face before deciding she'd taken her own life.*

Do you even know that your decisions have consequences? Perhaps you do, but you just don't care or maybe the fat pay cheques are all you're in it for. Now she's gone and it's too late for me to show her how much I loved her. You took her from me.

There was silence in the room.

'But . . . he raped her,' Swift said. 'Why is Cook blaming everyone else for Quinn's death?'

'Because if he didn't blame everyone else,' Ava said, 'he'd have to accept that her death was his fault. I read the non-harassment order papers. His behaviour seems to have veered wildly from abuse and coercive control, to adoration and obsession. He wanted her back, he wanted her to need him, he wanted to own her and he wanted to destroy her links to her family. None of it's about love. At some point, Quinn made him feel powerful. When he lost her, he lost that feeling and everything he's done since has been about trying to get it back.'

'He's fuckin' deranged,' Lively said, 'and he needs locking up.'

'Much as it pains me to agree with Detective Sergeant Food Debris,' Overbeck said, 'he's right. Tell me what you need and I'll get you the authorisations. Just find him, arrest him and get him here in one piece. No accidents along the way. Liam Cook is going to have to answer to the people of Scotland for the lives he's taken.'

Chapter Forty-Three

The walls of Liam Cook's apartment were adorned with photographs. Lively and Callanach stared at the lounge wall and absorbed the ordered chaos. The images had been captured on a mobile and printed on poor quality paper, but they were organised into sections, each of which showed a single photographic session. Each cluster had Quinn in one particular outfit, presumably representing one day. Shots of her at work, on the street, in a cafe, pushing a pram through the park. If those weren't disturbing enough, there was a whole section of her bedroom window, lights on, tiny glimpses of Quinn showing between slatted blinds.

Also pinned to the wall were various tickets showing entry to the cinema, a museum, gardens, a crazy golf venue. Taking pride of place was lingerie. Knickers and a lace bra were displayed as they might have been in a shop. Below it all was a photo album leaning against the wall.

Lively, hands gloved, began flicking through. 'Son of a bitch.'

Callanach peered over Lively's shoulder. 'Is that—'

'I'm thinking the answer's yes. Photographed from every angle at every possible distance. Must have been when he drugged her. The police report said there was no video on his phone and he claimed he'd destroyed the footage, but he took enough stills to remember it by. Must have used a different mobile.'

A couple of pages later the intimate body shots were replaced by grainy black and white images that were unmistakeably Quinn McTavish in bed.

'Do you think those were taken here too?' Lively asked.

'No. She's in a single bed. The only bed here is a double. These must be her at home,' Callanach said.

The next image showed two faces. Liam Cook appeared smiling sublimely as he leaned over a slumbering Quinn, his arm outstretched to take the perverse selfie. Stuck to the page next to the photograph was a lock of hair and a yellowing patch of paper.

Callanach leaned forward and sniffed. 'Perfume. He must have stolen it that night. So he broke in, photographed her as she slept, took whatever he wanted from her bedroom.'

'Do you think she had any idea?' Lively asked.

'I hope not,' Callanach said. 'But the poor girl must have been driven to the edge of her sanity. Stalkers rarely get what's coming to them.'

'This isn't just a stalker, he's a delusional psychopath who thinks drugging and raping a girl is proof that he loves her. There's no bomb-making equipment in here though. He must have been using the abandoned farm the whole time. Doesn't look like he's got so much as a tool kit in here.' Lively opened a drawer and pulled out a pile of papers. 'Pay notifications. Anyone know anything about a company called Consultech?' he shouted to the other officers.

DS Tripp wandered into the lounge, reading information from his mobile. 'Says here it's an engineering consultancy firm. You have a problem with large scale machinery, they'll send out an engineer to deal with it.'

'So he's got some technical know-how,' Lively said.

'Sarge!' The call came from the bedroom. Lively and Callanach went to see what had been found. On the bed were several shoe boxes at different stages of tattiness, some covered in dust, others more recently handled. 'These were under his bed,' an officer explained.

Callanach sifted through the contents of the scruffiest box. Photo after photo of the same young Asian woman, most taken around Edinburgh University buildings, several of her working behind the bar of some unknown pub, a couple of up-skirts Callanach assumed she was unaware of, and some of her in bed, fast asleep. Also in the box were a half-consumed pack of contraceptive pills and a lipstick.

'Same thing, different girl in each box,' Lively said as he set a couple more boxes aside. 'What's in that one?' He pointed at a box with its lid off that had been left on top of a chest of drawers.

Callanach put it on the bed. It was largely empty. In the bottom was a green silk hair scrunchy, next to a paper serviette with the blurred outline of a wiped mouth left in lip gloss. Only five images had been filed there, propped up against the side as if waiting for more to be added. The first, a woman climbing into a car, licence plate clear. The second, what appeared to be the same woman pushing her key into a lock, the car now parked on a driveway. The third was a close-up of the woman's face, animated, laughing, holding up a mug to sip. In the fourth, she was on a treadmill at a gym.

'He's moved on to someone new.' Callanach held up the fifth photo to make the point. 'This was taken in a cinema. I'm pretty sure that's the back of the same female's head. But look at the image on the screen.'

'What is it?' Lively asked.

'A scene from a movie that was only released three months ago,' Callanach said. 'We've got eight shoe boxes, plus the shrine to Quinn on the wall. What I don't understand is why his obsession with Quinn moved to psychotic levels when he's already stalking another woman.'

'Maybe something pushed him over the edge,' Lively suggested. 'The psychological profiler said there would have been a trigger for his behaviour. If we want to understand his motivation for the bombings, we need to identify that trigger.'

'All right,' Callanach said. 'Get these transported to the station. One team member per box as a priority to identify each woman, make sure they're safe and see what else we can find out. Most important is his current obsession. Maybe if we can find her, we'll find him.'

Tripp entered from the kitchen. 'All the food in the fridge is off. Not just the milk, but items with a longer shelf-life. The dishwasher was put on but hasn't been unloaded and the whole thing is bone dry. Likewise the washing machine. He must have put a load in, washed it, and it's completely dried out.'

'That would take a long time,' Callanach said. 'How long since he's been here?'

'I phoned the company Liam works for,' Tripp said. 'Initially he called in sick and their HR department told him he'd need a doctor's certificate. Two weeks later he texted to say he was still ill and wouldn't be in for another week. They haven't seen or heard from him since then. He's not replied to messages or emails. They put a letter of termination in the post. It's been six weeks since he last made contact with them.'

'Eight weeks total, which puts us back to around the time of Gavin Cronk's death,' Lively said. 'Perfect timing. So what's the plan?'

Callanach looked around. Officers were busy bagging the contents of drawers, a laptop, clothing and pharmaceuticals for testing.

'Have we located his vehicle?' he asked.

'Aye, it's on the street outside. Possibly he swapped over to the Nissan Qashqai, which isn't registered to him, so he's less traceable,' Lively said.

'Before previous bombings he got in touch when he was ready. In the last call at the press conference, he said there would be two more events. We can assume that one of those was meant to be the commissioner, so the question is: who's the final victim?'

'All I can think of is anyone from the Procurator Fiscal's office. They've been notified. Increased security will make it difficult for him to get access to a new victim,' Lively said. 'Liam must have another base somewhere. Hey, hold on!' He put out a hand to stop a passing officer who was holding a small plastic bag of green tablets. 'Where did you find those?'

'Above the kitchen sink, taped to the wall along with a tourist booklet,' the officer said. He held up a separate evidence bag with the brochure in.

'Give those to me,' Lively said. The officer handed them over. 'Let's see what we've got.' Callanach followed him into the kitchen. Lively took a glass from above the sink and filled it with cold water before taking one of the green lozenge-shaped pills from the bag.

'You're destroying evidence,' Callanach said.

'Nope, just changing its form. Forensics can test the liquid instead, if this is what I think it is,' Lively said. He dropped a pill into the water and they waited. The green outer pill dissolved to reveal a blue inner core. A couple of minutes later the water was tinted blue, pill nowhere to be seen. 'That's Rohypnol. The dye was added to help prevent druggings in bars. If your drink turned blue, you knew you were being roofied. Of course, in a reasonably strong cup of coffee, the blue dye would scarcely be visible at all. What odds would you give on these being the last drugs Gavin Cronk ever sold?'

310

'I think I'd lose money betting against that. Cronk sold five of them in that final deal. There's one dissolved in the glass and two more are left in the bag. The postmortem report said there were traces of Rohypnol in Felicity Love's system which explains how the bomber got her into the Lady Justice costume and tied her up. That makes four,' Callanach said. 'One left unaccounted for.' He turned to the officer who'd found the pills. 'Is that the brochure the pills were with?'

'Yes, sir.' He handed it over.

Callanach opened it up. Images of the Royal Botanic Gardens appeared in all of their glory, from the glass houses to extraordinary trees and rare flowers.

'Hold on a moment,' Callanach said. He disappeared into the lounge, checking through the memorabilia Liam had kept of Quinn. He grabbed another piece of paper from the wall, waving it at Lively. 'Cook visited the gardens once with Quinn. It was obviously an important place to them.'

'I see the link, but not how it helps,' Lively said.

Callanach studied the brochure. 'This must be a new brochure. It relates specifically to a temporary exhibition being held in the Woodland Garden.' He turned to the back page and stopped breathing.

'What is it?' Lively asked.

'The exhibition's only on for five days,' Callanach said, already pulling out his mobile. 'And one of them has been highlighted.' He turned the brochure around for Lively to see. The dates and times of the exhibition had been listed, and a bright orange line of ink covered the first of those dates.

'Shit,' Lively whispered. 'That's today. The bastard did leave us a message, after all.'

Chapter Forty-Four

The Royal Botanic Gardens were the jewel in Edinburgh's already substantial crown. Sitting grandly to the north of the city, the seventy-four publicly accessible acres were a haven for birds, insects and tourists alike. Now uniformed officers were negotiating with staff members and stopping the public from entering via either the east or west gates, as squads filtered in quickly and quietly.

The briefest mention of the word 'bomb' had the gardens' director panicking and running for the glasshouses, the oldest dating back nearly two hundred years and irreplaceable. The bomb squad stopped him short, insisted he return to his office, and went to perform sweeps of the buildings on site.

Callanach met Ava at the gift shop near the west gate, where they gathered the various units for a briefing. DS Tripp handed out photos of Liam Cook and plans of the gardens.

'We don't know who his victim will be or where any bombs might be hidden. What we do know is that there's a Rohypnol tablet unaccounted for in the batch he bought from Gavin Cronk, and we're assuming he used it to get his victim in here against their will. The gardens cover a vast area. Uniformed officers will escort out members of the public. We're avoiding a loudspeaker announcement because we don't want to alert Cook to our presence, or cause panic. Plainclothes teams will take the various sectors indicated on the map. Keep radio chatter to a minimum. Call in only when each sector is clear or when you find anything of relevance. Let's go.' Ava motioned for her MIT officers to gather round as the other units disappeared. 'We're taking the Woodland Garden,' she explained. 'You need protective vests on beneath your jackets. Remember what happened with Felicity Love. Don't take anything for granted.'

The Woodland Garden was the furthest point from the bulk of the buildings. They borrowed a gardener's truck and took the shortest path to the heavily treed sector. From a distance it appeared abandoned. Birds flew from branches as they approached and a rabbit dashed across the grass before them. On any other day, it would have been idyllic. The sun was out, the gardens lush, but Ava knew that death was waiting. The bomber hadn't yet failed to deliver. There was no reason to suppose he would today.

'Stop here,' Ava said. Eight of them approached the trees, splitting up as they moved under the canopy. The dappled sunlight took them from bright to dark with every step. 'There could be bombs attached to the trunk, the branches, or covered by leaves on the floor. Take it slowly.'

They formed a broken line to walk through side by side. It was quiet. Not merely peaceful, but utterly still. In spite of the patchy sun, the air beneath the leafy branches held a chill. Ava shivered. Everything felt wrong.

Callanach raised an arm up. Everyone froze.

'Listen!' he whispered. He pointed in a two o'clock direction. They waited. Thirty seconds became a minute, then they heard a whimper and the soft, wet noises of muffled sobbing.

Two officers began to move forwards.

'Stop!' Ava said. 'Spread out further. Approach with extreme caution. Remember, there are likely to be devices where you least expect them. Let's find the target, establish a perimeter and get the bomb squad over here.'

They expanded their line and began to circle around the area where the crying had originated. The first thing Ava saw was hands. They were tied together at the wrists by sections of entwined wire that disappeared around a tree trunk.

'All units be aware, we have located a victim in the Woodland Garden. Bomb squad only to attend. Other units, continue searching the remainder of the gardens. We must avoid a large congregation of bodies in one area.'

Ava moved closer to the bound wrists as Callanach sidled around to get a view of the front of the victim.

'There's something around his right wrist,' Ava said quietly. 'And the right hand has been taped up to form a fist. No sign of any explosives on the tree trunk but we don't know what's in the branches.'

Callanach stopped in his tracks as he came face to face with the victim.

'We've found Liam Cook,' he said.

Ava went to his side and Lively joined them.

'I don't suppose he could have done that to himself?' Lively asked.

'Not a chance,' Ava replied.

'So what the fuck did we miss?' Lively stared at the human bomb who was sobbing and pleading for help. 'I thought for sure we had our psycho.'

'Apparently not, but the suspect list just got shorter,' Ava said.

Liam Cook's face was a mess. His eyes were so swollen it was difficult to see the bloodshot whites. He looked as if he'd been crying forever. His back to the tree, he'd been strapped to the trunk by the wires but now they could see what those connected to. Cook was wearing what resembled a suicide vest, only he wasn't there in pursuit of some fiercely held belief. His upper body was naked. He wore trousers but had no shoes or socks. What they could see of his ribs were poking painfully from his emaciated flesh as he shivered in the shade.

'Liam, we're police officers,' Ava said. 'I want you to stay still and very calm. We have bomb squad officers coming to defuse the bomb.'

He cried harder, shaking his head. It was only when he attempted a scream that they realised his tongue was missing. Spittle flew from his lips. His throat was hoarse.

'Oh fuck me,' Lively said. 'He most definitely did not do that to himself.'

'Lively, clear a much wider perimeter and get every single unnecessary body away from here. Whoever did this is either still here or they've found a way to watch. We have to assume we're all targets. Only you, me, Callanach and vital bomb squad members will remain. Go.'

Lively went. Four bomb squad members came jogging through the trees.

'What have we got?' the senior officer asked.

'The bomb jacket is the only device we've found.'

'I'll get suited up,' he said. 'I'm going to approach alone first to see what we're dealing with. Move back behind those trees.'

'Do you think we're safe anywhere here?' Callanach asked as they moved further away.

'Chances are we won't know until it's too late. Who the hell did this, Luc? Everything made sense until now.'

'Liam's the thread that ties all the victims together. Whoever's responsible wants their grand finale. We can't even be sure Liam's the only person in the gardens wearing a bomb right at this moment,' Callanach said.

They fell into silence as the bomb squad officer approached

Liam. He did so with his hands in the air, showing he was holding no equipment. They had to assume they were being watched at every turn. He leaned down, keeping one hand up. The frustration was clear in his body language as he trudged back to them. He pulled off his mask and took a deep breath.

'You remember the electric shock device on Felicity Love's head?' Ava's only reply was a defeated sigh. 'Well, there's one around this victim's hand. It's wired to a cylindrical device that's been taped hard into his fist with his thumb on a trigger button. My guess is, we do anything to help and an electric shock will be sent to his wrist that makes his thumb twitch and hit the trigger. We can work on defusing the main device but if the bomber has eyes on us, then he could make Cook blow himself up at any given moment.'

'How long will it take you to defuse the bomb?' Callanach asked.

'Minimum of fifteen minutes. They've built in additional wires, and there's no colour pattern. It'll take a while to establish which is the live circuit and make it safe. We can't use a robot, it's too intricate.'

'Get ready to start but don't go in yet. Stand by for go ahead,' Ava said. He walked back to his team, and they began to rally round, gearing up. 'What does the killer want this time?' she asked Callanach. 'If it was just to kill Liam Cook, he could have done that privately, and as slowly as he liked.'

'Maybe just to continue spreading fear and panic. Pass on the message to the public that they're not safe anywhere. To disrupt life in Edinburgh. Who knows?'

'It doesn't feel like enough. Last time the target was the police. The killer had us where he wanted us. What's here?' Ava said.

Liam Cook began to shriek then, shaking his head like a

dog emerging from water, trying desperately to make coherent sounds. All he produced was a mush of vowels and misery.

'Mr Cook,' Ava shouted, 'we're formulating a plan to deal with the situation. There are paramedics standing by and plenty of people here to help you. Try to stay calm for a few more minutes.'

Cook responded with a new stream of sound and spittle. Behind him came a crashing from the trees. Callanach and Ava walked forward to see what was happening.

'I'm curious to know why you're helping him,' a voice called from between distant trees.

Callanach stepped backwards and got on his radio to alert backup as Ava moved forwards to identify who was addressing them.

'He obviously believes he's about to die. I have a duty to help anyone in those circumstances, irrespective of who they are or what they might have done. Is he about to die?' she said.

A shadowy figure leaned against a tree trunk, hands in his pockets.

'What do you think?' he replied.

'I think right now you're more interested in talking to me than you are in ending Liam's life, or he'd already be dead. I'm Ava Turner. Who are you?'

'Simeon McTavish, Quinn's father,' he said. 'We spoke before. You survived the last bomb because you were brave enough to run towards a woman you thought was about to die. Why did the police officers my daughter went to for help not do the same for her?'

Quinn McTavish's father was calm. There was no hint of pain in his voice. They might have been making small talk in a lift for all the emotion he was showing. Sweat trickled down Ava's back and she shivered.

'You want answers,' she said. 'For what little it's worth at this stage, I believe there were failings. I'm so sorry you lost your daughter.'

'Two daughters,' he said. 'One of them had yet to take her first step. And that was just the start of it.'

'Two daughters,' she corrected herself. 'I can't imagine what you've been through.'

'Yes, you can,' he said. 'That was the whole point. For all of you to witness it, and to feel the pain I felt. To suffer the loss. To have to look the families of the dead in the face, and to know that if Quinn had got the help she needed, every single one of those people would still be alive today.'

'That's true,' Ava said. 'I can see that. I also think you're owed a better review into everything that happened. It's within my power to arrange that.'

He laughed. It was the saddest sound Ava had ever heard.

'You mean you're willing to do something now that my girls are dead, now that you've lost some of your own. That's good of you. Can you also bring the dead back to life? Because if you can, I'll unstrap the raping bastard here and now.'

Ava said nothing. There were no words.

'Do you have children, Ava Turner?'

'I don't,' she said.

'A partner, then? Someone you've promised yourself to?'

A lump formed in Ava's throat. It was hard to speak.

'No,' she said.

Footsteps, a light crunching in the leaves, Simeon McTavish's face in clear view now.

'You're what, in your mid-thirties? I was married at twenty-three. What are you scared of?'

'All of it,' she replied. 'The enormity of it. The fact that I might fail. The amount of compromise required. Not being good enough.'

'Liar,' he said, but his voice was still amiable. 'You're scared

318

of losing it. I wasn't, more fool me. You were right and I was wrong. I thought that if I worked hard, if I was honest and loyal, that I could protect them. I just had to live a good life. Don't do it, Ava. That's my advice to you. You don't ever want to feel what I've felt.'

'Simeon—'

'You don't get to use my first name,' he interrupted. It was the first time there'd been tension in his tone. 'No one uses your first name when they're letting you down. There's this respectful use of Mr and Mrs. They elevate. I don't know if that's just so they can drop you from an even greater height.'

'You're right,' Ava said. 'About all of it. About me, too.' Simeon had a gentle smile on his face as she spoke. Utterly in command of himself. Almost a mask, carefully constructed, inscrutable. 'And yet I can't just leave that man bound to a tree and walk away. So where do we go from here? What do you want me to do?'

'That's very simple. I want you to watch us die. I won't overcomplicate things. I'm not even going to force a messy trial where I tell the world how my daughter was failed. I just need a witness.' A fresh burst of sobbing issued from Liam. Callanach reappeared and took a few step towards Liam. 'Don't do that,' Simeon McTavish told him.

'Stay back,' Ava confirmed.

McTavish took his hands from his pockets. In one of them he held his own black cylinder, thumb on the top.

'He does have to die. I'm sure you can understand that. Before the police incompetence, before I was told my girl had committed suicide, before you all put your hands over your collective ears and decided not to listen, one man caused all this misery. For that, he has to forfeit his life.'

'Don't do it,' Ava said, risking a step closer to McTavish. 'Please don't do it. Not for Liam's sake but for your own. It doesn't have to end like this. I can still gather evidence. It's not too late to have him tried for the rape. He should answer for what he did to Quinn.'

Simeon McTavish smiled again and Ava knew in her heart that it was all too late. Nothing she could say was going to change what happened in the next few minutes. She found herself wondering what Ailsa Lambert would say with her years of experience dealing with the raw, raging grief of the bereaved. But not even Ailsa could have stopped what was coming, any more than the train that crashed into Quinn and Dolly had time to brake.

'You don't deserve to die, even if he does,' Ava said. 'I lost people I loved very much. You killed them, but I still don't believe you should die. If I can understand it then other people will, too.'

Other units were appearing now. Ava could hear their approach from behind. Simeon gave his shoulders a preparatory shake.

'Keep back,' Ava called to them. 'No one intervenes.'

'I wish you'd been the police officer Quinn had spoken to,' McTavish said. 'You'd have found a way to get something done. I honestly believe that. You should stand clear now.'

'Don't do it,' Ava said.

Liam began to scream.

Simeon McTavish held the cylinder up in front of him and pressed the plunger. A series of bodies could be heard hitting the ground.

'Don't panic,' he said. 'When I release this trigger, there will be a five second delay. Use that time to make sure your units are all well clear. This bomb is designed for certainty. After that, Liam will experience an electric shock that will make his muscles spasm. If you have armed units out there now, tell them not to shoot. You'll only speed this up.'

He walked across to the tree where Liam remained bound by the wrists. He neither acknowledged Liam nor bothered to speak to him. No last words were necessary. Ava guessed Simeon had said all he wanted to Liam, long before.

Her feet were glued to the ground. What more could she possibly say to Simeon McTavish? That Quinn wouldn't want her father to do it? That the daughters he'd lost were the essence of goodness, hope, and everything beautiful? She couldn't bring herself to use such cheap, trite words. All around her, men and women were backing away, getting themselves behind trees.

Time slowed down. Callanach reached out for her, pulling her backwards by the elbow, getting her beyond the blast zone. McTavish watched her go with a gentle nod. In spite of his hatred, in spite of his need for revenge, he still wanted her safe.

The girl, no more than three years old, came out of the trees at full pelt, giggling gleefully.

Simeon was letting go of the trigger as he heard the girl shouting.

'Come and find me! Mummy, come and find me!'

The expression on Simeon's face was anguish and love, knowledge and sickness. Simeon moved before anyone else could. The girl was racing towards him, towards Liam Cook, and towards an explosive force that would obliterate them all.

Then the mother's scream, seeing, knowing the way only parents did – even without the facts, the background, the context – that their child was in mortal danger.

'Sassy!'

McTavish launched himself, flew through the air towards the girl who was still now, head tilted, confusion painted over her face. No fear yet. Then she saw the man flying at her, and she began to turn her head towards her mother. When Simeon

McTavish's body hit hers, there was a whomp of air from her lungs. They flew backwards together.

Everyone was screaming. The girl, her mother, Ava, a horrified choir of first responders. Loudest of all, Liam Cook. McTavish pressed his body down onto the girl, covered every part of her.

And the bomb exploded.

The force knocked them all backwards. Those not properly hidden behind trees were thrown from their feet. The greenery of the forest glade took on a crimson glow. The mother's screams were the first thing Ava heard as the ringing in her ears began to subside, then she was sprinting forwards, hauling Simeon McTavish's battered and bloodied body away.

The girl beneath him was shaking, reaching her hands out for her mother who pushed past Ava to get hold of her baby. They gripped one another and cried together. Ava watched, unable to speak.

Callanach was at Liam's tree, what was left of it.

'Clear the area immediately,' the bomb squad leader ordered. 'Several of these trees will have been affected by the blast. It needs to be made safe.'

'All units,' Callanach announced into his radio. 'Move away from the explosion site.'

Ava caught her breath and brought herself back into the moment.

'Come with me,' she told the sobbing mother, guiding her away from what remained of the two bodies. 'Let's get your daughter checked out. We have paramedics waiting.'

By the time they were out of the Woodland Garden area, the little girl had already stopped crying. Ava thought it might take weeks before her mother did.

'He saved me, Mummy,' Sassy said to her mother. 'I thought the man was going to hurt me, but he didn't. He saved me and then he stopped moving.'

'I know he did, baby,' her mother sobbed, pressing her own face into her daughter's hair. 'We'll tell his family thank you, I promise. I promise.'

Chapter Forty-Five

BEFORE

Simeon McTavish had lost four hours. At some point he'd sat down at the kitchen table, although he couldn't remember doing so, and that must have been straight after he'd come in from the garage. Now it was dark. He hadn't shut the back door properly and the house was freezing. There was a spider on the wall that had been exploring the area with a view to making a web and now the jerky silken spiral was fully formed, arachnid nestled comfortably at its centre. The clock said 8 p.m. He'd gone into the garage at 3.

His aim had been simple. There was very little drama to it. He'd sealed the doors, pushed rags along the cracks to seal the air flow. Sat in his car, opened the windows, turned the ignition, and waited for the pain to end. He'd left a note for his brother-in-law, Bobby. Sooner or later the car would run out of petrol and the engine would grind to a halt. It might be a few days before he was found, and that was okay too. There was no one left to attend his funeral. He'd left instructions for a quick crema-tion, no fuss, and for his ashes to be scattered on his wife's grave.

The truth was that he was still angry with her. Not for what she'd done. Only for the fact that she'd done it without him.

They'd buried their girls. He knew it had been the second worst day of his life but he couldn't actually recall much of it. They'd never recovered from the police at their door confirming the details of their vehicle. Telling them it had been wrecked on the train tracks. An officer asking, desperate hope in her eyes, if perhaps it had been stolen by someone unknown to them.

No, not stolen, his wife had said quietly. The officer had asked them to sit down, which was pointless. The red flags had been waved already. Tragedy was about to unfold. Brace yourselves. His wife had sat. He hadn't. Their deaths would have been instantaneous, they were assured, as if that somehow made it better. Quinn's body was found shielding Dolly's. They were together at the end, wrapped around one another, and that was how they'd buried them. Dolly in her big sister's arms, protected in death, lovingly held as she could never be by her parents again.

They'd lowered them into the ground and his wife had swayed backwards and forwards, as if pulled by the magnet that was her beloved babies, then dragged back into the living, grief-filled world by Bobby who was wailing at her side, and her husband who had yet to cry a single tear since his babies had left him.

It was the paperwork that had driven Simeon to fury. Dealing with the car, the insurance company, the police reports. As if the world hadn't stopped. As if filling in a form and verifying his details mattered.

His babies were dead. He didn't want to fill out forms. His babies were dead. He didn't want to pick out coffins and select music. His babies were dead. He didn't want to consider drafting an announcement for the local paper or writing to inform Quinn's college.

His babies were dead, yet they were everywhere. A stack of nappies on the changing table. Quinn's trainers by the front door, her coat slung over the back of a chair as if she were about to grab it and kiss his cheek on her way out. Dolly's comforters scattered all around – a tiny pink blanket, a cuddly penguin, a fluffy hat. He could neither bear to see nor touch them, nor could he contemplate a world in which he packed them away like corpses into little coffin boxes, to be stashed pointlessly in the loft forever.

He and his wife had drifted around one another, utterly lost. Picking something up, staring at it, putting it back down. There was no point doing, no point planning, no point being. His wife had clearly realised the latter before him.

The day after the funeral, the love of his life had run herself a bath, drunk enough gin and consumed enough paracetamol to dull the pain, and opened up her wrists into the water. Ever thoughtful, she'd taped a note to the bathroom door telling him not to enter and to phone the police. He'd smashed the wood, slipped his hand in to turn the lock and found her there. She'd propped photos of Quinn and Dolly at the end of the bath, surrounding herself with their joyous faces, with memories of their spectacular and overwhelming love, as she'd gone to join them.

Without him.

She'd gone on without him.

Had it not occurred to her to invite him too? He wouldn't have tried to stop her. They could have held each other on the journey, wiped one another's tears and laughed in the face of the brief and irrelevant pain. Instead, he had another body to bury, and there was a part of him that was incandescent at her for her selfishness, that felt betrayed at being left behind.

And at the end of it all was yet more paperwork. Life insurance.

Additional police reports. Another postmortem. An extra finding of suicide.

He'd buried his wife next to their children. The gravestones were an essay in tragedy and consequences.

Bobby had wanted to accompany Simeon back to the house after Cora's funeral. Simeon had insisted that he wanted to be alone. For the first time in decades of friendship, the two of them had come to blows. Neither had intended to hurt with the fists they'd thrown. Neither had known what else to do with their rage. The other mourners had stood and watched the fracas, attempting to intervene uselessly, then stepped back until they'd burned themselves out. Bobby had given in and driven himself home. Simeon had sat at Cora's graveside and watched ants crawling through the grass until, at sunset, he'd been informed that he would have to leave.

The next day, he'd sat in his car and tried to breathe in the fumes that would send him to sleep forever. It hadn't worked. There was something he'd neglected to do; some remnant of purpose that remained in the physical world.

This was how he'd found himself watching the spider spin its web in the kitchen, losing himself in the intricacy of it, the engineering, the beautiful trap.

In the lounge was a pile of the dreaded paperwork. It had seemed as good a place as any to find whatever he'd forgotten to do. Someone, presumably, had written asking for information or for proof of death. Wasn't that the ultimate slap in the face? It turned out that you actually had to prove to other people's satisfaction that those you loved had been brutally ripped from your life. It wasn't enough that it had happened. You had to produce the paperwork in triplicate with a stamp on.

He sighed, moved his wife's coffee shop loyalty card, and began at the top, making notes and separating the documents into piles. Throw away, box, action. Halfway down he came to the file he and Cora had actively avoided opening. It sat on his lap, a sad shade of grey, thick with photographs, maps, plans, technical reports and witness statements. Contained within were his daughters' last moments. This was the basis on which it had been decided that a desperate and confused Quinn had driven her car through the level crossing barrier with the intent to commit suicide, only to realise that her sleeping baby sister was in the seat behind. The car seat base and baby seatbelt had become jammed in the accident. The baby's death had been deemed accidental. Case closed.

Opening the file had seemed pointless. It was Bobby who'd requested it, as if knowing the details could somehow bring Quinn and Dolly back to them. It had been hand delivered by an officer, put on the growing pile of documents they didn't really want to read, and left.

Simeon opened it, resenting himself for so doing. There were reports of erratic, even dangerous, driving around the city bypass. Speeding. Weaving in and out of other cars. Taking junctions with no warning and hitting pavements as Quinn had headed through Kingsknowe. Other drivers said she appeared to be yelling as she drove the car, looking frantic and disturbed.

Quinn hadn't slowed as she'd approached the level crossing. The car had bent the safety barrier, scattered fragments of red and white plastic everywhere, and flown straight onto the tracks. The police expert said she hadn't even begun to brake. Eye-witnesses said Quinn had exited the driver's door seemingly unharmed, pulled the rear door open instead of running out of the path of the oncoming train, and stayed with the vehicle. What happened next needed no recap.

Simeon read the witness list. The name at the top was Liam Cook.

He dropped the sheet of paper. Stood up. Walked away. He went back, not trusting his eyes, certain the letters would have rearranged themselves. Convinced he was seeing demons everywhere.

But no. Liam Cook it was. First at the scene, the car directly behind Quinn's as she'd approached the crossing. She'd been trying to get away from him, and he'd pursued her. The clarity was a waterfall of ice to his brain. Quinn must have seen him outside their home, and run. Grabbed the keys from her mother's hands before they'd had a chance to take Dolly and the shopping out of the car. Then she'd driven to her death, trying only to get away from the man who was destroying her life. And what had the police done? Nothing. Had they even bothered checking back on their previous contacts with Quinn, looking at the train crash witness list and joining the dots? Of course not. The police response, as it had been since the day Liam Cook had begun ruining their lives, was pitifully negligent.

Quinn's death was no more a suicide than Dolly's had been an accident. His wife's passing, too. They had all been murdered. Slowly, day by day, from the moment Liam Cook had first laid eyes on Quinn, they had all unwittingly, unknowingly been inching towards a slaughter.

What Simeon understood then was that it had to end with Liam, too. He had the Portobello address and a mobile number – Quinn had provided those so her parents always knew how to get hold of her. The irony was poisonous. Formulating the rest of the plan was much simpler than he'd imagined. There was an empty farm with outbuildings in a rural area to the west of Gorebridge that he drove past regularly. Local gossip told of a tragedy that meant it wasn't going to sell any time soon, which made it the perfect place to get started.

He lured Liam there with the promise of a box of Quinn's belongings, and sure enough, Quinn's stalker was both bold and deluded enough to attend. After that, armed with Liam's mobile phone and the information he gave up so easily with

329

the application of just a small amount of pain, Simeon was able to find the other people who'd helped Liam destroy his daughter's life.

Cora's life insurance financed it, and his employer had already suggested he take a six month sabbatical while he, 'came to terms with his losses'. Insomnia meant he could research techniques and source materials twenty-four hours a day if necessary. And if he got killed by mistake partway through wiring a device? Well, halle-fucking-lujah to that. His wife would have hated him swearing, but he was alone now so it hardly mattered.

He made Liam watch it all. Gavin Cronk's abdominal surgery. Maura Douglas and the fake baby bump. Maura had begged and pleaded, and Simeon had wanted to listen. He'd actually tried. But there was a grave with both his daughters in it, and one at its side with his wife, and he just couldn't feel anyone else's pain. It had been impossible. When the barn was discovered he'd had to move his centre of operations to his garage. Using the family home had been a risk, but Simeon had never been scared of getting caught – only that he wouldn't achieve all that he wanted before that day came.

Now time was running out. He'd left a trail, and the police were finally catching up with him. Simeon was exhausted. Revenge was hard work, but worth it. Everyone involved had to be made to see what they'd done. They had to feel what he'd felt. Quinn's voice, ignored, stifled and derided when she was alive, deserved to be heard at last. The grief his wife had been unable to bear had to be shared.

His time was nearly up and he looked forward to it being over. Simeon wanted to rest. He dreamed of curling up next to his wife, seeing Quinn's smile once more and hearing Dolly gurgle from the crib. He knew they were somewhere, waiting for him, just over the horizon.

He left a note for Bobby in the bird box at the end of the garden by the back gate, where they always left him a key if they were out. In it, Simeon provided instructions to be followed after his death. Then he fetched Liam from the garage. They would be taking a trip together from which neither of them would ever return.

Chapter Forty-Six

Two weeks had passed since Liam Cook's death. Ava sat on the floor of her office nursing a whisky and wondering if she could cobble together enough cushions and blankets to make herself a bed for the night. The rest of the MIT team were still in a pub – they'd visited a stream of hostelries over the course of the evening – for Pax Graham's delayed wake. She'd gone along to honour their fallen colleague. Pax Graham's loss had left a dent in their team, one that could never be filled, but the traditional night out in his memory, telling funny stories and poignant anecdotes, felt wrong to her.

On her knees was a photo of Quinn McTavish hugging her dad. Ava could see the glint in her eyes and the broad shine of her smile. She was beautiful. Every part of her shone with expectation and joy. To have that destroyed for no reason at all . . . Ava couldn't bear thinking about it.

Next to that was a photo of Dolly in her mother's arms. The family resemblance between the women was marked, but Cora McTavish's face exuded calm. There was a tranquillity to her love that reached through the photograph. Ava touched Cora's face with her fingertips. In the image, she was kissing

Dolly's forehead. It was the definition of motherly love. Ava could imagine Simeon McTavish clutching that photo in the long hours he had to contemplate his loss. Holding it, crying over it, reconstructing the moment it was taken in his imagination. Both photographs had been found in the boot of his car along with a stuffed hippo, a cuddly penguin, and a bracelet they deduced had belonged to his late wife. Little things with big meanings.

Ava knocked back her drink and poured another. She couldn't drive tonight. Even if she could, home felt like the wrong place to be. Having a home to go to at all felt like too great a privilege. She stared into the face of the most prolific killer Edinburgh had ever known, and could find no evil in his eyes, nor any hatred for him in her heart. It was easier when cases followed a Wild West brand of morality. There was the good and the bad, and you knew which side you were fighting for.

Simeon McTavish was a good man who had done terrible things. Not crazy but crazed was how Dr Connie Woolwine had described him. Ava didn't know if that was luck or brilliance, but no one could ever have conceived just how accurate a deduction that would turn out to be.

Life had broken him. He'd endured more than anyone should ever have to. Slow burn at first – the stalking, the rape, the injustices, the failure of any agency to help his daughter, her mental anguish – and then a riot of pain. The death of not just one child, but two. The knowledge of Quinn's regret as she'd heard her baby sister's cry and known she couldn't let Dolly die alone. His wife's suicide. Attempting to take his own life and failing – the forensics team had found the evidence in the garage.

But also on her lap was a list of the dead. First responders and other victims – Ailsa Lambert's name at the top of the page. Her own loss still stuck in her throat, impossible to quantify or express. The cruel waste of it. She'd wanted to kill Simeon McTavish before she'd known his identity. Now she was mourning him, too. Both killer and victim.

At any stage in the chain of events that had made him a murderer, things could have changed. If Liam had stopped at a different shop and never met Quinn. If Quinn had been less of a gentle soul and refused his offer of coffee in the bookshop. A worse indictment on them all; if the police and the Procurator Fiscal had decided to proceed with the rape trial. If Maura Douglas had not been dying of a brain tumour and therefore less desperate for a few extra pounds to leave to her son. If Felicity Love had not stepped in for her colleague. If any complaint, anywhere along the line had been upheld. If Quinn's death had not been misconstrued as a suicide.

If, if, if.

Ava lobbed her glass across her office and watched it smash against the far wall. A pathetic, childish gesture in a world where a stalker had caused the death of so many heroes, sung and unsung alike.

And an imagined scene she couldn't get out of her head – Simeon McTavish packing a fake baby bump with explosives as he remembered his wife's growing stomach, putting his face down to talk to the unborn child who had been a late, unexpected blessing in their lives. Delivering the same death and destruction to the world that had been dealt to him. Simeon taking a single hair from his wife's hairbrush and letting it set in the glue he poured into the battery pack wired to Felicity Love's nightmarish crown. Ava let the tears fall. It was the least she owed Quinn and her family for a multitude of systemic failures.

Stalking cases were almost never satisfactorily resolved. They were hard to prove, hard to investigate, one person's word against another's. They rarely went to court, and even less often resulted in a conviction. Women were left to put up with it or run.

Ava picked up the bottle and drank from it directly. It was a shameful way to treat a twenty-five-year-old single malt, not that it mattered. She would have toasted each of the dead, but there were too many of them.

Only Liam Cook had deserved what had come to him. It was just as well he'd died in the final bomb. Had he survived, Ava suspected that she too might have ended up charged with murder.

At Ailsa's funeral, she'd promised her dear friend that she would find her murderer and make sure he could never hurt anyone else again. The promise had been kept, but it was a sticking plaster over a lost limb. Jimmy Douglas, Maura's son, had been found a secure place to live independently and a scholarship to university. The cash his mother had been saving for him, stashed under her mattress, wouldn't have paid more than six months' rent. Ava could only hope she knew her boy was safe. Allan Cronk had been allowed out of prison for the day to attend his brother's funeral. Dr Nate Carlisle was returning to his Glasgow post for a while but Ava thought there was a good chance he'd be asked to fill Ailsa's shoes eventually. Ailsa would have approved of that. A memorial was being erected to the fallen inside St Giles' Cathedral. Small victories, all.

There was a knock at the door. Ava didn't bother to answer it. Callanach walked in, followed by Natasha. No one said anything. They each took a seat on the floor, a little triangle of concern, each of them worrying for the others. Ava passed the whisky to Natasha who drank then offered it to Callanach. He declined and set it back down.

'I'm driving,' he explained. 'We came to take you home.'

'I'm not going home. May as well sleep here now. Easier to get to work tomorrow.'

'You're not on duty tomorrow,' Callanach said. 'You've got a day off. I checked your schedule.'

'I'm always on duty.' Ava smiled.

'You need a hobby,' Natasha said.

'Yeah? Well you should be in bed, so we're quits,' Ava snapped back.

'Luc told me all about this case. I know your head must be a mess but please come home. You and Luc helped heal me by cooking together, watching movies, arguing about whose turn it was to vacuum, and by leaving each other stupid notes stuck to mirrors. We can do it again. It's your turn.'

Ava laughed. 'You can't fix this, Tasha. It's not about me. The whole system's broken. We failed one young woman and look at the consequences. Do you know how many others we fail every month, every year?'

'You're not part of the problem, you're the solution, Ava,' Natasha said. 'You can rage against the machine all you like, but at the end of the day, the answer's not to blow the machine up, it's to fix it.'

'Don't make me a philosophy project. This isn't a soundbite moment. The combined number of children who have lost a parent in all this is twenty-nine. Six of the deceased also had grandchildren. That's monstrous. It's beyond reason.'

'And it was an anomaly,' Callanach said. 'Unforeseeable, bizarre in many ways. If the baby hadn't been asleep in the back of the car, Quinn would have walked away from that crash. If the baby hadn't been in the car, Cora McTavish might well not have committed suicide and Simeon might have found a reason to survive in the world without taking revenge. It was a series of consequences, and yes, we need to review how we failed Quinn, but the rest of it is pure tragedy.'

Ava sighed. 'I miss Ailsa. She wasn't involved in Quinn's case at all, did you know that? It was an assistant who liaised with the Procurator Fiscal to decide that Quinn's death was a suicide. Ailsa just happened to pay the price for it, like all the others.' She picked up the whisky bottle. 'To Ailsa!'

'Let's go,' Natasha said. 'You're not going to find any meaningful conclusions at the bottom of that bottle.'

'No, but maybe I'll forget what I was looking for. That would be something.' She smiled.

'What are you looking for?' Callanach asked.

Ava stared at him. She'd barely seen Luc in the final two weeks of the investigation, partly because they'd been following leads in different directions, but she'd also got the impression that he'd been avoiding her. She didn't blame him. Living and working with her at the same time was probably the world's least enjoyable combination.

'I'm looking for the motivation to carry on. Something to give me back my love of the job. In fact, I want it to stop being a job. It never used to feel like one. It was a reason to be the best version of myself, a purpose.'

'Now who's making this a philosophy project?' Natasha interrupted gently. Ava had the grace to acknowledge the moment with a dip of her head. 'Ava, the truth is that you gave your life to your work to an extent that most people reserve for their partner or their children. This can be your calling – I'm sure it is, you were meant for it – but it shouldn't be your reason for living. If you aren't a rounded, balanced person, how can you have the judgement you need to do the job? Do you really want to understand why Simeon McTavish broke, or why Quinn sacrificed her life to hold her baby sister as the train hit? Then you need to experience some of it. Stop being Detective Chief Inspector Turner and learn to be Ava again. We love you. We've missed you. It's been a while.'

'You make it sound so easy but I don't have time. I can't make a commitment to anyone or anything because I'll end up breaking it a week later. Who the hell wants to set up home with a woman who can't guarantee she'll be there to celebrate birthdays or anniversaries, who'll inevitably have to cancel holidays, and who will definitely bring her work home with her?'

'I want to,' Callanach said.

Ava laughed. Natasha didn't.

'Only because you do exactly the same,' Ava said.

'Which makes us a perfect match. We have no expectations of each other except to be kind and pick up the pieces as necessary. Marry me, Ava. You know me better than I ever wanted anyone to know me. I believe I know you as well as I know myself. No compromise required.'

'You're not serious,' Ava said.

'I'm pretty sure he is, actually,' Natasha added, unable to keep the smile from her face.

'Luc?' Ava asked.

'God, you're already the most demanding woman I've ever met. Being married to you can't be any worse than living and working with you. Are you really going to make me ask you twice?'

'I'm sorry, I'm either so drunk I'm imagining things, or you just proposed to me while I'm sitting on my office floor, having consumed half a bottle of single malt, with Natasha watching the whole thing, while we're not even vaguely involved with each other romantically.'

'I did,' he said.

'Oh my god.' Natasha wiped tears from her face.

'Don't you bloody dare start crying,' Ava told her. 'Luc, you're being ridiculous. We're still closing this case—'

'We're always starting, in the middle of, or closing up a case. It's what we do, but it's not who we are. I don't want this to be all I am. If you want the romantic part, then you can have it. I love you. You saved me when I came here. You gathered up all the broken parts of me and jammed them, fairly roughly, back together. We've fought side by side, won and lost. We've hurt each other and recovered. There hasn't been a day since I met you when you weren't in my thoughts, almost constantly. We already live together. I'm not under any illusions about how messy you are, and you know I don't like to be spoken to for the first hour after I wake up.'

'Will you still live with me if you get married?' Natasha asked. Callanach glared at her. 'Sorry, not the moment.'

'You want to know if I've actually thought this through, or if it's just because I'm worried about you? The truth is both. I don't think there was any doubt in my mind that I'd end up asking you this question. I just finally got fed up waiting for you to be ready to hear it.'

'So it's my fault now?' Ava asked.

'You always make everything your fault. What's new?' Natasha asked. Ava rolled her eyes. 'I'll shut up.'

'I have no idea what to say, Luc. None at all. I didn't see this coming.'

'Ugh, I have to be allowed to speak. Ava, I love you as if you were my own sister but you can be the most infuriating human on the planet. God only knows why Luc just proposed to you, but the simple fact that one of you came to your senses at last is worth celebrating. You're perfect for each other, if only because you're both equally dense when it comes to your private lives. Luc, Ava has been in love with you since the first day she told me about this moody, awkward French guy. She didn't mention your face at all. When I met you, I couldn't believe she hadn't told me how good-looking you were, and I knew then that she was so captivated by you – by what she saw inside you – that she hadn't really noticed your face, not the way other people do. And Ava, this man worships the ground you walk on. If I didn't love you both so much, I would have found the whole situation utterly sickening. As for getting married, you have been married in my mind for quite a while now. Nothing much is going to change.'

Ava dashed the back of her hand against her own tears. 'Do you mean it?' she asked Luc.

'Do you need me to put it in writing?' he replied.

She laughed. 'Can I have some time? Just to figure out if I'm ready.'

'Yes,' he said quietly. 'We've got all the time in the world.'

'Could we cap it at a week?' Natasha grinned. 'I can't wait more than a week, and I'm the one who has to share a house with you both in the meantime. Also, the tension might give me a second heart attack.'

'My moment, Natasha. Please zip it,' Ava warned her. 'Take me home. I think I need some sleep.'

Luc held out his hand and pulled her up off the floor.

Chapter Forty-Seven

A show of public unity was what the powers that be had asked Detective Superintendent Overbeck to deliver from the press conference. It resembled the head table at a high-powered charity gala. Various dignitaries sat in a long line, ready to have their images captured and reassure the Scottish people that they could now go about their lives without fear. The threat had been successfully neutralised. Overbeck had called Ava to her office earlier and given her a long, cool look before beginning to speak.

'I've considered the comments you drafted for the press conference this afternoon,' she began. Ava kept her eyes on Overbeck's nails which were painted beige with white tips. Understated. Not at all the superintendent's usual style. 'I'm not sure the tone you've adopted is what anyone really wants to hear. We have some politicians with us today. They'll be looking for a more positive message.'

'You don't want me to mention Simeon McTavish's motivation,' Ava said. 'You think the press would be better off not hearing about Quinn and Liam Cook.'

'I think this city and its people have suffered enough. Sometimes, closing the book firmly and forever is the kinder thing to do,' Overbeck lectured.

'But the truth—'

'Will remain the truth. No one can say any different. But do we need to make excuses for the most violent succession of domestic bombings in Scottish history? We do not. Our responsibility is to the families of those innocent victims taken before their time. Those are the crimes we were tasked with investigating. You did a good job, Ava. You led your team effectively and resolved an almost impossible case, but I cannot let you turn that into some pulpit-style lecture on societal responsibility and police failings.'

'Can't let me or won't let me?' Ava asked.

'Same thing. If you can't do this, then someone else will have to, and please don't turn it into another battle ground. In the grand scheme of things, I'm doing you a favour,' Overbeck said. Her usual dry smile was missing. In its place was an unfamiliar weariness. Ava didn't have the stomach for a fight she knew she couldn't win.

'Fine, you do it. Say whatever you've been ordered to say. I'll stand behind you and look deferential. Let the politicians have their day, pat one another's backs. Maybe you're right.' She stood. 'We can't honour the dead at the same time that we talk hard truths. But I can't be party to blaming Simeon McTavish for all the things he did.' She walked to the door.

'I don't want you to leave MIT, DCI Turner,' Overbeck said. 'There will always be politics and spin. Someone will always be tasked with packaging the unpalatable and making it smell like roses. You and I still know the truth. Occasionally, that has to be enough.'

'I'm not going anywhere. I just need to stop believing I can change the whole world and concentrate on the corners of it that matter to me. See you in the conference room.'

★ ★ ★

Overbeck was at the far end of the table, next to a variety of even more senior Police Scotland officers, three politicians, representatives of both the fire brigade and the ambulance services, the commissioner who had escaped McTavish's attempt to kidnap her, with the Procurator Fiscal, John Raskin, at the other end. Ava, uniformed, entered as late as she could. The room was stifling. Every possible space was taken. There were so many cameras and tripods that they'd been set up in a horseshoe formation around the edge of the conference room, their operators fitting lenses and checking their shots. Microphones were set up on the top desk. Photographers took the front rows of seating, and behind them were journalists furiously scribbling notes and calling out to one another.

Ava waited for the political spin to begin. There was a moment at the end of each major case when someone took the facts and bent them to their will. Every time, stock phrases were cut and pasted. The police had 'worked to the best of their ability in difficult circumstances'. They had 'overcome the odds to vanquish an antagonist, often at great personal and professional expense'. It was always a 'team effort – every squad, every department, proud of their own'. All as it should be. The facts that were omitted told a different story. Those omissions did not always make a lie of the press release, but they certainly painted the so-called truth in a different colour.

It was a more subdued crowd than when they'd been in the full throes of the investigation. The urgency had gone from the room, as had the excitement. It was no good dressing it up as anything else, Ava thought. Nothing like a high-stakes, life-or-death game of cat and mouse with a bomber to sell papers and fill airtime.

Her mind wandered as she waited for everyone to be ready. It had been the strangest of times at Natasha's house. Three days earlier Luc and Natasha had turned up to find her less than sober on her office floor. Just minutes later the man she'd been playing her own game of cat and mouse with had proposed marriage. They'd gone home and made her eat toast and drink water, before sending her off for a sleep. The next morning Natasha had crept into her room, climbed into bed with her, and waited for Ava to surface from the depths of her hangover to remember the question Luc had asked her. None of it had felt real.

On paper, it would have appeared the least romantic proposal in history, but somehow Luc had managed to apply his straightforward style and made it perfect. Natasha had been there to witness it and add the same brand of sarcastic exasperation that she'd contributed to the past twenty years of Ava's life. The proposal had come when Ava was feeling hopeless and useless, precisely when she'd needed it. She pondered it as a sympathy-proposal, then reminded herself that she wasn't doing Luc justice. He'd never patronised her, and she didn't believe he was merely trying to save her now.

'Say yes,' Natasha had said as Ava had grabbed the bottle of water next to her bed, mouth woolly, throat parched.

'I need coffee,' Ava had groaned.

'You need Luc,' Natasha had persisted. 'I know you do, you know you do. And he needs you. Say yes.'

'Natasha, please.'

'I won't stop. He held my hair when I was throwing up after chemo. He changed my bedsheets when I'd sweated through them. He carried me to my bedroom when I was too weak to climb the stairs. He's funny. He's also blunt, I'll give you that, but it's one of the things I love about him. If I could turn him into a woman, I'd steal him from you in a heartbeat. Say yes.'

Ava pulled the pillow over her face. 'Natasha, you can't talk me into this one. I asked for time, and that's what I need.'

'Why?' Natasha persisted.

Ava sighed. 'Because I screwed things up before. Luc and I tried to have a relationship. I've seen so many marriages fail when both parties are police. I can't imagine how it might feel to be that happy and then lose it.'

'That's just choosing not to live because you know one day you're going to die. Take it from someone who found out the hard way. Choose life, Ava. Choose every fucking day, pain and all, and live it. Say yes.' She slipped out of bed then and left Ava contemplating her choice.

Ava had got up, showered, dressed, pretended nothing had changed, and no one had mentioned it since. She'd watched Luc, though, when he was otherwise occupied, kissing Natasha on the temple almost every time he walked past her, wordlessly saying, 'You're still here, you're safe, you're loved.' Endlessly reassuring with the deft touch of a man who knew what it was to feel scared and lost. Watching him was nothing new. She'd been doing it for months, since they'd moved into Natasha's to look after her. She'd be an hour into a movie and realise she'd long since ceased concentrating on the screen and had been staring at Luc instead. He'd be cooking as she sat at the kitchen table playing cards, and realise she'd completely forgotten what she was doing in favour of studying the back of his neck or the curve of his shoulder blade. Still, they'd kept their distance from one another. If he'd had the proposal planned, he'd hidden it so well she'd had no idea it was coming. And yet, when he'd said it, it had seemed the most natural, normal, logical thing in the world.

Now Ava was one side of the room behind Overbeck, and Luc was at the far side behind the Procurator Fiscal. The clock was ticking. She had to give him an answer soon. The only question was how brave she could be. Run into a building with men holding guns and hostages? She'd done that. Walk into a room with a psychopathic killer who wanted to use her for leverage? No problem. Make a lifelong commitment to a man she thought she probably loved so much it terrified her? Now that was scary.

'Let's begin,' Overbeck said. 'Operation Blunt Sword has now been concluded. Simeon McTavish, popularly known as the Edinburgh bomber, died in the Royal Botanic Gardens when an explosive device he had attached to a man named Liam Cook exploded. McTavish was a technical writer for the armed forces. He was a civilian who had low level security clearance to write up military instruction booklets, technical specifications for vehicles, weapons, and so on. It's believed that is how he came by the knowledge to construct the explosive devices and weaponise the landmine. Mr Cook also died in the blast. No members of the emergency services or the public were seriously injured although a three-year-old girl was left shaken and with superficial cuts and bruises.'

No mention of the fact that Simeon McTavish saved the girl's life. No explanation that the last thing he wanted was for another girl – another daughter – to die.

'McTavish used a deserted barn on unused farmland as his base. He kept his kidnap victims there and built his bombs on that site. Thorns found in Gavin Cronk's feet matched a field in the vicinity and Maura Douglas' car was discovered there. After police discovered that location, he'd had no choice but to use his own home. Thereafter the bombs were constructed in the garage attached to his house. We're still searching for a blue Nissan Qashqai that was used in an attempted kidnapping and seen near the farm.'

The Major Investigation Team had arrived at the McTavish house within four hours of Liam and Simeon's deaths. They'd split up and taken a room each, but what had struck them all as they'd entered the house had been the hallway. There wasn't an inch of wall space left. Beautifully framed and carefully hung

346

photos of the family adorned the walls. Light dust frosted the glass but Ava had no doubt that through the years the photos would have been lovingly polished every week, and looked at with pride and joy every day. The images showed varying combinations of Simeon and Cora and Quinn and Dolly at each stage of their lives, always beaming with love. The place was alive with it, even after the tragedy. The hallway was a shrine to the power of family, to the extraordinary joy of belonging and knowing you belonged. Other people featured there too, some in just a few photos, others more regular. The McTavish family hadn't been selfish with their happiness. Ava had lost thirty minutes just staring into their faces, wishing she could turn back time and return those glorious people to a world before the hurt had started.

They'd left the garage to the bomb squad to make safe, then scenes of crime officers had moved in to preserve the evidence. A quick sweep of the house had shown that there were no more undiscovered hostages, no hidden bodies.

A young man had been standing outside as Ava exited. He looked washed out, beaten down by life. Ava saw herself in the disappointment on his face.

'Was it him?' he asked as she approached. 'Did Simeon do the bombings, kill those people?'

'He did,' Ava confirmed. 'Did you know him?'

The young man nodded. 'It wasn't his fault,' he said.

'Are you all right?' Ava asked.

'It was always going to end this way,' he replied rather than answering. 'Whatever we tried to do to keep her safe, he just kept coming for her.'

'You mean Liam, and Quinn?' He nodded. 'Could I ask your name? I'd like to put together a better picture of what they all went through. Maybe you could help?'

'Bit late for that,' Mark Devlin said, before walking away to start his shift at the shop. Ava didn't pursue him. He was right. Anything they did now was too little too late.

Overbeck was reading out names that Ava was all too familiar with. The list of the dead was too long and the damage to the city too grievous to pretend that Simeon McTavish's actions had been anything less than evil, but still Ava's heart ached.

She looked across at Luc, leaning against the wall, and found him already staring at her. Ava knew then what her answer had to be. 'Say yes,' Natasha said inside Ava's head.

It was the worst possible time. They were grieving personal losses. They were remembering those in their community who'd been brutally murdered. They were contemplating an ineffective system that without radical change would continue to fail stalking victims. Natasha was still not fully recovered and wouldn't be for some time. Ava finally realised that none of it mattered. Life went on. She could live for the job with her life on pause or choose to embrace it.

Luc tipped his head to one side, raised his eyebrows at her.

Ava gave him the smallest nod. She couldn't smile, not now with all the cameras pointed at her. Not when so many were still mired in grief. She watched his mouth, saw Luc suppressing a smile of his own and had to look away before their communication was noticed. She looked across the room instead, casting her eyes around the crowd.

One face puzzled her. She recognised him, but not from the usual ranks of the media. Ava gave the cameraman a longer look. He seemed to notice her and stepped closer in behind the tripod for cover. Ava glanced at Luc, frowning. His eyes followed hers to the camera operator just a few metres from him. He made the same expression she'd made. Recognition, but vague. Luc moved his head to one side for a better view. The man was wearing a press lanyard but it wasn't clear from which outlet.

The breath left Ava's lungs as Luc's lower jaw fell open. He began stepping discreetly to the edge of the room, out from behind the table, motioning to those in his way to move aside. The camera operator wasn't looking at either Ava or Luc. His was the same face that had appeared in many of the photos on the McTavishes' wall, that of a man with an arm often flung around Cora's shoulders. The physical resemblance had been clear and Ava had assumed at the time that she was seeing Cora's brother, Quinn and Dolly's uncle, whose gaze was now focused firmly on the Procurator Fiscal. Ava searched his camera for the tiny red light that would tell her it was recording, functioning as a normal piece of media equipment. There was none.

'Everyone down!' she yelled, reaching forward to push Overbeck's head to the desk and cover the superintendent's body with her own.

The Procurator Fiscal stood, looking around for the nearest exit.

Bobby Wilson thought of the family he'd lost, the brother-in-law he'd met at a military base, a quiet writer who'd taken a technical job for the money and who Bobby had introduced to his sister, knowing they would fall in love. Callanach tried to reach Bobby before he could detonate the bomb, but everyone was panicking, trying to move their gear and reach an exit.

Callanach pushed forwards, but got knocked back again in the ensuing panic. He struggled to keep moving towards the camera operator.

Then the room was a ball of bright, white light as the camera that had been hollowed out and packed with explosives ignited.

The walls were spattered red.

Finally, thick grey smoke consumed everything and the screaming began.

Ava did her best to exit from behind the table as people

panicked and screamed. There were two bodies slumped over the far end. One politician. The other, the Procurator Fiscal – John Raskin. She breathed in smoke as she leapt across the tabletop between the bodies. People cried out for help, others were crushed in the doorway. Closer to the camera were moaning, crumpled heaps of flesh. Ava fought to make out faces, but the smoke was too dense. Nearest the centre of the bomb blast were the bodies of those who never had a chance to survive.

'Luc,' she yelled. 'Luc!'

There was too much smoke and too many people in such a small space. The sounds of human misery were overwhelming.

A hand gripped her ankle. Ava knelt down, stopped herself from crying out. Luc was alive. That was a start. She shielded his body with her own and assessed his injuries.

'Hey,' she said softly. 'Stay still. Paramedics will be here in a couple of minutes.'

'Ava,' he whispered. 'Was that a yes?'

She forced a smile as she lifted his head onto her lap. 'It was. You didn't need to do the hero act to impress me. I'd already agreed to marry you.'

The smoke was beginning to clear. She could feel the blood soaking through his shirt and reached out to slip her fingers over his wrist. His pulse was thready and faint.

'Luc, look at me,' she said. Ava turned his head to see his eyes. Her hands met loose flesh and splinters of bone. As his head fell across her lap she finally saw the right hand side of his face. What was left of it.

Her tears fell into his hair.

'You don't get to leave me,' she told him. His eyes were closing, breath ragged. The blood from his chest was flowing down his arm and puddling on the floor at his hand. 'Luc, you fight and you stay with me. Paramedic!' she screamed with every ounce of power she had left in her body. 'Don't you dare leave me,' she cried. 'I said yes. Please, Luc, please don't die.'

She let her body fall over his, holding him to her.

New shouts could be heard. Someone was taking charge. People were giving instructions.

'I need medics here!' Ava yelled again.

She held the side of his face together with the force of her hand, and pressed her chest into his to stem the blood flow. She whispered her love for him into the smoky air and kissed him. Luc Callanach lay in her arms and Ava prayed for a future. Any future at all. As long as she could be by the side of the man she loved.

Can't wait for the next book from Helen Fields?

Then read on for a sneak peek of her next page-turning thriller . . .

Chapter One

Finding Adriana Clark's body was a shock, but not a surprise. I had, after all, been searching for it. The girl had been lost to her family for eleven devastating days and nights. I mention the nights because, in my experience, they outweigh the daytime in awfulness so greatly that the daylight hours become irrelevant. Families waiting for a missing loved one to return can fill their days. They can make telephone calls, put up posters, give pleading interviews to the press, bake bread or go to church. Everyone, everywhere has some sort of altar – domestic, professional or religious – at which to bend the knee in times of crisis during the day. But when I first met Adriana's family, I saw the horror of the endless nights they'd endured waiting for the phone to ring and the seconds to pass. Nighttime is not merely a lack of light; it is the darkness within each of us when we lose hope.

The facts of the initial case were not uncommon. A teenager had disappeared. Seventeen years old from a family living on the Isle of Mull, west of the Scottish mainland. An American family, which was one of only two aspects of the case that struck me as unusual. Had they been visiting Mull as tourists then that would have been one thing, but it seemed a bizarre place for a family from Southern California to have chosen to live. For one thing, save for a brief, blissful summer, there were many fewer hours of sunshine per annum, not to mention the lack of malls, coffee franchises and delivery options. Still, I thought, good for them. Personally, I was much happier in smaller communities rooted in nature and self-sufficiency than in oxygen-deprived cities, but then I'm a Canadian who hails from Banff. Much like Mull, Banff half tolerates, half welcomes the annual influx of tourists. I always managed to escape into the mountains in winter or to sit by a lake in summer when I needed peace. A call to investigate a case in Vancouver or Toronto was how I usually defined a long-distance trek. Scotland was a commute further than I'd anticipated.

So, to Adriana. One late September Saturday morning her parents awoke, assumed their daughter was sleeping in and became concerned only at lunchtime by her failure to appear. Her father put his head round her door and discovered an empty bed. No sign of her anywhere in the house. Her bike still in the garage. Wallet gone, but Adriana's passport remained in her mother's bedside table. No sign of her cell phone.

Five days later I landed at Glasgow airport and made my way overland to the ferry.

You're wondering if I'm a police officer. I'm not. Nor am I a pathologist or any sort of forensic expert. What I am is a private investigator – a title I'm not keen on – but it comes with a licence, and sometimes a piece of paper is useful when you're asking people to share information. I specialise in missing teenagers. Not the subset of work I'd had in mind when I started out, but I'm female and short – thus apparently unthreatening – and I have what's been referred to more than once as a 'cheerful, positive manner'. Also, dimples. Sadly, none of those things were ever going to bring Adriana back, or render her parents' grief less dreadful.

They let me into their home and told me everything they believed to be relevant about their daughter. Adriana was enrolled in an online educational course to complete her American high school diploma. She'd had a summer job at the local pub in Tobermory where they were renting whilst renovating a permanent home. Good student, no drug problem, no boyfriend, very social. Missing her friends in America to an appropriate extent. No red flags. She had a twin brother, Brandon, with furious eyes. That was okay. I couldn't imagine how it would feel to have a missing twin. He was suffering. Last was a little sister, Luna, four years old and the product of a union between older parents who believed that nature was taking care of contraception, only to be caught out. Cute, bouncy, with curly black hair, she was a miniature of her Latina mother, Isabella. Their father, Rob, was the American classic – tanned skin, baseball loving, avid barbecuer. They'd looked at me as if I were both the poison and the antidote: a greeting I was used to. No one wants to be in a situation where they need my help.

I'd been working as an investigator since graduating from my Criminal Justice course eight years earlier, and Adriana's corpse was the most upsetting thing I'd seen in all that time. Given that I'd found the remains from a mountain lion mauling and witnessed a bear attack in progress, that's a high bar.

It was little more than a hunch that had taken me to Mackinnon's Cave. To be fair, a guidebook and a decent understanding of teenagers had ignited my gut instinct. Not that it was inevitable that Adriana was there; it could have been any of the caves on the island. A twenty-two mile trek from Tobermory, the distance was probably the reason Mackinnon's Cave hadn't been explored by police earlier; but Adriana's peers were old enough to be driving, and at that age, the further you partied from home, the less likely you were to be discovered.

Mackinnon's Cave is a billion-year-old crack in the western

357

edge of the island that invades the land mass by some 500 feet. By early October, September's previously calm seas were washing up moodier and less predictable. There'd been a storm that morning with a high tide. Mackinnon's Cave was only accessible safely when the tide was out, otherwise the pathway required a swimming costume. I'm an outdoor sports enthusiast – skier, snowboarder, hiker, mountain climber. I've camped out in arctic conditions and endured snowstorms with nothing but a tent membrane between me and the elements. But a sea swimmer . . . at night? Not so much.

The cave was impressive. As I entered, the rock wall on the right leaned in, imposing. The entrance was a tall, thin break in the rock face that made my pulse dance in my wrist. The late sunlight was no match for the darkness inside, but I'd come prepared with a climbing helmet featuring multiple lamps. Stepping in, I knew my instinct had been right. The discarded cider can I trod on produced the distinctive metal crumpling sound that says 'teenagers' the world over.

The remains of a fire were just a few metres beyond – close enough to the fresh air that the smoke would be drawn out of the cave. More than one ring of surrounding stones, more than one type of wood burned – the makeshift fireplace had been used, relaid and reused perhaps over years.

Teenagers have places.

I'd already searched many of those places on the island. Favourite beaches, deserted farmers' huts, shells of castles, car parks with sunset views and privacy. But Adriana was waiting for me at Mackinnon's Cave.

My footsteps echoed through the mouth of the cavern, the sound sharpening as I entered the throat. Then into a substantial room, with natural shelves high on the rocky walls and ditches cracked into the ground at each edge. High-ceilinged, grand, imposing. I'd have missed Adriana if not for a break in the blanket of rocks that revealed the metallic glimmer of the teal toenail varnish her mother had said she'd been wearing. As I'd walked, the light from my helmet had lit the nail lacquer, producing the wild flash of a swamp animal's eyes at night. My feet, slower than my brain, had walked another few feet, and when I turned back the teal shimmer was nowhere to be seen.

On my hands and knees, I'd cleared the rocks away, wary of rockfalls, anxious not to seal my own premature coffin. Her body had been pushed down into one of the cracks, covered by a few large boulders, then shale, pebbles, dirt.

I touched Adriana's hand first. It was icy, the skin silken but firm, digits swollen. Closing my eyes a moment, the intimacy caught me off-guard. You always hope you're wrong, but I'd sensed her family's hopelessness. There'd been an undercurrent in their side-looks and the words they weren't saying. They'd been asking me to find a corpse, not locate a runaway. I'd felt it almost immediately.

I should have walked out of the cave there and then, let go of her hand and preserved the scene. Procedure, procedure, procedure. The problem with that is that private investigators have no rights. You don't get to consult with the forensics squad or the pathologist, you never see the police file (unless you're sleeping with a detective, and I'd sworn off them years earlier) and those first impressions are everything. It's almost all the useful knowledge.

Hands gloved, keeping everything in one place so as not to lose any trace fibres from the scene, keeping my knees in a single spot on the floor, I moved rock after rock until Adriana was laid out naked before me.

I'm glad the dead cannot see themselves. There's nothing peaceful about it. Being a corpse is an endlessly intrusive process.

Adriana had no obvious injuries to gasp or gape at. Forget bullet wounds, claw lacerations or the raging burn of rope around neck. Her skin, though mottled purple in patches, had a base tone of grey-white-green. There's no name for that colour but in my head, I've labelled it mortuary green. It's really the only place you ever see it.

Her eyes were open, whites running red, the former sparkling brown of her pupils covered by an opaque shield. Adriana's mouth was open, too. Spilling from it, like the cave's own vomit, was sand. Not the loose sand you kick up walking along a beach on a sunny afternoon, but the packed-down sand of a child about to turn over a full bucket to make a castle. Her lips stretched wide in a perpetual scream that mine threatened to copy.

It was not a feature of a drowning case. It was not a prank gone wrong. Nor had the girl stuffed her own mouth with sand in some grotesque drug-fuelled delusion. Sooner or later she'd have spat it back out and rolled onto her side. Adriana had had company at the moment of her death.

Her long black hair – her pride and joy by all accounts – was fanned out beneath her head, and wrapped into it, twined around, was seaweed. It was dark and stinking now, although the decomposing body won the competition for assaulting my senses. The seaweed was a grotesque crown: she was a dead beauty queen belonging to the sea. I took out my camera and photographed the body. I had the family's permission – carte blanche to do whatever was required. They would never have to look at those images as far as I was concerned, but I needed them as a record in the investigation. And there was one final, terrible task. Drawing the girl's legs up, I opened them to check for injuries. Adriana had been beautiful in life. She might not have reached the peak of her looks at seventeen, her body still growing into itself, but she was easily captivating enough to have attracted the attention of people whose motives were less than pure.

I hadn't wanted to look. When I did, I couldn't look away.

A large shell had been inserted into her vagina, half of it still visible. Swallowing my revulsion, the shame of witnessing such violation, I took more photos, hating myself, knowing I had no choice.

There was no blood on the ground beneath her, nor spilled down her legs. Her nails were intact, her hands free of the scratch marks of defensive wounds. Only the heels of her feet were damaged. She hadn't scrambled across rocks, barefoot and panicking.

Setting her body back the way I'd found it, leaving the rocks to one side, I searched the remainder of the deep cave. No clothes or personal possessions remained there, only the odd food packet, cigarette stubs; human debris. Someone had defiled her body then hidden her, just not well enough that she'd never be found. They'd tidied up after themselves and removed the clothes she'd been wearing, then left her in a place that felt both empty and watchful at once.

Shivering, I knew I'd taken all the time I could, but it pained me to leave Adriana alone there. It wouldn't be long until she was inhabiting a body bag instead, I told myself. Safe from predators on a morgue slab. That was cold comfort.

Emerging from the cave an hour after I'd entered it, I sat on a rock and dialled the number for the emergency services. No reception at the cave mouth. Regretfully, I moved away, leaving Adriana lying alone in the pitch black. I was halfway up the slope to the road before my call went out.

The island officer on duty overnight would be notified, I was told. They would be there as soon as they could. A scenes of crime unit would have to come from the mainland. Something about a request being put through to Glasgow. Could I remain in situ and attract attention so officers knew where the body was? I assured them that I would.

I'd said I'd found a dead body, but not the name. I owed it to the family to break that news to them myself, and on a small island word would get out the second the name was spoken aloud. I was going to be asked to give a statement, and to explain what I'd been doing there. There would be the inevitable grilling over my handling the corpse and moving the rocks. It was going to make for an uncomfortable working relationship with the police moving forward.

But that was why my services had been engaged in the first place. An unwillingness by local officers to send out search parties. A reticence by the police to believe that any foul play had been involved. The trite phrases, 'happens all the time at this age', 'she'll be back in a week, tail between her legs' and 'probably just partying in Glasgow' had been repeated to Adriana's parents ad nauseam. Also, something less irritating and more unsettling – a sense that the police were not counting the days until they really started investigating, but were in fact counting the days until the Clark family gave up and went back to where they'd come from. I'd met Mull's most senior police officer. The family hadn't been imagining the hostility.

Which was why they'd turned to the internet for help and found the name Sadie Levesque, investigator, teenager tracking specialist. Paid my ticket from Calgary International Airport. Booked me a room at a hotel. Agreed my fee.

Now their girl was dead. Mocked, hurt, violated, abandoned. I'd grown used to dead bodies, but I would never grow used to the cruelty some humans were capable of unleashing. Adriana's death was not only an assault on her, it would spread its unwelcome fingers to touch every family member, every friend, scarring them forever. There's no such thing as 'peace over time' for the loved ones of murder victims. I know that better than most.

So the police would come, they would express their standard sympathies to the family (for what little that was worth), and

362

an investigation would – finally, too late – be officially opened. The question I had for the police was not how they planned to catch Adriana's murderer, but, in a small, island community, would they really want to know which of their own had committed such a horrific, unspeakable act?

The new, heart-pounding crime
thriller from Helen Fields

The Last Girl to Die

Coming to all good bookstores
in September 2022.

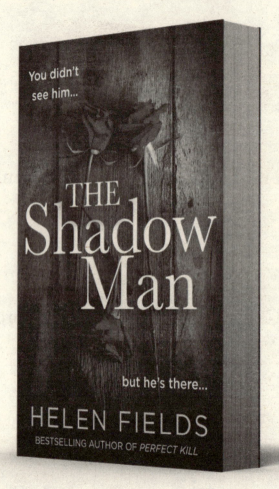

Welcome to Edinburgh.
Murder capital of Europe.

Book 2
Available now in paperback, ebook and audiobook.

The worst dangers are the ones we can't see . . .

Book 3
Available now in paperback, ebook and audiobook.

When silence falls, who will hear their cries?

It all ends with the final stitch . . .

'Highly recommended'
JAMES OSWALD

Perfect Silence

HELEN FIELDS

Book 4
Available now in paperback, ebook and audiobook.

Your darkest moment is your most vulnerable . . .

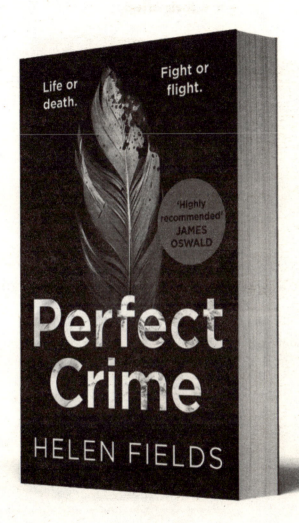

Book 5
Available now in paperback, ebook and audiobook.

He had never heard himself scream before.
It was terrifying . . .

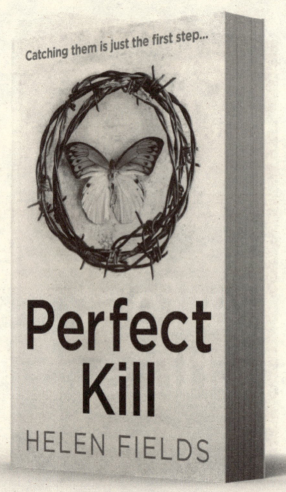

Catching them is just the first step...

Perfect Kill

HELEN FIELDS

Book 6
Available now in paperback, ebook and audiobook.